GW01339366

PRAISE FOR DONY JAY'S THRILLERS

FOR *MURDER BY HALF*

"Razor sharp, thoroughly captivating, and just one-more-chapter addictive. A perfect reason for thriller and crime fiction fans to stay up way too late. Give me more Nathan Press, please!"
—**Tosca Lee**, *New York Times* **bestselling author of** *The Line Between*

"With *Murder by Half*, Dony Jay launches a bold and brash detective series featuring Nathan Press—a brilliant yet unconventional hero who is a heart attack for criminals but also for his bosses in Major Crimes. High stakes and action-packed, *Murder by Half* will thrill fans of Marc Cameron's Arliss Cutter series and leave readers clamoring for the next installment!"
—**Andrews & Wilson**, *New York Times* **bestselling authors of** *Act of Defiance* **and** *Tier One*

"Entering a world where reality blurs and secrets lie just beneath the surface, Dony Jay's gripping and unpredictable new novel, *Murder by Half*, is a masterfully crafted thriller that will leave you breathless and reading well into the night."
—**Ryan Steck (aka The Real Book Spy), author of** *Out for Blood*

"Meticulous and masterful! With a level of precision and detail born only from real-world experience, Dony Jay has brought to life a police procedural that stands tall against the best out there! *Murder by Half* has tight, compelling action and riveting suspense. Do not miss this one!"
—**Ronie Kendig, bestselling author of The Tox Files series and** *Havoc*

FOR *ARTIFACTS OF CONSPIRACY*

"A smart, fast-paced thriller...fans of Joel C. Rosenberg will devour this book!"
—**The Real Book Spy**

"*Artifacts of Conspiracy* is all thriller, no filler. Guaranteed to satisfy the most discerning literary palate."
—**Joshua Hood, author of *Burn Out* & Robert Ludlum's *The Treadstone Rendition***

"Special Forces operator Reagan Rainey is back in *Artifacts of Conspiracy*, the exciting second installment of Dony Jay's Warrior Spy thriller series. Like Joel C. Rosenberg, Jay has found the perfect balance of well-crafted military and covert operations thriller and faith-based fiction. In Rainey we see an operator true to his faith, but with the frailties and weaknesses of all of us, making a realistic character we are eager to root for. Jay has masterfully crafted a non-stop trill ride that will keep you turning the pages well into the night. This second book in the series proves that Dony Jay is a rising star in the genre."
—**Andrews & Wilson, *New York Times* bestselling authors of *Act of Defiance* and *Tier One***

FOR *THE WARRIOR SPY*

"A fast-paced story, full of action and adventure."
—**Luana Ehrlich, USA Today bestselling author of the Titus Ray thrillers and Mylas Grey mysteries**

Murder by Half

BOOKS BY DONY JAY

WARRIOR SPY THRILLER SERIES
The Warrior Spy
Artifacts of Conspiracy

NATHAN PRESS THRILLER SERIES
Murder by Half

Murder by Half

A Nathan Press Thriller

Dony Jay

MHP
Merry Hill Publishing

MHP
Merry Hill Publishing

This book is a work of fiction. Any references to historical events, real people, or real places are used fictitiously. Other names, characters, places, and events are products of the author's imagination, and any resemblance to actual events or places or persons, living or dead, is entirely coincidental.

Murder by Half

Copyright © 2024 by Dony Jay

All rights reserved. No part of this publication may be reproduced, distributed, or transmitted in any form or by any means, including photocopying, recording, or other electronic or mechanical methods, without the prior written permission of the publisher, except as permitted by U.S. copyright law. Permission requests and all media inquiries can be sent to DonyJay@DonyJayBooks.com.

Published in the United States of America by Merry Hill Publishing.
Cover design by Alexander von Ness

For more information visit the author's website at DonyJayBooks.com.

ISBN 978-0-9969270-7-9 (hardcover)
ISBN 978-0-9969270-8-6 (softcover)
ISBN 978-0-9969270-9-3 (ebook)

For Jill, my true love.

And for God and country.

For nothing is secret that shall not be made manifest; neither any thing hid, that shall not be made known and come abroad.
—Luke 8:17 KJV

1

CHARLES STREET
PROVIDENCE, RHODE ISLAND
SATURDAY – 0130 HRS.

"Come on, Lance. It's all clear. Now grab an end."

"I thought I heard something." Lance Cheney stood beside the van, hands on his hips, peering into the severe darkness. He took one final drag from the cigarette then flicked it into the night. The little red ember arced through the air and sparked as it hit the dry pavement ten yards away. He turned, leaned into the side of the truck, angling himself for maximum leverage, and latched onto the spooled carpet. "Heavy sucker."

"You're just getting old... Or maybe it's all those filthy cigarettes," the other man whispered.

Cheney bristled but held his tongue.

Together, they lifted the unwieldy parcel from the cargo area and hustled it over to the creekbank.

"On three," said Cheney with a pained grimace.

The big man—Marcus Zug was his name—nodded wordlessly, his bulk creating a larger-than-life silhouette within the heavily shadowed parking lot.

In unison, they swung the item back and forth once, twice, three times then hurled it as far as they could. The splash seemed like a small explosion in the quiet of the night. They studied the bobbing lump in the undulating, inky water for several long seconds, then, satisfied with their handiwork, gazed briefly at their surroundings. Seeing nothing, they hurried back to the van, peeled off their rubber gloves, and deposited them into a heavy-gauge plastic garbage bag that already contained a wallet, datebook, and a pair of bricks. Zug tied a knot in the bag and dropped it on the floor between his feet.

Neither man spoke another word until they had rolled out of the empty lot, turned right onto Charles Street, and assumed a normal speed.

"I'm hungry."

"You're always hungry," said Cheney, firing up another cigarette.

"And *you're* always a nag," snapped Zug.

Soon the cabin was clouded with a gauzy haze, the glow from the clock on the dash coloring each of their faces with an ominous, green hue.

"And open a window for Pete's sake."

Cheney rolled his eyes. He cracked his window, tilted his head toward the opening, and stiffly exhaled a cloud of smoke into the chill night air.

"I'm serious, Lance. I'm starving over here."

"Look, we'll get something to eat later…after we search the guy's office, okay?"

Marcus Zug muttered something to himself then said, "Pancakes? Can we get pancakes?"

"Anything you want, but first we've got more work to do, and I need you to stay focused."

"You don't have to worry about me, Lance. I'm focused like a laser."

Cheney's cigarette flared as he shot a sideways glance at the large mass of humanity seated next to him. "On pancakes, no doubt."

Zug grinned conspiratorially and they both shared a hearty laugh.

As they traversed the College Street Bridge, Cheney slowed and veered close to the edge while Zug lowered his window, lifted the plastic trash bag from the floor, and heaved it from the vehicle into the Providence River below.

A few turns later, they spotted a cop car. The yellow directional light from the cruiser's otherwise dormant lightbar pulsed from right to left on its rear-facing side. Two uniformed officers were hovering over a trio of teenagers sitting on the curb. Each kid wore a backpack and a rebellious glare that suggested they had been up to no good. As they drew near, one of the boys barked something incomprehensible at the officers and tried to stand but was immediately helped back to the ground by a barrel-chested sergeant who did not appear to be in the mood to put up with nonsense.

Cheney gave the policemen a wide berth and slipped past them unnoticed. He studied his rearview mirror for a long moment afterward then focused his attention once more on the street ahead.

They parked the van far afield of their target destination—an office building on Dorrance Street—and the surveillance cameras that he and Zug knew dotted the area.

For thirty minutes, Cheney and Zug sat in total silence, assessing the street with their predator eyes. During previous stakeouts here, they had gathered valuable intel. As a result, they now knew who belonged, who didn't, which vehicles stood out, which blended in. Their intel collection also included mapping the location of every security camera within a 3-block radius in the unlikely event that that information would be needed. Preparation could cure many ills in a plan gone sideways.

"What do you think?" Zug said.

Cheney lowered the military-grade, night-vision binoculars. His fingers itched for another cigarette, but it would have to wait until later. He stowed the binos beneath the seat and clicked on a small penlight with a red LED bulb. With it, he studied a map that charted the layout of the top two floors of the office building. He glanced up and peered in several directions. Finally, he switched off the light, grabbed a small gear bag, and slung it over his shoulder. "It looks right. Let's be quick though."

After performing a quick weapons check, they each pulled on balaclavas and tactical gloves.

Then stepped into the night.

2

BROWN UNIVERSITY
SATURDAY — 1000 HRS.

Even from an early age, Nathan Press had been good at solving puzzles, but this one was proving to be a real head-scratcher. He read the letter again, trying to decipher its meaning and what on earth could have prompted its author to write it in the first place and in such an urgent fashion.

Press had discovered it in his mailbox yesterday, commingled with the daily post. Who'd put it there was not a mystery. Riley Talbert was one of the few criminal defense attorneys Press considered a friend. Though he was based in Providence, Talbert possessed the legal chops, furious work ethic, and track record of high-profile criminal trial successes that had garnered him recognition all across the country.

Press sighed as he examined the note for the umpteenth time. Talbert had handwritten it on a blue-lined, yellow page. The top edge was ragged, indicating that it had been swiftly ripped from a legal pad. The distinctive penmanship, the elegant, sweeping pen strokes even in their obviously hastened state left no doubt as to the identity of the letter's author. Press figured the blue ink had come from one of those insanely expensive pens Talbert was known to carry in his suit coat, the type all prominent lawyers and bankers and politicians waved around like swords: Montblanc, Visconti, Faber-Castell, or Montegrappa.

Frustrated, Press folded the letter, tucked it back inside his jacket pocket, and sipped at the coffee he'd bought downstairs at the Blue Room Café. He set his cup back down on the small walnut accent table beside him and leaned back in the burnt-orange club chair, parsing both his thoughts and the words in the letter. Whether it was a complex puzzle or a stone-cold whodunit-type murder case, he would not rest until he solved it or at least had exhausted every avenue toward its solution. He knew his extreme competitiveness and other aspects of his Type-A personality bordered on disorder, but he had long accepted those parts of who he was.

The third-floor mezzanine, in which he currently presided, overlooked the Leung Family Gallery, a grand room where Brown University students could often be found laboring away on their laptops or reading a book, sometimes even for pleasure. Most days sunlight cascaded into the large seating area via two great arched windows, which were situated on opposing walls. But today, with buckets of rain pouring from a leaden sky, the entire space appeared dark and gloomy. Regardless, Press was happy to see that the unwritten rule of studious silence was still in full effect just like it had been when he was a student here.

The corner of the mezzanine was a good vantage point for observing those who came and went below. It also made logical sense why Riley Talbert had suggested meeting here. Not only were they both Brown alums and knew the campus well, but Talbert still gave lectures here. Thus, it would not be out of character for him to pop into the Robert Center to grab a coffee or meet with a student group, faculty member, or fellow donor even on a Saturday morning like this one. Press reasoned that Talbert had certainly deduced as much. These disquieting facts ruthlessly tickled at his puzzle-solving nature. What was so important to warrant a clandestine rendezvous? Why all the cloak and dagger stuff?

Press paged through a cycling magazine, fully aware of his surroundings though outwardly appearing bored. At just a tick past 30, he had a face—and a persona—that some might label as anachronistic in a place like Providence. Toxic masculinity was taboo these days after all, at least in some circles. His face was handsome though not overly so, and his athletic musculature was more functional than what might register as garish. Turning wrenches, wrangling truck tires, and pulling debris spilled from a wrecked semi from the side of the road with his father and older brother all throughout his childhood—in all kinds of weather—had made him incredibly strong, both mentally and physically.

Today, he sported a faded and well-worn Brown University ball cap, a flannel shirt, blue jeans, and a pair of mid-level Danner hiking boots. The shoulder bag at his feet did well to suggest he might be a graduate-degree candidate or even a hip, young professor. Though most of them probably couldn't bench 225 pounds once, let alone complete a set of 20.

He checked his watch once more. Talbert was nearly 20 minutes late. Maybe he had gotten stuck in traffic. After another 10, however, Press concluded that his friend wasn't coming. Perhaps circumstances had changed. Certainly, Talbert had not forgotten about the meeting. He was not the type of man to lose track of such things. There had to be a very good reason for him not to show.

A knowing sense of dread settled into the pit of his stomach as Press gathered his things and stood. He took one last look around before leaving, haunted with a deep, dark foreboding.

3

**RIVER'S EDGE
NEAR SOUTH WATER AND PLANET STREETS
MONDAY**

The cell phone bleated from the nightstand, the glow from the screen painting the ceiling of the dark bedroom a bright mixture of blue and green. Press instantly sat up and grabbed at the offending device. As he did so, he squinted at the red numerals on his digital alarm clock.

2:17 a.m.

He cleared his throat and thumbed the green circular icon on the phone. "Hello?"

"Nate. It's Tevaughn."

"Hey, LT."

"We got a body."

He listened as Detective Lieutenant Tevaughn Gentry ticked off the details, though at this point there weren't many.

"I know that technically you're not due back to full duty until later this morning, but I'd like you to come in now, if you could."

Press yawned, rubbed his unshaven face, and again looked at the clock. "Sure thing, Lieu. I'll be right there."

Press rolled up to the scene a few minutes past 3:00 a.m. The street was alive with pulsing red and blue emergency lights. As he drew closer, he flipped a switch on the center console that activated the hideaway flashing strobes on his unmarked Ford F-150 XLT SuperCrew then just as quickly turned them off. Seeing this, a uniformed officer standing beside a patrol car, walked to the line of large traffic cones blocking off the street. The patrolman moved two of them aside and waved him inside the perimeter. Press squinted past the man's patrol car and its blinding red and blue LEDs. Rolling forward, he glimpsed the officer in the rearview mirror setting the cones back in place.

Press weaved through the other police vehicles and parked along the curb at an angle. After climbing out of his black pickup truck, he stared upriver at the exact spot on the pedestrian bridge where just six months prior, he and another man, locked in a battle to the death, had gone over the railing and plunged into the Providence River. Press with bullet wounds to his shoulder and thigh, the other man with a 165-grain .40-caliber slug in his abdomen and a primal determination to never go back to prison.

In the end, after fighting and thrashing with every fiber of his being for what had seemed like hours, Press managed to choke the other man out just before passing out himself. Thankfully, his partner, Josh Killian, pulled him to shore and rushed him in the back of a police cruiser to Rhode Island Hospital. There, a stellar team of doctors and nurses worked on him for hours and ultimately saved his life.

The other man drowned.

Pity.

Even now Press felt no remorse for his actions that night. The man had been wanted for a string of grisly murders from Portsmouth to Pawtucket. One involved a four-year-old child. He'd gotten what he deserved. The incident had garnered Press accolades from all over New England. There had even been a small blurb in some national news outlets. Everyone has their fifteen minutes of fame.

It was morbidly ironic that his first day back to full duty should be here at the river.

Now, as he stared at the bridge and the inky water flowing beneath it, all the feelings from that night came flooding back.

Press shoved them out of his mind and opened the back door of his truck. Before grabbing the leather-bound legal pad off the seat, he picked up his Streamlight rechargeable and pushed it into his back pants pocket. He made sure he had several pairs of nitrile gloves in his jacket pockets then swung the door closed and locked the truck with his key fob remote.

"Hey, look who it is," called Ollie Yanik, a senior patrol officer from District 9.

"What's up, brother?" Press ducked under the yellow crime-scene tape and shook the uniformed man's outstretched hand.

"Us, Nate. Us."

"I hear that." Press scanned the row of police vehicles parked along Water Street as Yanik recorded his arrival. "Floater, huh?"

"Looks like it."

"How did the call come in?"

"Dude out walking saw him, called it in."

"Who was first on scene?"

"Forrester." Yanik jerked his head. "She's down there by the water with the others."

"Good deal." Press glanced around, made several entries in his notepad before starting toward the riverbank.

"By the way...," called Yanik.

Press stopped, turned. The bald-headed patrolman was smiling.

"Welcome back. Glad to see you out here again. It's definitely bad news for the bad guys in this town."

"Thanks," Press said. "It's good to be back."

4

The fire department had erected lights in the grass just off the sidewalk. These and the equally powerful LEDs mounted to the side of the Providence PD Marine Unit vessel anchored offshore made the crime scene and the surrounding area bright as day.

Press waded through the tall grass by way of a trail, which the officers preceding him had made, to an area near where the victim lay. Several BCI—Bureau of Criminal Identification—detectives were huddled together nearby. Having already placed yellow tent markers bearing large black numerals at various locations, they were now preparing to photograph the scene. BCI housed the crime scene folks—highly specialized experts in anything and everything within the realm of evidence collection and evidence processing.

"There he is. The man, the myth, the legend." Press's best friend and squad mate, Detective Josh Killian, whom everyone called JK, greeted him with a large smile and a fist bump. "Welcome back, brother."

"Amen to that," said a short, raven-haired female detective. Gabriela Ibarra could do more pushups than most men her age, a credit to habits formed during her military service. And she certainly wasn't afraid to mix things up either. One of her hobbies was kickboxing and it showed. The only female on the squad, Gabby was every bit as fetching and intelligent as she was competitive. And that extended to the way she fiercely pursued each case. Press sometimes marveled at how similar their personalities were.

Detective Lieutenant Tevaughn Gentry stood beside a stocky patrol officer named Shelly Forrester, and a grim-faced, uniformed shift commander. Gentry picked his way over, shook Press's hand. "Hey, Nate. Thanks for coming out. I know I speak for everyone here when I say it's great to see you back in action. We all know your path to get here wasn't easy."

Gentry's words and sincere delivery along with the other officers' earnest faces now looking up at him struck an emotional chord. His path back hadn't been easy. In fact, the rehab had been especially grueling. The months of isolation from his peers and the job he loved had taken their toll as well.

He swallowed a knot of emotion. "Thanks, guys. But I *had* to come back. I couldn't let y'all keep having all this fun out here without me. Speaking of which, what do we have so far?"

"Well—"

"He's back!"

All heads turned as Laith Meredith jogged over. Meredith was the youngest detective on the squad. Everyone called him Tank because he was built like a compact, mighty Sherman.

When the fraternal banter was over and he had everyone's attention again, Gentry hiked up the duty rig on his left hip and turned toward the lifeless figure that lay face down ten yards to the north, next to one of the wooden pilings that supported the boardwalk above. "Like I said on the phone, it appears to be an adult male."

Press took a step closer. The man's lower half was submerged in the river, the torso beached in the stony, grass-covered earth.

"We're still waiting for the ME to show, so we can move him." Gentry shielded his eyes from the glare of the bright lights as he peered up toward the street.

"Who found him?" Press said, directing his attention toward Forrester.

"Timothy Hadley. Lives in the condos over on James Street. He works the graveyard shift. On his days off, he comes out here, walks the river. Saw him lying there. Just like you see now. Didn't touch him, didn't go near him. Told me he stayed up there," Forrester pointed to the boardwalk, "and called nine-one-one."

"What time did he call?"

Forrester slipped a pocket-size, spiral notepad from her uniform shirt pocket, flipped it open. "Zero one fifty."

Press jotted this down in his pad. "And we don't have any idea who our dead guy is, correct?"

"Not yet," said Gentry.

"No missing persons reports involving adult-age white males in the past three weeks either," said Gabby. "I already had Dispatch check."

Without moving closer, Press studied the corpse then scanned the ground, including that on which they now stood. Several yards away, a stretch of grass leading from the bulkhead to the water's edge was uniformly laid over. He looked at Forrester again. "Was Hadley out walking yesterday at the same time?"

"Yeah. Body wasn't here then. He's positive."

"What are you thinking, Nate?" said Killian.

"Well, he obviously didn't die here. There are no signs of a scuffle, no shoe impressions aside from ours or anything else to suggest he was carried here. We did, however, have a lot of rain this weekend. I remember seeing on the news that there was substantial flash flooding up north around Woonsocket and into southern Mass. I wonder if all that rain could have somehow been a factor in how he wound up here. Just thinking out loud."

"Maybe it's suicide. Guy did a header off a bridge?" Gabby offered. "Though most probably aren't high enough to kill a jumper."

"It's possible, I suppose. There's certainly no shortage of bridges here in the city to pick from. But I agree. I think it would be difficult to wind up dead simply from jumping from a bridge in this city, unless of course you hit your head on one of the stone or concrete slabs on the way down."

Press and the others stood by taking notes and exchanging ideas while a BCI detective photographed the scene. When the medical examiner and her medicolegal death investigator finally arrived, more photos were taken. As the examination of the body commenced, Press and his fellow detectives moved in closer.

"He's shoeless!" proclaimed Killian as the ME, assisted by her investigator and BCI detectives, hauled the dead man out of the water and rolled him onto his back.

"*Man*, somebody worked him over *good*," Tank said.

More photos were taken, then the ME, a shapely redhead of 40 years named Cassandra Berman, wearing purple medical exam gloves, went through the man's sopping wet pockets. "No phone. No wallet. No ID," she called out as Press and the other detectives scribbled in their notepads.

"Facial rec's obviously out, but what about the fingerprint scanner? Can we use it?" said Killian, referring to a fancy cell phone with an optical pad onto which a decedent's fingerprints could be rolled. It was linked to numerous databases and was often used in cases where other methods of speedy identification proved difficult.

Berman lifted the man's hands, studied the pads of his fingers. "Too soft and wrinkled to do here. We can try it when we get him on the table. Also, there's bruising on his wrists. See?"

"He'd been bound at some point," Press declared.

Berman nodded. "Based on the width of the bruising, I'd say it was probably done with zip ties or some type of thin cording."

"That watch he's wearing looks expensive," said Gentry.

"It is, LT. That's a Ball Roadmaster Rescue Chronograph. Swiss-made. Retails for between three and four grand."

Everyone looked at Killian with curiosity.

"What? Watches are one of my hobbies."

"Watches you'll never be able to afford," Gabby teased.

"Some people like cars. I like watches."

Press stepped closer, tilted his head. The man's face was chalky white and at the same time tinged in blue. The nose was askew, the jaw too, both were obviously broken. The left eye was immensely swollen thus leading Press to conclude that an orbital bone was likely fractured as well. As Berman opened the man's mouth, the teeth revealed more. Several were hinged inward at a grotesque angle. One, in morbid fashion, dislodged and fell into the back of the man's blackened throat causing Berman to utter a foul curse word. Hearing this, several of the uniformed onlookers chuckled.

Press took another step forward, bent over at a forty-five-degree angle. He lingered here for a few seconds before straightening to his normal six-foot three-inch height. "I know him."

"Yeah," Killian said. "He *does* look familiar."

Gentry tilted his head, squinted. "I'll be... Is that—"

"Riley Talbert, attorney at law," Press said, feeling as if the air had suddenly been sucked from his lungs. For some reason, he did not mention the letter. Maybe because Talbert, himself, had unambiguously warned against it.

"Well, now he's Riley Talbert, attorney at rest," Berman snapped. She was obviously in a peevish mood. "By the way, Dr. V will be handling the post. I'm going on vacation. I should have left already."

And now her crabby attitude made perfect sense, thought Press.

"Where're you headed?" Tank's muscled neck twisted toward her.

"Away from this place."

Several of them grinned. But not Press. He had been gone for too long already. But he could understand the feeling. This job—the hours, the stress, the weight of the work—was grueling for detectives and medical examiners alike.

Meanwhile, Gabby punched the lawyer's name into a mobile application on her smartphone and soon had the man's DMV photo on the screen. She held it up for Berman and the others to see.

"Well, at least we have someplace to start—we know who he is." Gentry turned his attention to Press. "I'm glad you're back, Nate. Because I want you primary on this."

Press stared down at the beaten, waterlogged body of his friend. "I wouldn't have it any other way, LT."

5

TALBERT RESIDENCE
126 HARTSHORN ROAD

Press gazed out of the heavily tinted passenger-side window. He had parked his truck at Central Station and was now riding shotgun in Killian's white, unmarked Chevy Malibu.

"So how well did you know him?" Killian said, pulling the steering wheel down with his left hand.

"Well enough to call him a friend. I faced off against him a handful of times...when I was a young buck. He was selective about the cases he took, and he was expensive. You didn't hire Riley Talbert just to enter a guilty plea, if you know what I mean."

"He definitely had quite the reputation."

"That, he did."

Riley Talbert had been one of the best criminal minds in all of New England. The tale of his legal exploits did not end there, however. Talbert had made a routine of taking on select cases in places far and wide from his native Providence—cities like New York, Philadelphia, DC, Denver, and Los Angeles, for example. Almost all of them were high-profile in nature. Highly intelligent, Talbert had been a dogged pursuer of truth, possessed incredible character, and exemplified what it meant to be an honorable steward of justice. An attorney with such qualities these days was hard to come by. At least, that was Press's experience.

"This is going to be a tough one, brother."

Press quietly nodded as he turned over the thoughts percolating in his mind. He had never worked the murder of a lawyer, let alone one of Riley Talbert's prestigious ilk. Doubtless few homicide detectives across the country—retired or active—could say they had much experience in doing so. Naturally, this type of investigation was rife with all kinds of complexities right off the bat. The number of people with a motive to see Riley Talbert dead had to be substantial. Could there be a more difficult case to solve?

Welcome back, Nate. Welcome back indeed.

"How'd you do against him?"

"What?"

Killian played with the knob on the police radio with the thumb and index finger of his right hand. "I hear he is...*was*...like a surgeon when examining someone on the stand. Before you knew it, your intestines were hanging out and you had no idea what on earth had just happened."

"He definitely put me through my paces, but I did okay." Press sighed. "Talbert was a good man. I know, I know. He was on the other side, but he did things the right way, didn't treat cops like the enemy. He did his job, and knew we had to do ours. One time, I even worked a case *for* him."

Killian shot him a sideways glance.

"It was one of my first cases as a detective, back when I was in GIU." The GIU, or General Investigations Unit, was responsible for investigating burglaries, thefts, financial and fraud-related crimes as well as other types of offenses not generally associated with violent crimes against persons and those that fit into other unique categories. "Someone broke into his wife's car and stole her purse from under the seat and her gun from the glove box. Used her credit cards all over to buy TVs, laptops, power tools, and cell phones."

"You get the guy?"

"Yeah, and the gun. It was a punk from Silver Lake and his junkie girlfriend. Real brainiacs. Anyway, it's not like I was *super* tight with Talbert, but I got to know him well enough over the years. He went to Brown… I know he's got two kids. They're grown obviously. All in all, a really nice family."

The Blackstone neighborhood was dark and quiet as Killian turned onto Hartshorn Road.

"What's the numeric, again?"

"One twenty-six," Press said. "There it is."

Built in the traditional Tudor style, the attorney's home was large and stately, complete with sharp roof lines and two front-facing gables. The nearly half-acre plot of land was immaculately maintained. Most of the lawns here were. After all, this was one of the most exclusive residential communities in the city.

Motion lights that had activated upon their navigating to the front door remained brightly illuminated as the doorbell chimed within the darkened entry hall. When no one answered, Press pushed the button a second time then gazed upward at the curtained windows, looking for movement or a light to click on.

"Doesn't look like anyone's home." Killian cupped his hands and peered inside the long, slender window beside the front door.

"What say we do a walkaround, make sure everything is ship-shape before we head out?"

"Sounds good to me," Killian replied.

All seemed secure and in its proper place until they reached the third door on the back of the house, the one closest to the pool.

"It's open," whispered Killian, his hand still on the knob.

Considering that Riley Talbert had washed up dead on a riverbank with clear signs of having been bound and tortured, it wasn't beyond the realm of possibility that his wife might be lying dead or dying somewhere inside the home or was otherwise in some kind of imminent peril.

Press drew his Smith and Wesson M&P 2.0 .40 cal. pistol from the holster on his right hip. It was outfitted with a weapon-mounted light. Killian did the same. Together they entered the residence and immediately called out "Police! Anyone here?!"

If there had been some clear indication of criminal activity afoot, they would have taken a stealthier approach. But this was a private residence in a wealthy neighborhood, and it was still well before dawn's first light. The last thing they wanted to do was get shot by a groggy family member or frightened service worker.

"Alarm's off," Killian pointed out in a hushed voice as they turned left past the alarm panel.

Moving in a practiced manner, they methodically cleared every room, which in a house this size took considerable time for two people to do properly. When they were satisfied that everything appeared normal, they holstered their sidearms and eased into a relaxed posture. As they were about to leave, Press noticed a sheet of paper on the marble island countertop in the kitchen. On it was a list of things Mrs. Talbert had ostensibly jotted down for her husband to do in her absence. She had also left several phone numbers where she could be reached. A quick internet search of the unfamiliar area codes via his phone's mobile browser suggested that she was in Florida.

Press snapped a photo of the sheet of paper with his phone. "Looks like the wife is out of town." He pulled the back door shut and made sure it was locked. "We'll try to reach her when we get back to the office."

6

Providence PD
Central Station

Press's phone buzzed inside his pants pocket just as they were turning onto Dean Street. The caller ID on the screen read *FBI-Hickman*. Before being recently promoted to ASAC (assistant special agent in charge) within the FBI's Boston Field Office, Clint Hickman had run the FBI Resident Agency in Providence as a supervisory special agent. Having worked with him closely on several complex cases that resulted in federal prosecution, Press knew him well and liked the man. Hickman was a consummate pro and was always quick to help when it was within his power to do so.

"Hey, Nate. I just talked to Gentry. He said you're primary on the Talbert deal."

"Word travels fast."

"You know it. Any leads yet?"

"Not yet. We're just getting started."

"Understood. Listen, Talbert was a good man. And considering his past cases and his role in some ongoing matters at the federal level, I just want you to know that if there is anything you guys need, the Bureau is here to help. All you have to do is call."

"I appreciate that, Clint. Is there anything you're aware of right now that would link to someone wanting him dead?"

"Nothing jumps out, but I'll start asking around and reviewing some of the Bureau's case files. If I land on anything that looks promising, I'll give you a shout."

"Sounds good. Thanks."

Providence Police headquarters, formally known as Central Station, was located at 325 Washington Street, within the modern three-story redbrick, concrete, and glass Providence Public Safety Complex. The building also housed the city's fire and communications departments as well as municipal courts. The block of offices and other rooms that constituted Detective Division's Major Crimes Unit could be found on the second floor.

The sunlight had begun to prevail in the morning sky by the time they called the last number on the list. All had gone to voice mail.

Press bellied up to his desk and scanned his unread email messages. They consisted of the usual. A large number he had received by virtue of his participation in an email group made up of detectives, investigators, and intel analysts from various law enforcement agencies in the region. Based on their subject lines, most of the emails had to do with efforts to ID suspects in cases ranging from armed robberies and burglaries to Felony Lane Gang-type activity and organized retail theft. Other emails were alerts for training tasks that were well past their completion deadlines. One of these was for something called "implicit bias." Reading the online course description, Press just shook his head. He was certain that the people who put these touchy-feely things together 1) had no clue about how actual police work was done; and 2) knew how to milk the current system for as much training and consulting grant money as possible. Such was the culture of modern policing. Law enforcement agencies at every level—local, state, and federal—were becoming overrun with two different types of leaders and both were toxic to the profession: bull-headed tyrants and spineless weenies. The former's only concern was anything that stood to feed their massive egos. The latter's attention focused on everything that had to do with public perception, chasing social agendas, and not hurting anyone's feelings as opposed to arresting dangerous felons and ridding the streets of crime. Nevertheless, most of the grunts on the ground, people like him, still knew what it took to keep America safe. And that didn't involve constantly reviewing policies and watching 30-minute training videos on how to be nicer to criminals or how to participate in—even celebrate—the cultural rot taking place all over the country. Press was a professional and relentless crimefighter, a cop's cop, and no one or no thing was ever going to change that.

He clicked on a few emails that interested him then disregarded the rest. Leaning back in his chair, he gazed across the large squad room, the groups of cubicles that formed the bulk of the unit's footprint. Most of them would soon be occupied, but for now the vast majority were dormant.

Press opened the usual databases and after sending several jobs to the office printer, straightened the stack of papers that would begin the victim section of the murder book, which was a simple industry term used to describe the comprehensive case file for a homicide investigation. He then made a duplicate of everything. The first collection of paperwork was for the original case file and would later be carefully placed into a large 3-ring binder. The second set—his working copy, he deposited into a deep, accordion-style file folder. This was the copy that he would carry with him into the field by way of a black, tactical messenger bag made by 5.11. It wasn't the way everyone did it, but it was his way. And he would not deviate from it.

Press checked the time on his watch. It was an all-black model, with the words "Protection" and "G-Shock" in blue lettering on its face, a color combination that appealed to his cop nature. In fifteen minutes, it would be 8:00 a.m.

"Hey, JK."

"Yeah?"

"Let's run down to Talbert's office, talk to the law partner."

"Ten-four. Let me grab another refill and I'll be ready to roll." Killian snatched the metal travel cup off his desk and headed for the unit's coffee machine.

There was something suspicious in the cadence of his voice though. Press watched him go and immediately detected whispering, a hushed giggle, and the shuffling of feet in the hallway just around the corner. Instantly, he knew what was coming.

It was at this time that a small army of detectives and a handful of civilian support staff from the various units within the Division led by Perry Everhart swept in with smiles on their faces. An administrative specialist, Everhart was one of Detective Division's friendliest and most outgoing personalities and for that reason everyone called her Sunny. Atop a wheeled cart pushed cautiously by Sunny and Gabby, was a gigantic sheet cake that proclaimed, "Welcome Back!" in large block letters. On it, too, were a set of handcuffs and a yellow-gold shield with his badge number—136—at the bottom, all of it crafted out of colorful icing.

"It's just a little something from all of us to show you how thankful we are to have you back." Sunny radiated pure joy. The detectives and other personnel that surrounded her all nodded, some offered comments of their own. One of them, a quick-witted guy from the Intel Unit, teased him about always needing to be the center of attention, which everyone knew was the furthest thing from the truth. This caused a ripple of laughter that urged on more banter.

"Thank you, everyone." Press smiled. A current of emotion rose within him as he registered the jubilant, expectant faces of his colleagues. Most of the Division detectives and staff were there, save for the guys and gals who worked the night shift or who had court. He took a deep breath while his eyes moved about the crowd. "It's good to be back here with you all. And thank you, too, for all the cards and goodies you dropped off and sent over the past several months. I'm going to have to up my workout routine for the rest of the year because of you people." He patted his stomach with both hands in a whimsical manner. "But seriously... Thank you. Without all your kind words and deeds, my recovery would have been a thousand times more difficult. I think of you all as family."

"We feel the same way about you," said Sunny, her face beaming.

Many of them shook his hand, some patted him on the back as the group slowly dispersed to their workstations and offices. But Sunny was different. Her joyful disposition and bold Christian faith set her apart from the usual grim-faced men and women that filled the halls and offices of Detective Division.

She remained until she was the last one there then paced over to him and, stretching up on her toes, delivered a warm hug. "You don't know how hard the people at my church have been praying for you. God has a special plan for you, Nathan Press."

Press had always thought of her as a mother figure. In fact, he often wished she *were* his mom. What might life be like with a mother like that? "Thanks, Sunny. You're the best."

"Why don't you join me on Sunday? I think a lot of the folks at church would appreciate seeing you and how God has answered their prayers."

"You tell 'im, Sunny," called Killian from his cubicle.

Sunny had been inviting him to church for years along with anyone else in the office who would listen. The truth was he had grown up in the Church. It was only after tragedy had struck his family that they stopped attending. After that he just sort of lost touch with his faith.

"I'll think about it." His words were polite if not patently non-committal, and thus he immediately felt a dagger of guilt prick his conscience.

Press walked to his corner cubicle and gathered up his gear with Sunny's words still echoing inside his head. He then mustered his squad and together they again ran through the details of the Talbert case. After issuing various instructions and outlining the general overall plan of attack, he released them. Press left to use the restroom and, when he returned, found Killian polishing off a second piece of cake.

Killian shrugged. "Someone's gotta eat it."

"It's eight o'clock in the morning."

Killian just smiled, blue icing on his teeth. "What's your point?"

"Cops," Press said.

"I know, right?"

7

LAW OFFICES OF TALBERT & DONAHUE
127 DORRANCE STREET

The law offices of Talbert and Donahue were located on the top two floors of a redbrick building originally built in 1900. A little over ten years ago, it was renovated in such a way as to preserve the building's historic charm while at the same time incorporating modern conveniences and mechanical infrastructure. As a result, the intricate, handcrafted woodwork remained. Press was thankful to not be the only one in Providence who appreciated quality craftsmanship and the careful preservation of history.

The elevator door chimed open, issuing Press and Killian into a rectangular chamber that had been fashioned into a lobby. A wood-and-glass door with brass hardware stood at one end. Etched onto the textured, frosted glass were the names of the lawyers that constituted the firm's namesake.

It was apparent from the moment they entered that something was wrong. The receptionist at the front desk wore an anxious look on her face as she spoke into the phone. Her eyes locked with theirs then fell to the guns and badges at their waistlines. She waved them over, said thank you into the handset then placed it back in its cradle.

"My goodness, that was quick," she said with relief in her voice.

Killian's face screwed up in confusion. "What do you mean?"

"I just called you guys like twenty seconds ago."

As the receptionist was engaged with Killian, Press peered down a short hallway. A door stood open at the end of it. The room, which he presumed was some sort of office, was in a state of disarray. A man in a suit swept back and forth into and out of view: Riley Talbert's law partner. He was irate, barking expletives to persons unseen, while bending down every few seconds and plucking papers from the floor.

The receptionist excused herself and ambled back to the open door; she stopped and knocked on the door frame. Straining his ears, Press could hear her sweet, gentle voice—a receptionist's voice: "Mr. Donahue, sir, the police are here."

Greyson Donahue's voice, harsh and direct, boomed from within the room. "Good! Send them back. And, Lydia, bring me some coffee."

They kept their voices low and their eyes up and alert yet casual, almost bored, in fact, the way police detectives often do. Killian tilted his head ever so slightly in Press's direction. "You ever face off against *him*?"

"Donahue? Yeah. You?"

"Mmm hmm. Guy is brilliant. He's also one arrogant son of gun."

Press nodded. "My sentiments exactly."

She must have been accustomed to Donahue's manner, because when Lydia the receptionist returned, she wore nothing on her face that revealed anything—embarrassment or shock or displeasure—save for a servant's heart.

"You'll have to forgive him, he's under a great deal of stress at the present." Press's inquisitive gaze urged her on. "He has a big trial starting today and now this. You may go right back, gentleman." She smiled and motioned with an upturned hand to the closed steel door on their left. Through it they accessed the hallway that ran behind the reception desk.

Framed photos of the firm's staff hung on one side of the hall, sailboats and ocean scenes the other. Press noted the firm's organizational structure by way of the positioning of the photos. The law partners, for which the firm was named, had expensive, decorative frames which were placed above a row of smaller frames of lesser quality. These were the associates. Each photo captured a lawyer in professional pose, some offered a smile, some did not. Press counted ten attorneys in total. In another grouping of portraits were the paralegals—the office grunts—of which there were six, as well as two legal assistants, an office manager, and the receptionist they had just met out front.

"I must say, you boys got here quick!"

Press and Killian exchanged glances.

"We don't know how they got in yet, but I have our security company checking into that. Lousy degenerate, good-for-nothing—"

"Excuse me, Mr. Donahue?" Killian interrupted. "What are you talking about?"

The attorney's face revealed bewilderment. "What do you mean? We called you. About the *burglary*."

"The office was burglarized?"

"No, our offices always look like this."

Press ignored the sarcasm and let his eyes wander about the room. The nameplate on the desk indicated this was the domain of Wendy March, the firm's office manager.

Placing his hands on his hips, the attorney fixed his eyes on the two detectives before him. "If you didn't know about the burglary, then why on earth are you here?"

This time Press spoke. "Mr. Donahue, sir, your law partner is dead."

8

"I don't understand. Riley? *Dead*? How? When?"

"Sir, is there someplace we can sit down and talk privately?" Press said.

"Yes, of course." Donahue led them upstairs to his office and closed the door. It was large and smelled of wood, leather, and power. He walked past a sofa fronted by an antique coffee table and pointed to the wingback chairs just off the bow of his yacht-size desk. As Press and Killian eased into them, Donahue circled around to his high-backed, leather chair.

"Let's start over. My name is Detective Press…" He often dropped the use of "Sergeant" when introducing himself, only adding it when he felt an extra exertion of his authority was warranted or when it offered some strategic value to a conversation. "…and this is Detective Killian. We're investigating the death of Mr. Talbert," said Press.

Donahue was much more subdued now. Every movement was slower, more deliberate. He swallowed several deep breaths, braced himself on the back of his desk chair with both hands before easing into it. He possessed the sudden sobriety of a wayward courtroom that had just been gaveled to silence. "How did it happen?"

"He was killed."

The attorney gasped. "When?"

"Preliminarily, sometime between Friday afternoon and early Sunday morning." Seeing the unspoken question in Donahue's facial expression, Press continued. "We'll know more after the autopsy."

"His wife, Gwen. Does she know?"

"We haven't been able to reach her yet. We've left messages for her to call us."

Donahue seemed to not know what to do with his hands. He straightened and re-straightened his desk blotter, then did the same with a walnut-and-leather double pen stand. "She's visiting her sister in Florida. I think she lives in Tampa. Goes there every year around this time. For a birthday or anniversary or something."

"We'll get ahold of her." Press crossed his legs and propped his notepad on his knee. "To your knowledge, had Mr. Talbert been having problems with anyone?"

"Are you asking me if I am aware of anyone who wanted him dead?"

Press nodded.

"No."

"What about anyone else at the firm? Anyone receiving threats, that type of thing?"

"Nothing to be taken seriously. What I mean is that the lawyers in this firm are involved in many high-profile cases. But just because a case isn't high-profile doesn't mean emotions don't run high. We sometimes get whackos calling in or sending emails. Social media is the worst. But if you're asking if I am aware of any specific, credible threats directed at Riley or *anyone* at the firm, the answer is a hard no." His eyes suddenly shot from Press to Killian then back to Press. "Do you think anyone else here is in danger?"

"To be honest, sir, I don't know."

A shock of fear flashed in Donahue's face even though he tried hard to disguise it.

Press switched gears. "How was his marriage? Any problems there?"

Donahue shook his head. "Riley and Gwen were high school sweethearts. They've been together forever."

"Nevertheless. Is there anything that you're aware of that we should know about? Either one stepping out?"

"No. They loved each other. You could always tell. I've known Gwen for years. She's such a sweet..." Donahue's bottom lip quivered but he quickly recovered. "This is going to kill her."

"What about their children?" Killian said.

"Riley, Jr. and Christine." The utterance of their names caused a pained look to appear on his face. "Riley spoke of them fondly. He and Gwen tried to visit them as often as they could. RJ lives outside Denver, I believe. Has his own medical practice. And Christine and her family live in Tulsa. I know she's expecting her third child."

Press scribbled several notes on his pad. "So, he and the kids got along then?"

"Yes. He was quite proud of them."

"Finances. To your knowledge, how was Mr. Talbert in that department? Did he owe anyone money?"

"We rarely discussed each other's finances aside from a few investments and charitable donations from time to time." The attorney gripped his face with his left hand.

Killian leaned forward in his chair. "Did Mr. Talbert gamble? You know, casinos, the ponies, football, that type of thing?"

"Riley had no vices, if that's what you're asking. Didn't gamble, didn't do drugs. He was the perfect law partner."

"So, let's talk work then. Any cases or specific people from over the years you think we should check out? Anything at all?"

Donahue stared off into space, slowly shaking his head. "I'm sorry. Right now, I'm just at a loss."

Press gazed at the file cabinets and bookcases in Donahue's office. None appeared to have been disturbed. "Tell me about the burglary."

"You think it's related to his death?"

Much of detective work involved analyzing probabilities. A normal person might call it a coincidence. But to Press and detectives like him, there was no such thing unless it could be proved otherwise. However, because he was not given to revealing his thoughts to anyone who was not law enforcement, especially at this stage of an investigation, he simply shrugged his shoulders and said, "Maybe, maybe not."

They had Donahue walk them through the entirety of the firm's two floors from front to back. Every office, file room, break room, server room, and bathroom. They concluded their tour at a door that issued onto Eddy Street at the rear of the building.

"Employees from most of the building's tenants generally use this door to come and go since the parking lot is right here."

Press glanced up and noted the CCTV cameras looking down at him from each corner of the building. He pointed at them with his pen.

"The property management company is already checking security footage for us," said Donahue.

"Anything taken?" Killian said.

"We're still evaluating that. Nothing obvious thus far."

Press scanned the nearby parking lot. "What about service workers? Anyone new or out of the ordinary been in the office recently? An HVAC company or maybe new cleaning personnel?"

"I will double check, but no, none that I'm aware of."

Once they were back in Donahue's office, Killian drew in a deep breath, let it out slowly. "You guys keep anything valuable here? Client payments? Petty cash? Lockboxes? Or what about some insanely rich guy's last will and testament?"

Donahue shook his head with resolve. "We have the best cybersecurity money can buy. Paper documents are under lock and key. But valuables? No, we have nothing like that here. Client funds are usually accepted either electronically or by check. Whatever cash payments do come in—consulting fees, retainers, that type of thing, are deposited at the bank each day. We are intentional about not keeping cash in the office."

Press said, "I'd like our forensic people to take a good peek at all the rooms that our actor rummaged through, but Mr. Talbert's office specifically needs to be carefully processed as that room is apparently the only one that has yet to be contaminated by staff." The remark was meant to be a subtle shot. Surely, Donahue had grilled a few police officers on the stand over the course of his career about the contamination of evidence.

Donahue made a sour face.

"Is there a problem?" Press said.

"It's just that there are a lot of confidential files in Riley's office, as there are in most offices in this firm. I want to accommodate you fellas, but I do have to protect the confidentiality of the clients we serve."

"What if we were to have someone from the firm alongside us as we look around and search for evidence? That way if there is something of a confidential nature in sight, he or she can alert us, and together we can take appropriate action."

Donahue considered this. "That may work. I'll summon Ms. March at once. She's our office manager. I can think of no better guardian of the firm's interests—she's been here longer than I have. Since the day Riley started this firm. She'll see that you get what you need, but nothing that is protected and may cause us legal entanglement or harm."

"Very well. That'll be fine."

9

Wendy March was a short, stern woman with wide hips and lips that formed a permanent pucker as if she were consciously trying to keep some deep, dark secret—one that would take the jaws of life to get out of her. She wore a heavy charcoal wool jacket over a plain white blouse buttoned at the neck, a matching wool skirt, and her gray hair pulled back against her head in an impossibly tight knot.

"Reminds me of the librarian at my high school," whispered Killian dryly as the woman soldiered down the hall toward them. A pair of old-fashioned reading glasses, dangling from a chain around her neck, swished back and forth with each clipped step.

Press offered no acknowledgment but found the remark to be spot on.

"Gentleman, would you please follow me." She never even broke stride, just whisked right on by.

March stopped outside the office door of the late Riley Talbert. With a soft grunt, she produced a ring of keys attached to a bright green lanyard, unlocked the door. Press seized hold of her wrist as she was about to grab the doorknob with her bare hand.

"Allow me," he said, drawing her attention to the blue nitrile gloves he and Killian were now wearing. "We're just going to pop in for a quick walkthrough. Okay?" Before she could object, he added, "Of course, we'll leave the door open, so you can keep an eye on us from here in the hall."

March wrinkled her nose. She was clearly not used to being ordered around by outsiders let alone police detectives.

"Or we can lock this whole place down, come back with a search warrant and make everyone wait outside on the street until we're through."

The puckered lips bobbed up and down.

"Thank you, Ms. March," Press said with a humorless smile. He carefully twisted the knob and eased the door open. As the two detectives stepped into the room, Press immediately detected the odor of cigarettes, not unburnt tobacco but second-hand smoke. He turned back toward March. "Had Mr. Talbert developed a recent habit of smoking?"

Killian now tilted his head back, sniffed the air.

"Absolutely not."

As Press scanned the room, Killian's gaze was drawn to the door and its latch. "Does the door to this office lock automatically when it's closed?"

"There's a small lever on the edge of the door. If it is flipped up, the door will lock automatically when someone shuts it." Her feet firmly planted in the hall, March hinged at the waist, squinted at the open door's exposed hardware before finally donning her spectacles. "And it is in the up position. So, yes, the door would automatically lock when closed."

"Was it commonplace for Mr. Talbert to close his door upon leaving for the day?"

"It was. In fact, I can't think of a time when he ever left his door open."

Press studied the door jam. "So, whoever was in here either had a key or knows how to defeat a lock. See here? No obvious signs of tampering. And they merely pulled it shut upon leaving. That makes more sense than the actor purposefully locking the door on exit."

March nodded at his reasoning.

Press jotted this down in his notepad then resumed his assessment of the room. It was much like Donahue's with respect to size and décor, but this one had a distinctly different feel. Family photos were prevalent, on bureaus and shelves, on the desk and on the walls, whereas in Donahue's office there were none. A lot could be learned about a man from the way he kept his workspace.

Files lay scattered on the floor. Drawers had been pulled out and dumped everywhere. The place was a wreck. Press maneuvered slowly around the room. When he had worked his way behind the dead man's desk, he stopped and let his eyes roam. A computer sat atop a second desk behind Talbert's leather executive chair. Press nudged the wireless mouse with his pen. Instantly, the computer screen came alive with a system prompt for Talbert's login credentials. Press documented this in his notepad. Finally, he said, "Ms. March, I assume you are familiar with Mr. Talbert's office. Would you know if something were missing or not just by looking around?"

"Probably. I am in here all the time, consulting with Mr. Talbert over..." The words caught in her throat as the woman surely realized she would never consult or do anything else with Riley Talbert ever again. She swallowed hard. "I'm sorry. The answer is yes."

Press looked up, motioned to her with two fingers. "Would you come in here please? Just don't touch anything." He and Killian watched her almost tiptoe into the room, now fearful of disturbing anything that might be important. "Back here, just watch your step." When she was next to him, he said, "I know the office is a mess, but is there anything obvious that isn't here or perhaps something that *is* here that shouldn't be?"

Hands on her hips, the woman gazed back and forth. Judging from the fierce look on her face, it was obvious she wanted to help. "I'm sorry, I..."

"It's okay. Take your time."

She sighed, refocused her eyes. Yet again her intense scrutiny yielded the same results.

"Okay. What about his caseload? Anything he was working on that jumps out? For example, an angry client or perhaps someone he declined to represent?"

"Gia would be the best person to ask about his caseload. She's one of our paralegals. She worked almost exclusively for Mr. Talbert. If anyone would be able to answer that question, it's her."

Press remembered the woman's name from the photo in the hall: Giavanna Paglione. "May we speak with her, please?"

"She's not in yet. Her ex-husband's mother picks up her daughter each morning. The woman oftentimes runs late. Gia thinks the lady does it on purpose so she'll lose her job and the ex can file for full custody. That man and his mother are such connivers. But with Gia's parents both deceased and no other family living in the area, her options right now are limited. She's looking for a trustworthy sitter. But so far, none have passed muster."

"Understood. We'll go talk to some of the others awhile. Flag us down when she comes in, please."

10

As the BCI detectives were doing their thing, Press and Killian set out to meet with each employee in the firm for the purpose of collecting statements. Those who weren't present in the office, they would track down later, including Gia Paglione.

As it turned out, the initial round of interviews was mostly unproductive. A small glimmer of hope visited them during the questioning of Roland Finley, a recently christened partner. According to his coworkers, Finley's courtroom arguments, motions, and witness examinations were akin to precision-guided smart bombs, which the detectives quickly learned was an apt metaphor. Finley was a former JAG Corps prosecutor and among that rare breed who had experienced combat as an enlisted man prior to his commission. Everyone with whom they spoke seemed to think the man had limitless potential. He was a rising star and could match wits with anyone within New England's stuffy, blue-blood legal circles. More importantly for Press and the investigation, Roland Finley was someone who routinely fraternized with the late Riley Talbert, especially after hours.

"Yes, Detective, I saw Riley just this past Friday evening. We always made an effort to meet on Fridays after work to unwind. You know how it is. He especially liked to hear stories about my time in the Service."

"Where did you go?" Press said.

Finley pointed toward the wall. "The GPub, right down the street."

"Either of you drive?"

Finley shook his head. "No. It's only a short walk there and back."

"Anything stand out to you from that night? Did he seem upset, concerned about anything?"

"No, he was his usual self."

"Meaning?"

"Kind of quiet, until we got to talking about our families or politics or jazz."

Press nodded. "Did you discuss cases? Anything work-related?"

"No. Friday evenings were for unwinding. We never talked shop on Fridays after work. It was one of the rules we had."

"What about something on a personal level?"

Finley shook his head. "Nothing of any consequence, no."

"Did he make or receive any phone calls? Anyone stop by your table?" added Killian.

Finley's eyes went up and to the left as he searched his memory. "No," he said, shaking his head.

Press said, "What time did you guys clear out then?"

"Must have been around seven thirty or so."

"Do you know where he was going after that? He say anything?"

"Home. He said he was going *home* to read by the fire." The mention of the word seemed to have a profound effect on the attorney. He was quiet for several long seconds. "He loved his wife, his family... I can't believe he's gone."

Press produced a business card. "If there is anything else you remember or think is important, anything you think we should know, please call me. The number for my cell is on the back and it works twenty-four/seven."

"Yessir. Will do." Finley's eyes dropped to the conference-room table in front of him then slowly rose to meet Press's. "I'm going to miss him. Riley was a kind of mentor to me. Took me under his wing, taught me a lot. He was all class, that's for sure. A true man of honor. Please find whoever did this to him."

"We're going to do our best."

They conducted interviews with several more employees; all the conversations were short and lacking in probative value. They were preparing to call upon a junior associate when Wendy March poked her head into the conference room and informed them that Gia Paglione had since arrived.

The detectives found Miss Paglione behind her desk—it was smaller than Talbert's by half. She had obviously been crying. Her eyes were red-rimmed and there were several balled-up tissues on the desk in front of her. She dabbed her nose, sat up straight, and adjusted her suit jacket to appear more presentable. Press noted the stacks of files on the desk and on the floor beside her. Gia Paglione was clearly one of the firm's worker bees.

They ran through the usual questions with minimal revelation. She could imagine nothing in Talbert's current or past caseload that would precipitate someone wanting to murder him. The whole matter just seemed unconscionable. It was one remark, however, that Miss Paglione made at the conclusion of her interview that would prove to be most interesting and would steer the investigation henceforth. She prefaced her comment by saying that she didn't know if it was important or not.

"I ran into Mr. Talbert at the zoo last week. He was coming in as we were heading out."

"We?" said Killian.

"I was with my daughter. She's four. She just loves the rainforest exhibit."

"Which day?" said Press.

"Sunday, the ninth. It must have been about three in the afternoon or so."

"Anyone with him?"

"No. He was alone. But..." She sighed and gazed toward the window.

"Go on."

"I don't know... I just got the sense that he was meeting someone."

"Why is that?"

"He must have checked his watch three times in the brief time we spoke. And," Paglione regarded them both, "he's normally so good with Haley, likes to pinch her cheeks, make her laugh. Treats her like his own grandchild, you know? But that day... That day he seemed preoccupied. He didn't pinch Haley's cheeks or tease her in the usual way. He seemed..."

"Yes?"

"All business."

When Miss Paglione could recall nothing else, they thanked her, handed her a business card, and took their leave.

They checked in with Buck Kauffman, the on-scene BCI supervisor, near the reception desk. So far, he told them, the crime-scene detectives had come up with a lot of nothing. A ton of prints, which was not surprising in a busy office, but none that seemed to have been left by the actors—the prevailing theory was that there was more than one and they had worn gloves.

"Are you guys done in Talbert's office?" Press said.

Kauffman nodded. "Just finished in there."

"Good. I want to check something." Press set off at a quick pace.

Killian looked at Kauffman and shrugged.

Press corralled Wendy March and Gia Paglione en route to Riley Talbert's office and asked them to follow him there. He veered inside and walked directly to the area on the left side of the late attorney's desk. A large desk calendar lay upside on the floor. He returned it to its proper place and examined it closely, focusing on Sunday, April the 9th, the day Gia Paglione had said she'd seen Talbert at the zoo. Beneath the doodle of a sailboat, Talbert had scrawled the letters, "S.B." They were scribbled out with a black Sharpie, but the letters by virtue of their impressions in the paper were still visible.

"The initials S.B. mean anything to you, Ms. March?"

She stared at the calendar, looked up. "No."

"You, Miss Paglione?"

"I'm sorry. They do not."

Press locked eyes with Killian, conveying to him that they had their first real clue.

11

The two detectives stopped in and spoke with each of the other businesses in the building but came up dry. No one was present at the time of the burglary save for the people responsible apparently.

They took the stairs and exited out the back of the building where they met up with Gabby and Tank. Press quickly briefed them on the burglary and what they had learned thus far. Everyone then split up and hit the pavement, canvassing the offices and businesses that surrounded the building in which the law firm was housed.

"How'd you make out?" Killian asked after they had linked back up.

"Fair," said Press. "Might have something from the judicial complex on Dorrance. They have a couple cameras aimed toward the parking lot which may capture the back door of the building. Staff are going to check their system and send me whatever they find. Also, the manager at the GPub gave me a copy of the footage from Friday night." Press held up a flash drive. "We can sift through it when we get back to the office. What about you?"

"About the same. I spoke to Goshen in the D-One sub. He and Campus Safety are going to review Jay Wu's cameras and let us know if they come up with anything." PPD's District 1 sub-station was situated inside the Johnson & Wales University campus facility at 270 Weybossett Street.

"What did you guys find?" Press said, turning toward Gabby and Tank.

Gabby shook her head. "Came up dry."

"Same here," added Tank.

"All right," Press said. "I think we're done here." A RIPTA bus negotiated a turn in the nearby intersection. Press waited for the loud transit authority vehicle to pass, then added, "JK and I are going to grab a bite to eat. You guys want to join us?"

"I have to get back," Gabby said. "I've got someone coming in for an interview in an hour for that Cortez homicide and I want to do some more prep work beforehand. It's a case from a few months ago. The guy's a crucial witness and he finally agreed to come in and talk."

Press looked at the little Sherman. "Tank?"

"Would love to, Sarge, but I have a prelim. this morning on a robbery case." He checked his watch. "In fact, I gotta jet."

"Well, I'm starved," Press said, directing his words now to Killian. They had been going strong since well before sunrise. Neither had eaten anything during that time aside from JK devouring two pieces of cake back at the office, but that had been hours ago. Press took one last look around the area, mentally checking off all the places at which to follow up. After confirming they had hit them all, he said, "Okay, JK. Let's go eat. Then, if you're good, I'll take you to see the monkeys."

Killian chuckled, "Oh boy!"

They stopped off at the Seaplane Diner on Allens Avenue. It was one of Press's favorite haunts in the city. He ordered a black coffee, western omelet with some strips of crispy bacon, and toast while Killian opted for a Dr.

Pepper, triple-decker turkey club, and fries. As they waited for their food, they chatted briefly about the case then moved on to the latest department news. Nowhere on earth did office gossip move faster than within a police department. After their meals were delivered and his coffee cup topped off, Press grew serious.

"You and Sunny go to the same church, right?"

Killian nodded. "Same church. Same service."

"She's been on me for quite a while now." He forked a hunk of his omelet. "What do you think?"

"About you going? I think it's a great idea, Nate. The people are terrific. There was such an outpouring of love and support after Ryan was killed. For me *and* my family. But I'm not telling you anything you don't already know. How many gift baskets, cards, and letters did they send you? And man, the *meals*... Some of those church ladies can really cook."

"Don't I know it." Press thought back to when he had heard the news about JK's brother, Ryan. He'd been shot and killed during a terrorist attack in New York City just this past December. But that wasn't all there was to the story. Ryan Killian had fought back against the jihadis and saved untold lives in the process. It had been major national and international news at the time. Still was, in fact. Fresh details seemed to emerge daily. Details that the mockingbird media trumpeted and dissected for hours on end.

JK's brother, Ryan, was the epitome of a hero. He had laid down his life to save others. Perhaps it was because JK, too, had lost a brother that Press trusted his opinion more than anyone's.

"And best of all, Nate, West Prov. Free preaches the Bible. That's *huge*. Lots of churches these days just want to pack the seats, make people feel good, and try not to offend anyone, so they water down the truth, preaching nothing but platitudes and the Golden Rule. Churches like that, those who conform to the culture and whatever is politically expedient, are to be avoided at all costs. They muddy the water, give Christians a bad name. Scripture warns about them.

"If you're asking me, bro, I say go. Sam and I love it there. The kids, too. The church has a lot of activities for the kiddos. For singles, too." He winked. "By the way, when *are* you going to get back on the horse and start looking again for Miss Right?"

JK had a way of cutting straight to the point sometimes. Press bit into a strip of bacon as a way of avoiding the question.

"Listen, I know Maggie did you dirty, but you can't live your life alone and in misery because of her bad choices. She's gone and not coming back."

"I know, I know." Press sighed. Maggie had walked out on him just over a year ago, opting instead for the company of a gangly ophthalmologist of all people, whom she had met at the gym. The thought of her in the sack with someone else still infuriated him. After the divorce was finalized, he heard that before the eye guy there had been others. He gave the idea of reuniting with his ex-wife no quarter in his mind. Yet searching for another life partner was an altogether different thing. The whole situation had made him gun shy. He couldn't help but wonder if his next relationship would end in shambles, too.

"It's time to move on, brother. I say that as your best friend."

"I appreciate that you care. I just don't know if I'm ready to start looking again. Besides, where on earth am I ever going to meet someone, especially someone I can trust?"

Killian smiled. "Like I said, our church has a singles class you may be interested in. They do activities as a group, too. It's not a date fix-up service. There is zero pressure. Just good, wholesome fun with other singles."

Press made a face that translated to "Are you kidding me?" before uttering a simple no.

"Well, you're not going to find the woman of your dreams out riding that bike of yours eight days a week or in those books you're always reading. You've got to make an effort."

Press added no further comment thus ending the current thread of conversation. In his heart, though, he knew JK was right.

There was silence between them for several minutes while they polished off their plates. Press dabbed his mouth with a napkin and leaned back in the booth. He regarded the other patrons in the diner as the waitress returned to the table and topped off his coffee again.

"So, what's your take so far on Talbert?" said Killian, circling back to the case.

"I don't know. It's too early to tell. You?"

"I'm thinking he got himself into a bit of trouble. With another man's wife, with the mob. Something he did obviously pissed *somebody* off."

Press nodded. "I would agree with that analysis. And somehow it connects to whatever was on his desk calendar...this possible meeting with S.B. at the zoo, assuming S.B. is a person."

12

Roger Williams Park Zoo
1000 Elmwood Avenue

It was 2:00 p.m. by the time they had worked their way through the zoo and entered the Sophie Danforth Administration Building. Their contact was a man named Brad Hoke, the zoo's chief administrative officer. Hoke was a medium-size fellow with ruddy cheeks and a round belly that pressed outward against his gray button-down shirt and purple necktie.

Press needed only to inform him that they were investigating a homicide, and the man eagerly offered whatever services he and/or the zoo could provide to assist them.

"We need to look at your camera system. It seems our victim might have met someone here at the zoo."

Hoke's eyes widened. "You mean the person who killed him?"

Killian smiled. "We don't know at this point."

"Can you pull up video footage for Sunday the ninth?" Press said.

"Time?"

"Let's start at two thirty. By the way, is there any time offset with the video feeds? What I mean is," Press explained, "is the time on the feed synched up with the true date and time?"

"Yes, sir. The times are synched."

"Good."

He and Killian looked on as Hoke monkeyed with the camera system controls on his computer terminal. A series of four large-panel flatscreens were mounted on the wall above the desk. Each displayed a gridwork that corresponded to numerous camera feeds. Press counted forty-two in total. The current system was installed just last year, Hoke informed them. It now consisted of all high-definition cameras and a fast computer to process the feeds. The system could also now be accessed remotely through the internet.

"It's a lot better than the one we used to have. Our insurance carrier recommended the upgrade."

"Focus on the front gate," Press said.

They stared at the bank of screens, waiting painfully for Hoke to click to the correct camera feed.

"Hey, Brad. I think we can manage here if you've got more important things to do." Killian looked down at the back of the man's head then turned to Press so that Hoke could not see the face he was making, which communicated impatience and mind-numbing boredom all at once. The two of them had been here more times than they could remember, peering over a store owner's shoulder as he fumbled through his ill-used surveillance system. They were no longer surprised by how few of them actually knew how to run their own systems let alone how to save a copy of relevant footage to a flash drive or DVD.

"No, no. This is more important than anything I need to do today. I want to help you guys."

"That's very nice of you," said Press, meeting Killian's gaze.

"Okay. Here we go. This is the front gate."

Hoke clicked the computer mouse several times as Press and Killian focused on the screen. The time on the frame for the front gate camera feed read 15:02:17 when Press instructed Hoke to stop.

"There he is."

"Mr. Talbert?" said Hoke. "*He's* your victim?"

"Yeah, why? Do you know him?"

Hoke's face revealed mournful shock. "Mr. Talbert is one of our faithful donors. Every year, he gives the zoo ten thousand dollars."

"Can you follow him? See where he goes?"

"Sure." Hoke's cheerful, upbeat disposition had notably darkened.

Press set his leather-bound notepad on a nearby table and crossed his arms, the glow of the monitors flashing against his pupils. Via the camera feeds, they followed Talbert from the gate past the zebra exhibit. Gia Paglione was right. Talbert did seem all business. His stride wasn't hurried, but it was certainly deliberate. The paralegal and her daughter seemed to have caught Talbert off guard. The impression that Press got as he watched their interaction was that the attorney was taking considerable pains to be polite. To an experienced police detective, however, it couldn't be more obvious: Talbert was preoccupied with something. He checked his watch, fidgeted with his hands, rotated his head back and forth, didn't focus on Gia or her daughter as they spoke. What was he so anxious about? Being late? Being seen? Both?

The detectives looked on studiously as the video documented Talbert's subsequent movement through the park. Outside the Meller-Danforth Educational Center at the back of the property, Talbert stopped, glanced down at his wristwatch, and scanned his surroundings. The attorney then ambled toward the glass doors, yanked one open, and disappeared inside.

"Pause it," said Press. "Are there cameras in there?"

"Just one." Hoke pointed at a frame displayed on the bottom of one of the monitors. "It covers the lobby just inside the ed. center's main doors."

"Got it. Okay you can play it."

Hoke let the footage roll. Now they saw Talbert from the opposite angle—he was coming toward the camera. He swept into the ed. center's entrance, hesitated in the lobby for a beat then turned to his left.

Twenty-two minutes had elapsed on the camera feed by the time Talbert emerged back on the video monitor. He was still alone, but now his countenance had changed. He looked concerned. Fearful even.

"I don't get it," said Hoke.

Press ignored the comment. He asked Hoke for a copy of the footage that would include the two hours prior to Talbert's arrival through an hour after closing.

"Anything to help you guys. Mr. Talbert was more than just a donor. He was a very nice man."

13

**PROVIDENCE PD
CENTRAL STATION**

The office was hopping now, even more so than a typical Monday afternoon. Based on the chatter amongst detectives on duty and a quick scan of the morning's flash sheet—a weekly department intelligence bulletin—the weekend had been a busy one for the PPD.

On top of the usual assaults, thefts, and B&Es, detectives were now working a fresh string of street robberies and a Sunday night shootout between gangbangers that had resulted in three people being hospitalized, one man—an innocent bystander—paralyzed from the waist down.

Press dropped his briefcase and slid into his desk chair. "Hey, JK. I'm pulling up the GPub footage if you want to see."

A few seconds later, Killian swung his chair around the cubicle wall and maneuvered it next to Press's. Press plugged the flash drive from the GPub into his desktop computer and navigated to the files that contained the footage of Riley Talbert and Roland Finley having drinks Friday evening. The clarity of the video was crystal clear. So too was the fact that nothing remotely consequential occurred within the confines of the GPub's walls. The phone on his desk rang, but he ignored it as he clicked through the footage again just to be sure he hadn't missed something. His head pitched slightly forward, Press scrutinized the screen with the same result. There were no curious behaviors by anyone on camera. No visitors to the two men's table. No awkward movements or expressions by either man as they engaged each other in friendly conversation. And neither man left the table for any amount of time for the duration of their afterwork unwind session. The conclusion? Aside from corroborating Finley's statement, there was nothing of probative value to the investigation here. Or was there?

He first saved the GPub footage to the appropriate department media server, pulled the flash drive free of his machine, and tossed it into a small manila folder, which he locked in his desk. He would log it into evidence later.

Press clicked back to the footage now safely secured on the media server, scrolled back through it until he found what he was looking for. He paused the video at various spots and snapped several screenshots of the frozen footage, copying each successive image to an often-used template he had created long ago and kept in his MY FORMS folder, which resided in his user-specific account on one of the department's servers. Press then closed the video file and set about cropping the photos and enlarging them in the new document.

"His shoes?" said Killian.

Press nodded as he added a heading to the document above the words UNCLASSIFIED//LAW ENFORCEMENT SENSTIVE – FOR OFFICIAL USE ONLY that were already there in red font. He next supplied a short narrative that sufficiently summarized the investigation, enough for the BOLO to make sense. At the bottom of the page, he applied the case number and his contact information. Satisfied after carefully proofreading his creation, he fired off a department-wide email to which he'd attached the document.

"Smart," Killian said.

A few seconds passed before Press noticed the red light blinking on his desk phone, an indication of a new voice-mail message. He checked the number in the phone's call history before playing the message. The first three digits were 813—the area code for Tampa, Florida.

He punched two buttons on the phone's console and at the same time lifted the handset to his ear. The message was from Gwen Talbert. The urgency and sadness in her voice was apparent. She had obviously heard that her husband was dead. She provided her cell phone number and said she would be waiting for his call back.

Press related this all to Killian, who agreed to take the flash drive containing the zoo's CCTV footage across the room to the unit's intel analyst, Carla Sheffield. With the aid of facial recognition technology, they would hopefully be able to identify anyone seen entering and/or leaving the zoo's educational center before and after Riley Talbert with the initials S.B. It would be a tedious process, but one that might give them the lead they needed to break the case wide open. Detective work was full of these types of tasks—time-consuming, meticulous sifting. There were no shortcuts to building a rock-solid criminal case. Yes, sometimes things fell in your lap unexpectedly, but usually results were born of plain, old hard work. Either way, the feeling of latching onto that one beautiful clue that resulted in the discovery of more leads and clues and the eventual arrest and conviction of the perpetrator was like nothing else. There truly was a thrill in the hunt.

"Hit me up if you guys come up with anything," said Press. "I need to call Mrs. Talbert."

"Will do."

The phone rang only once before a woman answered. Her voice was alert and halting.

"Mrs. Talbert, this is Nathan Press. I'm a detective with the Providence Police Department."

"What's happened to Riley? What can you tell me?"

"First, on behalf of the police department and myself, allow me to express my condolences. I knew your husband. He was a good man."

There was a pause followed by several sniffles. "Thank you, Detective."

"Ma'am, I would like to speak with you in person. The sooner the better. Do you know when you will be back in town?"

"I'll be on a flight in the morning. If all goes well, I should be back around ten a.m."

"How about I come by your place at noon? That way you have some time to get in and get settled."

"That will be fine. And thank you again, Detective."

Press hung up the phone and scribbled the time down in his notepad. He flipped the page and made several more notes about tasks that needed to be performed. Lists were a detective's best friend.

Near the top of this one was determining where Talbert went into the water, or at least doing his level best to do so. He picked up the phone and dialed a buddy in the Marine Unit of a state-level organization. They agreed to meet in an hour.

Press leaned back in his chair, which groaned in protest. Amidst the ringing phones, voices chattering away in various cubicles, and the otherwise general reverberations of the busy office floor, he mentally reviewed what was known thus far.

Talbert was last seen alive by Roland Finley on Friday sometime around 7:30 p.m. He was found along the bank of the Providence River on Monday at 1:50 a.m. According to the medical examiner's on-scene assessment, there was no obvious cause of death, but the consensus among the ME and detectives on scene was that Talbert had drowned after being severely beaten. It's hard for one to stay alive in a body of water when one is tossed into it unconscious. Press was banking on the fact that the ME would have more conclusive findings tomorrow after the post. It was scheduled for 8:00 a.m.

He next considered what had become of Talbert's car. It had been absent from the law firm's parking lot when he and Killian were there earlier. A black Mercedes-Benz AMG GLS that retails for well over a $100K doesn't just disappear. Presumably, Talbert had driven it from the lot after having drinks with Roland Finley.

Press logged back on to his computer workstation and then into the state's secure law enforcement portal. Once there, he searched Rhode Island's DMV records for all vehicles owned by Riley and Gwen Talbert. The document center along the far wall whirred. He paced to the machine and snagged a single sheet from the paper tray, noting the VIN number halfway down the page.

He returned to his desk and buzzed through the list of stored contacts in his computer. When he'd found the right one, he picked up his desk phone and dialed. The Mercedes-Benz representative dutifully took down his name and number and the information he was seeking and, in an efficient voice, said she could help. All she would need was a faxed request on department letterhead.

Press hammered out the requested document quickly via a template he had created during a previous case and faxed it to her. Soon afterward, he received an email attached to which was a full accounting of Riley Talbert's vehicle operation, complete with location information from Mercedes-Benz's robust telematics system. The data was limited in scope to the date of his death—Friday, the 14th—onward. The records showed that the connection with Talbert's SUV was offline as of the time the MB analyst had pulled it from the system, which was only a few minutes ago.

Press clicked on the hyperlink showing the GPS coordinates of the SUV's last known location. A map instantly appeared on his computer screen. Using the mouse, Press zoomed in on the spot. He printed what was on the screen then called out to Gabby.

She promptly joined him at the printer. "Yeah, Sarge?"

He pointed to an area he had circled on the printed map. "I need you and Tank to go check this area for Talbert's Mercedes. He handed her the other sheet he had printed previously, the one that contained the vehicle's make, model, tag number, and VIN. "I have to run out and meet someone or else I'd do it myself."

Gabby listened intently to his instructions. Intelligent and fiercely determined, she was one of the unit's best detectives. Like him her voice had remnants of an accent that was not native to Providence or even New England for that matter. Her parents had moved here from Costa Rica when she was seven. After school, she had joined the United States Army, quickly earning the rank of E-5. Gabby was a spunky, fit overachiever who loved life and America and took absolutely no crap from anyone.

"No problem," she said in her usual self-confident manner.

"Call me with whatever you find...or don't find."

14

Rhode Island Department of Environmental Management
235 Promenade Street

On the short drive over to Promenade Street, Press ruminated some more about Riley Talbert's missing shoes. How did they disappear? Where were they now? He had a strong suspicion of what might have happened to them thus the email he had sent out to all sworn PPD officers. Would it bear fruit? Only time would tell. What was more important right now, however, was to locate where exactly the attorney had gone into the water. The best way he could think to do that was to consult with Leo Korver.

He had first crossed paths with Lt. Leonard Korver during his time in the Patrol Bureau. Press had been a young patrol officer while Korver had been a field officer in the Marine Unit, one of the four units within the DEM's Division of Law Enforcement. Among its other responsibilities, the Marine Unit was known for its water-based search-and-rescue capability. One discipline that played a significant role in S&R efforts was mapping the water currents and flow rates around the state. And that specifically was what Press was hoping Korver could help him make sense of relative to the Talbert murder investigation.

The DEM offices were located inside an enormous, multi-story, redbrick structure that had once been home to a manufacturing plant. In addition to the DEM footprint, the campus contained numerous businesses and over four hundred luxury apartments.

Press found Korver in his third-floor office. The room was neat and tidy with family photos on the desk and a few framed news articles highlighting successful search-and-rescue operations on the exposed brick wall behind him. Several scale models of the unit's marine vessels were prominently displayed atop file cabinets along with numerous field manuals and an aluminum SOP binder.

"How's the family?" Press began. "Last I remember your daughter was looking at my alma mater for grad school and your son was about to finish his sophomore year at Penn State."

"You've got a good memory, Nate. Cassie ultimately chose MIT over Brown. She's pursuing her PhD in computational science and engineering."

"She always was a smart kid."

"Look who's talking." Korver smiled. "Brandon's in the police academy up in Boston."

"Just like his old man."

"But hopefully *he* will stay in and make a career of it."

"Why did you leave the BPD again?"

"It's a long story. And I'm not in the mood to tell it." Korver inched his desk chair forward. "So, what brings you to my house?"

Press explained the nature of events that had led him here. "Any chance you can help us narrow down where Talbert may have gone into the water?"

"I don't know. Usually we're working the reverse: We know where someone fell in or jumped and then we try to find the body. With your scenario, there are a number of factors to consider. Each of them presents a difficult proposition."

"Can you do it?"

Korver sighed, the wrinkles in his forehead revealing considerable mental calculation. "I can give you a number of educated guesses based on the current and flow rates, weather and the data you've provided, but that's the best I can do."

"Understood. I just need to make the area of our search more manageable. I'll take whatever you can give me."

"I assume you need it right away."

Press smiled.

"All right, I'll stay a few hours over tonight and see what I can come up with. I should be able to have something for you by tomorrow afternoon at the earliest."

They shook hands and Press headed out.

His phone vibrated inside his leg pocket the minute he stepped into the warmth of the spring sunshine. Press squinted into the screen as he walked to his truck.

"What's up, Gabby?"

"We found Talbert's car."

"Where is it?" He listened as she explained where they were. "Okay, sit tight. I'll be right there."

15

Lincoln Woods State Park
Lincoln, Rhode Island

Press shot north on Route 146 to Exit 4. At the end of the ramp, he turned left onto Twin River Road and again hammered the gas pedal. He slowed down as he entered Lincoln Woods State Park. It was a gorgeous spring day and as expected there were people all over the place.

He knew the park well. It was a place where he enjoyed hiking and mountain biking. The woods here, like much of Rhode Island, were riddled with giant rock formations. It was through these rocks and canopies of lush green forest that he snaked his truck.

Press turned off Table Rock Road, a narrow, two-lane ribbon of pavement that wound through the park, onto a dirt track that weaved upward through the trees to a point where it looped back on itself. Dusty bits of gravel crunched beneath his truck tires as he crept forward.

There at the dead end, he found Gabby and Tank leaning against the former's black unmarked Ford Fusion. They had already strung up yellow crime-scene tape to prevent vehicles or foot traffic from disturbing the area beyond her car. As Press exited his truck, he saw the dead attorney's Mercedes-Benz SUV, or what was left of it, there in the dirt circle. Now, it was nothing more than a burned-out husk.

Together they stepped closer to the vehicle, careful not to disturb potential evidence that might be on the ground. The pungent odor of melted plastics, gasoline, and other flammable materials—in a modern vehicle there were many—stung his nose.

"Not much left is there?" Press said.

Tank shook his head. "I'm surprised no one noticed it today."

"It's secluded up here," said Press, swiveling at the hips as he thoughtfully took in the scene. "According to the Mercedes records, it was nighttime when the signal was lost, remember?" He glanced up at the trees that skirted the circular dirt track. "Thankfully, the whole forest didn't burn down." Press slowly walked around the vehicle's skeleton. When he had drawn next to the front-passenger door, he stopped, leaned forward. "This is interesting."

"What is it?" Gabby walked to where he was standing, followed his gaze to the bare metal. "That a bullet hole?"

"Sure looks like it. Nine mil maybe? Look, there's another." Using his pen, he pointed to a creased perforation in the bottom of the vehicle's A-pillar.

"I don't get it. Talbert wasn't shot."

"No, Tank, he wasn't." Press straightened, scrawled some notes in his pad then slowly turned in a 360-degree circle, trying to visualize what whoever had torched the car and left it to burn might have seen when they were here, how they would have approached the area, how they would have left. It would have been very dark here during the night. The shadows cast by the raging vehicle fire would have made it difficult to see anything along the edges of the dirt path.

"State police are on the way," said Gabby.

"Good deal."

Tank folded his muscular arms—he looked like he was hugging a football and preparing to lunge into the endzone just like he had back in his glory days. Tank Meredith had been one heck of a tailback in school. He'd even been invited to the NFL Combine. But when his father died of a sudden heart attack and his mother was diagnosed with an aggressive form of cancer in the very same month, Tank gave up his dream of playing pro football. Instead, he chose to help take care of his terminally ill mother—a decision he never once regretted. He still loved football, but now his passion was all things CrossFit. "What are you thinking, Sarge?"

Mindful of his footsteps, Press paced toward the edge of the dirt road and began slowly examining the grass with his eyes. "Another vehicle could have been parked here. See how the grass is pressed down."

Gabby nodded. "Maybe whoever dumped the car here had a buddy pick him up. Or follow him here."

"I'd actually be shocked if there *wasn't* a second vehicle." Press was still taking in the scene when a raucous hip-hop tune bled into the serene environs. The three detectives turned their attention toward its origin. There, in the tall grass, not far from where Press inferred another vehicle had been parked, a cell phone lay face down.

Press regarded Gabby, and she him as Tank squinted back at them into the fading sunlight. As if directed by someone out of view, they all smiled in unison.

"I love stupid criminals," Gabby declared.

Press turned and took in the glorious sunset. "Me, too, Gabby. Me, too."

When the state police trooper had finally arrived and learned that the vehicle was linked to a murder in the city, he eagerly deferred to Press and the PPD. A BCI team soon responded. They snapped the necessary photographs, took some measurements, and completed various other tasks. Once the phone had been properly documented, examined for prints, and swabbed for DNA, the senior BCI detective carefully placed it into a Faraday bag and handed it to Press, who in turn passed it to Gabby.

Though it probably would yield few clues at this stage, Press had Talbert's vehicle towed back to the police impound. Maybe the BCI guys would be able to dig one of the slugs out of the vehicle. A check of the ground once the SUV had been moved, visually and with a metal detector, turned up nothing useful.

Despite a tedious search of the area for anything else of evidentiary value—a discarded cigarette butt, a dropped wallet, a cartridge case, even a thrown pistol, or an unfired round, they came away empty-handed.

"Well, at least we have an idea when the car was dumped here."

Gabby looked at Press.

"It had to have been driven here and torched sometime last night. The phone, too."

"The rain," she said.

Press nodded. "Yep. Phone's still operational. Also, there's no rust anywhere on the vehicle. All that rain we had ended late Sunday afternoon."

"So now what?" said Gabby.

"I want you to punch a ticket for that phone first thing tomorrow morning. Then get it to Paulie." Paul Martini was the PPD's resident cyber guru.

Press watched as Gabby and Tank drove off into the gathering darkness. He sat there in his truck for several minutes with the engine running and headlights illuminating the blackened earth where Talbert's SUV had been torched. Sporadic radio traffic crackled from the mobile unit in the center console.

Something suddenly occurred to him. He pulled up the morning's flash sheet on his phone. He remembered seeing something on it about the shooting from last night that might connect to the Talbert case.

Using his finger to scroll through the document, he finally landed on the post he was after. He read the summarized facts of the case then zoomed in on three slightly pixelated images detectives had culled from neighborhood camera footage that captured the suspect vehicle approaching and then fleeing the shooting scene. Based on the camera angles, the vehicle's tag was not visible, but to Press there was no doubt.

It was Talbert's Mercedes.

16

Providence PD
Central Station

The office was quiet when he arrived back at Central Station. Most of the detectives in the Division were either still out on cases or had gone home for the night. Throughout the various units, a few tireless souls still pecked away at their computer terminals, typing up that last supplemental report of the day or replying to the countless emails—tomorrow there would be countless more—before they would call it a night. Fewer still loitered in the corridors after their shifts had ended to chat about their personal lives, share a laugh or two, or complain about the latest perceived injustice perpetrated by the department brass.

Gabby was already busy at her desk typing up a search warrant for the phone they had recovered near Talbert's burned vehicle. Press breezed past her and continued around Killian's empty post to the corner of the room, where his large cubicle was situated. He let out a heavy sigh after dropping his messenger bag to the floor and rocking into his chair. It had been a long first day back and he was starting to feel its effects.

"Wonder how JK made out with the zoo footage," he called to Gabby over the cubicle wall.

"Good from the way it sounded. He and Tank just ran out to grab some pizza. Said he'll brief us when they get back."

Press hadn't even thought of food until now. Suddenly, he felt very hungry. While he waited for his dinner, he hammered out a search warrant of his own for Riley Talbert's cell phone records. Hopefully the location history would help determine where his killer or killers had first contacted him and maybe even where they had taken and tortured him.

With that done, he scrolled through some emails. Being out of the office for six months left thousands to sort through even after a week of light duty. After about fifteen or so, he leaned back from his desk, ran his fingers through his hair then stretched his back and neck.

Tank and Killian were laughing heartily as they emerged through the unit's main door. Both looked fresh and chipper, like they could go another day or two without a minute of sleep. Tank set the pizzas down on a table along with a stack of paper plates and napkins while Killian procured bottles of water for everyone.

When the detectives were all settled in and engaged with their supper, Killian began. "It wasn't easy, but thanks to Clearview AI we've managed to narrow it down to three people with the initials 'S.B.' who could have been at the zoo to meet Talbert: Sabrina Babcock, Seth Barnett, and Steven Brockenridge."

Gabby bit into a slice of pizza as Press continued to study Killian and a stack of papers the man was now indicating.

"I had workups done on all three." Killian wiped his hands on a napkin before passing out packets of paper bound with black binder clips to each of his squad mates in successive order.

"You like any particular person over the other two?" said Press, perusing the first packet.

"I've only had a chance to do a quick scan of each dossier. Nothing jumped out. None of them has a criminal history. And their social media accounts—the ones we could find—are anemic, to say the least. They all seem to lead rather boring lives. Babcock has family ties to Chicago. Moved out here about ten years ago. Her younger brother has been in and out of jail. He's locked up right now in the Ohio State Pen in Youngstown on drug trafficking and gun charges."

"Any link to Talbert?" said Tank.

Killian shook his head. "None on the surface."

Press held his finger on a particular data point. "Says here she runs a local non-profit."

"That's right. Their focus is on social justice issues, specifically gun control and climate change."

Gabby looked up from the papers in her lap and, with a straight face, said, "C'mon, Sarge, don't be shy. You know you've donated to that outfit."

Press turned toward her, his face lacking all emotion.

She smiled in answer; everyone did.

"Moving on," Press said.

"Right. Next cat is Seth Barnett. He's an MIT grad from Wisconsin. Far as I can tell, he works for some data company in town. Typical computer nerd from the looks of it. He's as vanilla as they come.

"And lastly, we have Steve Brockenridge." They all flipped to the third packet. "He's a Boston transplant. Ex-wife and kids still live there. He's had a handful of traffic offenses in the past few years, mostly speeding. Recently filed a civil case over a landlord/tenant dispute."

"Hardly seems like something Talbert would be involved with," Press said.

Everyone's body language reflected their agreement.

"Brockenridge is currently employed by Rhode Island Hospital as a nurse. Girlfriend is some hotshot accountant. She lives down in Swansea. Her family is *loaded*."

"And she's hot," offered Tank, holding up the page that displayed the woman's driver's license photo.

Gabby rolled her eyes.

"Right now," Press said, "I'm thinking that Brockenridge is our best candidate."

"I think you're right." Killian neatened his stack of papers. "There's a lot more digging to do, but that's about it for the thirty-thousand-foot view."

Their bellies satisfied, the detectives retreated to their desks to type up reports and prep for the next day. Press meanwhile continued pouring through the intel workups. He meticulously read each page, looking for anything that might be exploited or explored. The key to solving Talbert's murder lay with one of these three individuals. He was sure of it. What about him or her had led someone to kill? Nothing was glaringly obvious. JK was right. These people did seem to live boring lives. As things stood right now, Brockenridge felt like their best bet. But if there was one thing he had learned from his very first day on the job, it was that looks could be deceiving.

17

OFFICE OF STATE MEDICAL EXAMINERS
50 ORMS STREET

The main autopsy suite within the Office of State Medical Examiners, otherwise referred to as OSME, was cool and smelled of disinfectant and death. From a cabinet just outside the brightly lit room where the post-mortem examination would be performed, Press found booties, gloves, and other personal protective equipment, which he donned by rote. He had been here in the macabre bowels of the Chapin Building many times, having contributed in some form or fashion to close to 100 death investigations in his five years in Major Crimes. Each occurrence of post-mortem examination brought on renewed feelings of disgust and at the same time fascination. It was here perhaps more than anywhere else that he observed firsthand the evidence of God's awesome creation. The intricacies and complexities of the human body were infinite. Though his faith had long been dormant, he knew at his very core that God was real. The way everything fit and worked together to constitute a living, breathing, thinking human being proved it beyond all doubt.

Paradoxically, it was here, too, that he bore witness to the perversities and perniciousness of the Devil's handiwork. The fact that evil existed in the world proved that Satan did, too. He had seen it in many forms. Nowhere else, save the field of battle, could the evil in the hearts of men be seen up close and personal more so than a pathology lab.

These thoughts and more skittered through his mind as Dr. Nandkishore Vijayasekharan, the forensic pathologist, whom everyone called Dr. V for obvious reasons, and his assistant readied the nude, chalky white form of the late Riley Talbert. In this case, it was the assistant, a garrulous yet whimsical former Attleboro police officer, who did most of the prep work. Once the body was photographed, rinsed, and opened, Dr. V set about his duties, which he carried out with meticulous precision. Press regarded the conscientious physician warmly, as warmly as anyone could in such a chilling setting.

Aside from the assistant's occasional attempt to provoke a laugh or, at the very least, a comment or two, Press remained quiet and looked on with thoughtful consideration. At various times, he iterated the findings from the scene where Talbert had been found and added to those a description of the life and lifestyle of the decedent. All these things Dr. V documented in his notes, which lay atop a metal podium of sorts with wheels.

Press leaned against a desk in the corner as he observed Dr. V remove Talbert's brain and vital organs, weigh them, and carefully exam each. Sections were taken and placed in special containers for further testing.

It was during the examination of the heart that Dr. V waved him over. "See this?"

"Yeah, but I have no idea what I'm looking at."

Dr. V stepped over to a counter, pulled open a drawer. When he returned, he handed Press a powerful magnifying glass. "Here, use this." Dr. V maneuvered his thin stainless-steel tool to an area of the heart he had opened for close inspection. He tilted his head back so the bifocals he wore could better focus his eyes on the tissue he was now indicating. "This is the left ventricle. It's the heart's main pumping chamber. You see this here?" He moved the tool back and forth in a U motion as Press adjusted the angle of the glass.

"Yeah?"

"It's abnormally thick. It's what we call hypertrophy."

"You're saying he had heart disease?"

"Yes. Actually, I was expecting to find something like this."

"What do you mean?"

Dr. V lowered his head and looked at him over his spectacles. The surgical mask somewhat muffled his voice. "The blunt injuries to the head and trunk are considerable in number but largely superficial. None caused internal injury sufficient to explain death. An example of that would be a subdural hematoma. You follow?"

"So far."

"Rarely do we see the stress of an assault such as this, severe as it was," he motioned toward Talbert's body, "singularly causing death by the triggering of an arrhythmia—an irregular rhythm of the heart. Usually, we see some pre-existing heart disease like coronary atherosclerosis or cardiac hypertrophy, which is what we have here in the heart of Mr. Talbert."

Press looked from Dr. V to the organ, which lay atop a faded teal surgical cloth on the stainless-steel table.

"What happens in a case like this is that the stress from the assault causes the body to release adrenalin. Adrenalin in turn causes the heart to beat faster and the blood pressure to increase. These physiologic changes can cause an irregular rhythm of the heart and, in fact, cause the heart to stop."

"You're saying he died from a heart attack?"

"Brought on by the assault, yes."

"So, it's a homicide."

"Assuming the tox comes back normal, my ruling for cause of death will be cardiac arrhythmia due to physical altercation complicating hypertensive cardiovascular disease with the manner of death being, yes, homicide."

Press removed his outer layer of gloves and scribbled the medical lingo onto his notepad as fast as he could. "What about time of death?"

"Based on what you've told me about the case thus far, in addition to the water temperature and, most importantly, the state of the body, I put time of death somewhere between nine p.m. Friday night and three a.m. Saturday morning."

Press nodded as he continued writing. "Someone from BCI will be over to collect the DNA standard, fingernail clippings, and clothing."

"Very well. One last thing, Detective."

"Yes?"

Dr. V gazed down at the body on the table before turning back toward him. "Catch the savage who did this."

Press looked him dead in the eyes. "That's the plan, doc. That's the plan."

18

SWAN POINT CEMETERY
585 BLACKSTONE BOULEVARD

It was near the grave of Sullivan Ballou, a Union Army major and native Rhode Islander killed during the Civil War, where they were to meet. The sound of birds shrieking back and forth to each other filled the air. Somewhere off in the distance a lawnmower hummed.

Lance Cheney took in the pleasant scent of flowers and freshly cut grass as he glanced down at the earth around him. His eyes moved to the shoes on his feet as he rocked back on his heels. He took care to wipe the wet clippings and a few fallen cherry blossoms from the toes of his brogues as he ruminated. With all that glorious April sunshine cutting through the trees, the well-groomed grounds seeming to roll on forever, busy wildlife scurrying about, he couldn't help thinking how ironic it was for a place reserved for the dead to convey such energy, such life.

A bumble bee buzzed about his head as he continued to study the serene, idyllic landscape. There had been a time in his life when he would have swatted at it repeatedly, letting the white-hot rage within him pour forth through profane speech and wild, aggressive actions until the insect was nothing more than a smear on the blade edge of his balled-up fist. But his time in the Diplomatic Security Service, where he routinely worked alongside US

Special Forces types, had changed all that. It had taught him to channel his anger, be strategic in its design, and ruthless in its deployment. Add to that the highly specialized training he had received over the years, most notably from his current employer, and the result was a man who was at the top of the food chain with respect to his chosen profession.

"You sure he said ten hundred?"

Cheney's eyes flitted toward the big man standing in the shade of a yellowwood tree. "Yes."

Zug wrinkled his nose. As he adjusted his posture, the muscles beneath his tightly stretched polo shirt flexed. "He's late."

Cheney consulted his Suunto Core wristwatch. It was three minutes past. "He'll be here."

"Holy pupkis, it's hot out." Zug lifted each thick arm into the air in quick succession. Sweat was beginning to dot his black shirt at the armpits.

"Relax, Nancy. You won't melt." Cheney squinted in the glare of the sun. "And it's only seventy degrees out here. How could you be sweating?"

"Man, I hate the waiting. Especially in the sun."

"Then go wait in the car," snapped Cheney.

"It's hotter in there than it is out here."

Marcus Zug wasn't a thinker. He was a veteran front-line soldier, one who fearlessly charged the enemy without a thought in his mind save to kill. It was this trait alone that made him a lethal professional. Cheney had realized early on that they made a good team, warts and all.

Zug pinched the front of his shirt and pulled on it several times in quick succession, allowing the air to access his skin beneath, then stood with his hands on his hips, legs spread like an athlete waiting for play to resume after a timeout.

Cheney couldn't blame him. He abhorred the waiting, too. The trick was not to think about it but to stay sharp and focus on the job at hand.

Another two minutes expired before a dark sedan turned onto the long leafy lane that snaked through cemetery. The bright sunshine and the darkly tinted windows made it impossible to see the vehicle's occupants.

Zug stepped beside him and together they prepared to greet the man for whom they worked.

Just as the vehicle lurched to a halt on the pavement and its rear door swung open, a red fox emerged from behind a distant headstone. It silently skulked into a snatch of brilliant sunlight. The snout rotated toward them, explored the air. Cheney shifted his gaze to Brenner for only a blink. When he glanced back at the fox, it was gone. He considered the metaphor he'd just witnessed. Robert Brenner was that red fox.

Dressed in a starched, white button-down shirt, pleated khaki trousers, and simple, rubber-soled shoes with laces—Agency men like him never wore loafers, Brenner paced toward them, his eyes scanning the environs as he moved.

"Hey, boss." said Zug, a goofy grin on his squinting face.

Brenner glared at them. He did not suffer fools kindly. Neither did he engage in small talk. He was all business all the time. Cheney wondered if that was how he had been during his time as a spook. Despite years of working for the guy, there was still much he didn't know about the man or his background. And it wasn't for lack of digging. Aside from attaining coveted deputy director status, the man seemed to have no history. What Cheney did know from the myriad myths and legends that circulated amongst his friends and colleagues was that for thirty years Brenner had worked for the CIA in various capacities, was fluent in several languages including French and Arabic, and was an expert in black operations. His curriculum vitae also included targeted assassination, running spies, intelligence gathering, and information warfare. Brenner had imparted much of his wisdom and tradecraft knowledge to him and Marcus and others in the company. Cheney wasn't afraid of much—people or things, but he did fear Robert Brenner. By all accounts, the man was a dangerous and very intelligent sociopath.

"What's the latest?" Brenner said without preamble.

Cheney gathered himself while feigning nonchalance. "We still haven't found him."

Brenner's intense, dark eyes swept from Cheney to Zug then back to Cheney. "He's not a ghost, gentleman. Find him. Or I'll find people who will."

"We will, boss," Zug said with a half-hearted smile.

"See that you do. And remember, I need him alive." He held their gaze for a moment to underscore his order.

"Yes, sir." Cheney could feel sweat running between his shoulder blades.

And that was that. Brenner turned, walked to the waiting sedan, and climbed inside through the rear door, which his Marine-like driver/bodyguard had dutifully propped open. Cheney watched the broad-shouldered man in the gray suit snap the door shut, pace around the vehicle, duck inside, and drive off.

"Boss didn't look happy. We had better find him," said Zug. "And fast."

Cheney regarded the big man then joined him in staring at the sedan as it glided over a slight rise in the paved lane and disappeared through the trees.

19

**TALBERT RESIDENCE
126 HARTSHORN ROAD**

With the search warrant for Talbert's cell phone records signed, stamped, and fired off to the service provider, Press and Killian hopped in his pickup truck and headed for the Talbert house. Barely out of the parking lot, they copied a radio broadcast for an apparent drug overdose. The patient was believed to be deceased, according to the dispatcher.

Press dialed Gabby and asked that she and Tank respond to the scene and follow-up on any leads that might point to a drug dealer. They would all link back up later at the office. You had to be light on your toes in this business. There was always something or someone ready to rip you away from your current plans, work-related or otherwise.

Now pulling to a stop in the driveway, Press switched off the engine. As Killian reached for his door handle, Press said, "Hold up a minute."

The detective turned back, exhibiting a questioning gaze.

"I need to tell you something." Press stared at the dash. "He wrote me a letter. Before he died."

"Who did? *Talbert*?"

Press nodded.

After several contemplative beats, Killian said, "What did it say?"

Press recited the letter's contents from memory.

"I don't understand. What did he want to give you?"

"I don't know. But it obviously has something to do with his murder."

Killian relaxed back in his seat, considering this new information. "Are you going to tell the family?"

"Not yet. In fact, right now, you're the only one who knows. I'd like to keep it that way for the time being."

Killian studied the home's front door.

"Not to get all spooky on you, but just in case anything happens to me, the letter is locked in the bottom drawer on the left side of my desk. It's tucked inside a manila envelope beneath a stack of legal pads."

"All right." Killian chewed his bottom lip.

"I apologize for not telling you sooner," Press said.

Killian shrugged, nodded. "You were just being cautious."

JK never wavered in his loyalty. He always had a positive outlook, always had his back. Their friendship was ironclad.

"Ready?" Killian said, extending his arm.

Press completed the fist bump. "Yeah."

He checked himself in the mirror upon exiting the truck. The last thing the widow Talbert needed to see right now was a piece of food stuck between the teeth of the man investigating her husband's murder.

The neighborhood was quiet and somber as if it too were somehow grieving. A few houses over, a large dog let out two deep barks, declaring their arrival, then grew silent.

Press picked up the folded newspaper in the driveway and followed Killian to the door. They waited patiently on the porch after engaging the doorbell.

Killian glanced around the front yard as Press stood ramrod straight and stared at the door.

To be sure, speaking to the victim's family was his least favorite task in a homicide investigation. Truth be told, he hated it. Notwithstanding, it was oftentimes one of the most important and productive things an investigator could do in developing a clear and total picture of the victim, his activities, his friends, his enemies, the list went on. In the parlance of criminal justice professionals, this was called victimology. Indeed, the family could be a wealth of information about the victim and just might provide that one fateful lead or crucial clue, knowingly or unknowingly, that would send the case down the path that ended at the perpetrator's doorstep. The converse was also true. Sometimes the family didn't know a jot about their loved one, the life they led, or events and circumstances that may have contributed to their untimely demise.

The latter scenario is the one in which Press found himself this time around. Or so it seemed from the outset.

Gwen Talbert and her daughter, Christine Hampton, greeted them at the door. They marshaled the detectives into a large, elegant sitting room that consisted of two leather sofas, a walnut and glass coffee table between them, and four wing chairs that were carefully positioned in pairs and equidistant to each other at either end of the table. The floor was Brazilian hardwood. A giant Persian rug was spread out beneath the coffee table; it looked handmade and expensive. A black baby grand piano stood in the corner of the room. On top were an assortment of framed pictures that documented numerous family members in various stages of life. Some were professionally done portraits. Others were quite obviously taken impromptu, and showcased adults and children alike engaged in all manner of activities. Floor-to-ceiling bookshelves lined one of the walls. Each held a bountiful supply of tomes, more photos, and a tasteful assemblage of trinkets—glass and brass and porcelain, objects that doubtless had been collected over the years and held untold significance.

The widow Talbert was a picture of grace and class and quiet wealth. She played with the pearls at her neck briefly as they first sat down. Though refined and stately, she exhibited a meek kindness. A few inches taller and a touch thinner in the hips, her daughter was a younger version in every possible way, aside from the obvious baby bump.

Press crossed his legs and propped his notepad on his thigh.

Hampton remained standing. "May I bring you gentlemen some coffee or tea?"

"Coffee, please," said Press.

"Same," Killian added. "Thank you."

The elder woman sat huddled on the sofa, her hands clutching a balled-up tissue. She exhibited a sorrowful smile. "My daughter has been such a help."

Press nodded. "It's always good to have family around at a time like this."

"Christine's husband took the children to the park. He wanted to be here, too, but we thought it best to spare the little ones from hearing our conversation. My son, RJ—Riley Junior—and his family are coming in later this evening. He may wish to talk with you at some point, if that's okay."

"Absolutely. I'll leave several of my cards when we're done. If anyone else in the family has questions or wants to share information, please convey to them that they can contact me anytime. We're here for you all."

"That's very gracious. Thank you, Detective."

Christine soon returned with a silver serving tray, which she set down carefully on the coffee table. She offered the men their beverages then retreated around the table and eased herself down beside her mother. Both women now looked expectantly at Press.

"First of all, on behalf of the entire police department, Detective Killian, and myself, I want to extend our condolences to you and your family. I knew your husband, ma'am. He was a class act, a very kind human being."

"Thank you."

"I'm not sure if you remember, but I was involved in that case a number of years back in which the guy and gal broke into your car and stole your purse and—"

"Press. *Nathan* Press. You're the young man who caught the people who smashed out my car window. You got my pistol back!"

Press offered a courteous smile. "Yes, ma'am."

"Oh, Riley was so grateful for that. We both were."

"He was a good man, your husband."

A fresh tear broke from the corner of her eye. Seeing this, Christine wrapped an arm around her.

"Before we get into some specific questions that I need to ask, I would like to bring you up to speed on the case, what we know, and what's been done thus far."

With Killian adding supplemental details and compassionate commentary, Press recounted everything that was known to the investigation up to this point.

"The firm? Ransacked?"

"I'm afraid so, Mrs. Talbert."

"And you think that may have something to do with…Riley's passing?"

"We're considering that possibility very seriously. The odds against it, I submit, are quite high. I should add that the firm is fully cooperating with our investigation. If there is a link, we'll find it."

Though he had been in this position many times before, Press found it especially difficult to watch Mrs. Talbert and her daughter as they heard how and under what circumstances their husband and father had been discovered. He didn't dive into the details of the specific injuries but summed them up by saying, "It was evident that he had been restrained and severely assaulted prior to his death."

"Are you saying my father was tortured?"

Press felt the muscles in his jaw contract but did well to conceal the emotion rising inside him. At the same time, he looked Christine Hampton in the eyes. They were red and tired. "Sadly, yes. That's what the evidence indicates."

"What was the cause of death?" Christine probed as she wiped tears from her cheeks.

"Pending toxicology, the preliminary cause of death is being ruled," Press flipped several pages back in his notes, "cardiac arrhythmia due to physical altercation complicating hypertensive cardiovascular disease. In other words, a heart attack brought on by the assault."

The women consoled each other as they unsuccessfully fought back another wave of emotion.

Killian leaned forward, pushed a box of tissues on the table closer to them as Press waited to continue.

"I need to ask some questions now, if you're feeling up to it, that is. Some of them might not be pleasant, but it's important that we ask regardless. I'm sure you understand that we need to be thorough in our investigation."

"I understand...and thank you. Feel free to ask me anything you wish." Gwen Talbert turned to her daughter. "Are you okay, my dear?"

"I'm good, Mother. Go ahead, Detective. Anything we can do to help catch the animal who did this to my dad." Resolve flared in her face.

"Had Mr. Talbert been having problems with anyone recently? Any threats, that type of thing?"

"No, no one in particular. Depending on the cases he had going, we would get the occasional angry call or letter or email. That was common. But there hasn't been anything like that for some time."

"Any current or past clients you feel we should take a look at?"

The older woman shook her head. "He discussed his clients occasionally but never in great detail. And while he worked many hours at home, writing briefs, motions, that kind of thing—I'm sure most attorneys do—he tried to keep work life separate from home life, which I can attest wasn't exactly easy for him. Most of his cases were high-profile in nature and garnered lots of attention especially from friends and relatives. But he knew the meaning of discretion well. And was adamant about his clients' confidentiality. It was one of the things for which he is best known."

"That and his record. He's only ever lost four cases in his whole career," added Christine with a glimmer of a smile. She was clearly proud of her dad.

"What about people coming to the house? Servicemen, food delivery drivers, that type of thing. Anyone like that been here who maybe rubbed you the wrong way, made a strange comment, or gave off a weird vibe?"

Mrs. Talbert thought for a moment. "No, I'm sorry."

Killian leaned forward, placed his elbows on his knees. "I know this might sound personal, Mrs. Talbert, but how was your marriage? Were you having any concerns? Any problems?"

Gwen Talbert shook her head vehemently. "Not a one. I loved Riley with all my heart, and I know...I *know* he loved me as well. We had no issues. None throughout our entire forty-two years of marriage. We were very happy." Tears rolled down her face.

Press gazed at the photos spread around the room. What he saw was clear evidence of a joy-filled, stable, loving marriage. He couldn't help thinking how his own had ended so badly in such a short amount of time. "Yes, ma'am. We believe you. It's just one of those questions we had to ask."

"I understand," she uttered as Christine rubbed her arm and cinched her closer.

Press motioned to Killian, who read off the three names that had surfaced as a result of the zoo footage analysis. "Do any of these names stand out to you?"

Gwen Talbert thoughtfully considered each one. Finally, she said, "No. Again, I'm sorry. Should they?"

Neither Press nor Killian mentioned how the names had come up. And it was entirely on purpose. Sometimes details like that were withheld for strategic reasons. In this case, they didn't feel it was necessary to reveal the names' significance. If Mrs. Talbert had recognized one of them then their calculus might have been different. It was clear from her countenance that she had no idea who any of them were.

"Is there anything we haven't asked that you think is important for us to know?" Press said. It was a question with which he concluded all interviews.

She thought for a long moment, the grandfather clock ticking behind her discourteously. "No, I don't believe so."

"Very well." He handed several business cards to Mrs. Talbert and her daughter. "If you don't mind, would it be okay if we take a look around before we go?" Press related that he and Killian had been to the house yesterday early in the morning and had found the back door unlocked and the alarm turned off but that nothing seemed amiss, thus, it had seemed to them to have just been an oversight.

The mention of this appeared to cause Mrs. Talbert a good deal of alarm. Her eyes widened and a hand shot to her mouth.

"Ma'am? Are you okay?" said Killian.

"We as a family have always been very safety conscious, Detective. Riley was fastidious about such things especially because of the work he did and the types of cases he took on. How 'bout it, Christine?"

"My mother's right. Daddy never would have left the back door unlocked let alone the alarm turned off."

Press stood. "You're sure?"

"Absolutely certain."

Mrs. Talbert sat up straight. "Are you saying that someone has been in our home?"

20

Press and Killian explored the house with Mrs. Talbert and Christine in tow. The two women had been given explicit instructions to indicate whether anything was missing or seemed to have been disturbed.

The guided tour began in Riley's study, which seemed the most likely target for an interloper given that the firm had been ransacked. For several long minutes, Press slowly and silently paced about the room as the others looked on with curious expressions. At one point, he lowered himself to the floor and began crawling around on his hands and knees.

"He's part bloodhound," quipped Killian dryly from just inside the threshold. His audience did not laugh. They weren't in the mood for police humor, innocent as it was.

"Aside from Mr. Talbert, is there anyone else who uses this room?" said Press from beneath the desk.

"No. I use the writing desk in the bedroom. Even our cleaning woman isn't permitted in here without specific instructions she may enter. And only then it must be when Riley is present. Like I said, Detective, my husband was fastidious about client confidentiality."

Press stood. "You trust her?"

"Implicitly," she said. "She's been with us for years. We pay her well and she's never stolen so much as a penny."

Methodically, they trekked their way through the first floor. Stopping briefly by a back door, the same one he and Killian had found unlocked yesterday morning, Press peered outside and leveled his gaze on the lawn. Two red-breasted robins were pecking the grass. Sunshine glistened against the cover of the in-ground pool that abutted the covered flagstone patio.

During their ascent up the front stairs on their way to the second floor, Press said, "I suggest changing the alarm code...just as a precaution."

"You think they might come back?"

"Probably not, but in all honesty, it's impossible to be certain one way or another."

"Is my mother in danger, Detective?"

They stopped on the landing. Worry riddled Christine's face.

Press said, "We have no information to indicate she is, but I think it only prudent to employ some simple safety measures."

"I'll have my husband change the code as soon as he gets back with the kids. What else do you recommend?"

"If you're so inclined, cameras are always a good idea. You don't need a large, expensive system for it to be effective. A few strategically placed cameras work well."

Christine looked at her mother, nodding. "We'll talk to the alarm company. I believe they do camera systems, too."

"They're not the end-all, but most folks feel that cameras do offer an added sense of security."

"Anything else?" The question was directed this time at Killian.

He didn't hesitate. "Big guns and big dogs are the best security measures in my opinion. Dogs, especially, act as a good early warning system and as a deterrent. But I think Sarge's ideas are spot on and the most appropriate right now."

Press took the lead down the hallway, continuing the conversation over his shoulder as they moved as a group. "I'll have patrols increase their presence on your street for the foreseeable future. And barring any major emergency calls, I'll arrange for a car to be parked outside at least for a few days."

Mrs. Talbert's pained expression relaxed. "That would be fantastic. Thank you."

Christine mouthed the words "thank you" from behind her mother to which Press replied with a perceptible nod.

Thus far, none of the second-floor rooms sparked any interest from the detectives, and Mrs. Talbert found nothing amiss. They finished in the master bedroom. The room was clean and decorated handsomely. It could have easily featured in one of those magazines or television programs that showcased large, elegant homes and artfully styled living spaces.

Press motioned to the jewelry cabinets on the dresser. In response, Mrs. Talbert strode past and checked each one but found nothing out of place and said as much.

Killian stood next to the door to Mr. Talbert's walk-in closet. When given the okay by Mrs. Talbert, he pushed it open, revealing a space as big as some folks' bedrooms. Inside, four very large and doubtless very heavy safes stood shoulder to shoulder, with chests out and chins up, like soldiers waiting for inspection. Each was roughly five feet in height, three feet wide and three feet deep, and, based on the badging at the top corner, could withstand temperatures up to 1700 degrees for a full hour.

Wanting to leave no stone unturned, Press respectfully asked if Mrs. Talbert could check the safes just to verify that everything was in order. Again, she stepped forward, unlocked them, but upon a sudden swell of emotion, discharged herself from the closet and back to the side of her daughter.

"Please, you gentlemen do it. Going through Riley's things, standing next to his clothing, smelling his aftershave..." She brought a tissue to her nose. "I'm just too emotional right now."

Press suggested another time or even that Christine glance through the safes. But they both insisted he conduct the examination. "How about we make lists of the contents of each safe, have you look them over when we're done?"

"That will be fine. I'm sorry for..." Her voice caught in her throat. She took a deep, cleansing breath, lips and lungs quivering.

"Not at all."

The widow Talbert smiled through tears and, cradled by her daughter, left the room.

So then, with Killian acting as scribe and intuitively shining a flashlight on Press's careful sifting, the two detectives catalogued everything. The first two safes contained fine jewelry with accompanying photos and insurance documents, a rather surprising amount of gold and silver bullion, several banded bricks of cash in $100 denominations, and firearms large and small, some of which were valuable collector editions.

Affixed to the third safe was a digital climate-control unit. Upon swinging its heavy door open, Press found it to be entirely full of rare, leather-bound first editions bearing names such as Milton, Chaucer, and Sophocles. Being an avid reader himself ever since early childhood, in addition to his late grandmother having been a longtime librarian, Press recognized them immediately. They had to be worth a fortune.

The last safe was empty but for the top shelf. On it were three accordion folders that contained birth certificates and various other important documents including investment and bank-related papers. Press flipped through them and quickly deemed them to be of little consequence to the murder investigation.

When he finally stood, his back and knees ached, and his neck was stiff. He spent several minutes stretching and twisting himself back into shape before he and Killian returned to the front sitting room, where Mrs. Talbert and her daughter were waiting somberly. Once settled, Press issued several property record forms that Killian had used to document the contents of the safes, then, reading slowly, ticked off each item from the yellow carbonless copies.

"As far as I can remember, everything is as it should be," declared the widow Talbert. "Thank God for that."

Killian stood facing a bookshelf that took up an entire wall. "Mr. Talbert sure did love his books, didn't he?"

"Oh yes. The law and books were his two biggest passions. He was always reading," Christine said. "It's from him that my brother and I inherited *our* love for books." She dabbed her nose with a ready tissue.

Press focused his attention on the wall above the piano on the far side of the room. On it hung a miraculous oil painting beneath a small brass light fixture. It was a portrait of a galleon amidst a tumultuous sea. The vivid brushstrokes brought to life the riotous froth and foam. "And just so we're clear, there is no other location in the house—or elsewhere—where Mr. Talbert might have secreted important documents or valuables?"

Mrs. Talbert shook her head. "No."

"Very well. Thank you, ladies," said Press. "And again, our deepest sympathies."

21

They didn't speak until Press had turned onto 8th Street. The truck jumped slightly as he goosed the accelerator and came out of the turn. Cops were always in a hurry even when they had no place to go.

"So, what do you think?"

Press pulled his sunglasses from the visor, slid them on. "Someone was definitely in that house. And they were looking for something."

"How can you be sure? The place looked untouched."

"There was a film of dust on the lip of the desk drawers; it had been disturbed." He reminded Killian that Mrs. Talbert had said she never used the study, and, because of the confidential nature of her husband's work, it was off limits to the cleaning lady. "Also, I noticed tiny fragments of mulch in the carpet beneath the desk, the same kind that was in the flowerbed by the back door we found open yesterday. Someone sat there at the desk and rummaged through the drawers. Whoever it was wore gloves—there was no ridge detail in the dust." He checked his mirror before changing lanes on North Main Street then clicked on his blinker as he prepared to turn onto

Smithfield Avenue. "There were also bits of mulch in the closet carpet...in front of the safes."

"That's why you were crawling around..." Killian said it almost in a whisper.

"Do me a favor. Check with the alarm company," continued Press. "They should be able to tell us when the alarm was disabled. At least, I hope they can. It was probably sometime over the weekend...*after* Talbert was killed. I get the sense that Talbert's death surprised his captors. When that happened, they were forced to go looking for whatever it was they were after."

"I'll call them as soon as we get back to the barn." Killian made a note in his pad. "By the way, did you smell any cigarette smoke in the Talbert house?"

"No, I didn't."

"Why would we not be able to smell smoke at the house but could smell it at the law office?"

Press considered this. "You're assuming it was the same people who did both places. But for the sake of argument, let's say it was. Could be several reasons. Maybe they didn't smoke before entering the house and they did prior to dumping the office. Maybe they wore different clothing. Or perhaps the air circulates better in the house than at the office. The building that houses the firm is much older."

Killian, wearing similar wraparound sunglasses, gazed through the windscreen at a red Nissan sports car that was sitting at the stop sign on Collyer Street. The thumping bass from its stereo continued to intrude on their conversation even after they had glided past. "You think they got into them, the safes, I mean?"

"Hard to say. It stands to reason that if they had the alarm code, they would have had the safe combinations, too. But they clearly weren't interested in stealing from the man. At least not in the traditional sense. It's likely that whatever they were after was informational in nature. Perhaps more valuable than the items contained in those safes."

"Agreed." After a moment of thoughtful silence, Killian added, "Wonder what they were looking for. And if they found it?"

Press nodded behind his shades, thinking.

They were cruising south on I-95 at speed, the dome of the statehouse on their left, followed by the Renaissance Providence Hotel and the VETS, a well-known performing arts center, when the phone in Press's pants pocket buzzed. Seeing the stored contact in the caller ID, he immediately answered the call.

"Nate. It's Leo."

"Yeah, buddy. What's up?"

"I might have something for you. You know… With the case you're working."

"Sweet. I'm just passing you now. You good to meet in about five?" Press twisted in his seat and glanced over his right shoulder then jerked the wheel in the same direction, guiding the truck through traffic and onto the ramp that shot past the large redbrick building complex that housed Leo Korver's office.

"Yeah, that's perfect. See you in a few."

22

**Rhode Island Department of
Environmental Management
235 Promenade Street**

Leo Korver met them in the hall, a stack of papers tucked under his arm. He directed them to his office. Once inside, he plopped the papers on the corner of his desk, which was crowded with an array of folders and computer printouts. Propped on a metal chair behind him were various charts and maps, some splashed with color. The man had obviously been busy.

"I apologize for the clutter. But I wanted to make sure you had the information as quickly as possible." He was slightly out of breath. "I will send over a polished report at some point, but this here is the nuts and bolts of what you wanted, I believe." He handed Press a stapled photocopy of the city's river system displaying various statistics. On the last page was a colorful map with a number of points plotted in red ink.

Press thumbed through the sheets of paper then flipped back to the first page and began scanning the documents more carefully.

"I know what you're thinking. It's still a lot of areas to search. How does this help me? Am I right?"

Press looked up.

"If you'll grant me a few minutes, I might be able to sharpen your focus. Many of the points you see there on your map are simply possible locations where your dead guy *could have* gone into the water. I listed these to cover all the bases. You know, CYA." He swiveled in his chair and selected one of the larger maps from those grouped behind him, placed it on his desk. "If you'll gather around, please, detectives…"

Press and Killian took up a position on either side of him, each of them leaning forward, palms pressed against the desk.

"Here is where your body was discovered." Korver now slid his finger upward, going in a northerly direction on the map. "By the way, thanks for the information from the forensic pathologist, Nate. That helped a great deal."

Press had called Korver immediately upon leaving the ME's office and noted how long Dr. V approximated Talbert had been in the water prior to his body being discovered along the river. He continued to stare at the map as the Marine Unit man went on.

"I began by looking at the river's average daily stream gage, discharge, and streamflow then factored in this past weekend's rainfall. What I came up with put your body well north of the Steeple Street Bridge."

With his eyes, Press followed Korver's two index fingers. They were touching at the bridge, but then split in different directions as they traced the upstream paths of the Woonasquatucket and Moshassuck Rivers.

"Now, if you consider spots in which a vehicle has ease of access—no one's carrying a body across open ground in this city very far unless they are just plain stupid—you end up with these possible locations." He glanced up at them.

"That's still a lot of possibles," Killian said.

"Agreed, Detective. But if you take away all the places where someone would be easily spotted dumping a body you are left with these." Korver leaned forward and snatched a freshly printed paper from the corner of his desk, placed it in front of them. There were far fewer red dots."

"That's manageable," noted Press.

"Yes," Korver agreed. "Based on everything I stated previously and these additional probabilities, I conclude that your dead guy likely went into the water at one of the sites you see marked here with only one qualification."

Both detectives' heads rotated toward Korver.

"If Talbert was hung up on something at any point, it throws all of my calculations out the window."

"Well, let's hope he was a smooth floater. That's good work, Leo."

"Thanks, Nate." He grinned, adjusted his eyeglasses. "Just to be clear, I've listed all the factors that played into my analysis on the second sheet there in your packet. Here are the updated maps. They just came off the printer. Like I said, I'll shoot over my final report when it's finished."

23

**Providence PD
Central Station**

Press gathered up the Talbert case file materials. As with all homicide investigations the paperwork seemed to grow exponentially by the minute. He paced down a short corridor and into the Major Crimes Unit's conference room.

Gabby joined him a few seconds later. While he spread out his things and started making notes, she filled him in on the overdose death that she and Tank had been out on earlier. Sadly, there wasn't much that could be done investigation-wise. Aside from a heroin kit, the kid had nothing in his possession but a cheap Tracfone, a lighter, and a stick of Chapstick. A quick scan of the unlocked phone's contents, she pointed out, revealed nothing remotely useful in identifying his dealer. No recent calls or text messages with talk about a purchase. No nothing. From what they had been able to gather, the nineteen-year-old Mapleville native had simply walked into the bathroom of the Atwell's Mini Mart in Federal Hill, locked the door, and that was that. They'd found the used needle at his feet and no signs of foul play. It was open and shut. The death would be ruled accidental. No drug dealer would ever be held to account. And the case would go down as just another sad statistic. They both knew it wouldn't be the last. In fact, there would be many more throughout their careers. It was just an unfortunate reality of the job.

"What's all this? It looks like you got a fresh lead." She shifted her weight and rested her right hand on the butt of the pistol in her duty rig.

"That's why you're a detective, Gabby." He glanced up and smiled, which in turn caused her to do likewise although with a good dose of sarcasm. He handed her the packet that Leo Korver had produced. "This is a map of likely spots Talbert's body entered the river. I want to go over everything in detail here before I start making phone calls."

"Phone calls?"

He nodded. "If everything goes smoothly and I can arrange it, we are going to search each of these locations tomorrow. You might want to dress down by the way." He smiled again, this time adding a look that suggested he was prone to mischief. "We might get a little dirty."

"Well, you know me, Sarge. I'm always up for whatever."

"What's the status of the phone we found near Talbert's car?"

Gabby was already flipping through the pages of Korver's preliminary report. "Paulie's got it hooked up to the GrayKey. Said if it's locked with a four-digit code he'll be able to crack it rather quickly. I'm hoping to have the dump by tomorrow at the earliest."

Press nodded as he continued sorting piles. "If we're lucky, I'll have Talbert's cell phone records back by then, too. Any luck in tracking down our three zoo lovers?"

"Not yet. We've left messages, but so far none has called back."

Head down, he was now scribbling reminders and labels on a pad of yellow sticky notes, tearing them off and affixing them to the various piles. "JK is working on Talbert's financials. Why don't you and Tank run by their homes or workplaces and see if you can make contact in person. I don't have to tell you…it's important that we figure out who met with Talbert at the zoo. Are they a suspect, a witness, or is there something else that explains their initials being on Talbert's calendar? The sooner we know the who, the quicker we can start drilling down on the why."

Gabby dropped the stack of stapled documents she was perusing on the table. "Roger that. I'll let you know how we make out." She tossed a dry smile over her shoulder as she left the room. "Have fun with your paper."

Every cop hated paperwork. It was the part of the job that wasn't sexy or fun but was every bit, if not more important in some regards, than hitting the street and wearing out the shoe leather. If investigative actions were not documented properly in an orderly fashion for not only the prosecutors to understand, but defense counsel, and who knew who else down the road—feds, civil litigators, et cetera—even a great case could sink faster than the Titanic. Documentation was the key to a successful prosecution and conviction and for surviving any rigorous appeals.

Press began by making a list of the people and resources that would be needed to search the spots Korver had indicated. Gabby's and Tank's voices carried from across the unit's office suite and into the conference room as they headed out to the street. He lifted his head and his pen and listened for a few seconds. The two were trading jabs and laughing. Part of him wished he could go with them. He loved being out of the office and chasing down leads, feeling the rhythm of the street. But someone had to do the nitty gritty, too.

Almost two hours later, Killian ducked into the conference room. "I ran through Talbert's financials, also spoke to several senior analysts at the banks that hold Talbert's accounts."

"Yeah? And?"

"No sudden large deposits or withdrawals. Or any other strange activity for that matter. Everything seems to be in order, Nate."

"All right. Well at least that's done."

Killian turned toward the door then stopped. "Oh, and the alarm company finally got back to me. The alarm at Talbert's place was deactivated Saturday night at twenty-two fifty-three."

Press scribbled the information down on a yellow legal pad beside him then leaned back in his chair. "That jives with what the law firm told me—they called earlier. Their alarm was turned off at exactly zero two hundred Saturday morning."

Killian nodded slowly.

"So, just based on the timeline, whoever did the firm, probably didn't find what they were looking for. They or one of their pals went to Talbert's house later that night when it was dark and rainy. My guess is they had him and the house under surveillance."

"How do you figure?"

"They knew Mrs. Talbert wouldn't be home, because she was down south visiting her sister."

"How do you suppose they got the alarm codes?" Killian asked.

Press tented his hands and rested his lips on his fingertips. "Again, they could have surveilled him, or perhaps they beat the information out of him. Or they could have bypassed the alarm some other way. With technical know-how."

"You think it's a *they*?"

"I'm going with that theory for now. Snatching Talbert probably required at least two people. Someone drove, someone managed their captive. Dumping the body, too, likely took two guys—Talbert wasn't a small man. Then you figure the tasks of tossing his office at the firm, searching the house, and the way they were each done. One place was messy—a brute-force search, the other almost surgical. It feels like at least two people, maybe two *groups* of people."

"Yeah. You're probably right," said Killian.

"Do me a flavor."

"Name it."

"Check in with the firm and the other businesses we hit over there and see if any of their security footage is ready yet? Hopefully, at least one camera *somewhere* captured something useful."

24

Kettle Point Apartments
Captain John Jacobs Road, East Providence

A small suitcase in hand and a duffel bag slung over his shoulder, Lance Cheney strode across the parking lot and headed toward the western-most apartment building, one of five in the complex. Each had four floors and housed modern, elegant living spaces. He entered through a glass door with the numeral 38 stenciled in white on the transom window above it.

Cheney wore a light jacket, blue jeans, casual loafers, and a crimson Harvard Rowing Team ball cap pulled low to shield his face from the cameras he knew were perched high above on the corners of the various buildings. He and Zug had recce'd the place in previous weeks, waiting for the target to leave or take a visitor, to step out on the walkout balcony for some fresh air or to water a potted plant. Anything to confirm he was there. But each time they came up dry. They concluded the obvious: He had vanished.

One night nearing 4:00 a.m., they had attempted to slip into the apartment to toss it for intel, but the neighbor's little Bichon Frise was a fearless and watchful little sentry, sounding the alarm with an incessant yipping that forced them to bail on the idea almost immediately.

So it was that Cheney, a slight hunch in his malingered posture, now took on the appearance of a weary traveler. If pressed by anyone he would say he was the kid's father visiting from out of town. Age-wise it made sense and would be an easy enough explanation as to why he was here—a stranger suddenly showing up at the apartment. He stepped to the door and huddled over the doorknob. He was about to get to work on the lock when he suddenly sensed the door behind him swing open, and the little canine began its shrill, unrelenting siren.

"Hush up, Pookie. Hush, now! Can I help you?" The voice came from the neighbor, a middle-aged woman with gussied-up blond hair and thick mascara. She gazed at him suspiciously, the stuffed-animal-looking dog held close to her smothering breast. The tiny white puffball had at least stopped its infernal barking. It now stared at him, too, between alternating bouts of panting, teeth licking, and short growls.

"Uh, yes. Hi. I'm Seth's dad. I'm visiting for a few days. Just got in." He motioned toward the door. "I knocked, but he doesn't seem to be home." Screwing his face up in apparent confusion, he continued. "Seth said he would be here, but maybe I misunderstood." He pulled his phone from his jacket pocket. "He isn't answering my calls or texts either. Probably got tied up in a meeting or something at work."

"I'm Barbara." The dog whined. "And this is Pookie."

"Hi, Barbara. Hi, Pookie." He made exaggerated kissing sounds and extended his hand to scratch its head, but the dog only snarled and snapped.

"Pookie! *No.*"

Cheney chuckled. "Protective little guy. Nice to meet you both. Name's Gerry."

She warmly returned his ready smile and her school-hall-monitor demeanor softened. "Do you have a key?"

He always could charm the ladies. "I do, but it's in my suitcase. Let me see here... He grunted and moaned at the same time muttering something about a bad back as he climbed out of his shoulder bag and hinged at the waist for the suitcase at his feet. He sighed then made like he was going to dig through his things right there in the hall.

"No, no, no. Here. I can let you in."

"Oh, that would be great. Thanks, Barbara." He smiled again. "You're a sweetheart. You, too, Pookie."

Nice woman. Not all that bright, but nice, Cheney thought as he slipped on a pair of nitrile gloves and appraised the apartment. He registered the faint smell of bananas.

He left his suitcase and shoulder bag by the door and quietly drew the SIG Sauer P365X from the holster at the small of his back. It didn't take long to verify the apartment was empty just like he and Marcus had figured.

Cheney secured his pistol then walked the apartment with a much more discerning eye starting in the kitchen, which was a better hiding place than most people knew. But in this case, all he found was a cupboard full of ramen noodles, canned chili, and rice. He found a couple of unopened boxes of cereal and packets of instant oatmeal in yet another. The fridge was relatively empty. Only some cheap beer, a package of string cheese, and a neat stack of nearly expired yogurt cups. The kid hadn't been to the grocery store in a while.

A few crumbs from what seemed like toast dotted the counter by the pop-up toaster. Next to that was a ceramic bowl of greasy, blackened bananas. And in the sink, a few dirty dishes.

Cheney pulled open the slide-out cabinet left of the sink. He lifted the plastic waste bin from its housing and dumped the contents on the kitchen table. He spun around, walked to the counter, and selected a long, thin boning knife from the wooden block next to a tree of K-cups and methodically sifted through the pile of refuse. A couple of ripe eggs shells. A few torn-open envelopes from the daily post. Soiled paper towels that looked to have been used to sop up spilled coffee but were now dry and brittle. Remnants of a cellophane wrapper and... *This is interesting.* A balled-up receipt from a local Walmart store, evidence of a recent cash purchase of a prepaid Motorola smartphone. The box was nowhere in sight. Barnett probably disposed of it elsewhere or perhaps took it with him since it bore the various numbers associated with the phone and its operational components.

Cheney shoved the receipt into his pocket. With only his eyes, he examined the kitchen again for locations in which someone could secrete things. Finding none he hadn't already explored, he moved on to the living room.

Here, he first yanked the cushions from the couch, then pulled it from the wall. There was nothing behind or beneath it. Cheney smiled, flicking open his Spyderco Military Model G-10. The blade made quick work of the sofa cushions. Then he turned the sharp instrument on the large flatscreen TV on the credenza just because he felt like it. All of it would send a message to the kid should he return to the apartment in the meantime: They were coming for him.

In a short, two-drawer file cabinet in the bedroom, Cheney came upon a few file folders for bank and credit card statements and some other documents of lesser value. He cast the ones in which he had no interest on the floor. Then turned his attention to the bed and smiled again.

The rest of the apartment was devoid of anything useful, much like he had assessed it would be. He took note that several dresser drawers were empty and a good number of clothes hangers in the bedroom closet were curiously bare. It was obvious: The kid had split town. Now they just needed to find out where he had run off to.

Hopefully, the burner phone he'd purchased would tell them.

25

Gabby and Tank alighted from the latter's unmarked gray Chevy Tahoe. A minute ago, they had been trading jabs. Now, they had their game faces on.

The pair had already made contact with Sabrina Babcock and Steven Brockenridge. Babcock lived in Mt. Pleasant and had said she didn't call detectives back because she downright wasn't fond of cops. Despite the buckets of attitude she had emptied upon them, they were comfortable in crossing her off the list. She literally had no idea what they were talking about when they arrived at her door and began asking about Riley Talbert. And her body language proved it.

Brockenridge was a similar story though his disposition was much more amicable. They had found him at the hospital in Upper South Providence, where he worked as an OR nurse. With all the overtime he had been forced to endure lately, he had simply been too busy and too tired to remember to call. Sure, he had heard of Riley Talbert, Nathan Press, too, in fact. As it turned out, Brockenridge had been one of the nurses on duty when Press was hurried into surgery six months back. On the noted Sunday afternoon, he had been at the zoo with his girlfriend and her niece and nephew. But a meeting with Talbert? Heavens, no.

Which brought them to Seth Barnett. Living at the lower end of East Providence, he was the last one on the list and therefore the only viable candidate left.

"He's on the third floor," said Gabby. The sunlight was beginning to fade, the spring air turning chilly. She tugged the zipper up on her jacket as a breeze swept in from the Providence River, which was just off to the west.

As they strode into the elevator car, a man carrying luggage stepped out. He begged their pardon for his artificial girth and headed for the main door through which Gabby and Tank had just come. Though they knew it not, the man paused only briefly and glanced back at them as the elevator doors were closing.

Lance Cheney gathered his things then gave the apartment one last look. Satisfied he had uncovered all there was to exploit here, he shouldered his bag, turned the doorknob, and cracked the door. He peeled the gloves from his hands, shoved them into his pants pocket, and grabbed the handle of his suitcase. In one smooth motion, he pushed open the door, hooked it with his foot, and swept into the hall. He was several doors down when Seth Barnett's door clicked shut and little Pookie began his vigilant protest anew.

Approaching the elevator, he decided himself fortunate. The car had already been called up and was empty of its passengers. The doors were just now beginning to close. He forged into the narrow gap, forcing the doors to open. Once inside, he turned and stabbed the button for the first floor with a knuckle on his right hand. Here, he adjusted the brim of his cap, making sure it would again hide his face from the lobby cameras.

When the car finally lurched to a stop and the doors whooshed open, he found himself staring face to face with the law. In a moment of quick calculation, he decided to play it cool.

The one on the left—the lady cop—was Hispanic and pretty. Her dark hair was pulled back in a ponytail and seemed to funnel attention to her face and neckline. He looked at her long enough to notice bright, coffee-bean eyes, full, determined lips, and a confident, if not, feisty spirit. The other cop was a shorter version of Marcus but with a buzzcut. Judging from the size and shape of him, Cheney figured him for a former wrestler or a practitioner of mixed martial arts. He appeared to be a rather powerful human being.

Cheney politely disembarked from the elevator and headed for the main entrance, resisting the urge to spin around and check out the female cop's backside. It wasn't until he had reached the door and leaned into the glass with his shoulder that he glanced back at the police detectives.

In a minute more, he was stuffing the suitcase and duffel bag into the back seat of a black Ford Expedition and climbing inside next to Marcus Zug.

"It's just as we figured. He's flown the coop."

"He's gone?"

"Yeah. But I think I know how to find him."

Zug smiled. "It's about time."

Tank struck the door repeatedly with a hammer fist. The force of his efforts was so severe that it seemed to rattle the walls of the entire corridor. Who needed a door ram with Tank Meredith on your squad? He *was* a door ram, thought Gabby, standing with her back along the wall, gazing at the door across the hall from Barnett's apartment. Behind it, an energetic little dog whipped itself into a frenzy, scratched at the floor and door trim, only hesitating now and again to sniff the thin space between the bottom of the door and the floor.

Tank stopped knocking and joined her in listening for telltale sounds of life in Barnett's apartment. But the neighbor dog's incessant yapping made it impossible to hear anything else.

Finally, the neighbor's door swung back and a woman with bountiful hair piled atop her head and a scrappy little fighter pressed to her bosom eyed them with curiosity. "The police," she said with instant recognition.

"Hi, ma'am. I'm Detective Ibarra. This is Detective Meredith. Providence Police. We're trying to reach your neighbor, Seth Barnett?"

Her eyes narrowed. "Is he in some sort of trouble?"

"It's hard to say, ma'am." Gabby offered a professional smile as Tank petted the dog, which seemed strangely taken aback by the muscled man's unfazed attitude toward it. "Do you know if he's home…I'm sorry what was your name?"

"Barbara. Barbara Stanley. I do know that Seth isn't home. But his father should be. He came by about an hour ago. Said he just got in from out of town. I didn't hear him leave, so I'm assuming he's still inside. Then again, I've been doing laundry, so…"

Gabby nodded, flashed a business card. "Can you give us a call if you happen to see Seth or his dad? It's important."

"Okay. Yes."

"Thanks, Ms. Stanley." Gabby waited until the neighbor had retreated into her apartment then wedged another business card in Seth's door just above the knob.

Tank stared down the corridor, pursing his lips. "How 'bout we check in with the leasing office downstairs? Maybe they'll have an emergency contact listing for our guy."

"Good idea."

Five minutes later, Gabby was dialing the phone number for Gerald and Marsha Barnett, who, per the leasing agent, were Seth's parents.

"Voice mail," Gabby mouthed to Tank, before leaving a short, generic message that conveyed without alarm that the police department was trying to reach their son. She asked for a call back when it was convenient and then wished them a good evening.

26

East Providence, Rhode Island

It was nearly 10:00 p.m. when Press turned down Boyden Boulevard. Two blocks on, beneath a canopy of trees, the road dog-legged to the left and became Sunnyside Avenue. He followed the leafy street past Park Road to its terminus where Sunnyside intersected with Waterview Avenue. Here, he nosed his truck into a small, blacktop driveway. His home was a one-story affair with white siding, black shutters, and a front porch with railings that extended on either side of the centrally positioned front door. A redbrick chimney stretched skyward on the far side of the house. His ex-wife had once described the place as "tastefully cute."

He stopped in front of the detached garage, which was tucked slightly behind the house. It, too, was white with black shutters. Press switched off the truck's engine and grabbed his bag from the seat beside him. He stepped out and scanned the night air. The neighborhood was quiet just how he liked it.

Press walked to the mailbox, collected the post, and slipped it into his shoulder bag. Even now, as he strode to the side door, he kept his right hand—his gun hand—empty. To Press, exercising sound police tactics was a healthy habit whether on duty or off.

Inside, he bolted the door then looped his keys onto one of the wall-mounted hooks in the kitchen. The shoulder bag he placed next to the small, dining-room table, which he had long ago converted into a desk. There was no hot meal awaiting him or even leftovers to warm up in the microwave, no one to welcome him home after a long day's work. It had been this way for well over a year now.

He selected a bottle of mineral water from the fridge and walked out the back door to a pair of Adirondack chairs. They were angled toward a stone-ringed firepit, which lay dark and mute with black, sooty half-burned logs. At the far reaches of the yard, the grass gave way to thick brush and sloped precariously downward to the East Bay Bike Path and the Providence River beyond. He dropped into one of the chairs and gazed toward the docile water, following it with his eyes to the city lights winking on the horizon to his right. The view was glorious and one of the main reasons he and Maggie had fallen in love with the place.

He recalled some happy moments the two of them had shared out here. She, sitting across his lap on this very chair, the two of them sipping wine and stealing kisses while taking in the view of the river in the bliss of fresh matrimony. These memories buoyed his spirit for a time. For several long moments, he thought nothing of the Talbert case or any other case for that matter. Then like a thief in the night, regret was upon him. What could he have done differently? Maybe she never would have left him. He failed to mention this to anyone, even JK, but recently he'd heard Maggie and the ophthalmologist had gotten engaged. It was Maggie herself who had told him. She had called one evening while he was at work and left a message just to let him know. It was classless and entirely spiteful.

Though it had taken some time, he was no longer bitter toward her. That feeling had passed. He now fully understood that she had never loved him, never *really* loved him anyway. The job was what did them in, or so she'd said. The long hours. The midnight shifts. The ruined get-togethers with friends, canceled dinners with her parents. The callout on their very first Christmas as a married couple. Add to that the daily emotional baggage that is constant companion to seeing the worst of humanity. Being a cop's wife isn't for everyone. It's not even for most. In truth, he couldn't blame her for leaving him. He was equally guilty. He had let her get away. He could have quit his job, tried harder to salvage the marriage. Ignored the cheating. Forgiven her. And...

It was no use, he decided. What's done was done. The divorce had cut him deeply, but he knew he had to move on with his life. He had decided the same thing six months ago when he nearly died. The scars were there as constant reminder of the pain and suffering, but he had pulled through. He had survived. And that's exactly what he intended to do emotionally with the situation with Maggie.

Despite the risk of additional heartbreak, he *did* want to love again. But who? How? He wasn't exactly a social butterfly. The conversation with JK at the diner returned to him. JK was right. He wasn't going to find someone special on a bike ride or in the pages of some book. He had to at least make some amount of effort.

A cargo ship lumbered up the river, its lights shimmering against the calm water. Scalloped swells rippled outward from its stern. From the looks of it, Press guessed it was likely headed to ProvPort for road salt or maybe cement.

Just like that his thoughts shifted to his mother. Where was she? Why had he not heard from her in years? Did she still love him? Did she even remember that she had another son? The last he'd heard, which was close to two years ago now, she was in San Francisco getting drunk and high. It was Vegas and LA before that. How could she have devolved so swiftly, so unexpectedly? But he knew how. Or at least why.

Press was about to head inside and call it a night when he suddenly remembered something. He dipped his hand inside his pants pocket, grasped his phone. His face glowed in the screen light as he searched his stored contacts for Tony Miller. When he'd finally found him, he stabbed at the green telephone icon.

As the call rang, he pictured in his mind the child on the flyer: Vonna Miller, age four. The bright blue-eyed, little girl with blond pigtails had gone outside to play in her backyard one day and simply vanished without a trace, never to be heard from again. It had been one of his first cases in Major Crimes and still haunted him and everyone else in Detective Division to this day. He could scarcely believe it had been five years already. During that time, he made a point of speaking to her parents once a month and always on Vonna's birthday, which was today, to discuss any new information that might have come up or to talk about new ideas that might keep the case in the community's collective mind. Though it was still technically open, the case had gone cold long ago.

"Hello?"

"Mr. Miller. It's Nathan."

"Hi, Detective." The voice sounded distant, subdued, tired.

"I apologize for calling so late. I meant to do so earlier today, but I've been busy on a fresh murder case."

"The attorney?"

"Yeah."

"We saw it on the news. Tragic to say the least."

"Yes. It is." After a pause, he said, "Is Mrs. Miller there? I'd like to say hi to her as well."

"She's already in bed, I'm afraid."

"Oh, yes of course. Well, please pass on my regards. Again, I'm sorry for calling so late."

"Nonsense. You're a busy man. We know your heart. We know you are doing and will continue to do everything in your power to find our little girl." There was a pause. "I'm sorry. It's been an emotional day."

"Yes. I'm sure it has." He wished he had the magic words that could wipe away all their sorrow and grief. He wanted to bring Vonna back to them safe and sound more than anything.

"It was good of you to call, Detective. Vicky and I appreciate your hard work and friendship. God bless and stay safe out there."

"Yes, sir. Will do. Thank you."

The call ended and Press lifted his eyes to the river and further still to the starry sky. He imagined what could have become of the little girl. Would he ever know? And so it was, there in the solitude of his backyard, he shed a few tears for Vonna Miller, her mom and dad, and all the missing children and their families the world over. And after that, he shed a few more while thinking of his big brother. He missed him terribly.

27

Mustique

Robert Brenner arrived in Barbados under cover of darkness by way of his private company jet, a handsome Gulfstream III. He had purchased it recently from a wealthy sultan against whom he had often conspired during his years at the Agency, unbeknownst to the emirate. Briefcase in hand, he quickly deplaned and traversed the apron at Grantley Adams, where his employer's exclusive Beechcraft King Air 360ER was waiting for him to board. It would ferry him the rest of the way to his destination.

Brenner preferred traveling at night. He had spent the large part of his existence in the shadows while working in the American intelligence community and considered its anonymity central to his very being. By all accounts, he had excelled at clandestine activities, influence operations, and the occasional targeted assassination. But now instead of doing his nation's bidding, he worked for a select clientele who paid exceedingly well, as evidenced by his sprawling horse farm in Northern Virginia, the luxury brownstone in New York City, the beach house on Nantucket, the toney London flat, and the recent acquisition of the G3.

At first, the light was nothing more than a pinprick on the horizon, but soon swelled, until eventually he could make out a distinct pattern of illumination, one to which he had grown accustomed these past two years. The pilot uttered something over the built-in speaker system, but Brenner was too focused on his objective to recall what was said. It was of no consequence anyway.

At the exact moment of touchdown, a white Land Rover bumped onto the tarmac and waited for the plane to taxi over. New arrivals normally had to check in with Island Security, but in Brenner's case that would not occur. For the man he had come to see owned the island, though he did so through a veil of shell corporations registered in places like Delaware, Guernsey, Gibraltar, and the Isle of Man. This plane and anyone on it would be dutifully left alone.

Mustique was his employer's private paradise and Brenner envied him for it. At least as a contract employee he was afforded the privilege of indulging in its many delights, which included the island's beautiful maidens. But any indulgences would have to wait until later. There was important business to discuss. And he did not wish to disappoint his master with further delay.

The drive from the airport to the southern end of the island took twenty minutes. The engine whined as the driver feathered the gas pedal. The vehicle responded, pawing its way up an incline by way of a dirt track that sliced through the tropical vegetation. In a minute more, the foliage fell away, and a monstrous, palatial estate came into view. The driver nosed the SUV across the crushed gravel onto a paved stone pad beneath a glorious canopy. Here, guests could dismount safely in the event of a passing rainstorm or a curious drone piloted by a speculating civilian or, more sinisterly, a military or intelligence service from any number of governments the world over.

Brenner gripped his briefcase and forged to a set of massive oak doors. There, a house manager greeted him officiously and issued him inside. He was shown to a comfortable suite to wash and tidy up after his long trip. Then it was back outside where his master presided in a cushioned rattan-and-bamboo chair that could easily pass for a throne. Two young women were swimming shamelessly in a mammoth, cloud-shaped pool complete with rocks and fountains and overhanging fronds. The lights beneath the undulating water seemed to add to their erotic display.

Brenner blushed as the women were ordered from the pool and strode past him, each of them meeting his gaze and doing so without a modicum of self-awareness. He watched them gather their towels and flip-flops and eventually disappear through an adjacent cave-like walkway of white-washed stone.

"So. Tell me. What is the latest?" The host's voice was deep and direct. He was not one to dawdle with idle dialogue. In that regard they were quite similar.

"I spoke to our mutual friend." Brenner said.

"And?"

"This business with the attorney has her on edge."

The man in the chair lifted a thick cigar to his mouth. The end of it burned a brilliant red for a long second before fading into the darkness concentrated beneath the portico. "You're handling that, am I right? You assured me there would be no more complications."

"The kid's smart, but my people are on his trail. We believe we'll have him soon."

The cigar glowed again. "See that you do. If anyone ever finds out what we're doing, there will be hell to pay." The man spoke these words sans emotion, as if he were moderating a business meeting of the world's most powerful and influential people—the politicians, the kingmakers, tycoons, and robber barons alike—and he were its chairman, which was in a way, very close to the truth.

Hands in his pants pockets, Robert Brenner angled his body toward the majestic panorama before him, a sudden breeze jostling his thin, linen shirt and tousling his carefully styled hair. The sea, dark and undulating, stretched out beyond the treetops that cascaded from the mountaintop estate. There in the distance, perhaps a mile and a half from shore, an anchored mega yacht slept. He wondered briefly who might be aboard her.

"You think he'll talk?"

"They all talk. Eventually," Brenner said.

The cigar flared. "We can't afford any setbacks."

Brenner stared intently into the obsidian darkness.

"How is the distribution coming along?"

"Good. We've got nearly all of the product and associated materials in place and will be pushing them out soon to the various vendors through our agents-in-place." He may have left the CIA three years ago, but the parlance of the intelligence world was much harder to abandon.

"Excellent."

"Now, how 'bout a swim?" The man beckoned to the house manager and soon the two young women returned, arm in arm and giggling. In the next instant they slipped into the pool and commenced splashing each other playfully.

The corners of Brenner's mouth crept upward. For a moment, his eyes flitted toward the sea and the dormant yacht, then, with a growing amount of fervor, returned to the luminescent water of the pool. Finally, he focused his attention on the two objects moving sublimely within it.

Then he staidly disrobed.

28

**Providence PD
Central Station**

The day had been warm and sun-rich, which in large part had aided in their search. Despite the pleasant weather, however, they had nothing much to show for their considerable efforts.

Press had commenced the early morning briefing with an optimistic bent, as his investigative and personal constitutions commanded. Now he felt they might not ever find the dump site let alone the place where Talbert was murdered, which would make the case considerably tougher to solve.

Their waterside expedition had not been entirely unfruitful, however. Leo Korver's maps had led to the unearthing of countless bottles and cans and other articles of trash, fishing line and bobbers, an old wooden buoy, a bicycle from a bygone era, a rusted floor safe which had been pried open and thrown into the water long ago. The search party had also netted two cell phones, a squeeze coin purse—it was empty of course, numerous hypodermic needles, the rotting carcass of a female deer, a tube television, and no less than three mangled umbrellas. More interesting finds included a gold necklace with an inscribed pendant and two handguns that would later prove to be stolen.

With daylight rapidly fading, the searchers had reconvened at the command post—a large parking lot near Central Station. Press stood facing the exhausted, forlorn faces of nearly every detective in the Division in addition to the twoscore and nine police academy cadets who'd been called in to assist. "I just want to thank everyone for coming out and giving up your day. I know the Talbert family appreciates all your sacrifice and effort as do I. We may not have found what we were looking for today, but we'll stay at it. As we always do. Until the job is done." Press asked if anyone had anything for the good of the order. When no one chimed up, he dismissed them.

Two crusty veteran detectives, though not outright belligerent, clearly weren't happy to have been dragged away from their heavy caseloads and instead forced to march along the riverbanks all day, slopping around in mud and skidding on wet rocks. The first, a portly and not-so-agile detective from Squad 1, had twisted his ankle along the Woonasquatucket near the Acorn Street bridge. He limped past now, grimacing and avoiding eye contact with Press. The other man was from Squad 2. His clothing was still damp and clinging to his body. From what Press had been able to gather from overhearing JK and Tank's earlier snickering, the man had slipped and gone down in the water altogether. For this, he would be ruthlessly ridiculed for days and weeks to come. It was just the cop way.

Press remained straight-faced as the Squad 2 man approached. "And thanks, Wally. I always knew you to be a dogged investigator. But searching *beneath* the water goes way above and beyond. I'm going to put you in for an award." Immediately, laughter broke out amongst the men and women within earshot.

The wet detective issued him the one-finger salute in response. To which Press simply grinned from ear to ear.

When everyone had finally cleared out, Press climbed into his truck. He sat there in silence for several minutes, allowing his muscles to rest for the first time all day. He was already ticking down the list of things to do next. He considered going home, but what was the point? There was no one waiting for him, eager for a kiss and a long embrace. He checked his watch and decided to head back into the office.

Once there, he made a quick trip to the locker room, where he splashed some water on his face and changed into a fresh set of clothes then headed back upstairs to forage for food. He found two remaining slices of pizza in the break-room fridge that were probably at least a day old. He quickly devoured them and chased it all down with a bottle of iced tea from the vending machine in the hall.

Feeling somewhat invigorated, he sat down at his desk and sorted through a stack of items that had been placed there by others in his absence. There were several phone messages Sunny Everhart had taken down for him. He flipped through them. One had to do with an unrelated case that would soon be going to trial. Several were from a nut who kept reporting to him and every other detective in the Division that her neighbor was stealing her cable TV, hacking her phone, and spying on her through her vehicle's nav system. The public had no idea how many whack jobs cops dealt with on a routine basis.

A note from Paul Martini lay next to his keyboard. Paulie had texted him earlier in the day to let him know he had placed the extraction report for the phone found near Talbert's burned-up vehicle on his desk. Gabby had mentioned it, too, but the day had been a busy one. She was planning to dig into it first thing in the morning, but he knew she wouldn't mind if he got a jump on it. Besides, he was the primary on the case, *and* he was her supervisor.

The report was housed in a blue folder, the PPD patch stamped onto the front cover. Tucked inside the left inner pocket were copies of Gabby's search warrant and the department lab submission form she had completed. This detailed the specific data detectives sought from the phone's stored contents, whether the phone was locked or not, and some other required information. In the right pocket was a paper report Martini had attached that documented his credentials, methodology, and common technology-related terminology, along with some photos of the phone, front and back, with a short plastic L-shaped ruler beside it.

Press scanned the report, noting Martini's recorded actions and conclusions, which in typical fashion essentially directed the reader back to the primary investigator to determine if the contents of the phone were relevant to the specified case and in what way.

A flash drive was included. It was inside a small manila envelope, which Press now opened. He inserted the device into his workstation and began clicking his way through the extraction report. He quickly deduced that the phone did not belong to the late Riley Talbert, unless of course he had a secret obsession with hip-hop culture and street gangs. Press scrolled through the images found on the phone. The themes were clear from the start: illegal drugs, thugs with guns, pornography (lots of it), fast cars, and tattoos. Though there were no selfies broadcasting the identity of the phone's owner—that would be too easy, he did find numerous photos of one particular female. And her, he did know. Shaniqua Banks was baby mama to a verified Providence-area thug named Vontavious Green, who was known on the street as "Boom" for obvious reasons—he was a shooter.

Press recalled first seeing his name in flash sheets about three years ago when Green had come to the attention of the Narcotics Bureau. He had his own run-in with Green back in September, the month before he'd gotten hurt, while investigating the shooting death of a 17-year-old gang member in Washington Park. Since then, Press learned as he sifted through the PPD records database, that Green's name had surfaced in upward of six recent shootings in Providence, two being murders of what detectives knew were rival gang members.

He ran Green's name through a number of additional databases and soon had built a complete intel workup on him that was now piling up in the printer tray. Even at Green's young age, his criminal history was extensive.

He'd already been arrested for assault, robbery (twice), PWID (also twice), and firearm-related offenses, as well as numerous misdemeanors most of which were thefts. His triple-I record showed additional arrests in North Carolina for retail theft and sexual assault. Press noted that most of the charges in his criminal history had either been nolle-prossed, plead down to lesser offenses, resulted in not guilty dispositions, or were otherwise conspicuously incomplete in their resolution. Probably because most of his victims refused to cooperate with police, or because they'd been too afraid of Green to testify in court. Or maybe it was because of the no-snitching way of the street. Or some combination of the three.

A recently entered data point in Green's records put a grin on his face. Apparently, Green had gotten himself locked up yesterday afternoon after attempting to flee from officers up in Smithfield. Press walked over to the printer, snatched up the stack of papers, and flipped through them until he landed on the Smithfield PD report that documented the incident. The report revealed that Green had assaulted a man outside the Barnes and Noble store just off Putnam Pike then fled the scene. This while driving a stolen car. There had also been a warrant out for his arrest at the time for a PV. The database didn't provide details on the specific parole violation but did have a notation about Green's violent tendencies.

Press recognized the name of the state parole agent listed in the Smithfield PD report; officers had contacted him following the arrest. He dialed the agent's cell phone number and waited for the call to connect.

"State Parole. Jolley speaking."

"Otis. It's Nate."

"Nate, my man! I heard you were back in action. Great to hear from you!"

"Thanks. It's good to be back. Hey, I won't keep you long, I know you're probably about to head out the door if you haven't already."

"No sweat. What can I do for the PPD's best detective?"

"Vontavious Green. He's yours, right?"

"Yes, sir. What a piece of crap. He's one dangerous dude. Just got locked up, thankfully. Filed the detainer on him this morning."

"I know. The reason I'm calling is that his name has come up in a murder case I'm working."

"Yeah?"

"Tell me, what was his original PV for?"

There was the sound of a file cabinet closing in the background then Jolley said, "He no-showed for his last office appointment. Then cut off his ankle monitor. On top of that he's now got new charges."

"The assault in Smithfield."

"Right on. He also fought with officers when they were taking him into custody."

His spirit buoyed with the possibility of a fresh lead, Press said, "When did he cut off the ankle device?" He waited as Jolley checked the file, already thinking ahead to his next question, which related to Green's location history and how it might tie into the Talbert murder, or if nothing else, put him at the scene of the burned-up Mercedes.

"Three weeks ago. March twenty-fourth…it was a Friday…at ten oh three a.m."

"*Dang* it. Okay. I appreciate you looking."

"Sure thing. Let me know if there is anything else I can do to help."

"Will do. Thanks, Otis."

Press sighed and for a moment leaned back in his chair and stared at a particular spot in the ceiling tiles as he considered his next move. More specifically, he was running down the list of questions that had spontaneously formed in his head. Thirty seconds more and he suddenly checked his watch. Then reached for his phone. If all went well, he'd be staring across the table at Vontavious Green in the morning.

29

The Intake Service Center was on Slate Hill Road down in Cranston. Normally, it was a fifteen-minute drive from the jail to Central Station, but because of morning rush-hour traffic and a crash involving a tractor trailer on I-95, the two patrol officers tasked with transporting Green were sorely delayed.

The extra time though had given Press a chance to shoot Talbert's cell phone records over to Carla Sheffield—they had popped into his email inbox as he'd been walking into the office. With her tech tools and intel analyst savvy, she would set about mapping the phone's geo-location history and parsing his calls, texts, and emails. The woman never ceased to impress with how much information she could cull given a short block of time. She was an invaluable asset to the unit.

Press also had time to scroll through Green's known social media accounts. When he heard the officers call out over the radio that they had arrived at Central Station, he dipped into Interview Room A and made sure everything was just how he liked it—the positioning of the chairs and such—then grabbed his prepared notes and a fresh notepad.

Three minutes later, the elevator door out in the main hallway opened and two uniformed officers led a handcuffed and shackled Vontavious Green into the Major Crimes Unit's office suite. The officers guided Green to a chair inside the interview room with his back to the wall and his face to the camera. Here, they removed one handcuff and secured it to a thick steel loop built into the table, which was bolted to the floor. They locked the door from the outside and approached Press, who was now studying Green via a CCTV monitor on the wall near his cubicle.

"How was he on the ride over? Any issues?"

"Nah," said the shorter of the two transport officers. "He was pretty quiet."

"Okay. Thanks for running him in. You guys are welcome to hang out up here, grab some coffee. I'm not sure how long I'll be."

As the two unis headed off for the break room, Press turned back to the monitor. With arms crossed, he studied Green for several more minutes. He usually liked to let the person in the fishbowl begin to ruminate before going in. Sometimes they said stupid or even incriminating things. They almost always offered some kind of information about themselves. It was during this time that Killian joined him.

"He's going to be a tough nut. I know when I worked narcotics, he always got mouthy with us."

"Just so long as he doesn't go mute," Press said dryly. He was just about to head in when Lt. Gentry appeared.

"Hey, Nate. Someone's here to file a missing person report."

"Can't patrol handle it? I'm about to step into an interview."

"It's Seth Barnett's parents."

Press exchanged thoughtful glances with Killian then nodded. "Send them up." When Gentry was gone, he waved Gabby and Tank over and explained the new development. "I need you guys to interview Barnett's parents. JK, you know Green. I want you monitoring my interview with him. Everybody good?"

The three detectives answered in the affirmative and the huddle broke.

Press slid back the two deadbolt locks and entered the interview room. Green sat with his head on the table and his eyes closed. Whether he was asleep or just acting the part was difficult to determine. Frankly, Press didn't much care. It was a known fact in this business that the guilty ones could easily fall asleep in the midst of police custody. Innocent folks didn't like being caged up and accused of things they hadn't done. Whatever the case, in a somewhat casual yet authoritative tone, Press ordered Green to wake up then took a seat opposite him.

Squinting, Green slowly sat back and flexed his neck from side to side. With a short, guttural croak, Green hawked up a wad of phlegm and held it in his throat. For a split-second Press thought he was going to spit—at him or on the floor. Instead, Green just swallowed it down as he continued sizing him up. Looking as if he were trying to act bored—and by extension tough, Green wiped his nose with the side of his index finger on his well-inked right hand. Despite the unflattering oatmeal-colored prison attire, Press could tell that Green frequented the prison weight room during his recurring periods of incarceration. But it was something else that had drawn the bulk of his attention, something on the back of Green's hand. For now, he would make no mention of it. He would come back to it later if need be.

"Mr. Green, my name is Detective Sergeant Press."

"Yeah, you're that *po*lice was in the news. The one who got shot. I know who you is."

"Very good. I'd like to talk with you about—"

"Yo, muh. I already done told those pigs, I ain't got *nuthin'* to say."

Inside Press wanted to punch the guy in the mouth, but outwardly he maintained his composure. Green was a predator. A dangerous gang member. A known shooter. His eyes revealed it, too. He was not at all intimidated by the presence of the police. In fact, it was evident that he enjoyed challenging authority. What's more, it was clear that he believed he was smarter and tougher than everyone he encountered. On top of that, Green demonstrated an attitude that suggested he didn't care about anything or anyone but himself.

"If you'll let me finish... This isn't about what happened in Smithfield. I'm here to talk to you about a murder."

"Yo! I ain't did no *murda*, bruh. Is that why you dragged me up in this joint?"

Press clipped his pen to his notepad and crossed his arms. He had a way of showing his intent with his eyes as well. "How about we do it this way. I'm going to talk and you're going to listen."

Green mirrored him by crossing his arms, too, then sneered. But otherwise remained quiet.

Press knew that during an interrogation most thugs like Green were equally interested in hearing what police knew or wanted as much as they were hellbent on denying any criminal involvement.

"A lawyer by the name of Riley Talbert was found dead early Monday morning along the river just south of the Crawford Street Bridge. He was murdered."

"And you think I did it?! Yo, muh... You *trippin'*."

"His SUV—a Mercedes-Benz AMG GLS 63—was recovered up at Lincoln Woods State Park. Someone drove it there then torched it. We found evidence that links you to the scene." Press paused for a moment to let that information sink in, all the while watching for a reaction in Green's face. At the exact moment Green was about to speak, Press held up his hand. "You know how this works. If you want to talk with me about any of this, you first have to sign this. It's a Miranda waiver form. Press read what was delineated on the form verbatim then presented it to Green. "Again, you can stop at any time."

"Gimme a pen."

Arrogance. Press loved using a suspect's own foolish arrogance against him. With the way he had presented the facts, leaving out just enough detail in order to make Green curious, he knew the young thug wouldn't be able to resist.

With the signed Miranda form safely tucked away, Press began the interview anew. *Just get him talking. Let him tell whatever story he wishes.* Locking someone into a lie was almost as good as getting an admission. And oftentimes equally damning in court.

"Let's start with what you were doing with the attorney's SUV."

"I didn't kill no *law*yer, mofo!"

"Tell me about the SUV."

"I didn't have nobody's ride. I'm *telling* you!"

Press just looked at him, revealing nothing with his face. Finally, after nearly a full minute, Green spoke. The silence had apparently gotten to him. Most people felt compelled to fill it.

"How you gonna say I had dude's whip if it was all burned up?"

"Is your phone in your property over at the prison?"

"Whatchu mean?"

"Exactly what I said. Did you have your phone with you when you were booked?"

Green said nothing now as if he were thinking.

"What if I got a search warrant and went through your property over there? What do you suppose I'd find?"

This remark caused Green to smirk. "Knock yoself out, mofo. You can't tie me to *nuthin'*. 'Specially no murda."

"Has your phone ever been out of your possession? You ever let someone borrow it?"

"Ain't no one have my phone. Know wh' I'm sayin?" He paused. "What you gettin' at, *po-lice-man*?"

Press continued, "When was the last time you were at Lincoln Woods State Park?"

"I ain't never been up der."

"Never?"

Green spewed a couple vulgarities then with his whole body said, "*Never, yo*! What kind of frame job is this?!"

"And if I go look in your property bag out at the jail, your phone will be there, right?"

Green grew quiet. Again, it was apparent that he was thinking things through. Or was trying to anyway. "Yeah," he said at last but without conviction.

"You're sure?"

"Yeah, mofo!"

Press read off a number from his notes. "That's your cell phone number, correct?"

"Yeah. So?"

Press now produced a close-up photo of the cell phone they had recovered near the remains of Talbert's SUV. He placed it on the table and slid it toward Green. "Stay with me, Vontavious." Green's eyebrows knitted together. "Your phone isn't in your property bag at the jail. I'll tell you exactly where it is. It's in police custody right here at Central Station."

"Where you find it?"

"Where do you think we found it?"

Green's attitude changed. He was less sure of himself now.

"I'll tell you only because I don't have all day. We found it next to the dead lawyer's burned-up car." He let that fester in Green's brain for a few seconds then said, "Now, you want to start being honest with me?"

Green's head dropped and his shoulders folded inward. He leaned forward with his elbows on the table and shook his head back and forth several times. "Look, muh. I had the car, but I didn't kill no lawyer."

"Lay it out for me. Because right now it's not looking too good for you. In fact, I could make a strong case to say you did."

Satisfied he had wrung all he could out of Vontavious Green, Press stepped out of the interview room and sought out Matt Casteel from Squad 1. After bringing him up to speed, which included telling him about the scabbed over wound on the back of Green's right hand, Press turned over the interrogation to him since Casteel was the detective in charge of the weekend shooting investigation.

Press hit the coffee machine for a refill then paced back through the bullpen of cubicles to an area that detectives long before his time had converted into a makeshift lounge. The mismatched sofas and chairs were nothing much to look at, but they were comfortable and fostered a collaborative, team atmosphere. Soon, Killian, Gabby, and Tank joined him.

Press briefed them on the information he had extracted from Green. "He says he found the car in the street with the engine running."

"Where?" Gabby said.

"Over on Prospect Street near Brown U." Press handed her the crude street diagram Green had drawn. "Almost right in front of the Rochambeau House."

"What was he doing over there?" said Tank, peering over Gabby's shoulder. "I doubt he was visiting the university library."

"He was selling drugs to students. He didn't say that specifically, but he might as well have." Press breathed in the pleasant aroma of freshly brewed coffee as he brought the cup to his lips.

"You don't think he had anything to do with Talbert's death." It was a statement, not a question.

"You're right, Gabs. I don't. But he *was* involved in Matt's shooting from the weekend." Seeing their quizzical looks, he continued. "He's got a slide bite on the back of his right hand."

"Meaning he's recently fired a semi-automatic handgun," Tank added.

"From the looks of the scabbing, I'd say Green was doing his trigger pulling on or about the date of Matty's deal. Add to that his admission about taking Talbert's SUV, the CCTV footage turned up in the canvass, the bullet holes in the car, and most damning of all, the geo-location evidence from his cell phone. How much you want to bet it'll put him at the scene? More investigation is needed, but Matt's got solid PC for an arrest warrant. And don't think *we're* not going to crap all over Green, too. We've got him dead to rights for stealing Talbert's car, arson, criminal conspiracy, and that's just for starters."

Tank leaned forward on the sofa, his elbows on his knees. "So, if he didn't kill Talbert, who did?"

"I don't know, but Green did give us something to work with and it's big." Press took another sip of coffee, watching the suspense build in their eyes.

But Killian beat him to the punch. "He's given us the place where Talbert was abducted."

Press pointed at him. "Exactly. I think that spot on Prospect is precisely where Talbert was snatched. It's along the route he likely would have taken going home from the GPub. We need to hit the streets out there, look for cameras. Maybe someone's got it all on video for us." He turned to Gabby. "Before we do though I want to hear what Barnett's parents had to say."

Gabby grinned as if she were about to share some deep, dark secret. "Ready for this, Sarge?"

30

KETTLE POINT APARTMENTS
CAPTAIN JOHN JACOBS ROAD, EAST PROVIDENCE

Seth Barnett's apartment was in a state of disarray. Press stood beside Killian, Gabby, and a large-framed East Providence PD detective lieutenant named George Lamb just inside the entryway, each of them taking stock of what the scene had to tell. Sights, sounds, smells. All of it.

Meanwhile, Tank was waiting downstairs with Barnett's parents in a small meeting room inside the leasing office, which the property manager had graciously offered them to use. The couple had already signed a missing person declaration and a consent form permitting police entry into the apartment.

Because the Kettle Point Apartments were within Lamb's jurisdiction, Press had reached out to him on the ride over. Lamb was nearing retirement age, but with three kids in college, he had no plans of heading out the door anytime soon. Wearing a navy suit, plain white shirt, and blue-and-orange-striped tie, Lamb was old school and a big guy—he had Press beat by an inch or two and at least forty pounds. Lamb had seen his share of homicides over the years and had cleared most of them by arrest. Press had worked closely with him on a handful of occasions, most recently on a series of armed convenience-store robberies that had culminated when Lamb drilled the offender twice in the chest with his duty weapon during the execution of a search warrant on Hobson Avenue. Lamb was a hard-nosed investigator and knew how to work the angles of a case. Like Press, he understood the big picture when it came to the art of solving crime. Professional law enforcement was a collaborative effort that transcended egos and territorial boundaries. Therefore, it came as no surprise when Lamb eagerly offered his agency's assistance.

"So how does this kid, Barnett, play into your murder?" Lamb said, eyes still moving about the apartment.

"We're still trying to figure that out." Press snapped on two pairs of nitrile gloves. "But he's looking less and less like a suspect."

"Looks like you've got a real mess on your hands with this one."

"No argument here." Press tilted his head toward Gabby. "Can you call back to Central, explain what's going on, and have BCI respond over?"

Lamb stepped aside as Gabby returned to the corridor to summon the troops then again drew shoulder-to-shoulder with Press and Killian, each of them visually combing the open space for every available detail. Lamb didn't balk at the idea of an outside agency coming in to process the apartment and Press knew why. With his level of experience, Lamb understood that it was more efficient for the continuity of the case to have Providence PD's evidence techs process the scene. Chain of custody protocols dictated that the fewer hands in the pot the better. Even though East Providence now officially had a missing person case and an obvious burglary on their books, Lamb deferred to Press and the ongoing homicide investigation. The cases were clearly linked, but murder trumped all.

Lamb's phone chimed. After consulting it, he said, "Well, Nate, let me know if you guys need anything. I'll have one of our uniforms camp out downstairs until you're finished." He tapped a quick text message reply into the device. "I'm going to go ahead and clear. I wish I could stay, but we just had a bank robbery and one of the tellers was roughed up pretty good."

"Understood. Thanks, George."

As Lamb opened the door to leave, the frenzied yelping of a nearby little dog became more apparent. Press and Killian waited until the door had clicked shut and all but muted the dog's shrill clamor then began their scene assessment anew.

"You smell that?" said Killian.

Press returned his gaze and nodded. "First thing I noticed."

"Wonder if Barnett smokes."

"We're about to find out." A few steps more into the apartment, Press said, "I'll start in the kitchen. See what you can find over there." With the tail end of his flashlight, he pointed toward the living room. "Looks like someone had some fun."

The kitchen was neat but spare. Here, Press found a pile of garbage on the table. A long, thin knife lay beside it. He leaned closer. Using the beam of his Streamlight, he studied the blade from various angles. It bore no evidence of blood, or at least none that he could see with the naked eye. Turning slowly in a semi-circle, he noticed a wooden block of knives of similar design on the counter. It seemed obvious now that someone had dumped the garbage and sifted through it, perhaps in search of something. A particular item. A clue even. But a clue to what?

All signs indicated that Barnett was not a smoker. There were no cigarette butts or empty packs in the trash atop the table or anywhere else for that matter. No ashtrays, either. Press called it out to Killian as he added this information to his notepad.

The fridge was mostly bare. Nothing inside smelled of being past the date of expiration. Aside from the rotten bananas on the counter, the rest of the kitchen was similarly stocked. If Seth Barnett had money, he didn't spend it on food or drink.

Standing next to an enclosed set of bookshelves in the living room, Killian motioned to the knife-carved TV and sofa. "Seems like someone is trying to send a message. Wouldn't you say?"

Press nodded as he slowly walked past, his focus now on a desk opposite the TV. From the voids on its surface, it was obvious that a computer and printer were missing. He hesitated by the glass door to the walkout balcony as he scribbled down some more notes then tucked the leather-bound pad under his arm. With one gloved finger he tried the door handle, careful not to disturb any potential latent prints. The lever-style handle didn't budge under the pressure. "Door is locked. Nothing out there but a small table, a flowerpot, and two plastic patio chairs."

He next checked the hallway closet on his way toward the back of the apartment. It was mostly bare. Just some old boxes of junk that had been collected over the years, a folding chair, and a hodgepodge of jackets including a thick parka that hung from a white metal rod. Press pushed the coats aside and examined the floor along the right side of the closet. Something had been stored there but was now missing. Linear impressions in the carpet formed a rectangle with two symmetric square notches on one of the long sides. The missing item was quite obviously a suitcase.

The light was on inside the bathroom, but otherwise the room was unremarkable in comparison to the next one. The lone bedroom in the apartment seemed to have suffered the brunt of the interloper's aggression. Bed pillows had been sliced open and their contents—hundreds of white, sponge-foam peanuts—were strewn all over the room. Papers were scattered about as if someone had simply pulled them from the small file cabinet next to the bed and flung them in one motion as hard as they could. Curtains, the rods, too, had been pulled violently from the windows. Eerily, however, the bed appeared untouched. This seemed at odds with the rest of the wanton vandalism. On a hunch, Press carefully pulled back the duvet and discovered next to an empty tube of blue-green toothpaste, a message written in a crude cursive font: "You're dead!"

31

As the BCI folks took photos and did their thing, Press called Lamb and related what they had found. While listening to the East Prov. lieutenant's response, he gave a thumbs-up to a BCI detective who was indicating that she had collected Barnett's toothbrush for later DNA comparison in the event it became necessary.

"Hey, George. Can you check your guys' system for any records involving Barnett as well as the apartment complex that suggest any kind of violence or similar behavior. I would also be interested to know if you've had any burglaries or thefts in the immediate area. You're probably not going to find anything, but I have to ask...just to cover all the bases. You understand."

"No problem, brother. Gimme a sec. I just got back to the office."

"Any leads on your bank robber?"

"Actually, patrol snagged him a few blocks from the bank. The momo."

"Nice." The clickety-clack of a keyboard and a chair squeaking under the big man's girth filtered through the receiver. Press pictured the fifty-year-old right now hunched over his desk stacked with case files, suit jacket thrown over the back of a nearby chair, tie and shirt collar pulled loose at the neck.

"We got nothing at the complex, Nate, aside from a bunch of fraud complaints—mostly tax-related crap, some reports of stolen mail, a handful of barking dog calls, and some domestic disputes between a mother and her teenage daughter from back in February. And I'm showing zero incidents involving Seth Barnett for anywhere in East Prov."

"Okay. Thanks, George. I appreciate you checking for me." Press slipped the phone back into his pants pocket and joined Killian by the apartment door.

"What do you think? Drugs?"

Press shook his head. "Nah. This doesn't feel like a drug case."

"You're right. Too neat. Too clean." The kid's clearly no addict. And by the looks of his expenditures, he's no dealer either." He stared at Press who was slowly sweeping the room again with his eyes. "Then what? Gambling? You think he owes somebody money?"

Press hooked his thumb on the grip of the pistol holstered on his right hip, turned back toward the kitchen, and focused on the trash spread out on the table. "I don't know, JK. I don't know. But I do know this: We're not the only ones looking for Seth Barnett." He mentioned again the missing suitcase and clothes from the closets and drawers, the message scrawled in toothpaste on the bed. "I'd say he knows it, too."

"Well, assuming he's still alive, we had better find him first."

Press headed downstairs as Killian began knocking on doors. Halfway there he ran into Gabby. He asked her a series of questions then directed her to link up with Killian. If the woman who lived across the hall from Barnett wasn't home, they needed to start making phone calls. There was something nagging at him, and he needed to address it.

Tank and the Barnetts were still in the small meeting room; it appeared to double as a break room. They all looked at him as he rapped his knuckle on the door and immediately entered. Mr. Barnett stood in a corner of the room with his hands on his hips while his wife was seated across from Tank. Her eyes were heavy with worry. Several empty paper cups were strewn on the wood laminate table. Two unwrapped breakfast sandwiches lay in their midst. The scent of coffee and French vanilla creamer hung in the air. So did a cloud of anxious tension.

"I'm sorry to have kept you all waiting." Press introduced himself and slid into the chair next to Tank. "I understand you spoke with Detectives Meredith and Ibarra earlier this morning, but I'd like you to run through again just what brought you folks to Providence."

"What do you mean? Our son is missing for cryin' out loud! *That's* what brought us here!"

"Yes, sir. And it's my job to find your son and make sure he's okay. You've seen his place. He's apparently in some kind of danger." Press didn't mention the overt threat scribbled on the bed in toothpaste; he was positive the couple hadn't seen it. "I apologize for having you go over this again, but it's important that we have all the information, so we can move quickly."

Marsha Barnett turned to her husband. "Sit down, Gerry. Please."

Gerald Barnett paced to the chair beside her and sat, his face a mix of anger, impatience, and concern. Though not quite as tall as Press, he was a large, burly man. The shade of his skin indicated that he spent lots of time outdoors. He also worked with his hands, for they were thick with muscle and bore the type of rough callouses that one collects through fierce labor. He wore a green-and-blue, grid-patterned twill shirt with button-down collars and dark blue jeans that seemed seldom worn or were possibly brand new. Press figured him to be the construction-worker type—a general contractor, an excavator, or a brick mason perhaps. He was the owner of the business, too, or at least had a position in management. In either case, he was someone accustomed to barking orders. The man immediately reminded him of his father.

"Let's start at the beginning."

Mr. Barnett, still simmering, rotated toward his wife. Her hands were folded on the table as if she were about to pray. She took a breath, let it out slowly. "We talked to Seth by phone about a month ago. He usually calls every Sunday afternoon."

"You folks are not local. Is that correct?" Press already knew the answer to this question, their midwestern accent said as much.

"We live in Stevens Point, Wisconsin. Seth attended MIT on a scholarship then got a job up here right out of school. He graduated at the top of his class, had offers from all over, dontcha know. But he fell in love with this area, the ocean being so close and whatnot."

Mom was clearly proud of her son. "Please, go on."

Marsha Barnett looked at her hands as she focused her thoughts. "At first, when he didn't call, we figured he was just busy at work or with friends, *you know*. I texted him," she pulled a phone from her purse, tapped the screen several times, "back on the tenth, but he didn't respond. Again, I figured he was busy or just forgot to text back." She glanced at her husband. "Then... When was it, Gerry?"

"Tuesday, the very next day." Gerald Barnett's voice was strong and deep, in contrast to the light, airy timbre of his wife's.

"Yes, so on Tuesday the eleventh, his work called—someone in HR, right dear?"

Mr. Barnett nodded. "I don't remember the name. It was a woman. Said she was trying to get ahold of Seth. Said he hadn't been to work for several days and was not returning their phone calls, text messages, or emails. Since we were listed as his emergency contact, she asked if we had heard from him. I told her we hadn't spoken to him in several weeks. I asked if something was wrong. The woman said she didn't know, just asked that we have Seth get in touch with them if he were to contact us."

"And he hasn't called, texted, or otherwise communicated with you since?"

Mr. Barnett shook his head. "Not since..." He motioned to his wife to hand him her phone. When she did, he donned a set of reading glasses and brought up the phone's call history. "Not since Sunday, March nineteenth."

"Ever since that woman from his work called, we've been calling, texting, and emailing him." The muscles in Marsha's chin quivered. "I've left him probably twenty voice-mail messages and sent a hundred texts, dontcha know. So far, he hasn't responded to a single one."

"We finally decided to come out and see what was going on," said Gerald Barnett. "That's when we discovered his apartment."

Press leaned back in his chair, his notepad propped on his crossed legs. "And just to be clear, that was when exactly?"

"When we discovered the mess in his apartment?"

Press nodded. At that moment, his phone buzzed with a new text message. It was from Gabby: *Found her. She just got home.*

He tapped back a quick reply: *OK. Bring her down to mgt ofc. Knock when you get here.*

Her response was immediate: *On our way.*

"Sorry about that. You were saying... You discovered the mess in his apartment..."

"Right before we came to the police station." Mr. Barnett looked at his wife. "It was probably something like seven forty-five, maybe eight o'clock this morning."

"Our flight landed around six thirty," she added.

"Was there a particular reason you didn't go to the East Providence Police?" They looked at him like he had two heads. "The apartment complex is situated in their jurisdiction."

"Uff da!" blurted Mr. Barnett. The exclamation was followed by a filthy curse word better suited for a construction site or a police interrogation room. He shot a glance at his wife as if the mistake was her doing. "You mean you can't help us?!"

"No, no. I was just asking a simple question. I know jurisdictional boundaries can be confusing. Technically, this is East Prov's domain, but I count it as good fortune that you came to us. I'm going to be straight-up with you folks. I'm investigating the murder of a prominent attorney that occurred in my area. This may come as a shock to you, but Seth's name has popped up in my case and thus you can understand our interest in his whereabouts."

Mr. Barnett's face had gone red, while his wife seemed utterly confused. "What do you mean? Are saying Seth is a *suspect*?" she said.

"Based on everything I know right now I am confident that he is *not* the doer—the person responsible for killing the lawyer. Nevertheless, it's important that we find your son to one, verify his safety, and two, learn the nature of his involvement in all of this. Now, I just have a few more questions for you folks." He didn't wait for them to respond. "Where does Seth work?"

"Donstar Data Specialists."

"And what does he do there, ma'am?"

"Something with computers. He's a…" She looked at her husband for help.

"A *data security analyst*, I think is what he told me."

Mrs. Barnett nodded. "He's super smart with computers."

Press wrote it all down. "Sir, did the woman who called give you a number at which to call her back?"

There was a knock on the door.

"Come in," said Press, twisting in his chair.

The door opened and in walked Gabby with Barbara Stanley following closely at her heels.

Press waited a few seconds then apologized before asking the new arrivals to step back outside. He would be with them shortly. Gabby's face screwed up for a second until finally she seemed to understand what Press was doing.

"We'll be upstairs, Sarge."

"Very well. Thanks, Gabby." Press turned back to the Barnetts. "I apologize for the interruption."

Mr. Barnett looked at him vacantly. "What was the question again?"

"Did the woman who called about Seth give you a number where she could be reached?"

"Right. No, she didn't. She just said to have Seth call the office. I do remember the caller ID showing a number though if that helps."

"Yes, thank you." Press obtained additional background information on Seth Barnett from his parents to include his cell phone number, email addresses, known social media accounts, and the names of the places where he did his banking. He asked if Seth had any significant others past or present, any other close relatives or friends, especially any in the immediate area, with whom they felt he should speak. He also asked if Seth had any known enemies or had been having problems with anyone, any difficulties at work or elsewhere. The information they provided was sparse. He'd had a girlfriend in high school, but they had broken up before his senior year. They knew of no close friends or girlfriends in college, but then again, he was quiet about those types of things. Enemies? He had none that they knew about. And work seemed to be going just fine, so much as they were aware.

Press scribbled into his pad then looked up. "Finally, does the name Riley Talbert ring any bells? Did Seth ever mention him in any previous communications, et cetera?"

The Barnetts regarded each other as if they were thinking jointly. "No, I'm sorry," the wife said. "Is that the name of the man who was killed?"

"Yes."

"How did Seth's name come up in your investigation, if I may ask?"

"Well, ma'am, it seems that Seth had met with Mr. Talbert—the attorney—on Sunday, the ninth. His body was discovered the following Monday—the seventeenth—along the Providence River."

"But why?"

"That's a good question, ma'am. And it's one we intend to answer."

"Anything else you think is important for us to know?" Press waited until both replied in the negative then said, "Very good. May I ask what your plans are for the short term?"

Mr. Barnett had already stood. "We're not leaving town till we get some answers, I can tell you that much."

"I understand. Where are you staying? Can we give you a ride to your hotel?"

Again, they looked at each other. "We haven't even gotten that far."

"Well, ma'am, I am happy to recommend some hotels in the city." After doing so, Press supplied each of them with a business card. "Please call me directly if you have any questions or concerns about anything, or if Seth would happen to contact you. My cell phone number is on the back."

32

Press knocked and was immediately greeted by the sharp warnings of a dog he would soon learn was called Pookie. Gabby let him in after Barb Stanley scooped up her little friend.

"All good?" she said quietly. "You want me to go help Tank and JK canvass the complex?"

"No. I want you here," he whispered back.

Holding the dog like a football, Stanley led them into the kitchen, where they all sat down at a table not unlike the one in Seth Barnett's wrecked apartment. Though this table had a glass top and was not covered in trash.

Press guessed her to be in her late forties or early fifties. She had shoulder-length hair turned blond from a bottle. Her ivory shirt and khaki pants conveyed a touch of class as did the general décor of the apartment. Whereas Seth Barnett appeared to be at odds with how to get by in an expensive city, Barb Stanley was clearly at ease in her station in life.

Press would soon learn that, like him, Stanley was recently divorced. She, however, seemed to be embracing her new-found freedom or at least her ex-husband's money.

"So, the man said he was Seth's father? Is that right?" Press said.

"Oh, yes. Seemed like a nice gentleman. I let him use my key, so he could get into the apartment."

Press sipped the weak coffee she had supplied them as Gabby left hers on the table in front of her untouched. Pookie, meanwhile, sniffed their shoes and offered intermittent growls. At one point, Gabby reached down to pet the little guy if for no other reason than to be polite. The toy-size dog lowered his head, dodged, and scurried off only to return just as quickly as if it were a game he enjoyed playing.

Press focused his attention squarely on Barb Stanley. "Now, do you remember the man and woman you saw just now downstairs in the office? The couple with whom I was speaking when you and Detective Ibarra entered?"

"Yes. Why?"

"This is very important, Ms. Stanley. Was the man in the room downstairs the same man you saw entering Seth's apartment? The man who said he was Seth's father and was in from out of town?"

"No." Her eyes flicked back and forth from Press to Gabby, searching for meaning. "I don't understand. What's going on?"

"The folks downstairs… *They* are Seth's parents."

The gravity of the information now hit her. "You're telling me the man I let into Seth's apartment was *not* his father?"

"Looks that way."

Her hands began to tremble. She brought them to her mouth. "Did something happen to Seth? Is he okay?"

"We hope so. Right now, he's missing." With his posture and facial cues, Press endeavored to convey a sense of concern and compassion, which was hard to do, because at this very minute Pookie began ripping and snarling at his shoelaces in a sporting game of tug-of-war. Thankfully, Gabby came to his aid. She reached beneath the table for the dog, but once again he dashed off to safety, which now was a place at the top of the sofa. Tongue hanging out and tail vibrating from side to side, the white furball appeared to be smiling as he waited for the game to resume.

"I'll be straight with you, Ms. Stanley. We're Providence Police detectives. We work major crimes, which include *homicide*."

He might as well have picked up the flower vase from the sideboard next to him and tossed it into the middle of the floor. The effect was the same.

She recoiled, a look of horror now on her face. "*Homicide*?! Oh my. Is Seth...?"

"We don't know. Like I said, right now he's missing. We were hoping you could shed some light on what may have become of him."

Stanley swallowed hard and sat up straighter in her chair.

"When was the last time you saw Seth?"

"I don't know. Um, let me think." She squinted and looked at the ceiling then the floor then Pookie. Finally, she said, "I don't know. Maybe a week. I'm sorry."

"How well do you know him?"

"Seth? Well, he's my neighbor. We're friendly with each other. Share keys, you know...in case one of us gets locked out. He's a nice young man. Pookie adores him."

"Anything else?"

"I know he works in the city at some computer firm. I can't remember the name of it. He's smart. *Really* smart. I know *that*. What do they call it...? *Techy*. He's techy. Fixed my computer a number of times when I was having issues...*and* my cable TV. Did it for free. He's just a sweet boy."

Gabby chimed in. "Did he have many visitors?"

"No." Stanley scooched forward in her chair. "There was a girl who used to come around."

"A girlfriend or just a friend?"

Stanley's eyes widened as she shrugged her shoulders.

"When was that?"

"Oh gee, I haven't seen her in two, maybe three months."

Press held his pen over his notepad. "What did she look like?"

"Medium height. She had long, blond hair. Glasses. Very pretty."

"Anything else?" Press said.

"She had a tattoo on her ankle. The right one, I think. Yes, the right one. Of a sunflower."

Satisfied that Barb Stanley had no other relevant information to give them, Press handed her a card. "Contact me if you think of anything else."

"I will." She sniffled back a tear. "Please find him. He's a wonderful boy."

33

Providence PD
Central Station

Press spent the remainder of the afternoon reviewing CCTV footage from the apartment complex as well as Talbert's law firm and of course catching up on paperwork. More than once during that time, Deputy Chief Winthrop Dennison Fantroy prowled into the Major Crimes Unit offices and reminded him and some other detectives to complete their required departmental online training modules for the latest and greatest police reform initiatives. Most of them had to do with implicit bias and gender fluidity nonsense. With the chief being out on medical leave due to another bout of cancer and likely not to return any time soon, if ever, Denny Fantroy had been christened acting chief and as such saw himself as the heir apparent to the throne. The consummate brown-noser, Fantroy took special pride in wielding as much power as the elevated rank, however long it might last, allowed.

Fantroy turned his attention to Press. "I believe your superiors have told you a few times already this week. At least they should have. You need to get this stuff done, Sergeant. You're already long past due."

Press leaned back from the keyboard and looked at him. He maintained his silence but couldn't hide his absolute disdain for the man and his skewed priorities. Press had no respect for people like Fantroy. To a guy like that, police work was all about checking off boxes, smiling for cameras, and riding the political winds. Not solving crime and locking up bad guys. He doubted Fantroy had seen more than a year of street time in his entire career. Surely, he had no comprehension of what it was like to be out dealing with victims and investigating violent crime.

"I don't care for that look, Sergeant." Fantroy stepped closer. "Just because you collared a serial killer last year and were shot in the process, doesn't mean you are immune to the rules around here. In fact, had you followed *policy*, you never would have been injured in the first place."

Press kept his face emotionless and simply replied, "Okay."

Fantroy glared at him as if trying to decide whether Press was being intentionally provocative with his clipped response. Finally, he turned in his polished black Chukkas and walked off.

"Thanks, Mantoy," Press said as he resumed typing. "I'll get right on that, Mantoy."

Killian chuckled from the other side of the cubicle wall. "It's not like we don't have anything better to do."

"That guy right there personifies everything that is wrong with American government these days. Totally focused on his own power and has no genuine care or clue about us in here or the people out there. What's worse is that he can't even see it. Leadership is much more than a title."

"Here, here," said Killian.

Aside from taking up a lot of time, the apartment complex and law firm footage proved nothing more than what Press already knew in his gut. The people involved in Talbert's murder and the sudden disappearance of Seth Barnett were professionals. The fact that his team had uncovered zero footage from the place on Prospect Street where they'd concluded Riley Talbert had been abducted—Sheffield had since related, per her analysis of Talbert's cell phone records, that his phone had gone dark in that same area—only bolstered this belief. And raised more questions. What was it that linked Talbert and Barnett? What's more, what kind of circumstances would manifest the involvement of professional criminals? Press hoped to find some answers at Barnett's workplace in the morning. Maybe by then, too, the kid's cell phone records would be back from the service provider.

The video footage from the canvass around the law firm wasn't completely useless, however. From it, Press now had a general description of the two men who'd burgled the law firm and perhaps the Talbert home as well, although he still strongly suspected there were two different groups of actors at play. One of the men was medium-size and lean, the other massive with muscles all over. The second man was also curiously light on his feet. Because both men had worn gloves, dark clothing, and balaclavas, nothing more could be quantified.

After some more musing over the collected footage, Press wondered if the smaller of the two men was the same guy with whom Barb Stanley had stood face-to-face in the corridor outside Seth Barnett's apartment. He retrieved one of the yellow legal pads from his shoulder bag and flipped to the relevant page. Forehead scrunched in thought, he added to one of his lists the task of having the woman sit down with one of the BCI detectives to develop a computer-generated composite photo of the man. While he was thinking of it, Press dialed her and confirmed she would be available to respond to Central Station first thing in the morning.

As he was finishing the phone call, D/Sgt. Enrico Ramos and Det. Matt Casteel paraded in. Their squad mates, Det. Jimmy Dalton and Det. Ling Zhao, spilled in a moment later. Each man was carrying numerous evidence boxes and bags and seemed to have a pep in his step.

"What's good, Nate?"

"You tell me, Rico."

Ramos smiled. "Green admitted to being in the car that was involved in our shooting over the weekend. Well, *you* know...it was your vic's SUV. He didn't want to sign up for being the trigger man but said enough for a search warrant. We shipped him back to the ACI then punched a ticket for his place. Found a *bunch* of goodies." Ramos ran down the list of items they had seized, highlighting the most damning: firearms, boxes of ammunition, drugs and packaging materials, and several cell phones.

Press lifted his nose to the air. "Smells like smoke mixed with some kind of accelerant."

Ramos nodded. "Clothing from the floor of Green's bedroom. He probably tossed it there after torching Talbert's car."

"What a dummy. You get anything else?"

"Two other mopes with warrants and now a list of new charges of their own. Both rolled on Green as the shooter, for now anyway."

"Any mention of Talbert?" Press had to ask, but he already knew the answer.

"Nah. They both said they hopped in after Green already had the vehicle. Then helped him burn it after the shooting."

"We did get these!" Dalton held up an AK-47 with a folding stock then motioned to Zhao to do likewise. The detective lifted a suppressed AR pistol into the air high enough so Press and Killian could see it over the cubicle partition. "Got a Glock with a switch, too."

"Daggone. I think the ATF guys might be interested in Boom and his peeps," said Killian.

Ramos snickered. "To be honest, I think those two clowns we found inside the apartment made a little boom-boom in their pants when SRU breached that front door."

There were chuckles all around.

Casteel said, "Those turds are going to be doing some serious time."

"I think you're right," Killian said. "Nice work fellas."

Ramos squirted some anti-bacterial gel into his hands and rubbed them together. "All thanks to Nate."

Press smiled. "Teamwork makes dreamwork."

Soon the squad room was quiet but for the clicking of keyboards and the crinkling of paper evidence bags. Occasionally voices would cascade down the outer corridor and find a way into their coveted space. Sporadic traffic from the portable radios each detective kept close to them at their desks played like background music to the daily drama.

"You want to join me and the family for dinner tonight?" called Killian when they were alone and preparing to call it a day.

"I appreciate the offer, JK, but I've got plans. Go home to your wife and kids. Give them my best."

"You sure? They won't mind."

Press patted him on the shoulder. "Yeah, buddy. Tonight, I'm going for a long ride. I need to recharge my batteries."

34

EAST PROVIDENCE, RHODE ISLAND

Press found the nip in the air invigorating. After arriving home, he had shed his clothes and slipped on his bib shorts and yellow high-vis jersey specifically designed for night riding. Carefully, he'd traversed down over the bosky slope behind his house to the East Bay Bike Path, clipped into his pedals, and set off southward with Bristol in his sights. When he'd reached Warren, he decided to push on all the way to the coast. Just like old times.

Press did some of his best thinking on a bike. The rhythmic sound of his breathing, the buzz of the tires against the pavement, the occasional clicking of his shifters, and the whisper of the chain spinning the sprockets beneath him, issued him into an almost hypnotic state.

The brisk wind on the Mt. Hope Bridge cut through his jersey, sending a bolt of cold through his body. The only way to counter it was through more exertion. Traffic was light, so he pressed his advantage. He reached nearly 50 mph coming down off the bridge and thankfully managed to catch the green light at the intersection. Press slowed only slightly as he zipped by a couple of waiting vehicles and continued onto Boyds Lane, a narrow road that stretched across Rhode Island's idyllic rural countryside. Here, he picked up even more speed while pedaling down the long slope.

Drawing near to Mello's Farm and Flower Shop, he applied the brakes and cut left onto Anthony Road then again bore down on the pedals. The droning sound of fast-moving cars and trucks on the nearby Fall River Expressway grew louder. Being from a small town in West Virginia, he used to find the constant din of traffic distracting, but he'd long since grown accustomed to life in the city.

As he increased speed, the headlights from a passing motorist set the adjacent golf course aglow, enabling him to catch the glint of four sets of eyes. One deer lifted its head, but the other nimble beasts continued grazing as he whisked by.

In short order, Press swept across the Sakonnet River Bridge and onto Central Avenue then turned right onto Main Road, heading for the expanding countryside and quaint farmland. Long fieldstone walls skirted the road, conjuring up images of Civil War battlefields. This area of Rhode Island was known as Little Compton. He'd always thought the name did the endearing community here an injustice. Little or not, there could be no greater contrast to the California city which shared its namesake. For that was a place of violence, drugs, gangs, and mayhem. Here, there was none of that save for the wanton tumult of a winter nor'easter.

Press coasted by the gray-brown clapboard building that housed the Sakonnet Yacht Club and curled around the small harbor behind it. A few lighted fishing boats were just now burbling out of the marina. He took a left onto a narrow, unmarked lane ambiguously called Rhode Island Road, following it past cottages and some large homes to its terminus. Here, he switched off the bike's powerful LED headlamp, unclipped from his pedals, and dismounted. A chain-link gate loosely secured with a rusty padlock barred people from going any further. Press thought nothing of it. He simply hefted his bike onto his shoulder—the blue, gray, and black Orbea Orca M20iLTD was incredibly light, climbed over the barrier, and trekked down to the beach of small stones and sand. He leaned his two-wheeled steed against a large rock, draped his helmet over the stem at the handlebars, then forged further out onto the craggy coast. His clipless shoes forced him to concentrate on each step. Molded plastic and slick, wet stone did not play nicely together. Finally, he parked himself on a rock and from a pocket on the lower back of his jersey he plucked a TORQ bar. He took a generous bite, which he washed down with a large gulp from his water bottle.

The sea was lively. The wind stiff and swirling. Waves crashed against the rocks hurling jots of sea spray onto his exposed skin.

The historic Sakonnet Lighthouse stood about a mile from shore. Press gazed toward its silhouette and into the darkness beyond. In the moon's meager crescent light, he could scarcely discern where the ocean ended and sky began. All at once, inky black seawater plowed into the rocks nearest him with the din of a thousand symbols then fizzed and gurgled as it receded impotently into the spasmodic, undulating tide.

His pulse was normal now, the film of sweat on his forehead wiped dry. He took a long sweeping view of the darkened sea, following the blurred horizon from left to right. Here, his gaze landed squarely on the distant outline of the Gilded-Age monster mansion known famously as the Breakers. To many it was a gaudy symbol of New England, if not American, opulence brought about by greedy industrialists on the backs of slaves and the poor, working class. To the Vanderbilts, who'd had it constructed in the late 19th Century, it had been a mere "summer cottage." Today, the Breakers was owned by the Preservation Society of Newport County; it was one of the area's main tourist attractions. Just to the left of this behemoth, on a sprawling plot of land due south, was where his mother's sister resided. At least for six or seven months of the year anyway.

Emerald Crest Manor, as it was known, included a stately castle-like home every bit as garish as the Breakers, cavernous garages, a guest house, pool house, and bathhouse all arranged within and around grand stone courtyards and marvelous gardens with ornate sculptures and carefully tended topiary.

An exquisitely manicured lawn stretched from the granite stairs of a tiered central terrace all the way to an imposing bulkhead of cement and stone that guarded the estate from wind, erosion, and riffraff alike. Atop this wall was an elegant wrought-iron fence with signs that warned away determined gawkers who frequented the adjacent Cliff Walk—a burdensome public access area that snaked for three and a half miles along the coast. The pathway allowed anyone and everyone to peer at the ostentatious, coastal dwellings. Homes like the Breakers and Emerald Crest Manor. Thus, the need for a high wall to obfuscate the inconvenient interloping.

His mother's family had always been wealthy, but it wasn't until his Aunt Cordelia married Langdon Burke of Burke Holdings, Burke Investment Group, Burke Financial Advisors, and about a hundred other companies, that the Caulfields gained true prominence among the elites of society. Cordelia Caulfield-Burke was now the richest woman in New England. Press and his family often referred to her as the Countess of Emerald Crest. The sobriquet was clearly meant to be a pejorative, but it bore more truth than irony.

What grated him most about the Caulfields was how they viewed everything and everyone through the prism of economic status and treated them accordingly. Their little Genevieve had eschewed it all—the wealth, the private-school education, the country-club lifestyle—when she married his father, a blue-collar West Virginian who had since built his own tow-truck business into a solid, profitable operation quite literally out of blood, sweat, and tears. They were an unlikely pair to be sure, his mom and dad—how they'd met and fell in love was a whole other story. Of course, the Caulfields blamed his father for Genny's precipitous slide into alcoholism following Danny's death. The fact was that they'd detested his father since the dawn of their courtship, a sentiment that extended to this very day and even included his progeny.

For these reasons and more, Press kept his distance from the Caulfields. He had told no one at the department about his aunt or her insane wealth, save for JK. Press had only begrudgingly listed her name on the personal history packet he'd been forced to complete during the PPD application process. The man doing the pre-employment background investigation back then either hadn't registered who Cordelia Caulfield-Burke was or didn't care.

Press now realized he was now gritting his teeth and therefore averted his eyes. He wanted nothing to do with any of them. Despite the current rift between him and his father, Press much preferred the old man's blue-collar existence to that of privilege, condescension, and sanctimony. Though he was of shared blood, he'd never really been a part of their lives anyway. And couldn't fathom any circumstances that would ever change that.

Another wave smashed into the rocks, spritzing his face with cold salt water. His gaze swept out to the far recesses of the sea as he considered his mother, her warm smile from years long past. Where was she? Seriously. How could a wife, a mother, just leave? Did she not love him? Did she not care to know the man he had become? He pondered all these things for several long minutes. The vastness of the sea often caused him to turn introspective. Was it this way for everyone?

With the smack of another wave, he gathered himself and prepared to head back. He stood and one last time took in the glory of the nighttime seascape. Before he had gotten hurt, it was not uncommon for him to ride all the way to the beach, do a three-mile swim and ride back. He wasn't quite back to that type of form yet, but with time he would get there.

He harbored no doubt.

35

**Providence PD
Central Station**

Press brought the navy-blue, thermal-insulated metal cup to his lips. He had topped it off at home close to an hour ago, but the coffee was still lava hot. He swallowed quickly, the liquid burning all the way down, as he glanced at the clock on the wall again. It was 8:15 on the nose. He hated when people were late.

Barb Stanley had agreed to meet him here at Central Station at 8:00 a.m. to help draft a computer-generated composite sketch of the man she'd met face to face outside her apartment door. The same man who had posed as Seth Barnett's father to gain access to his home. Press was planning to put the image out to New England-area detectives and maybe even the media with the hope of it ginning up some leads. Someone had to know the guy.

After waiting another fifteen minutes, he dialed Stanley's cell. It went to voice mail after six rings. He ended the call without leaving a message, waited 30 seconds then called her phone again. This time a gruff male voice answered.

"Who's this?" Press said.

"I was going to ask you the same question," the man said.

Press identified himself then listened intently as the man related what had occurred. He caught JK spying at him over the cubicle wall, listening in on his side of the phone conversation. Press made a hand gesture and shook his head. "Okay. We'll be right there."

"What's up?" said Killian when the call had ended.

"Barb Stanley. She won't be coming in for a computer sketch."

"Why not? She decide against helping us?"

"Worse. She's dead."

"Oh, *crap*."

"Yeah. No kidding. Let's go."

Press parked his truck in the grass along the tree-lined shoulder. The lane leading into the leafy apartment complex was already crowded with emergency vehicles. A hundred fifty feet up the hill, the roadway was completely shut down. Yellow crime-scene tape had been strung up. It now fluttered and twisted in the misty breeze.

Yesterday's happy sunshine was nowhere in sight. Instead, it was a gloomy, overcast mess of a morning thus far. A cold intermittent rain that had begun sometime overnight greeted them with spiteful disdain. It began to pick up now fittingly.

Press and Killian took in the scene as the truck's wiper blades flung water from the windshield. Finally, they stepped out, zipped up their hooded jackets, and began forging up the hill toward the tape line, each man plowing his own path through the rain with a golf umbrella.

They checked in with the officer manning the crime-scene log. She was doing her level best to keep herself and her paper form dry beneath a white canopy that had been erected on the pavement. Here, too, stood several crime-scene technicians. Press and Killian acknowledged them when they glanced up from their kit boxes, which had been piled atop a folding table. One of the techs grumbled something about the conditions being "wicked awful" before turning back to his labor.

George Lamb marched down the slick grassy bank through the steady downpour and thickening fog. The soles of his shoes skidded at one point, causing him to bolt backward and at the same time drop his umbrella. Fortunately, he managed to catch himself before losing it right there in front of everyone. He bellowed a string of choice words for good measure, snatched up his umbrella, then flung the yellow tape over his head and ducked under the canopy. He did not look happy.

"Cream, no sugar. Right?" Press held out an extra-large coffee from a local Dunkin' Donuts—a peace offering of sorts.

The large detective wiped his bald head and wet face with a towel he had stowed on the table then accepted the coffee without pretense. He popped off the lid and took several quick gulps ignoring the doubtless scalding effect of the liquid then pressed the lid back on. "Morning, fellas. Thanks for coming out."

"What do you know so far, George?" said Press.

"Come on. I'll show you."

They followed him up the rise to the edge of a wooded area. Another canopy had been erected over the body of Barb Stanley, which was a few paces into the bosky bank. She was fully clothed. Her hair, slick with rainwater, was slung about her head. Her face was not visible as it was currently pressed into the thick brush and further obscured by clumps of dead leaves from the previous autumn. She had been shot. Press counted three apparent bullet holes in her torso. When the ME rolled her over, he tallied two more: one through her right eye, the other to the forehead just above it. Execution-style.

"We believe she was out walking the dog. Neighbors said she routinely took it out to do its business around eleven. Probably just before the time she normally went to bed."

"Where's the dog?" Killian asked.

Lamb shrugged. "I'm thinking she let go of the leash after the first shot and it ran off."

"Who found her?" Press said, nodding.

"A woman leaving for work this morning saw her foot sticking out of the bushes. She stopped to investigate and discovered her like this." With his hand, Lamb gestured toward the ground.

"Looks like she was shot over there then dragged here, tossed into the bushes." Press pointed to a spot about fifteen yards away from the body.

"Ayuh," Lamb said, following the tracks of lightly disturbed sod with his eyes.

"Rain's already washed away the blood trail." Press turned in a semi-circle, further taking in the landscape. "I bet it's nice and quiet out here late at night. Rain didn't start until what...maybe two, three o'clock in the morning?"

"Yeah, about then," Killian said. "At least that's what the forecast had been."

"So, it was dark and clear." Press studied the body as the ME continued with his duties. "Five shots... Looks like three eighty or nine mil. That'd be pretty loud especially at that time of night. Someone must have at least heard the shots."

Lamb shook his head. "We're continuing to canvass the complex and the adjoining area, but so far, it's been the same story from everyone we've spoken to. No one heard a thing."

"That's weird," said Killian.

But for Press it just confirmed what he already knew. They were dealing with professionals. He related as much.

"Are you telling me Barb Stanley was assassinated?"

"Look at her, George. My guess, those first three shots put her down, but she was clearly still alive—she tried crawling for a spell. See the broken fingernails, the dirt on the toes of her shoes? Two taps to the head. Kill shots." When the older detective said nothing, Press continued. "She saw the man's face in the building, George. He probably killed her because of it. There's your motive. Five shots that nobody heard. I'd bet JK's salary here that the killer used a suppressor, maybe even subsonic rounds, too. Ballistics on the cartridge cases you collected and the projectiles you pull out of her will doubtless be a lost cause. That gun's probably already at the bottom of the Providence River. I'm telling you. Whoever these people are, they're professionals. Count on it."

"*Jeezum crow*," Lamb muttered, shifting back and forth in his water-logged shoes. Finally, he looked up from Stanley's ruined body. "You guys have anything more on the Talbert murder? Any word on the Barnett kid? Clearly this is related."

"No," offered Killian. "So far, we've got nothing."

All three detectives turned silent, their collective gaze fixed upon the late Barbara Stanley as the worsening rain pounded their umbrellas with the rhythm of a chain-fed minigun.

They had to find Seth Barnett. He was the key to all of this.

36

**Memorial Boulevard
Providence, Rhode Island**

They had moved to a different hotel following the inconvenient death of Riley Talbert and yet another after they had been forced to eliminate the woman from Seth Barnett's apartment complex. Normally, after a hit they would exfil out of the area immediately, but the fact that they still had not located Seth Barnett required them to stay and develop the situation. The kid was somewhere. Someone had to know something.

Cheney press-checked his pistol, a model identical to the one he had used on the woman, though this one carried supersonic rounds and was not outfitted with a Silencer Central Banish 45 suppressor. He shoved it into the IWB holster on his right hip and covered it with his shirttail along with the fixed blade he wore in a Kydex sheath at his appendix.

Marcus Zug grunted from the other side of the room. For the last hour, he had been toiling away with a modified workout of squats, lunges, curls (using two chairs for makeshift dumbbells), and various forms of pushups. Cheney fingered the pack of cigarettes in his pocket as Zug hefted his large gunboats on the bed. The mattress sagged under his considerable bulk. When Zug finally hissed "one hundred," he dropped into one of the chairs and guzzled an entire bottle of water. His face was red and dripping with sweat, the jugular veins in his muscled neck swollen with the heavy flow of blood. Another minute ticked by before Zug stood, grabbed the small duffel bag off the floor and came toward him.

Cheney leaned back against the TV stand as Zug brushed past, the smell of the large man's exertions drafting in his wake. "You stink."

Zug made a show of sniffing his armpits and smiled broadly. "That's what happens when you work out."

"Some of us have to do the thinking."

Zug shrugged. "Gonna take a quick shower."

"We don't have time for that."

The big guy turned in the threshold to the bathroom and stared at him. "You need to relax, Lance."

"No kidding. Now, come on. Get a move on."

Zug smiled again. "You're like a woman, you know that?"

As the bathroom door clicked shut, Cheney appraised himself in the mirror above the bureau and frowned. Marcus's little put-downs chafed him to no end. He loved the man for what he brought to an operation as far as fearlessness, brute strength, and fighting ability, but Marcus sure knew how to push his buttons. What's more, he constantly needed to be poked and prodded along. He had no fire under his feet. The man seemed to worry about nothing.

Through pursed lips, Cheney expelled the air from his lungs over the course of several seconds, switched on the TV. A local news segment was just starting. He listened as a reporter sketched out the mysterious circumstances surrounding the murder of prominent New England attorney Riley Talbert. Police were stymied, she said. A few brief clips of an interview with the Providence PD's acting chief of police from earlier in the day followed. The reporter then segued to her colleague in East Providence who was covering the violent shooting death of a local woman there. Police were withholding the name until her next of kin could be notified. The reedy, hair-gelled man explained that police were also not releasing the exact number of times the woman had been shot. "But according to one unnamed source with knowledge of the crime scene, quote: 'The whole thing reeks of mafia-type violence.'" The reporter added, doubtless at the direction of the police, that authorities were certain the unfortunate woman had been targeted, and that the public at large was not in any danger.

Tell that to Barb Stanley.

Cheney looked at his watch and powered off the TV. He marched to the bathroom door, rapped his knuckles on it. As he did so, the sound of the shower spray stopped. Soon the door swung open, and a wall of steam flowed into the rest of the hotel room.

Zug emerged in the haze, pulled a towel off the rack, and wordlessly walked past him buck naked and dripping wet to his suitcase on the far side of the room.

"I'm going downstairs," Cheney huffed. Frustrated, he did not bother to turn around to see whether Marcus had anything on before pulling open the door and stepping into the quiet of the hallway.

"I'm right behind y—" called the big gorilla as the door swept shut.

Cheney was still bristling over how easily Marcus could get under his skin as he entered the cobblestone footpath beneath Memorial Boulevard and drifted past the Wall of Hope, a local monument of remembrance for the lost souls of 9/11. The big, freshly showered ogre trailed him at a pace that kept him out of sight but close enough to provide a watchful eye or a quick armed response if things got dicey.

It was 7:45 p.m. and people were already crowding the railings and walkways that skirted the Woonasquatucket River at the Waterplace Basin. Not surprising since it was Friday night, and the weather was gorgeous.

Cheney stopped just outside the opening on the far side of the underground passage. He fished a Zippo lighter from his right pants pocket, brought it to the end of the Avo cigar clasped between his lips. The tightly rolled tobacco was fickle but soon took the flame, glowing a brilliant shade of crimson with each familiar draw. Cheney snapped the lighter closed and placed it in his left pocket. With the signal delivered, he waded in a westerly direction through the growing mass of people to an open spot along the rim of the basin. Here, he leaned against the railing, peering toward the rippling water as the crowd's anticipation of a full lighting of the famed WaterFire exhibit buzzed up and down the riverside. Squinting through a cone of smoke that flowed out of him, he casually spied Marcus. The big man had taken an elevated position on the steps by the blue-tiled wall just outside the tunnel opening. It was a good yet discreet vantage point that yielded plenty of coverage with adequate sightlines in the event of trouble. Like his guardian angel, Cheney outwardly appeared calm and at ease though his senses were fully engaged.

A minute later a figure drew alongside him, placed a hand against the railing.

Their inside man.

Clint Hickman wore a Red Sox ball cap and a charcoal-gray sweatshirt with the hood pulled up. With temps being in the low fifties, he looked like hundreds of others out here.

Both men kept their eyes leveled toward the darkly dressed ceremonial forms in the slow-moving boat, who, by way of long torches, were lighting the braziers that hovered just above the surface of the water.

"Any news on the kid?" Hickman intoned.

"That's the question everyone is asking." Cheney rolled the cigar between his fingers, drawing a steady drag of nicotine-rich smoke into his lungs, pulled it from his mouth, and let a thick, nickel-colored cloud escape between his lips as he spoke. "According to Brenner, the phone still hasn't been powered on." Based on the information culled from the receipt Cheney had found in Barnett's apartment and some subsequent hacking by Brenner's small team of computer geeks squirreled away in the basement of a tan brick-and-glass building on a leafy cul-de-sac in Fairfax, Virginia, they had been able to identify the pertinent details of the phone. Its serial number, operating system, and more importantly the IMEI as well as the IMSI and MSISDN numbers on its SIM card.

"What about his bank accounts, credit cards…his socials?"

"Socials haven't been touched. And he's only made a few withdrawals in the past few weeks. Nothing substantial. Zero activity since he went ghost. Same for his credit card accounts."

"The kid's smart. He's staying off the grid."

Cheney glanced at his cigar before letting his eyes drift to the other side of the river. "You hearing anything?"

"About the kid? Cops are looking for him hard. Same as us."

"You think he's still in the area?" Cheney said.

"Where would he go? Where *can* he go?"

The intoxicating scent of woodsmoke permeated the night air as onlookers marveled at the firelight cast from the numerous braziers now set ablaze.

"The way his place looked… I'd say he isn't coming back any time soon. At least not to the apartment."

Hickman peered over his shoulder toward Zug, who gave an almost imperceptible nod.

"His only two centers of gravity are here in New England and back home in Wisconsin. Brenner's got people there watching the parents' place," Cheney said.

"They're actually here in town right now. Met with Press's squad yesterday and reported the kid missing. It doesn't seem he's been in touch with them about his whereabouts according to what Press told me on the phone this afternoon." Hickman had called to check in, keep up pretenses, and get a sense of where things stood. Also to share that there was nothing on the federal ledger that would indicate Talbert had had a target on his back.

Cheney used his teeth to scrape a fragment of tobacco leaf from his tongue, spat it toward the water. "If he *is* still in the Renaissance City, he's doing a good job of staying out of sight. My gut says he's holed up somewhere completely off our radar?"

"How are Damian and his guys making out?"

"They're keeping vigil on the girl. So far, all signs seem to indicate she doesn't have a clue about what's going on. They've been inside her apartment, her phone, and laptop. They haven't found any comms with the kid. Not one text, DM, or snap. Zilch. Seems he really did drop her cold."

"Like I said. He's smart." Hickman glanced back toward a pretty woman standing next to a young girl and boy, who appeared like they could be twins. The children seemed to be mesmerized by the numerous bonfires, the firelight reflecting against the glassy water. "I still haven't been able to gather anything more on the letter. Press hasn't even entered it into their system yet as a piece of evidence."

"How do you know that?"

"I had a contact at the PD send me a copy of the case file from their RMS." It had been a stroke of good luck when Damian Rogowicz, a man also in the employ of Green Castle, Inc., had stumbled upon the legal pad in Talbert's study—the same legal pad the lawyer had used to draft the letter to Press. What's more, Damian had been able to decipher the letter's contents from the impressions left in the blank page beneath. It was old-school sleuthing to be sure but still an effective technique.

"You think Press has found whatever Talbert was talking about in the letter?"

"If he hasn't discovered it yet, he will. I've worked with him a good bit over the years. Press is the type of guy who doesn't give up. You think Barnett's smart? So is Press. He's got a master's degree in applied mathematics from

Brown of all places. He aced the SAT in high school. Twice. Eventually he's going to find whatever it is. Count on it."

Cheney considered this while nursing his cigar. Finally, he said, "All right. I'll let you get back to your family. Keep us posted."

37

**Providence PD
Central Station**

Press and his team had spent the rest of the day catching up on paperwork and going over the CCTV footage from the judicial complex near Talbert's law firm. But it was all for naught. The two shadows that had entered and exited the building were clearly aware of the cameras in the area. Aside from the size and shape of their silhouettes, none of the cameras caught anything worthwhile—a vehicle, a face, nothing. Again, the word "professionals" reverberated within his mind.

There was no treasure in Barnett's cell phone records either. The only thing they revealed was that he had called Talbert's office on several occasions in the week leading up to their meeting at the zoo. But after that, the phone had gone dormant. Further analysis of the phone numbers in the call detail record only proved that Barnett regularly dialed his parents and a bunch of local restaurants with delivery service. Press figured, like most people his age, Barnett communicated through encrypted texting apps like WhatsApp, Signal, and Telegram. There were other popular messaging apps the young kids were using, too, though less secure, such as Snapchat and Discord. But those would only show up on the phone records as data usage. It would take more digging and more legal process to uncover accounts linked to

Barnett's phone number. Even after all that, it was still a crap shoot whether those efforts would return any probative information. Nevertheless, Press had asked Gabby and Carla Sheffield, the unit's intel analyst, to collaborate on that angle of the investigation.

Putting the finishing touches on the last supplemental for the day, Press used the mouse to click several places on the screen by rote, which set the printer behind him whirring to life. He logged off his workstation and retrieved the thin stack of paper—it was still warm to the touch—from the printer tray. Press stapled the pages of the first copy together and initialed the bottom of the first page. This would stand as his original report. He then placed it in a file bin for Gentry to review and approve. After that, he repeated the process, firing a staple into the duplicate stack, before dropping it into one of the manila folders that would travel home with him by way of his 5.11 briefcase.

His first week back had been a full one. As always, Press felt guilty when the weekend came calling and there was still much to do on a case. But it wasn't possible or practical to run nonstop. The department wouldn't and couldn't write blank checks for endless overtime even if detectives wanted to work it. Each of his squad mates had already logged upwards of 70 hours for the week. They needed a break. He needed a break. As important as the work they did day-in and day-out was, it was equally important to relax and recharge, enjoy time away from the rigors and stressors of the job. Time with family, friends, or hobbies was critical in that regard. Considering what the job had done to his brief marriage, he was especially sensitive to this. He and his team would get back at it on Monday morning. It didn't mean that during their days off they wouldn't be thinking about their cases. Far from it. All good detectives lived with their caseload 24/7. They might be driving in a car, pushing their son or daughter on a playground swing, or in his case furiously riding a bike on a desolate, sand-swept road, all the while their subconscious brains were turning over pieces of the puzzles, testing theories, reasoning over, around, and through obstacles in an investigation, and strategizing next steps.

He had planned to go home first, fix himself something to eat, and maybe read for a few hours then go out for another night ride this time east to the Assawompset Pond. He was already contemplating his route when Tank and Gabby swung into his oversized corner cubicle.

"Hey, Sarge. Gabby and I are hitting Corky's for dinner. You want to come?"

"JK's got plans tonight," Gabby added. "Something with the kids."

Press considered the expectant looks on their faces. He was not predisposed to large gatherings or crowded pubs with loud music and louder patrons, especially when those patrons were consuming alcohol. But he knew Corky's was a place where he wouldn't run into one of the many people he had arrested over the years.

"All right. I'll be along in a few minutes. I'm just packing up now."

Gabby smiled. "See you over there."

Press went downstairs to the department locker room, grabbed a quick shower, and changed into a comfortable button-down shirt he kept on hand, one that didn't have the department patch embroidered on the chest and was also long enough to cover his sidearm. He never went anywhere unarmed, not even on bike rides. Not these days.

It was nearly dark outside when he climbed into his truck and fired up the engine. For a moment, he considered heading home instead but finally decided against it. Perhaps he needed to spend more time out with friends. His ex-wife had left a bitter taste in his mouth. The thought of forming any kind of new relationship left him feeling insecure, hopeless, depressed, and frankly exhausted. But the truth was that he did want to meet someone new. But where? How?

What JK had said the other day came to him at once. *"Well, you're not going to find the woman of your dreams out there riding that bike of yours eight days a week or in those books you're always reading. You've got to make an effort."*

You're right, JK. I need to make an effort.

38

Corky's Impound
Atwells Avenue

Corky's Impound was a favorite watering hole of local first responders, especially cops. Situated in Federal Hill, not far from Central Station, the three-story, redbrick building had been an art studio until about ten years ago when the former owner, suffering dire financial straits, had been forced to sell the property. Retiring Providence Police Captain Grady Corcoran saw the opportunity and ponied up a large portion of his life savings to set sail to his dream of owning a sports bar. He and his wife, Dalisay, were finally enjoying the fruits of their labor.

When Press arrived, Gabby and Tank were already seated in the back with their paramours along an exposed brick wall. Each was dressed to spend the night out on the town. Gabby's hair flowed down over her shoulders. Her taupe-colored, V-neck blouse revealed a rather unexpected amount of cleavage, but nowhere near as much as Tank's. His shirt collar was opened nearly down to his belly button, exposing his well-defined CrossFit torso. Such a lady's man.

Yeah, I'm going to fit right in here.

Large television screens were mounted to various walls nearby. A pre-game show for a first-round NBA playoff match-up played on some. Others displayed highlights from last night's Bruins' game. Advertisements from local businesses ran silently in a loop across still others.

Everyone looked up as he approached. Tank swung over a chair from a neighboring table, perched it at the head of their booth. This was the part he especially did not enjoy, being the only one without a partner. He very much felt like a third wheel. And yet he didn't outwardly reveal his thoughts.

Press eased into the chair just before a woman in a purple T-shirt and tight, faded blue jeans popped into view beside him. Wanda was her name according to the tag on her left breast.

"Evening folks," Wanda said. "What can I get for you?"

Press offered a polite smile. "Club soda with lime, please."

The others asked for a pitcher of beer. Wanda smiled with a nod and promptly disappeared. Next thing he knew Tank was holding out a deck of playing cards. It drew an instant smile from everyone at the table. All eyes were on Tank now...and his hands. Tank Meredith was famous for his magic tricks. A master of sleight-of-hand techniques that boggled the mind, he was always working on new skills and material.

"Pick a card, Sarge. Don't let me see it but hold it up so everyone else can get a good look."

Press did so then, when prompted, slid it back into the deck.

"Good?"

Press nodded and glanced at the others. They could all sense something mind-bending was about to occur.

Tank shuffled the cards carefully all the while making small talk about Press's drink selection, now the tattoo on Gabby's arm, the shirt Gabby's fiancé was wearing. At every turn, he injected a dry-witted remark that resulted in hearty chuckles.

"What's wrong with my shirt?" Eli implored.

Tank made a funny face that was perfect in its subtlety. This caused Gabby and Jordyn, Tank's girlfriend of roughly a month, to come down with a bad case of the giggles. All the while, Tank kept a straight face as he shuffled the cards. He was naturally likeable and certainly had an innate gift of gab, something that often came in handy during interrogations. Finally, Tank placed the cards on the tablecloth and kept his hands where all could see them. Next, he reached into the small plastic tray by the wall and selected a packet of sugar, handed it to Press and, while making eyes at Jordyn, began waxing on about the need for everyone to have a little sweetness in their life. His ability to talk at length about seemingly nothing at all was comical in and of itself. Soon, Tank opened a paper napkin, laying it flat on the table, then motioned for Press to tear open and dump out the contents of the sugar packet onto it.

Press did so. Along with the white sugar crystals that poured onto the napkin was a small piece of paper, which had been folded numerous times into a tiny square. Knowingly, Press peeled back each fold in the paper, doing it slowly for added dramatic tension, something he was sure Tank would appreciate.

He stared at the hand-drawn seven of diamonds—the very card he had chosen from the deck—on the center of the paper then laid it on the table for all to see. Gabby and Jordyn erupted in gasps while Eli shook his head back and forth repeatedly. Tank simply smiled as if he had been doing this trick for years and was familiar with the reaction it generated.

"How did you *do* that?" Jordyn raved.

"Magic."

Eli picked up the paper and sugar packet, studied them with genuine amazement.

Amidst the marveling and natter, Grady Corcoran glided up to the table and slid a plate of appetizers in front of them. "On the house, folks. Enjoy." They all graciously thanked him and chatted briefly about the happenings at the department in the years he'd been gone. "Glad I'm out," he said. "I don't envy you guys one bit." He patted Tank on the shoulder. "You know, kid, you're pretty good. Ever give any thought to doing live performances on stage?"

Tank considered this. "Actually, yeah, I have. I've been toying around with the idea of a little side hustle."

"Let me know if you ever want to do your hustle here. I think it would go over well."

"Will do, Corky. Thanks."

"Do another one," Jordyn said when Corky was gone.

Tank winked at her. "Okay. But for this next trick I'm going to need some help."

The hook had been set. All eyes were again on Tank Meredith.

He made a show of his hands to prove they were empty, squinted as if he were entering into a state of deep concentration. Then dropped all pretenses and said, "I'm going to make this plate of Cajun fries disappear." And with that he scooped up a couple, plunged them into the cup of cheese sauce, and shoved them down his gullet. "Come on. Dig in," he said chewing.

Jordyn elbowed him in the ribs and laughed, then carefully plucked a fry from the plate and dipped it into the gooey cheese. She turned her attention to Press. "So, Nate, are you seeing anyone? I have *lots* of girlfriends..."

Press felt the blood rush to his face for a moment then offered a polite no. "But I appreciate the random offer."

As if she hadn't heard him, Jordyn plowed onward. "I know someone who would be *perfect* for you." She looked at Tank and his eyes widened as if they were suddenly of one mind.

"Tabitha," he said.

Jordyn eagerly nodded.

Press betrayed no emotion unless you were to count the slight show of discomfort in his features, something Tank must have perceived from having spent so much time working with him.

"Oh, come on, Sarge. Tabitha's a knockout. Believe me. You'd love her. She works at Jordyn's school. Teaches third grade." Tank consumed another handful of fries.

"No thanks, Elrod."

Jordyn's face took on a quizzical expression and this time it was Tank who blushed.

"Elrod? I don't get it," she said.

Press locked eyes with Tank. "Elrod. Laith. Meredith."

"That's your real name?" she said, now thoroughly distracted. "Elrod? No wonder they call you Tank."

"Thanks, Sarge."

Press shrugged his shoulders and grinned.

The rest of the evening at the Impound was full of laughter, great American fare, and not thinking about dead bodies or investigative tasks. Despite the awkward moments and sense of intruding on their double date, Press was grateful for the night out and the opportunity to spend time away from work with his squad mates. JK had missed a fun time.

While driving home, he resolved himself to the idea of going to church on Sunday. It would be his first time sitting in a pew in more than fifteen years. He imagined what it would feel like. He also imagined the look on Sunny's face when she saw that he'd finally decided to take her up on her offer. JK's, too.

A twinge of anxiety soon set in. Was it due to guilt? The uncertainty of where his life was headed? Maybe the time he'd wasted on empty pursuits. Somewhere in the back of his mind, he knew that God had more in store for his life—something good—somewhere over the horizon.

39

East Providence, Rhode Island

That night, sound sleep eluded him. The case would not rest in his mind. Somewhere around 3:00 a.m., Press finally dozed off after turning to an old stand-by method to induce sleep, one he'd discovered early on in his career: reading the dictionary.

It was 8:47 a.m. when a piercing sound caused him to stir on the sofa. He threw back the colorful afghan his grandmother had crocheted for him years ago, snatched his phone from the coffee table, and stabbed at the screen.

"Hello," he mumbled.

"Sergeant Press? This is Hannah Marchand over in District Eight."

"Hi, Hannah. What's up?" He rolled onto his back and yawned, eyes blinking away the fog of slumber. Birds outside chirped happily. Sunshine splashed into the tiny living room via the windows above the sofa. One particular sunbeam caught in an empty drinking glass on the coffee table, projecting a bright, thin bar of rainbow light onto the opposite wall.

"I saw the email you sent out about the Talbert case. You know, with the photos of his shoes?"

"Yeah?"

"I'm pretty sure I found them."

Press was instantly awake. He swung his legs from the couch, propped himself into a sitting position, and listened intently as the young patrol officer recited her account. "And you're there now?"

"Yes."

"I'll be there shortly. And Hannah. Great job."

Press arrived at the car park on Stevens Street in record time. As he nosed into the nearly vacant lot, he spotted two PPD cruisers straight ahead, parked along the grass. He twisted to the right and saw a young woman in uniform waving at him from beneath a stand of trees. Her blond ponytail bobbed as she turned back toward another officer, a black man with thick, muscled arms and wraparound shades. He looked to be ten years her senior. The male officer, whom Press recognized to be Xavier Pierce, glanced in his direction now, too, both thumbs hooked onto the arm holes of his load-bearing vest.

A man with a thick, rowdy beard, who was clearly homeless, sat in the shaded grass between them. A tattered blue tent that had been fortified in places with strips of duct tape, stood near a worn set of poured-concrete stairs with pipe railings that led back up to the street.

"Xay, how're you doing, brother?"

"Life's good, Nate. Wife's pregnant again."

"Oh, man! Congratulations!"

Pierce smiled brightly. "Keisha and I need to have you over again soon. By the way... Welcome back."

"Thanks, my friend. Tell you what... They gave me a good one for my first case back."

"Ah, you'll get 'er solved. Ain't no doubt."

Press patted Pierce on the shoulder, turned to the female officer. "Hannah?"

She shook his hand when he held it out. "Morning, Sergeant Press."

"Please. It's Nate."

Hannah Marchand smiled. "I'm sorry for calling you out here on a Saturday."

"Not at all. In fact, I'm glad you did." Marchand seemed to be a bright bulb. Her youth and enthusiasm suggested she was not long out of the academy. He led her a short distance away, then, with Pierce keeping an eye on the homeless man, said, "Can you run through again what you said on the phone now that I'm fully awake?"

"Sure. Like I said, I saw the BOLO you sent out about the victim's missing shoes. The homeless angle you noted in the email made perfect sense. So, every shift I've been checking homeless camps and shelters in my district. I also put the word out to some people I've come across to keep an eye out for anyone suddenly in possession of expensive men's dress shoes. This morning, one of the women I'd spoken to flagged me down. She told me I should check out Bermuda Bob and that he could be found over here.

"When Ofc. Pierce and I pulled up, Bob was still inside his tent. We identified ourselves and asked him to come out and talk to us. We were playing it real low key...*you* know. As he came out, I got a good peek inside his tent. Along the left side near the front, I noticed a pair of men's brown dress shoes just like the ones in your email."

"That's good work, Hannah. Seriously. Great job."

"Thanks. By the way, his real name is Robert Nailor. He has a bench warrant for failure to appear for a public intox charge he picked up last year, but I figure we can hold off in serving it for the time being. Might come in handy if we need to use it down the road."

"You've got good instincts, Hannah. All right, one more thing. Is your body cam still running?"

She looked down at the small pager-size device affixed to the center of her load-bearing vest. "Yep. Good to go."

Press and Marchand walked back over to where the homeless man sat. Bermuda Bob looked up, eyeing them now with growing suspicion. He began shifting around in the grass, looking back and forth from the parking lot to the nearby Moshassuck River, which was more stream than river. He was getting antsy.

Press drew closer, registering a tired pair of watery, gray eyes and a face that was leathery and creased from having endured too many years outside in the elements. Whether Robert Nailor was here because of bad choices or because of some cruel twist of life circumstances, he knew not. However, it was common knowledge that some homeless folks could be dangerous. Many suffered from mental illness or substance abuse in some form or another. Thus far, Bermuda Bob had been compliant. But every cop knew that compliance could change in a heartbeat.

With Marchand and Pierce serving as cover officers, Press leaned forward and offered the man his hand. He ignored the strong stench of body odor and baked-in filth. Nailor was a human being and Press would treat him with respect regardless of whether he could help with the case or not.

Bermuda Bob shook his hand without resolve. His skin was rough as tree bark, the grip limp and non-threatening.

"How y'all doin'? My name is Nate. I'm with the police department."

"Bob. Pleasure to make your acquaintance." He said it with a feigned aristocratic tone and a voice that revealed he smoked far too many cigarettes.

"They call you Bermuda Bob, right? How's come?" Sometimes the native West Virginia dialect came in handy. Press had found that it often put folks here at ease, or at least a little off their guard. He didn't know why. Nevertheless, he thought now might be a good time to lay it on thick. "I understand y'all might have come across some shoes recently...the ones right there in your tent."

Bob's eyes narrowed.

"I'll be straight up with you, Bob. Those shoes are pretty gol dern important. A man was killed. A friend of mine, matter of fact. Now, I'd be real appreciative if you could tell me where you found them there shoes." He paused. "And I just want to be clear here, Bob, you're not in any kind of trouble. I just need to know about the shoes, because, well...it might help me catch whoever killed my friend."

After several long seconds, Bob's suspicious eyes softened. "Found 'em."

Press remained quiet, hoping his silence would urge him on. It worked.

"Up there." Bob turned ninety degrees and pointed to a spot through the trees that was further upstream.

"Can you show me?"

The homeless man stared at him.

"It would help me a great deal, Bob."

Five minutes later, they were standing beside a thick wooden guard rail in the northern-most corner of the parking lot behind the American Mathematical Society on Charles Street. Press and the other officers peered through the trees and over the wooden barrier to a spot in the river at which Bob was now pointing.

"They threw him in right there."

Press looked at him. "You actually *saw* them?"

"I was fishing a little further down...from the other side of the water. I do som' my best fishing at night. Good time to catch crayfish, too."

"What did you see exactly?"

"Well now... I seen two fellas drive up in a van, park right here. They pulled him out—he was rolled up in a carpet. Walked to the riverbank and chucked him over." Bob made a swinging motion with his arms. "My heart never beat so fast."

"I bet. Then what happened?"

"They got back in the van and drove off. When I was sure they were gone, I walked up through the water to, you know...see what they had thrown over. See if it was something I could use. That's when I seen it was a body. Poor guy's feet was sticking out the one end."

"And you figured you'd help yourself to his shoes," blurted Pierce.

"He wasn't gonna be needed 'em."

Press stepped forward, subtly blocking Bob's line of sight to Pierce. "What can you tell me about the men who did this?"

"Well...it was dark. I didn't really see their faces too good, but I *can* tell you they was white guys. One was wicked big. I'm talking *gigantic*...with muscles coming out of his shirt. The other guy, the driver, was normal size. Looked like me a little in fact, 'cep no beard. Might've been a little older than the big guy and seemed to be in charge based on the way he was talking."

"Do you remember what either of them said? Anything at all."

"Nah not really... Now, wait. The big guy called the smaller guy, Lance. Yeah. That I do remember. And he smoked. The smaller guy, I mean. Flicked his cigarette right over there."

Press motioned to Pierce to go check for a cigarette butt, though considering the amount of rain that had fallen since then, figured it was almost assuredly long gone. "What about the van? Can you describe it? Make, model, color, any markings, that type of thing?"

"It was plain-Jane. Looked white or maybe gray or silver. Like I said, it was wicked dark. Coulda been a Ford, I guess. With a sliding door."

"Anything else? Did it have a roof rack? A dent in the fender? Maybe a sticker on the bumper? Anything to make it stand out."

Bob shook his head.

"Okay. What about the time? Can you tell me at approximately what time this occurred?"

Bob shrugged and stroked his brambly, salt-and-pepper beard. "It was Friday night sometime. Late. The bars were still open though."

"How do you know they were still open?"

"You can always hear cars peeling out of Snookers at closing." Snookers, the sports bar a couple of blocks away. "It was nice and quiet till I was back inside my tent."

When Press had massaged every last bit of information out of the man, he drove him back over to his campsite. "Now, Bob, one last thing."

"You need the shoes."

"Yes, I do. But because you were nice enough to help me, I'm going to buy you a brand-new pair. Shoes that are far more comfortable and actually your size."

Marchand and Pierce agreed to stand by with the man while Press ran to a nearby store. Meanwhile, a BCI detective responded to photograph the shoes and collect them as evidence as well as a buccal swab from Bob for elimination purposes. Press returned a short time later as the BCI detective was wrapping up. He thanked her then walked over to Bob who was reclining in the freshly cut grass not far away, taking it all in. Press handed him a sturdy backpack, inside which he had stuffed some packs of new underwear, socks, three pairs of blue jeans, several shirts, and an assortment of toiletries. He had also slipped 10 $20 bills he'd pulled from an ATM into the outer pocket.

"And here are your new shoes as promised." Press passed him a shoebox.

The man accepted the box and excitedly glimpsed inside it. Then unzipped the various pockets of the backpack, tears welling up at the sight of the clothing, cash, and sundries.

Press smiled. "You stay safe out here. Okay, Bob?"

Nailor shook his hand, this time with conviction. "Bless you. Bless you, all," his voice cracked.

Press gave Marchand another attagirl before heading out in search of CCTV cameras that might have captured the mystery van entering or exiting the Mathematical Society parking lot. He struck out with the cameras at the gas station just to the south, thus he deduced that the van had to have come from the north and left the same way.

He slowly followed Charles Street in that direction, craning his neck back and forth. He spotted a camera outside a business that sold intimate products on the other side of I-95. Inside ten minutes, the owner had pulled up the store's footage and emailed him a twenty-second video clip. The footage revealed a van turning right onto Corliss Street after the body dump, but with the dark of night plaguing the street, Press was unable to determine anything further.

With the aid of the cameras outside the Post Office and several other businesses on Corliss, he tracked the van as far as Barbara Leonard Way. But that's where the trail went cold. If nothing else, he now knew the van was a mid-2000s model Ford. The color was either white or light gray, it was difficult to tell which amidst the dimly lit streets and wash of occasional headlights from oncoming traffic. Unfortunately, there was nothing that distinguished it from any of the doubtless millions of other similar vans in America.

Nevertheless, it was something. A hopeful jolt to his morale. And it perfectly corroborated Bermuda Bob's account.

40

West Providence Free Church
Johnston, Rhode Island

The man and woman who greeted him at the door that Sunday morning radiated pure joy. Their smiles were warm and heartfelt, not at all contrived. It was as if they'd known him for years, shared some degree of kinship even.

Press continued into a large, carpeted lobby that had been freshly vacuumed based on the smell. The aroma of freshly roasted coffee beans struck him next. People were everywhere. Old people. Young people. People with kids. People with no kids.

Despite its size, the place felt warm and cozy. The generous smiles and enthusiasm set in and around the tasteful wingback chairs, sofas, and low-slung wooden tables had much to do with this. Brass sconces, framed mirrors and prints of fields and flowers and waterscapes added an artful aesthetic.

As Press proceeded further, corridors shot off this way and that. Small, burgundy placards with directional arrows and white lettering pointed toward the main sanctuary, the mezzanine, adult and children's classrooms, restrooms, gymnasium, and church offices. To his left he spotted an area dubbed, "Common Grounds," in which a team of ladies was merrily serving refreshments. An impressive selection of gingers snaps, crème cookies, brownie squares, and juice boxes were arrayed on a long counter. On another, stood a row of commercial-type machines that dispensed coffee and hot chocolate. At either end were stacks of insulated paper cups and napkins and tubs of various condiments.

Press had never seen such a thing. It felt like he had walked into a Starbucks. This was a lot different from the small, simple country church he'd attended during his childhood. He was still gathering his bearings when a familiar voice called out.

"Hey, brother. Long time, no see."

Press pivoted to his right in time to see JK in a blue golf shirt and jeans walking toward him. His wife, Samantha, and young son and daughters followed in his wake. All of them were smiling, eyes full of surprise.

"So glad you came. You even got all spiffed up and everything."

Press rocked back on his heels, taking stock of his coat and tie. "Yeah, I'm feeling a bit overdressed now." He waved to the others. "Hi, Sam. Hi, kids."

Little Jon-David, age seven, was a smaller version of his father. The two missing front teeth conveyed pure boyish mischief. And the girls, Laura (4) and Lexi (2), were picture-perfect, golden-haired little angels.

"I should have told you... It's pretty casual here."

Press shrugged. "Guess it's just the way I was raised."

"We were just heading in now. You want to sit with us?"

"Long as you don't mind."

Samantha Killian leaned forward, touched his arm. "Don't be silly, Nate. We would love for you to sit with us."

After they had marshaled the kids to their respective classrooms, JK and Sam led him into the vast, tiered auditorium that served as the church's main sanctuary. At the front was a well-lit stage with instruments including drums and shiny guitars set against the back wall that featured a tall wooden cross fashioned out of roughly hewn timbers. Large sections of padded chairs—not pews—upholstered in muted burgundy were separated by aisles much like you would see at a handsome performing arts venue, each of the multiple levels angled toward the stage. Press paused and took it all in. An upper floor—the mezzanine—ran the width of the sanctuary, a partitioned booth cloistered at the midpoint. Inside the small room, two men wearing headsets sat behind a bank of buttons, dials, and switches.

"Wow, this place is *huge*."

"Yeah, it's big, but we like it. The music is really good, and they have a lot of programs for the kids. But like I told you the other day... The most important thing is they preach the Bible here."

They found a seat in the middle section about ten rows from the front. JK and Sam had turned to their right and were chatting with another couple he assumed sat next to them each Sunday. Press let his eyes wander. He soon spied Sunny Everhart in a neighboring section. She had not yet registered his presence. She was laughing and gabbing with a tall, slender woman with long, blond hair who at present stood with her back to him. Judging from their mannerisms and the general way in which they interacted, the two women appeared to be good friends.

As people continued to filter into the sanctuary, a man with trendy glasses and a green polo shirt bearing the church's logo appeared on the jumbo flatscreens on either side of the stage. He welcomed everyone then made a series of announcements about coming events.

Soon the lights began to dim just as the last stragglers were settling into their seats and the buzz of lively chit-chat diminished.

Suddenly, with great verve, the sound of guitars and drums filled the sanctuary. A captivating young woman with brunette locks flecked with caramel highlights that shimmered beneath the stage lights, slipped behind the piano, adjusted her ear monitors, and pulled a microphone close to her mouth. She began to play, tilting her head to the left of the mic as she addressed the congregation. "Welcome, Church! Please stand as we honor

God in worship." All in attendance rose. "We lift our voices now to You, oh God. For You are worthy of honor and glory and praise."

The woman set off in a smooth, confident alto voice in the lower register with the song quickly building toward the chorus. When it came, her powerful voice took flight, causing goosebumps to form on Press's arms. Pitch-perfect and soaring with a slight rasp, it was nothing short of miraculous. Whoever this woman was, she commanded his full attention and not just because of her killer voice, though he was a little ashamed to admit it here in a place of worship.

Press tried to follow along with the words on the screen, moving his lips in synch with all those around him, but no sound came out. Right now, nothing could pry his eyes off the beautiful singer. As he studied her, he couldn't help noticing that she looked somehow familiar, but he couldn't quite place her.

The next song was more of the same, lively and loud, with some in attendance raising their hands to the heavens, but the one that followed was slower and featured the woman with the big voice even more prominently. It was just her and the piano for several moments until the chorus kicked in and the voice, now accompanied by the guitars and drum kit, began to soar once more.

When the song ended and another one began, he leaned over to Killian and said, "Who is that? She looks familiar."

"That's Avery Gwynn." The din of the congregation's singing grew louder forcing him to lean closer.

"Avery Gwynn? The pro mountain biker?"

Killian nodded with a broad smile. "The one and only."

"Wow, does she have pipes."

"Sure does."

Press mused about the gorgeous woman with the monster voice all throughout the sermon, which happened to be a compelling message about forgiveness delivered by a man with gray hair, a trimmed beard, and an easy but booming baritone of his own. He remembered JK once telling him that the pastor had been a Marine and had served in Iraq in the early 2000s during some hard-fought battles.

Despite the visions of Avery Gwynn bouncing around in his head, Press followed along with the sermon, dissecting each of the pastor's impassioned and well-reasoned points. Numerous times, he found himself relating the message to areas of his own life and his own history. Sensitive moments like those following the death of his brother when anger and grief had gripped him like a vice; the quick and subsequent disintegration of his family; his mother turning to the bottle and ultimately just up and leaving one day never to be heard from since. *I should forgive her? What about Maggie, the way she ran off with that other dude. Her? I'm supposed to forgive her?* And yet he knew in his heart the answer to each of these questions was an emphatic yes.

Before closing, the pastor segued into the message of salvation. To underscore his final point, he read from the book of Romans a verse that despite all the years Press had been away from Church and the Bible and all the things of God, he still remembered verbatim. *"But God demonstrates His own love toward us, in that while we were still sinners, Christ died for us."* It was a powerful verse that the pastor used to drive home his earlier words on forgiveness. Press suddenly sensed a tugging at his heart he had not felt for some time. Memories of the good times with his mom and ex-wife entered his mind's eye, sparking a tremor that rippled across his chin and bottom lip. At the same time, the muscles around his eyes contracted. He gritted his teeth, fending off this wave of emotion all throughout the benediction, which ended with the pastor declaring, "And all God's people said..."

"Amen," the congregation replied in unison.

Everyone stood and began filing out. By the time Press had reached the aisle, he had regained his composure.

"What'd you think?" said Killian with a pat on the shoulder.

Press considered the entirety of the first church experience he'd had in more than fifteen years. "I liked it."

"Awesome. You think you might want to come again next week?"

"Yeah. I think I might."

41

Having just bid the Killians a good day, Press stood outside in the foyer by a table displaying bulletins and church flyers. He glanced up in time to see Sunny and her tall blond friend advancing toward him.

Sunny threw her arms around him, beaming with joy. "You came!"

Press was not one to broadly advertise his emotions, nevertheless, he reciprocated Sunny's warm smile.

"You didn't tell me you were coming. You could have sat with us."

"I sat with JK and his wife."

"Oh, good." Sunny stepped sideways. "Nathan Press, this is my friend, Kelsey Gwynn. Kelsey, Nate's the detective who got hurt catching that serial killer and the one we've been praying for. He's all better now though, thank God."

They shook hands. "It's great to finally meet you. Our small group, our entire church really, has been praying for you for quite a long time."

"That's what Sunny tells me. I really appreciate everyone's thoughts and prayers. It was great knowing so many people were in my corner and pulling for me." Press figured the woman to be in her mid- to late- forties and close to six feet tall. "Gwynn. Your daughter's Avery Gwynn?"

"Yes, that's right. How do you know Avery?"

"I'm into cycling, so I know that she races mountain bikes. I had no idea she went to church here or could sing like *that*. Her voice is amazing."

"That's very nice of you to say. She's been singing and playing the piano since she was a little girl. Plays a little guitar and drums, now, too."

"She ever decides to move on from racing, I think she could easily have another career on her hands."

Just then Avery Gwynn walked up and joined her mother and Sunny. The three ladies stood facing him in a semi-circle. Avery was a good bit shorter than her mother. He put her at about five foot five. She was stunning on stage, but up close, she was literally breathtaking. Her eyes dominated his attention. Colored with an entrancing starburst of cerulean blue and turquoise, they were right now focused directly on him. The moisture in his mouth suddenly vanished. No one had ever had that effect on him before. Not even Maggie.

Kelsey Gwynn said, "Avery, this is Nathan Press. He's the police detective we've been praying for."

"Oh, yeah. Right."

"He was just saying how much he liked your voice."

A big smile erupted on Avery's face. Her teeth were perfect. *She* was perfect.

Breathe, Nate. Breathe.

"Aw, thanks! That's so sweet."

Kelsey Gwynn leaned forward. "You know, Detective, I'm having Sunny and some friends from church over for lunch today. You're welcome to join us. If you don't have any lunch plans, that is."

"Um, n—"

"You and Avery can talk about bikes," Sunny said, a sparkle of mischief in her eye.

"Uh, sure. That'd be great. Thanks."

"Excellent," said Kelsey. "Now, I've got to run home and finish getting everything ready. Avery can give you the address."

"What's your number?" asked Avery.

He could feel heat radiating beneath his shirt. "My number?"

"Yeah. I'll text you the address."

An hour later, having shed the jacket and tie, Press wound his truck upward through a forest of eastern white pine, red oak, and maple trees off Hemlock Road not far from the Ponaganset Falls near the southern end of the Barden Reservoir. Soon the trees opened up to a wide, crushed-gravel driveway. Facing him was a large Craftsman-style house dominated by stone and earth tones. Connected to the home's left flank by way of a covered walkway was a four-car garage. On the right, down a small footpath, a barn peeked through the woods. The house, garage, and barn were consistent in their exterior design.

Press stepped out of his truck to a happy chorus of birds and the faraway drone of a prop plane. The isolation and tranquility reminded him of his childhood home in West Virginia.

"You can come in." Avery Gwynn stood in the threshold of the front door, hands on her hips, as two rowdy Jack Russell terriers shot like missiles past her. She giggled as he bent down and tried in earnest to pet the little white-and-brown moving targets.

"What are their names?"

"This is Rosie and that one," she pointed to the dog he was now scratching behind the ears, "is Captain Jan."

"Ha. *Captain*."

Avery smiled, rolled her eyes. "My brother named her."

She showed him inside, to a grand living room with hardwood flooring and exposed wooden beams that arched overhead. Here, a serious-looking man not quite as tall as him stood beside a stone fireplace that lay dark and dormant. Bookshelves were everywhere. Avery quickly made the introductions and then excused herself to go help her mother in the kitchen.

Lester Gwynn looked to be around fifty and in far better shape than men half his age. There wasn't a shred of fat on him. His hair was shorn close to his head but allowed for a slight spike at the front. His sun-tanned face was naturally resolute, the chin probably crafted from carbon steel. A powerful handshake. Dark, piercing eyes conveyed a sense that Mr. Gwynn had seen untold violence in his life and perhaps had doled it out as well. What was the saying: It takes one to know one?

Neither Sunny and her husband nor any of the other invited guests had arrived yet, putting Press at the very center of the Gwynn family patriarch's attention. Strangely, he felt like he had stumbled into an interrogation room and this time he was on the wrong side of the table.

"Have a seat." Mr. Gwynn motioned to the nearby sofa.

"You've got a great place here. It's very quiet and the house is beautiful."

Mr. Gwynn said thanks but otherwise remained silent.

"So, what is it that you do, sir, if I may ask?"

Lester Gwynn's voice was deep and deliberate. "I have my own business." He didn't elaborate on what that business was, and Press got the sense that he didn't necessarily care to share that information freely either.

"I see."

The two men stared at each other without further comment for the next several minutes. In Press's case it was a bit awkward, but Mr. Gwynn seemed perfectly at ease. Thankfully the doorbell soon chimed, and Sunny and her husband swept in with much fanfare.

Soon, others arrived, and more introductions were made. Press was relieved to see Mr. Gwynn's disposition remain the same when interacting with people he supposedly knew well. The man shook a few more hands then excused himself to go fire up the grill.

The meal consisted of steaks, burgers, and hotdogs, as well as numerous delicious trimmings followed by cakes and cookies that Sunny and some other wives had baked. A large, enclosed room with lots of windows, which could not be seen from the front of the house, accommodated everyone. It was here around a rustic farmhouse table that seemed to stretch on forever, that Press met Cooper, Avery's younger brother. They were seated next to each other and on several occasions brushed elbows mainly because of their similar builds. Press recognized him as the drum player from this morning's church service. He would also learn throughout their lunchtime conversation that Cooper was a local high-school, three-sport dynamo but was undecided yet about going to college to continue his athletic career or joining the military like his old man.

"It's a sore subject," Avery said. They had finished lunch and were now strolling down the short footpath toward the modernized barn.

"Your dad wants him to join the military?"

"No. He feels he should stay in school and pursue football. Says he could play in the NFL someday if he continues to work hard and stay healthy. Cooper's been compared to a young Josh Allen by college scouts."

"Josh Allen? From the Bills? Wow. He must be pretty good."

"He is." They walked past a brand-new, navy-blue, four-door Chevrolet Silverado 1500 ZR2 Trail Boss with 20-inch wheels. The truck was backed up to the barn beneath a car port with room enough for two more vehicles.

"Wow, there's a nice truck."

"Thanks. It was a gift from one of my sponsors."

"That's *your* truck?" Press said, looking back over his shoulder.

She giggled. "Yeah. I like your accent, by the way. Where are you from originally?"

"A little town in West Virginia called Gauley Bridge. It's about forty-five minutes south of Charleston."

"I've raced in West Virginia a bunch of times. It's a beautiful state. In fact, I have a race down there in a month or two."

Avery unlocked one of the barn doors then pushed it open and together they stepped into the building. She paused to disengage an alarm via a keypad on the wall, flicking on the lights in the process. Numerous bicycles were lined up on racks. A large workbench with cabinets above and below ran along a wall. It was stacked with various tools and bike parts. Banners and posters and decals from sponsors and well-known bicycle industry brands decorated the space.

"So, *this* is how a pro mountain biker lives," Press said, still taking it all in.

"My mom said you're into cycling. Do you ride a lot?"

"When work doesn't intrude."

"On road or off?"

"Both actually. But I tend to ride my road bike more during the work week. Days off are usually when I hit the trails."

She led him further inside, so he could check out the bikes. Most of them cost as much if not more than a small car. A fast-looking, teal Santa Cruz Hightower with orange lettering on the down tube was propped up on a bike repair stand. The back wheel had been removed. Press examined the cassette and rear derailleur, trying to determine the specific work that was being done on her.

"You got a few broken teeth here."

"Yeah, it needs a whole new cassette."

Hands in his pockets, Press's attention was only partially focused on the bike. Avery's athletic curves were thoroughly distracting. In fact, they were intruding on his thoughts this very minute. He forced himself to look away from her lest he embarrass himself.

This caused him to notice a metal door marked "Crew Lounge – Pilots Only." When he mentioned it, Avery smirked and led him through it, into another room. Shelves were chock full of binders, model airplanes, and aviation-related trinkets. Maps and navigational charts and aerial photos of various locations peered down on them from the walls. Some he recognized as being popular New England hotspots. Others he could scarcely discern were even in the United States.

Next to a Sporty's catalog and a David Clark headset was a navy-blue rucksack. Avery's name was embroidered on it. Press commented about this with curious fascination.

"Oh yeah, that's my flight pack."

"What a minute. You're a pilot, too? Is there anything you *can't* do?"

Avery's face lit up. "My grandfather was an airline pilot. He taught my dad and they both taught me. Once you start flying, it kind of gets in your blood."

"What kind of plane do you fly?"

"I learned on a little trainer, a Cessna 172 Skyhawk. But ever since I got my commercial multi-engine license, I fly mostly a Cessna SkyCourier. It belongs to my dad's company. Sometimes I get to fly my grandfather's plane—a 208B Grand Caravan. Regardless, I try to fly whenever I'm not busy with bike stuff."

"What does your dad do again?"

"He's got his own business."

"Yeah, but what *kind* of business? He seems pretty successful."

"Well, he was in the military for twenty-three years. Formed his company when he retired. It's multi-faceted...different divisions do different things. Some do contract work for the government, some conduct various training schools for military units, specialized law enforcement groups, and others. You should see the training complex out in Idaho. It's really neat. Let's see.

What else? One division does private security work. Another—one of the newer ones—tests and develops different types of gear and equipment. There are other facets of the company, too. Some are even *classified*."

"James Bond stuff, eh?"

"More like Mitch Rapp."

"Oh, you're a reader, too. I'm impressed."

"Both of my parents have put a high premium on reading ever since I was a little girl. My older sister and her husband own a bookstore in Boston. My family *loves* books."

"I could tell from all the bookshelves in the house. I've always loved to read," Press said. "My grandmother was a librarian for years. She was always giving me and my brother books."

"Is your brother older or younger than you?"

Press's smile faded. "Older... He, uh, passed away when I was in ninth grade."

"Oh, I'm so sorry."

"No, you're fine. Danny used to race sprint car. One night at Lincoln Speedway in Pennsylvania, there was a terrible crash involving several cars. Three guys were seriously injured. Danny..." Press looked off into the middle distance. "He didn't make it."

Avery studied him in earnest. "I can tell you two were close."

Press offered a polite smile. "We were."

They left the heavy moment in the aviator room and walked back to the bicycles. Press ran his hand over one of them.

"We should go riding sometime," she suggested.

"You and me?"

"Yeah. Just don't give me a ticket for speeding. Text or call me. I promise not to embarrass you." She gave a wink with a straight face, which melted into a warm smile. Dimples and all. For a moment, he thought his knees might buckle.

DONY JAY

She had issued him a dare.
The question was: Would he take it?

42

DONSTAR DATA SPECIALISTS
PROVIDENCE, RHODE ISLAND

Press and Killian strode across the cavernous lobby of the Superman Building at 111 Westminster Avenue. Built in the 1920s, the 26-story Art Deco-style office tower was Rhode Island's tallest and most recognizable building. The entire structure and several others nearby had been acquired a few years ago by an investor group, the name of which Press could not recall. The building had since undergone considerable repair, which included a complete restoration of its Indiana limestone façade. Aesthetically, both inside and out, it now exuded the youthful exuberance of its glory days.

With only modest signage, Donstar Data Specialists claimed four floors near the top of the building. When the elevator dinged on the 20th floor and the gleaming brass doors swept open, he and Killian hooked a left, passing by a wall of windows that looked out over the city. A row of chairs and wooden benches ran beneath them. Rays of sunshine splashed about, bathing the intricate tilework on the floor in magnificent light.

They stopped at a glass-encased reception desk, which was equipped with a stainless-steel pass-through slot for paperwork. It reminded Press of a modern and very secure bank-teller window. The glass was quite thick, as if designed to withstand persistent gunfire. Rather curious for a computer firm.

Press flashed his credentials and asked to speak with Seth Barnett's supervisor and/or whoever was in charge. After fifteen minutes of waiting by the windows, the detectives were permitted entry and guided into a small, quiet, and ultramodern conference room with high-backed, abstract-looking chairs and a table of shiny metal and glass. Here, they were asked to wait some more.

After another fifteen minutes, a woman with jet-black hair and oversized, amber-colored spectacles entered. She was petite, olive-skinned, and fiercely attractive. Without the sky-high, burgundy leather heels, she was probably the same height as Avery Gwynn. The woman had long since shed her jacket—if she wore one at all. Her top, the color of clotted cream, showcased lithe, toned arms, while a pair of runner's calves screamed from beneath her black, high-waisted, pencil skirt. Two plastic keycards and a shiny flash drive dangled from a lanyard that hung between the swell of her breasts. Clipped to her trim waist was a laminated photo ID card on a retractable badge holder that identified the woman as Donstar's president and CEO, Dr. Janelle Holt.

Press explained why they were there.

Holt slid into the chair at the head of the table after briefly excusing herself to retrieve a file from her office. "I can't tell you much, gentlemen. Security is very tight here. You understand."

"Seth is missing. And we have reason to believe he is in danger."

"Yes. We've been worried about him. He's not been in to work since," she opened the thin manila folder and consulted a single sheet of paper before looking up, "Thursday, the sixth. And he has not called or otherwise contacted us about his status."

"What do you guys do here? You're a tech company, right?"

"That's right. We do all sorts of things, Detective. IT support, systems administration, systems and network design, cybersecurity, and many things in between. Our client list ranges from small, medium, and large corporations in the private sector. And a growing contingent of entities in the public sector."

"What was Seth working on?" Press said.

"I'm sorry, but I'm not at liberty to discuss that. Much of our work is of a highly confidential nature. Some is even classified."

"You can't tell us what he was working on?" Killian asked.

"I'm afraid I can't go into specifics or reveal client names."

"How about giving us a general overview?" Press said.

"If I had some inkling that what Seth was working on was somehow relevant to his *situation*, I would certainly be willing to share that with you, gentlemen, but I don't see how the work he was doing here could in any way be germane to your investigation."

Press knew when he was being fleeced. But arguing with the company CEO wouldn't do any good. Frustrating as it was, he offered a polite smile and nodded. "May we see his workstation?"

"And why would you want to do that?"

Killian leaned forward. "You would be surprised by what you can learn about a person from the way they keep their workspace."

"There may be a clue or something he kept at his desk that might be valuable to our inquiry, Dr. Holt," Press said. "Sometimes we don't know what we're going to find that may be important until we find it."

The woman scrutinized them for a moment longer then said, "I guess I can allow it."

Soon they were standing beside a cubicle that was completely empty. Stripped bare, to be precise. Even the name placard had been removed from the outer side of the chest-high wall that denoted the boundaries of Barnett's workspace. To be sure, Press gazed around the office floor at the other cubicles in the immediate area. Each of them had a navy-blue name placard affixed to the outer wall of his or her tenant's domain. Seth Barnett's was the only one that did not.

"There's nothing here," said Press.

"Yes, well. We had no idea if Seth was coming back. Our clients have high expectations, Detective, and so do we. One of the reasons this firm is in the position it's in is because we enforce a strict code of conduct. And that starts with showing up. To answer your next question, we tried reaching him numerous times. He never responded. It's rather unfortunate in light of his situation, but...we were forced to terminate him."

"I don't like that woman. I don't like her one bit," said Killian.

"I'm with ya, brother. She's definitely holding back."

They had just emerged from the building and were headed toward Press's truck when his phone buzzed. Press consulted the screen, which simply read "Unknown Caller." He decided to answer anyway. "Hello?"

The caller was male, spoke in a hushed voice, and wasted no time getting to his point. "I heard you asking about Seth. I believe I can answer some of your questions. I also might be able to provide some additional information you may find useful."

Press listened for another minute then hung up and turned toward Killian.

"I know that look. What's up?"

"I'm afraid I can't go into specifics."

"Oh, shut up."

Press smiled.

43

Pawtucket, Rhode Island

It was nearing dusk. The sun, drooping well below the treetops, created a spectacular kaleidoscope of colors across the western sky. Spring was in full bloom, but tonight's cool air felt like a desperate last gasp of winter's breath. Press found the weather to be rather splendid and wished he could have been out putting miles on his bike, but once again work prevailed.

He eased past the tennis courts and parked along the street near the Daggett House, one of the oldest standing structures in all of Rhode Island. Slater Memorial Park was still full of people despite the fading sunlight. It was a popular spot in Pawtucket especially for those who lived or worked in the city and enjoyed spending their evenings out of doors. Weekly musical performances were held here during the summer, and come Christmastime, the public could catch a dazzling light display near the carousel. Press had been here on numerous occasions by virtue of the park's vicinity to the East Bay Bike Path, thus, he was familiar with the layout.

A woman unseen struck a tennis ball with gusto and at the same time uttered a high-pitched shriek. As if in answer, a dog bellowed from the dog park across the treed parking lot.

JK had wanted to come along, but Press had overruled him. He didn't want the Killian kids' night of baseball and gymnastics practices ruined, especially when there was a good chance the tipster would fail to show.

Press chose a bench near the circular, granolithic bandstand on the western brim of the large pond at the center of the park. Here, he waited for close to twenty minutes. Occasionally, he checked his phone for emails, texts, and missed phone calls all the while remaining vigilant of his surroundings. He glimpsed his watch again. The tipster was late by ten minutes already. Soon he would need a flashlight to find his way back to his truck.

After several minutes more, a white swan glided into the pond, cutting a V that expanded in ripples across the glassy surface. Water along the shoreline in front of him teetered back and forth. The parking lot was now alive with headlights crisscrossing the darkened landscape as people fled for home. He was just about to stand when the metallic rattle of dog tags caught his attention. A man led by a leashed, butterscotch-colored Labradoodle approached.

Press allowed him—the dog not the man—to sniff his shoes and then his open hand.

"Detective Press?"

"That's right."

With a suspicious gaze, the man surveyed the surroundings. "I'm... I'm Braxton. I'm the one who called." He didn't bother to introduce the dog.

Press remembered seeing the name on one of the cubicle placards at Donstar. *Braxton Keefer*. "How do you do, Braxton?"

"I'm sorry for being late."

"Not a problem. Have a seat." When they had both reclined on the park bench, he gently pressed onward. "You said you had some information? About Seth?"

Keefer nodded, still scanning the empty park. The dog was sitting now, too. The ghostly swan had obviously caught its eye and though the four-legged animal remained focused on it, she made no attempt to bark or lunge into the water in hot pursuit.

"Are you recording this?"

Press reached for his shirt pocket. "I can turn it off if you'd like."

"No, it's okay, I guess."

A brief, contemplative silence fell over them before Press nudged the conversation forward. "You come here often?"

"Every night for our walk. Rain or shine."

That explained the dog's easy regard for the swan. Press, too, was familiar with this place. The place where that first, elusive trickle of information came forth like a mountain spring. One he hoped would grow into a small stream then to a raging river and finally a deluge that no force on earth could stop. Thankfully, in the case of Braxton Keefer, the stream began to flow soon enough.

"I heard you asking about Seth today." He lifted his gaze toward the water as if he were steeling himself for a weighty decision and sighed with his whole body. "What do you want to know?"

"First, I just want to say that I appreciate you agreeing to meet with me. You're doing the right thing." Press sensed Keefer's confidence beginning to blossom. "What does...or did...Seth do at Donstar?"

"He's a computer systems engineer. But he can do it all. Develop systems architecture, he can code, design software, build networks, troubleshoot. You name it. The guy is brilliant. He finished top of his class at MIT. Like I said, he can do it all."

"Do you know what he was working on before he...before he disappeared?"

Keefer wrinkled his nose. "Yes and no. I don't know specifics. Projects are highly compartmentalized even among team members. What I mean is... If there is more than one person working on a project, not everyone on the team will be privy to the full scope of what the project is or what the different components of the project are or do. Generally, Dr. Holt assigns a project to a small team that consists of anywhere from two to five people. But, if the scale of the job is small enough, it might just be one person who is assigned.

"And a job could be anything. A software problem to solve, a system to design, maybe a vulnerability to patch up, even red team an entire network or ecosystem. You know, look for holes to penetrate and exploit. It's all determined by the client's goals and objectives. During an initial briefing at the project onset, we are usually asked to sign an NDA—a non-disclosure agreement." He paused to scratch his canine friend's head. "After that, we get to work. Dr. Holt usually holds regular meetings with staff to go over status updates, or in some cases, issue follow-on instructions from the client.

"If he's anything like me, Seth had a number of projects going simultaneously."

"Any idea what any of them are? Or who the clients are?"

"No, but if you ask me, Seth's disappearance has something to do with Albert."

"Albert? Who's he?"

"Albert Roten, another systems engineer. He and Seth were like this." He held up two crossed fingers.

"Why do you suspect Seth's situation has anything to do with him?"

"Rumor has it that Albert was working on some kind of primo assignment. Security around it was the tightest I've ever seen at Donstar. Nobody knew what he was doing except for Dr. Holt and *maybe* her executive staff."

Press didn't recall seeing the name Roten on any of the cubicle walls at Donstar's offices and said as much.

Keefer shook his head. "You didn't for good reason. He's dead. Killed in a climbing accident in Colorado this past November. It was right before Thanksgiving."

"Say that again?"

"Albert died in a climbing accident in Colorado. Black Canyon." He shot Press a doubtful look. "At least that's what they say."

"Who says?"

"Dr. Holt, the news media, everybody really."

Darkness had enveloped them. "You don't believe that to be true?" said Press.

"Albert was Swiss. He grew up in Switzerland...you know, the Alps? And was an expert rock climber."

"Accidents do happen. Even to the best of them."

"Normally, I would agree," Keefer said. "But... See, first, there was Albert's blowout with Dr. Holt. I don't know what they were arguing about, but it was *heated*. Then he takes a trip and conveniently dies while climbing, something he had been doing since before he could walk. And now...Seth is *missing*. The mathematical odds of that happening on top of Albert's death are astronomical. The only sensible conclusion is that Albert was killed. Had to be. I only hope the same fate didn't befall Seth. He's a super nice guy. They both were. Are. Whatever."

"Anything else? You have no idea what Albert was working on? None whatsoever?"

"I'm sorry. If I knew, I'd tell you. It's just... Albert seemed anxious in the days prior to his trip. The argument with Dr. Holt must have rattled him pretty good. I would bet my life that Albert confided something to Seth, something relating to the project he was working on. Like I said, they were the best of friends."

Press peered across the oscillating, mercury-like water. "Anyone else you think I should talk to? Another close friend, a girlfriend maybe? I'm told he was seeing a blond with a sunflower tattoo on her ankle. Ring any bells?"

Keefer looked at him.

"You know her?"

44

Her name was Ocean. And when she wasn't in school, she served as a barista at a popular coffee shop in The Arcade, which was directly across the street from the Superman Building. About 99 percent of Donstar's employees frequented the place and Seth Barnett was no exception, according to Keefer. Ocean was every male's favorite. Or almost every male's—this was Rhode Island after all. Her hair was knotted or pinned or braided in a fresh way nearly every day, he said. She had a smile that could light up a room and curves that drove men bonkers. Ocean was the reason some of the Donstar staff had begun drinking coffee in the first place.

Keefer told him about discussions they'd had at the office about her. How everyone drooled over her, bragged that they were going to be the first to ask her out, but none had worked up the nerves to do so. Until one day Seth did, and she said yes.

"They were pretty hot and heavy for a while. Inseparable, in fact."

"They're no longer together then?" said Press.

"Broke up a couple months ago. I don't know what happened. But I can tell you that Seth was really bummed about it. Seemed different after that."

"Different?"

"Sad, distracted, even a little short-fused."

"Anything else?"

Keefer studied the ground in front of him. "You saw his cubicle, right?"

"Yeah?"

"I was working late one night. Dr. Holt and a couple of her goons were rooting through Seth's things. His desk, his workstation, his drives. They took everything. Every scrap of paper. Cleaned out every drawer. Didn't leave so much as a paperclip."

"When was this?"

"Thursday night. The sixth of April."

"The sixth. Are you sure?"

"Positive. I made a note of it."

"Did they give you any indication about what they were doing or why? They say anything?"

"No. I don't think they even knew I was there. I had clocked out but decided to stick around to complete some paperwork which I was behind on."

When Keefer had nothing more to add, Press handed him a business card. "I appreciate your help. And so does Seth's family."

Keefer stood, kneading the dog's leash with his fingers. He looked up, met Press's gaze. "I hope you find Seth."

Press was standing now, too. "You just make sure you stay safe. Don't talk about this with anyone. You hear me? *Anyone*."

Keefer pushed his free hand into the pocket of his windbreaker. "Yeah. Okay."

The Arcade closed at 7:00 p.m. Instead of waiting until tomorrow and trying to catch her there, Press slipped his phone from his pocket and scrolled to the number for the cell phone that the Brown University Department of Public Safety shift supervisor carried. A man with a high-pitched voice answered. When Press explained who he was and what he needed, the man eagerly agreed to help.

"Hold on, Detective. I'll check the computer."

Keefer had said that Ocean was a grad student at Brown. Press was hoping DPS could give him her local contact information.

In a matter of minutes, the shift supervisor came back on the line with a smile in his voice. "Ocean Enberg. She's in River House. Apartment five nineteen." He recited her date of birth, cell phone number, and email address as well. "Anything else?"

"Nope. That's all I need." He thanked the man and clicked off.

Press found the apartment building easily enough. Though he had never lived in the upscale, modern housing complex during his time at Brown, he knew River House lodged graduate and medical students.

He dialed Ocean's number. An intelligent, mature female voice answered. He immediately pictured a gang of computer nerds sitting in the corner of the coffee shop, studiously watching her every move. After a brief introduction, Ocean agreed to meet him in the lobby. She wasn't home now, but she could be there in about twenty minutes.

While he waited, Press scoured the internet via the mobile browser on his phone for articles about Albert Roten and his unfortunate demise in Colorado. He found several, but the one from the *Montrose Daily Press* had the most detail.

A Rhode Island man fell to his death while rock climbing yesterday afternoon. Albert Julian Roten, 37, was solo climbing "Russian Arete," an 1800-foot rock cliff on the north rim of the Black Canyon at Black Canyon of the Gunnison National Park. His body was discovered by hikers at the bottom of the canyon at dusk. Darkness and dangerous terrain prevented rescuers from retrieving his body last evening, the coroner said. Assuming the weather cooperates, the recovery is expected to be completed sometime later today, according to officials from the National Park Service and Montrose County Sheriff's Office.

Originally from Switzerland, Roten moved with his family to the United States during his high school years. After graduating from Carnegie Mellon University with a degree in computer engineering, he went to work for Google and then an emerging tech giant in Silicon Valley. For the past ten years, he was employed by Donstar Data Specialists, a small but well-regarded IT firm headquartered in Providence, RI.

Family members described Roten as an expert rock climber and avid adventurist who had climbed routes at Black Canyon several times previously. "He's been climbing since he was six years old. He took every precaution and was meticulous with his gear. We are devastated," said his father. "We don't understand how this could have happened."

Press clicked on the link to a follow-up article that indicated authorities had investigated the fall and determined that a climbing cam had failed. Not surprisingly, Roten's death had been ruled accidental.

Press caught movement in his periphery. A woman with a purple backpack slung over her shoulder and blond hair pulled back in a messy ponytail had entered the lobby and was now walking toward him. Her heather-gray sweatshirt with "Brown University" in red block letters across the front could do nothing to hide her feminine curves never mind the thin Lycra leggings. He immediately recognized what Keefer and his fellow Donstar employees saw in the woman. She was indeed beautiful.

"Miss Enberg?" He saw the recognition in her eyes. "I'm Detective Press, Providence PD." Without making a show of it, he opened his jacket and allowed her to see the badge clipped to his belt.

"I don't mean to be difficult, but do you have photo ID?"

"Yes, of course." He pulled a thin wallet from his pants pocket and allowed her to view his department credentials. "Is there some place quiet we might be able to talk in private?"

She led him to the elevator and then down the hall to her fifth-floor apartment, apologizing for the mess when they entered, though he saw no sign of such a thing. "Finals are in a couple weeks, and I haven't had much time to clean."

"If you call this a mess then I don't know what you'd call some of the places I've been in." This caused her to crack a slight smile and at the same time seemed to put her at ease.

The apartment furnishings were nice but spare—the typical billet of a serious student. The living room smelled of jasmine and had a light, airy feel to it. A few framed photos hung on one wall. Others were arranged on a small table that stood beside the modest sofa. Most of the people in them appeared to be family and close friends from high school, some of whom had apparently played soccer with Ocean at one time or another. A man in military garb featured prominently among the photographs, his attire ranging from tactical gear to official dress blues.

Press leaned toward what looked like an official military portrait. "Your father's in the Navy?"

"He was." Ocean drew alongside him, her head angled toward the photograph, which had been placed in a position of prominence on the wall. "He was killed in Afghanistan when I was ten." She pointed to another photo. In this one her father was standing with five other men, all of them in BDUs and heavy loadout gear, suppressed carbines slung across their chests. "He was a Navy SEAL...DEVGRU." She said this with pride. "My mother says I have my dad's eyes and his competitive spirit."

Press gazed at her face, nodded. "I believe her."

She left him examining the photos and paced into the kitchen.

"What are you studying?" he said from around the corner.

"Chemistry. I've got one more year to go to get my doctorate."

"Nice. Say, is Dr. Orlov still around?" Press stepped further into the room to a spot where he could see her and still maintain a proper level of decorum. He would not move closer unless prompted to do so.

"Yeah, he's still teaching. I had him for Math 180 during my undergrad. I see him around campus all the time." She wrinkled her nose. "He's kind of an odd duck."

"No doubt. But he's a mathematical genius." Press recalled some of the professor's antics and mannerisms in class. "Man, that guy was old when *I* had him."

"You went to Brown?" She seemed genuinely surprised.

"It's the accent, right?"

Ocean blushed. "That's not what I meant."

"I know. I'm just teasing,"

"What did you study?"

"Applied mathematics. I did the four-year concurrent-degree program."

"Wow. So, you have your master's in applied math? How on earth did you end up as a cop, if you don't mind my asking?"

"It's a long story." He canted his head and smiled as though the matter was shrouded in secrecy yet had a humorous bent.

She had already set down her backpack beside the rectangular kitchen table, which she clearly used as a desk. Books and notepads, a cup of pens and highlighters, and a stapler were neatly arranged on it, all evidence that indicated this was where she did most of her schoolwork. She offered to make him tea or coffee, but he politely refused. When she motioned to one of the empty chairs, he slid it out from the table and eased into it.

"I'm investigating a homicide and Seth's name has come up."

"I don't understand. A *homicide*? You think *Seth Barnett* is involved?"

"No, no." Press weighed his words carefully. He did not wish to frighten her or cause her undue stress. "When's the last time you spoke to or saw Seth?"

"A couple months ago. When we broke up."

"And you haven't seen him since? Haven't spoken with him? Maybe received a text or phone call?"

"No."

Press studied her. "Are you aware that Seth is missing?" He watched for subtle cues in her body language that were known to portend deception.

"*Missing*?!"

"He failed to show for work on Friday, the seventh. No one's seen or heard from him since, including his parents. I've been to his apartment. Someone tore it apart as if they were looking for something." Press let this sink in before he continued. "Did he ever mention the name Riley Talbert? He was an attorney here in the city."

"No."

"Did you ever get the sense that Seth was in some kind of trouble?"

She again responded in the negative. Ocean was extremely bright. To be a graduate chemistry student at Brown she had to be, but right now she seemed at a loss as she tried processing all of this. Then a spark of recognition fired in her eyes.

"What is it?" he said.

"I didn't understand it. Things were going so well between us. We were growing closer and closer." She reached for a box of tissues that were on the end of the kitchen counter. "We had been together for about nine months. Then it was like someone flipped a switch. He suddenly became distant and cold. He argued about the most inconsequential things. He was difficult to be around. I didn't know why. He never said. After about a week of this, he said we had to break up. I was so confused, I still am. He loved me, I *know* he did. I just..."

Not wanting to disrupt her thought process, Press waited for her to continue.

"I thought maybe he had found someone else, but he vehemently denied it."

"He never gave you a reason for the breakup?"

She shook her head. "He just kept saying we *had* to break up."

Press considered this for a moment then forged on. "Is there any place you can think of where Seth might be? Some place he may have chosen to hide out?"

"Hide out?"

Press answered with silence.

She slowly shook her head as she contemplated the shockwave of information. A sigh. "The only place I can think of is *maybe* the lake house. But I really don't think he would go there. It's three hours away."

Press's steady gaze urged her on.

"My grandparents have a cottage on Lake Winnipesaukee. It's in New Hampshire. Seth and I were there once last year. He raved about it for weeks after."

Press left a card with Ocean and asked her to call him in the event she heard from Seth or remembered anything else she felt was important. He rode the elevator to the lobby, pushed through the two sets of double doors, and embarked into the night air. Once inside his truck, he fired up the engine, jotted down a few additional notes from his conversation with Ocean, then dialed Killian.

"Nate. What's up, man?"

"Good news."

"You still working?"

"Yeah, well... Listen. I tracked down Barnett's ex-girlfriend."

"Nice. Has she heard from him?"

"No, but I think I may know where he is. It's a bit of a long shot, but right now, based on everything we know, it's the place that makes the most sense."

"Yeah? Where?"

Press heard JK's daughter in the background begging him to read her a book for bedtime. "You know what? It's getting late. I'll brief you in the morning."

"Well, you're just a great big tease, aren't you? All right, brother."

"I need to run it past the LT but be ready for a little road trip tomorrow."

"Should I pack my slippers?"

Press chuckled. "Yeah. And your nightie. Have a good night."

45

River House
1 Point Street

Her chemistry textbook lay open on the kitchen table and next to it a spiral notebook filled with formulas and symbols, what might appear to most people to be a strange, foreign language. Ocean had just highlighted a portion of text in the thick book, snapped a photo of it, and sent it to a fellow student who commonly came to her for chemistry help. She could easily earn extra money tutoring if only she had the time to do so. Still, Ocean liked to help those in need of her considerable knowledge. For she had once been in their shoes and was thankful when older chem majors had come to her aid.

The other girl texted a thank you and after Ocean replied with a thumbs-up emoji, she set her phone aside and dug back into an assignment that was due tomorrow afternoon. The interview with the police detective had already interrupted the study time with her lab partner, a girl from New Jersey named Tia, who was high-strung and easily frazzled as it was. Ocean was thirty minutes into a Zoom session with Tia via her open laptop when her phone came alive once again, its ringtone jingle-jangling one of her favorite K-pop tunes.

"Go ahead if you have to answer that," Tia said on the Zoom feed. "I have to go pee anyway."

"Okay." Ocean muted herself on the laptop and accepted the call despite the caller ID showing that it emanated from a restricted number. Part of her wanted it to be Seth.

"Hi, is this Ocean?"

"Yes. Who's this?"

"Hi, Ocean." The man supplied a name she didn't recognize. "I work with Detective Press and as you know we're trying to find Seth. Detective Press is busy right now on another matter, so he asked me to give you a buzz and see if you could come downtown to Central Station to answer a few follow-up questions. He said it shouldn't take long."

She raked a hand through her hair and sighed. Apparently, she wasn't meant to get anything done tonight. "All right. I'll be there shortly."

"Thank you, ma'am. Ask for me when you get here."

Ocean waited till Tia was back on the laptop screen then broke the news that she had to go—the police needed to speak with her again. She apologized and assured her that they would be fine despite the interruptions this evening. They still had the entire morning to wrap things up for the project.

The time on the microwave read 9:19 p.m. Ocean quickly checked the mapping application on her iPhone for the location of the Providence Police Department's Central Station. It was just a short distance away, but too far to walk alone or ride her bike especially at this time of night. She grabbed her wallet—a slim case on a colorful lanyard that contained her student ID, driver's license, and credit card—and her key ring, attached to which was a canister of pepper spray in a ruggedized, powder-blue, plastic shell.

She exited the lobby doors of River House, hurried across the parking lot, and turned west on South Street all the while staying vigilant of her surroundings. At the corner of a large redbrick building known as South Street Landing, she cut north and kept to the lighted forecourt. The parking garage was half a block further. Once there, she climbed the stairs to the second level and stepped out onto the landing. It was quiet here but for the traffic noise drifting up from the street.

Suddenly, a ghostly clatter erupted behind her, and her hands involuntarily shot up to her chest. At the same time, she spun and readied herself to fend off whoever or whatever was threatening to attack. She grasped for the pepper-spray canister in earnest, her hands trembling and clumsy. She looked back and forth but saw no one, then glanced up to the recesses of the ceiling where countless birds were cloistered and jostling for position.

Ocean drew in a deep breath and let it out all at once, a nervous smile forming at the corners of her mouth. She imagined if someone had seen her just now, what they might think.

Embarrassed, she made her way to her car, a tan, little Toyota Corolla with 90,000 miles on it, and circled around to the driver's side. A large SUV with dark, tinted windows was backed in right beside her car. The vehicle did not belong there. She knew this because each resident of River House was assigned a specific space in the garage. She was still contemplating this when a similar SUV rounded the corner at the end of the line of vehicles. It was crawling toward her now. Ocean ignored it and, without further delay, hurried to her driver's door while attempting to calm her nerves.

The approaching SUV, its brakes noisy with a squeal that echoed throughout the garage, stopped and the driver called out to her through his open window. "Excuse me, Miss. Are you Ocean? Ocean Enberg?"

She spun and took quick stock of the man. He was thin, in his early forties maybe, with a full head of short, premature gray hair. Ocean opened her mouth to speak when suddenly she heard shoes scuff the concrete behind her. This time she didn't think, she just reacted, dispensing the pepper spray with reckless abandon and at the same time shrieking as loud as her vocal cords would allow.

If her target had been any ordinary-size man, the cone of aerosolized mayhem would have hit him directly in the face, but instead the spray struck only Marcus Zug's upper chest and neck. By this time, his meaty paws had already latched onto her.

But if Zug thought she would go easily he was sorely mistaken. Ocean fought with fury, a fury unlike any she would have ever guessed she had inside her. She swung her fists and elbows, clawed, bit, and kicked for her life. She had played soccer for years and knew how to use her feet and knees. Wiggling and writhing in the monster's grasp, she managed to free herself just long enough to land two rapid and powerful kicks to her attacker's nuts. The man grunted and immediately let go of her, reaching now for his battered genitals.

Frantic and breathing heavily, Ocean spun around toward the gray-haired man and saw only an open door and an empty driver's seat. In the next instant, she registered a blur coming at her and just like that everything went black.

Lance Cheney hated working without a well-designed plan, but sometimes in this business you just had to flex and do what had to be done. Time was a ruthless dictator.

Damian had called only a short time ago and explained that Nathan Press, the detective in charge of the Riley Talbert murder investigation, had just come from Ocean Enberg's building. They had kept her under sporadic surveillance on the off chance she might lead them to Seth Barnett. Thus far, she'd seemed to know nothing of Barnett's whereabouts. It had been only by sheer luck that Damian had seen Press talking with her in the lobby of River House. When the detective had finally exited, his bearing betrayed a subtle glimmer of optimism. He had learned something. Something useful. At least that was Damian's belief, and he had the training and experience to detect such things.

A hasty plan had been formulated to grab the girl. Once the call had been made to entice Ocean out of the apartment, it was all but a done deal. To her credit, the girl was a fighter.

Cheney could only countenance the struggle for so long before he decided to act. He didn't want someone hearing the commotion and running to her aid, least of all a cop or some brave citizen with a concealed firearm.

"Oh, for Pete's sake," he muttered.

With Zug doubled over and gripping his undercarriage, Cheney leapt from the SUV, sprinted over to the girl, and just as she turned back toward him, hit her squarely in the jaw with a closed fist. She dropped to the deck with just one punch.

Game over.

Together, they bundled her inside the SUV with Zug reeking of pepper spray and still whimpering about his bruised bits.

"Well, that was ugly," Damian said as he walked over from his lookout position.

"Shut up," hissed Zug.

Damian climbed into the parked SUV, fired up the engine.

Cheney gave him the high sign, yanked his door shut, and dropped his vehicle into gear. The large SUV lurched forward, jostling Zug and the girl in his rearview mirror. Both vehicles curled around the next corner, and after spiraling down to the street, vanished.

46

East Providence, Rhode Island

Press arrived home with a spice of enthusiasm. Finally, he had a solid idea of where Seth Barnett might be. He was the key to all of this. Finding him meant coming one step closer to the people who killed Riley Talbert and learning why. Press already had a running theory about that but didn't have all the pieces yet to be certain. Barnett had gotten himself wrapped up in something bad and had sought out Talbert for some reason, likely legal protection. Perhaps he himself had done something for which he couldn't go to the police. Whatever the case, it all centered on Donstar and what Barnett—and Albert Roten—did there.

Press nosed into the driveway, grabbed his 5.11 briefcase from the passenger seat, and approached the side door. The bulb in the light fixture beside it had burned out again; they sure didn't last as long as they used to. The darkness was severe. He found the right key and inserted it into the deadbolt lock. This action alone caused the door to swing inward. Knowingly, he reached out, ran his hand along the door jam. Small fragments of splintered wood pricked his fingers. Someone had broken into his home.

Press quietly set down his bag, drew his sidearm, and leaned forward in a slight crouch. He stepped inside the doorway, which issued into the kitchen, shuffled two steps to the right, and stood stock still for nearly a minute just listening while his eyes adjusted to the obsidian darkness.

He heard nothing, felt no vibrations underfoot.

His pistol was outfitted with a weapon-mounted light, but if he used it now, it would ruin his night-vision. Equally important, it would give away his position, making him an easy target to shoot at. He would use the light but only sparingly and when there was no alternative.

Press crept through the kitchen and small dining room, circling into the foyer by the front door and clearing the coat closet. Next, he stalked down the hallway. On his left was the bathroom; it was empty. At the end of the hall were three small rooms. One he used for storage, the other two were bedrooms. The door to the storage room was closed, so he started with the spare bedroom at the front of the house. He approached the threshold of the door all the while clearing what he could within the room without stepping inside and committing himself. Then in a quick, smooth motion, he swung his left leg in and power-stepped to the right, rotating his torso at the waist and sweeping his muzzle wherever his eyes went. He eased open the closet door, keeping the gun close to his right side, so even if someone did suddenly appear he could pump rounds into them without them grabbing his pistol.

Press next moved quietly back to the threshold of the bedroom door and retook the hallway. His calculated movements—those that were honed throughout his seven years on the Special Response Unit—were neither slow nor hurried. He stepped around the corner and pushed into his bedroom fully expecting an intruder to shoot or launch an attack from behind the door, beneath the bed, or inside the modest walk-in closet. Again, he was met only by darkness and total silence.

The storage room was more of the same. As was the basement. There was no one here but him.

Press holstered his pistol and walked through the house, clicking on lights as he went. The place was in a shambles. Whoever had been here had ransacked the entire house. Seth Barnett's apartment instantly came to mind. So, too, did Riley Talbert's office at the law firm. Yet the damage done here was far more comprehensive. Drawers had been yanked from the dressers, their contents dumped on the floor. Books pulled from each shelf and thrown haphazardly about. Pictures knocked from the walls and tables and stripped of their frames. Even the toilet tank had been searched; its porcelain lid lay broken on the bathroom tile.

The desktop computer was gone from the dining-room table, his printer, too. A drawer in the nearby credenza, normally full of notepads, flash drives, and DVDs, had been emptied then chucked hard across the living room, leaving an angular hole in the wall just above the sofa.

In the basement, his American Rebel gun safe hung open, but as far as he could tell none of the firearms inside had been plundered. Who could access a safe like this but professionals?

Press walked outside to the detached garage. It, too, had not been ignored. The driver-side doors of his 4Runner stood open. The cabin lights inside glowed against the darkened space, adding a haunting aspect to the infuriating violation. Press flipped a switch on the wall and the overhead fluorescent lights flickered on. His tool bench, cabinets, and storage shelves had all been raided, their contents shoved about. The interior of the 4Runner was a mess, but otherwise appeared unharmed. The same could not be said of his bicycles. It was at this time that he felt a shot of unbridled rage course through him. He knelt and closely examined the carnage. The frame of his Orbea had been sawed open in several places. Why would anyone take the time to do that? His mountain bike—a gunmetal gray Specialized Stumpjumper—was stripped of its wheels and drivetrain and lay beaten and broken on the chipped concrete floor, left for dead like a casualty of war.

Fighting the urge to put his fist through something, he secured the garage and went back to the house, dropped into a chair in the dining room, and for several long minutes sat there sullen and brooding. His call to George Lamb connected after several rings. The East Providence Police detective lieutenant did not sound pleased to hear from him so soon after the scene of the Barb Stanley homicide.

"I hope you've got good news," Lamb said.

"Someone broke into my house. The place is a mess."

"What?"

"You heard me. My house is turned upside down."

Lamb was silent for several seconds. "Could it be kids or some turd drug addict?" It was an obvious first question for any police detective, but his words lacked conviction. Kids had nothing to do with this. And drug addicts didn't saw bikes apart or leave guns behind, let alone possess the expertise to penetrate an otherwise impenetrable, high-quality gun safe.

"Not a chance. This has to do with the Talbert case. A hundred percent. And whoever is involved just made this personal."

"I'll round up the troops and we'll be over shortly."

Press ended the call and dropped the phone on the table. He stared at the damaged door jam, already knowing that the odds of finding any forensic evidence here that would lead to the identity of the perpetrators were long indeed.

There was no doubt about why his home had been ransacked. Whoever killed Riley Talbert knew or had somehow learned about the letter he had written Press. And that meant they knew Talbert had something. Something that he'd intended to give to him. Maybe they thought Press now had it in his possession. The evidence to suggest such a thing was staring him in the face.

Press was thankful he had locked the letter in his desk at work. He pictured it now: the blue-lined, yellow paper ripped from a legal pad; the sweeping, artful penmanship scrawled from an expensive pen in blue ink. Something had immediately jumped out upon that first reading. Despite the elegant handwriting, the author's prose was rushed. Riley Talbert was a brilliant legal mind, a masterful litigator. His vocabulary and command of the English language were unrivaled. The man's motions, legal briefs, and oral arguments were something special. He had also been a gifted orator. Even a casual conversation with the man bore that out.

And now, even though the physical letter was safely locked away, Press revisited the words on the page. He had memorized them verbatim upon his first reading and could see them clearly in his mind's eye.

Nate,

I have something important that I need to give you and only you. Meet me tomorrow in the mezzanine at the Robert at 10 AM. Come alone. Tell no one! Trust no one! Don't try to contact me. It isn't safe. If something should happen to me in the meantime, I've put the item someplace safe. I trust that you'll be able to find it. Again, trust no one! I'll explain when I see you.

Riley

A knock on the front door shook him from his reverie. Gun in hand, he walked toward it and recognized a familiar face through the glass panes. Morty Sherman lived next door. He was a crusty, foul-mouthed, old Marine who had fought in Vietnam in the late '60s, the Battle of Khe Sanh no less. The man had some wild stories. He had taken a shine to Press after learning he was a cop and that he hailed from West Virginia. They helped each other on occasion with car repairs and other jobs around the house that required an extra hand. Sherman's wife, Evangeline, often rewarded him with homemade baked goods. Her chocolate-chip cookies, apple pie, and peanut-butter cake were his favorites.

Press held the door open and welcomed him inside. "Hey, Morty."

"What in tarnation?!" Sherman, mouth agape, gazed at the mess.

"Someone broke in and had some fun."

"I can see that. Boy oh boy. I'm really sorry, Nate."

"Thanks."

"No, I mean I should have done something."

"How's that?"

"Evangeline said she'd heard some strange noises coming from your place earlier but dismissed it, thinking you were probably just working in your garage. I just got back from helping my son-in-law fix his boat motor and something told me to come over and make sure everything was in order."

"I appreciate you thinking of me, Morty."

"Man, if only I had been home… I might have been able to catch those little pukes."

"Or you might have gotten yourself hurt. Kids didn't do this."

"How do you know?" Morty said.

"Years of experience."

"Well, you need some help cleaning up?"

Press put his hand on the old man's shoulder. "I'll be fine. My place needed a good housecleaning anyway." He smiled. "Again, thanks for checking up on me."

Sherman shook his hand, offered condolences once more, then took his leave. Press watched through the window until the old vet disappeared from view.

While he waited for the East Providence officers to show, Press dialed JK and related what had happened.

"You call it in?"

"Yeah. George and some East Prov guys are on their way over. But I highly doubt they're going to find anything."

"Is there anything I can do for you?"

"No, I'm good. Just a lot of cleaning up to do after they leave. I do have one question though."

"Shoot."

"Did you tell anyone about that thing I mentioned to you outside Talbert's house?" Press didn't want to talk specifics over the phone, that *thing* being the letter Riley Talbert had written him.

"No."

"You sure?"

"I'm sure. I haven't told anyone. Not even Sam."

"I was afraid of that. Okay. Thanks."

Notepad in hand, George Lamb stood in his kitchen, attired in a khaki Harrigton jacket, untucked East Prov. PD polo shirt, and blue jeans, plain black tennis shoes—the attire of a detective who had been rousted back to work from off-duty status. He leveled an inquisitive gaze at Press. "You said nothing of value was taken. Well, that may be, but Nate, clearly whoever did this," he made a motion to encompass the whole house, "was looking for something. You have any idea what it might be?"

Press had to be careful here. He did not want to lie to his friend, but he also did not want to discuss Riley Talbert's letter. There were just too many unknowns yet regarding its object. For now, he would heed Talbert's wise counsel and trust no one outside of Killian regarding the existence of the letter.

"I don't have anything here of any importance. Certainly nothing that would cause anyone to do this." The statement was a hedge, but it was the truth. He decided to direct the conversation to safer ground. "Any developments in the Barb Stanley case?"

Lamb scratched at the stubble on his face, clipped his pen into his shirt just below the bottom button, and pocketed his notepad. "We're looking at the ex-husband. He was in town on business this week and doesn't have an alibi that anyone seems to be able to corroborate. I'm told the divorce was a contentious one and that the guy had a temper. There's a long history of domestic violence from when they lived in Worcester. She moved down here after the divorce to be closer to her son and his wife."

"I still say that her case is linked to the Talbert murder," Press said.

"And this mess has something to do with it, too?"

Lamb was skeptical, but Press knew the man trusted and respected him. "I have no doubt."

47

Tingley Street
Providence, Rhode Island

She awoke in total darkness on a floor that was hard, rough, and cold, concrete perhaps. Her head throbbed, her jaw was swollen and burned with a sharp pain that radiated down her neck and deep into her shoulders. Ocean tried to move but found it exceedingly difficult to do so. She had been stripped out of her Brown University sweatshirt. When, she knew not. The remaining thin, white cotton T-shirt and leggings did nothing to keep the bone-chilling cold from seizing her. Her hands were bound. So, too, were her ankles. She could not see them, but the bindings felt thin and very strong. Likely zip ties. She had seen them used in movies and police shows on TV.

As she slowly climbed out of the abyss of unconsciousness, she recognized the coppery taste of blood in her mouth. She used her tongue to slowly assess the damage. A crust of dried blood had formed over a rupture in her bottom lip. A similar line ran beneath her nose. The muscles in her face were stiff and sore. As she attempted to flex her jaw, a tooth wiggled back and forth inside her mouth. Instantly, tears began to flow from her eyes—her left one was nearly swollen shut—and her body shivered with fear.

Suddenly, a bright light burst forth from somewhere above her, a door yawned open through which a draft of cold air invaded the room. Heavy footfalls scuffed across the floor toward her. More than one set.

The voices at first sounded distant as if they were coming from the end of a long tunnel. A firm hand gripped her arm and hoisted her up into a sitting position, causing lightning bolts of pain to shoot through her head, neck, and shoulders.

"So...you're awake. Good."

Ocean struggled to focus her eyes on her captors. A man was kneeling beside her. He wore a callous expression upon his face. She recognized him immediately. He was one of the two men from the parking garage, the man with the gray hair. Someone else stood behind him, a large bear of a man with massive arms that hung by his side like Christmas hams—the one she had pepper-sprayed and kicked in the nuts.

"You're a pretty, little thing," said Lance Cheney. I hope for your benefit that you cooperate. It would be a shame to have to ruin that face permanently."

Cheney stood and Marcus Zug stepped forward, grabbed her, and pushed her into a metal chair next to a table. She was in what looked like a basement or perhaps a small warehouse. She couldn't be sure. The room had no windows and only one door. Painted a dismal gray that was peeling in various spots, it looked thick and secure like the door of an armored truck.

"Feel free to scream and shout if you'd like, but I can assure you it will do you no good. These walls are too thick and this place too desolate for anyone to hear."

It was true. Her first, primal instinct was to scream for help, but Ocean was intelligent enough to know it would be of no use, at least at this moment. Her mind was in a bit of fog from the heavy blow to her face, yet she understood her predicament fully. Though she could not fathom what it was these men wanted aside from the obvious: her body.

"What do you want?" she muttered through the side of her mouth that wasn't puffy and crusted with dried blood.

"Ah, yes. Well, that, my dear, is simple."

She studied him, trying to summon the spirit of her late father. *Be tough. Do what you must to survive. If given the chance, fight for your life. Fight to the death.*

Now seated across from her, Cheney said, "I want to know what you told the detective tonight."

Ocean squinted. "What?" Her mind struggled to recall that portion of the evening, something her interrogator must have interpreted for feigned ignorance.

"Pity." Cheney nodded to Zug, who instantly stepped forward, gripped her shirt in one of his massive fists, and slapped her across the face with an open hand as if he were merely swatting a fly.

The blow knocked her out of the chair and into the wall. Her head erupted in excruciating pain. She saw stars. Her loose tooth had been knocked from the gumline to the back of her mouth. She nearly choked on it. A well of blood-mixed saliva, mucous from her nose, and now tears, flowed over her chin and onto the floor, the tooth included. Her bottom lip and mouth ran red with blood, giving a morbid tint to her remaining teeth.

Ocean now cried freely and without inhibition.

Zug again grabbed her by the shirt, which now drooped low at the neckline. He dropped her into the chair, shifted her into an upright position like a baby doll being readied for a tea party, then resumed his place along the wall.

"Shall we try again, Miss Enberg?" Cheney drew a knife with a serrated blade from his waistband. He made a show of turning it over in his hands several times.

"Please! No more!" She gasped for breath. "I will tell you whatever you want to know." Her words were slurred due to the swelling in her face and newly fractured jawbone.

"That's better." With his elbows on the arms of his chair, head tilted slightly to the side, the inquisitor drilled her with a withering gaze. "The detective. What did you tell him?"

"He wanted to know about Seth, my ex-boyfriend," she cried, saliva and blood spilling from her mouth like drool.

"Go on."

She was cold, so very cold, and felt as though she had just been hit by a train. A wave of nausea and fresh pain shot through her. Ocean thought of her father, leaned forward, and bore down until both sensations passed. *Do what you must to survive.*

"My grandparents...have a cottage. In New Hampshire. It's the only place...I could think...he may have gone."

"Where is this *cottage*?"

Her head hung over the table, saliva and blood dotting its surface. "Wolfeboro."

I'm sorry, Seth. I'm sorry.

"Give me the address."

When she did, Cheney slid back in his chair, tented his fingers to his lips and appeared to be thinking. Then he abruptly stood and stormed toward the door.

"Come," he said.

"What about her?" called Zug.

"Leave her. For now."

48

In the Air, Northbound

Robert Brenner ruminated about the latest development, while sipping Woodford Reserve from a squat, round glass aboard his company jet. He would soon be on Nantucket. From there, he would monitor the operation to nab Seth Barnett. They finally had a bead on him, at least a promising lead anyway. And Brenner would not squander it.

Using his laptop, he pulled up a series of maps from a database his company utilized and began assessing the target location. It was remote yet close enough to civilization to suit one's basic needs. Perfect for a man on the run. Wolfeboro was a small town popular with tourists visiting Lake Winnipesaukee. The presence of an outsider this time of year would not raise suspicions from the locals. Another reason Seth Barnett might have chosen to go there.

He wondered how Barnett could have managed to drive there undetected by the numerous automated license plate readers he would have doubtless passed along the way. One of the data points his analysts had been keeping tabs on was Barnett's plate number. So far, it had not popped up on their radar. Brenner theorized he must have switched out his plates for someone else's. That's why he had avoided detection. He was smart, this kid.

Zooming in on the house, Brenner calculated the necessary manpower. He could probably get away with sending more men, but he didn't want to draw unwarranted attention. The operation needed to be low-profile. Wolfeboro wasn't New York City or some other major metropolitan area. And Seth Barnett did not have the adequate skills or training to evade capture from experienced, ruthless operatives such as his. Six capable, armed men would be plenty.

He clicked on the computer's touchpad and read the details that appeared on the screen, jotting bits of information into a spiral notebook as he developed his plan. Once Barnett was in custody, he would dispatch a small company jet with obscure provenance to Skyhaven Airport, a Lilliputian airfield just outside Rochester, New Hampshire to retrieve him and bring him to the island for a proper interrogation.

His cell phone vibrated against the table as he was scribbling in the notebook. It was Nina this time. Nina Marlowe had been a staff operations officer when he was at CIA. Eventually, she'd become disillusioned with the backbiting and politics of the Agency and left in search of greener pastures, landing at a well-known, DC-based think tank. Due to her unique skillset, she was one of his first recruitment targets when he retired from the CIA and formed Green Castle, Inc. All it had taken to steal her away from her new post was more money and the freedom to run things her way. Nina was his Swiss Army Knife. She could do it all. She was particularly good at juggling administrative tasks and that translated well to sometimes acting as a forward hub for Green Castle field operatives. He'd recently decided to deploy her into the fray since things were starting to stretch his available manpower in the region. Nina would manage the moving parts on the ground locally and report back to him.

"Yes?" he said.

"Lance and Marcus are on their way north. What do you want me to do with the girl?"

Brenner looked out the cabin window. "Keep her alive for now...until we see how this thing plays out. We may need her down the road."

"Understood."

"Are Damian and his team back yet?"

"Yes, sir. They're right here."

"Good. I have something else for them to do." Brenner explained what he wanted then clicked off.

He could see the darkened outline of Nantucket in the distance. Some described its shape as an elbow or a triangle, but Brenner had always thought of it as a spearhead, a weapon of war, just like him. He'd operated in the shadows nearly his entire adult life. His record of success was one of the best among his peers, even if it had earned him the label of a man without a conscience. He got results and that was all that mattered in the intelligence business. The fact that he now worked for someone like Henrik Vandenberg did not change that. And never would. In the end, people like Vandenberg ran the world anyhow. They controlled governments by virtue of their command and manipulation of politicians, banks, and countless global corporations. And they paid exceedingly better than the CIA ever could.

Nina waved over Damian Rogowicz, as she finished the phone call with Brenner. "Okay. We'll take care of it."

Damian cocked his head. "What's up?"

"Take the others and go back to the house."

"Go *back*?"

Marlowe nodded. "I know, I know. But Brenner's orders. He wants whatever it is that Press has. If we didn't find it there, it means the detective has it hidden away somewhere else."

"What if he really doesn't have it?"

"Brenner's convinced that he does or at least knows where to find it."

Damian said nothing. He was clearly a little peeved to have to drive all the way back to the place from which he and his men had just come.

"Make him tell you where it is. Just don't get caught. Is that understood?"

"Perfectly. And after he does?"

"Kill him."

Damian smiled. "I know just what to do."

49

East Providence, Rhode Island

Lamb drummed the side of his leg with his flashlight. "Well, it's just as you predicted. We didn't find anything. No prints, no shoe impressions in the grass outside. No nothing. And none of your neighbors' cameras capture this side of the house, so... No doubt, that's the way the perps approached your place and how they left."

"Like I said. Professionals."

"Yeah, well... You going to be good for the night?" It was already well past midnight.

"It won't take long to repair the door."

Lamb nodded. "I'll have patrol keep an eye on the house for the next few days and nights."

"Thanks, brother."

"Give me a buzz if you have any further problems or if you come up with a reason as to why someone might have targeted your place."

"Will do."

After Lamb and the other officers had left, Press rigged a temporary lock for the door that would suffice until he could run to the hardware store and fix it properly. It was late and he was exhausted, so his efforts to clean up the house were limited to the most pressing tasks. He finally showered and collapsed on the bed sometime after 2:00 a.m. At first his sleep was fitful, thoughts of the case, his wrecked house, and disfigured bikes conjuring up swells of frustrated logic and rage respectively, but soon his mind relaxed and he descended into a deep slumber. So deep in fact that he did not hear the men entering his home for the second time.

Damian Rogowicz was a former FBI agent. Three years ago, he had been assigned to the Bureau's Intelligence Branch in DC. The work wasn't all that bad, but the pay and the numb nuts to whom he answered left a lot to be desired. One day, rather serendipitously, Robert Brenner came along and managed to lure him away with better money and promises of greater opportunities that would satisfy his thirst for action. Damian was good at finding things and conducting difficult surveillance. He was also not afraid of the rough stuff. In fact, it was this part of the job with which he had a keen predilection. Whatever this schmuck detective had that Brenner wanted, Damian would surely unearth.

Damian and his team had crept back into the neighborhood two and a half hours ago and taken up various posts so that they had 360-degree coverage of the target. They had watched the house since then. During their vigil, they had seen the detective—he was a big, athletic-looking guy—come and go several times from the detached garage. At one point, using sophisticated listening devices, they heard what sounded like a cordless drill. Damian figured the man had been fixing the damaged door frame. No worries, they would utilize a different method of entry this time.

It was close to 4:00 a.m. when the uniformed cop, parked at the corner of Sunnyside and Waterview, cleared out. He was probably headed off for more coffee or maybe to take a much-needed piss. Damian knew full well what it was like to sit on a stakeout for hours on end.

But for the high-pitched squeal of a frog and some screeching crickets, the neighborhood was quiet, movement on the street nil.

It was time.

Damian radioed his men to move in.

Press jolted awake as a powerful, gloved hand clamped down over his mouth and men began to pummel him in his darkened bedroom. He was instantly in scramble mode, though fighting back or even defending himself was all but impossible. Two men held the blankets tightly against the bed as a figure every bit his equal in size swung a hard object, repeatedly striking him on the legs and hips. Press wiggled and writhed, trying as much to avoid the blows as he did to lessen their intended effect.

He violently shook his head, arched his back, and kicked wildly. By sheer will, he managed to force open his mouth. The taste of dusty rawhide was immediate. He chomped down on the leather glove like a rabid dog and did not let go. At the same time, he thrashed and bucked as if possessed by evil spirits. The man wearing the glove let out a primal roar and instantly loosened his grip. Seizing on the opportunity, Press snapped his head forward and landed a brutal headbutt to the man's temple. The man staggered backward into one of the two men holding him down. Press felt the blankets on that side of the bed go slack. He kicked hard that way with both feet and somehow managed to twist free. In a rage, he burst from beneath the blankets, launching himself into his closest attacker. A lamp fell to the floor and shattered. The bed and nightstand scraped loudly against the hardwood planks, adding to the raucous clamor.

The fight was on.

Barefoot, Press leapt to his feet, swung his fists, kicked at thighs and knees and shins. Some of his blows connected, others merely kept his attackers at bay as they themselves waited for an opening to strike. He now fully perceived the enemy: four athletically proportioned men. One wielded a baseball bat. Each of the intruders wore dark clothing that included balaclavas and gloves. In the dim light, they assumed the appearance of shadows.

The man with the bat advanced toward him, reared back, and swung for his head with a two-hand grip. Press ducked at the last second, avoiding the death blow, then exploded forward, grabbed the man by the shirt and in one fluid motion, spun and threw the guy across the room. The man was half upside-down when he crashed into the dresser. All that time working on cars, hoisting engines, and lifting truck tires with his dad and brother as a kid, had forged incredible strength. Press quickly rotated back toward movement in his periphery just in time to parry away another attack with a stiff jab and a push kick. An unseen punch from a third man caught him on the chin and knocked him a few steps to the side, but instead of trying to regain his position, Press allowed his momentum to carry him toward the fourth man. Press rocketed into him, driving his shoulder into the man's torso at the same time wrapping his hands around his thighs and lifting him off his feet. Press continued forward, both men now in the air. With his shoulder still planted in the other man's sternum, the pair slammed onto the floor. A simultaneous crunching sound erupted from the man's chest as Press's full weight forced all the air from his lungs and doubtless cracked more than a few ribs.

Press was scrambling to get up when a hard object struck the back of his head. The blow caused him to pitch forward onto the man still trapped beneath him. Press did not lose consciousness, but now much of the fight had left him. He saw white blotches and had an instant migraine accompanied by a severe sense of nausea.

"Enough!" said Damian, a pistol in his outstretched hand.

The attacker beneath Press shoved him away and climbed to his feet. When he had gathered himself, he began kicking Press, hissing profanity with each exertion while at the same time grimacing through the pain of his broken ribs.

Press instinctively drew his arms inward to cover his head and curled into the fetal position while absorbing the blows as best he could despite his gauzy state. Each powerful kick landed with surprising accuracy sending sharp explosions of pain coursing through his body. He was woozy and helpless. Death was now a certainty. He prayed it would all end quickly. A few stray memories strangely flashed through his mind. A particular time he had gone hunting with his late brother, and another when the two of them were elbows deep in a car engine, a radio along the wall of the garage blaring their favorite country tunes. In a distant voice, Danny was right now urging him to stay in the fight and telling him he was proud of his little brother. Press next saw the visage of his irascible father. Ever since Danny had died the man never once smiled. Even now, appearing cynical and tired, his dad just looked on and shook his head. Then, there was his AWOL mother. And lastly, the wife who had left him for another man. He could hear her muttering something unintelligible. What would they all say when they heard the news of his death? They would know he was a failure. Everyone would.

But then the kicking ceased and the man with the pistol stepped closer. He shoved the muzzle hard against Press's temple.

"Where is it?"

"Where's what?" Press mumbled, his breathing stunted and heavy.

"Don't play stupid with me. The thing Talbert gave you. I want it. I know you have it. You're not going to walk out of here unless you give it to me."

"I have...no idea...what you're...talking about."

The man with the gun turned, nodded, and the soccer star went to work again. After just two kicks, a terrific blast lit up the room—a shotgun—though Press was too out of it to register from where the thunderous sound had come. The attacker who had been doing all the kicking fell to the floor beside him, his head nearly blown clean off. The man holding the pistol spun to fire, but he too caught a blast to the chest that made him jolt and crash to the floor. There was a scuffling sound, boots shuffling to and fro, men grunting and shouting. The pop of a window breaking. Press felt glass sprinkling over him and instinctively shielded his face. In truth, he was still searching for his senses. Then came another blast. And another. Two, three, four more. No, these were not blasts but piercing cracks. Like those from a pistol. Who was shooting?

Press remained flat against the floor as the cobwebs started to clear. He took stock of his surroundings. Two men lay dead in the room. The other two attackers had apparently smashed out the bedroom window and fled through it. Propping himself on an elbow, he reached up and gently touched the back of his head where the gunman had pistol-whipped him. His fingers came away slick with blood that appeared black as motor oil in the darkened room. Then he saw him. Morty Sherman—his neighbor—lay prone just outside the bedroom on the hallway floor, a shotgun by his side. Press scrambled over to him, taking a quick peek over his shoulder for any remaining attackers. He saw no one.

Press smacked at the light switch on the wall, so he could see better. Sherman was leaking badly from his right arm. If not immediately treated, he would bleed out in a matter of seconds.

He firmly pressed into the man's bony arm at the bicep with both of his thumbs thus lessening the flow of blood by constricting the brachial artery against the humorous bone.

"Nate." The old Marine grunted, tried to sit up. "You all right?"

"I'm good, Morty. Look here, you're hit. I need you to keep pressure on that arm right where my fingers are. You understand?"

"It's bad, huh?"

"Yeah, it's bad. But you're going to make it. You're a tough old dog."

Morty forced a smile. "Hurts like hell."

"I know."

Crouching down, Press ran to his closet, grabbed a leather belt, and raced back to Sherman's side. He looped the belt around Sherman's damaged limb, ran it up to his armpit, and cinched it down tight. Press then grabbed an old D-cell Maglite from the bottom drawer of a nightstand, slipped it under the belt and twisted it several times until the blood stopped flowing altogether.

Morty grimaced but didn't complain.

With one hand keeping the flashlight from spinning free, Press reached for his pillow atop the bed. He clutched the pillowcase at the closed end and shook it several times until the pillow inside fell to the floor. He scooched forward and placed his knees in such a way that would stabilize the flashlight while he tore the pillowcase in long strips, which he used to finish securing the makeshift tourniquet. After this, he eased the pillow under Morty's head. "How's that?"

"Exactly how I would have done it."

The old man still had a sense of humor. That was good.

"I ever tell you about the time I was shot in Vietnam?"

"You can tell me later...after you're all patched up. Right now, I need you to save your strength."

"You're a good kid, Nate."

"You're not too bad yourself."

The old man chuckled.

"Thanks, by the way," Press said. "You saved my life."

Sherman analyzed Press's handiwork. "I'd say we're even."

Finding no other bullet holes in the old man, Press next pulled open another drawer in the nightstand and armed himself with his duty pistol. He slammed a magazine into the grip and charged the weapon. Now, he could properly defend Sherman and himself should any of the attackers return.

Press crab-walked to the other side of the bed, where he found his phone still plugged into the wall, and quickly dialed 911. As the call connected, he heard the distant growl of a car engine and the screeching of tires from somewhere out on a neighboring street. The sound of the fleeing car soon ushered in a loud silence interrupted only by the pounding of his heart and the voice of the 911 call-taker in his ear.

50

Press sat on the back bumper of the ambulance, an EMT assessing his wounds. She urged him to go to the hospital for X-rays, but he graciously declined. Minutes ago, another EMS crew had hurriedly loaded Morty Sherman into their vehicle and sped off.

George Lamb approached as red and blue emergency lights flickered against the black, early morning sky. He was a special kind of pissed. Not only had the officer tasked with keeping watch over Press's place abandoned his post, but Lamb now had two dead bodies, a messy crime scene, and a royal cluster of a situation on his hands. So screwed up was it that the East Providence chief of police now roamed the cordoned-off street barking at anyone and everyone who crossed his path. There would be an internal investigation, doubtless a few suspensions. The young officer who had left his post would probably be fired. The media would feast for days if not weeks on this type of thing.

"Any idea who they are?" Press said with a grimace.

"Not yet. We didn't find any ID on either of them, and nothing is coming back on the fingerprint scanner. We'll keep checking. Something is bound to pop."

"Don't bet on it, George."

"Because they're professionals, right?"

Press nodded.

Lamb shoved his pad and pen into his jacket pocket, sighed. "Yeah, you're right. They probably are. So, what now?"

"Find Seth Barnett, then round up all these jokers and bring them to justice."

"Easier said than done. Listen, I'm glad you're all right, but if there is anything you are holding back, I need to know about it."

Press remained quiet.

Lamb studied him but did not dwell on the subject. "Well, you know how to reach me if you change your mind."

Press flinched as the medic dabbed at the back of his head. "How's Morty?"

"Alive thanks to you."

"I wouldn't be sitting here if he hadn't first come to my aid."

Lamb said, "I'm heading over to the hospital now. I'll keep you updated on his condition. And I'll do what I can to keep the media wolves at bay. Oh, and just so you know, officers are going to be posted on your doorstep day and night until I say otherwise. And this time no one will be leaving their post. I promise you that."

Press nodded.

"I'll let you know when we're done processing."

"Thanks, George." Press turned his attention to a dark-colored, unmarked Ford Explorer that had just rolled to a stop on the other side of the yellow crime-scene tape up by Park Road. Emergency red and blues were pulsing from the inside edge of the windshield as well as the corners of the headlamps. The lights were cut, and a figure emerged from the driver's door. At the same time, another car abruptly pulled up and parked behind the Explorer, its headlights illuminating the figure. Lt. Gentry didn't wait for Killian before ducking under the tape and marching toward an officer who was maintaining scene security. The officer said something to him then pointed at the ambulance.

By the time Gentry was within earshot, Killian had caught up to him. Press could see them exchanging words as they stepped in tandem into the wedge of light that projected from the open back door of the ambulance.

"What happened?" said Gentry. His facial features and body language evoked deep concern.

Press briefed him, while JK's eyes flicked back and forth from Press to the various goings on at the busy scene. As he finished, Gabby and Tank appeared with equal amounts of shock and concern on their faces. Neither said a word as Press finished relating the early morning events, the blood splashed across his T-shirt authenticating his grisly account.

"Are you okay?" Gentry finally said.

"Banged up and sore, but yeah. I'm all right."

The medic leaned forward and again dominated his field of view. "Are you sure you don't want to go to the hospital, Detective? The laceration on your head will heal better with a couple of stitches and you took some pretty good licks to your hips and legs. Again, I strongly recommend some X-rays."

Gabby moved closer. "I think it would be wise to go get checked out, Sarge."

"I appreciate it, but I'm good. Thanks."

"Well, at least come over to my place so you can get some rest while they finish processing the scene," Killian said.

"I'm too wired to sleep right now." Press told Gentry and his squad mates about Ocean and the house outside Wolfeboro, New Hampshire. "We need to get up there. ASAP."

The lieutenant said, "Absolutely not! Out of the question. Look at you. You need sleep and at least a few days to mend."

"I'm fine. Just a little sore is all." Press pointed in a northerly direction. "The kid is up there, Lieu. I know he is. It's the only place that makes logical sense," Press reasoned.

Gentry bristled. "We'll call the locals up there and have them check for the kid. How's that?"

"By the time I finish explaining what's going on and who they're looking for, we could be up there checking for ourselves. Besides, there's probably only a handful of cops working in that town anyway. And there's no guarantee they will give this the proper attention it requires. Plus, if we find Barnett, we can transport him back immediately."

Gentry unhappily considered Press's argument.

JK said, "I'm with Nate, LT. The sooner we find Barnett, the sooner we start getting some answers."

"I don't need to tell you, Lieu... If these people find Barnett first, he's a dead man. Time is of the essence."

Gentry squeezed his eyes shut and ran his hand in circles on the top of his bald head. "*If* I agree to this, I want all of you to go. If someone is after this Barnett kid the same way they are Nate, I think it only makes sense to have numbers. You really need to watch each other's backs."

"Agreed," said Press now standing, a current of adrenalin once again washing through him.

"And Nate sleeps on the way," said Gentry.

Press threw a thumbs-up over his shoulder. He was halfway across the lawn, headed toward the officer in charge of the crime scene, a slight limp in his gate.

"How far of a drive is it to Wolfeboro?" Tank said, turning to JK and Gabby.

"Three hours," Press called without hesitation, still pacing away from them.

"I have a feeling I'm going to regret this."

Gabby looked up at Gentry, her game face on. "You won't, Lieu."

"Uh-huh. Just please be careful. All of you."

51

**TINGLEY STREET
PROVIDENCE, RHODE ISLAND**

They had a crisis on their hands. Moments ago, Stevenson and Diehl, two of the four men who had been sent to Press's home, had returned with their tails between their legs. Damian and Hector were dead. They did not get anything out of Press least of all any item Talbert had passed to him. Nina Marlowe was hot with rage. She stormed outside the room and leaned against the wall of the seemingly endless warehouse corridor, trying to marshal her thoughts. She rubbed her sleep-starved eyes. Damian was a former FBI agent. Hector had worked briefly as a cop in Los Angeles. Both men's fingerprints had been scrubbed from the state and federal repositories at the time of their employment as had their facial recognition profiles. Brenner had seen to it when they were first hired. Nevertheless, this was bad. Very bad.

With Hector losing his head, he would be tougher to identify, but someone would surely recognize Damian when detectives eventually shared a photograph of him with their peers at the local, state, and federal levels. Could they somehow weave a narrative to accommodate the revelation when it came? Brenner would know how. He was a master of information warfare.

Marlowe looked at her watch as she lifted the phone to her ear. Brenner would be on Nantucket by now. A vehicle engine purred through the phone as she broke the news to him. The former CIA deputy director took it surprisingly well or so she thought.

"What do you want me to do?" Marlowe said.

"Sit tight. I may have something for you later. We'll get Press one way or another. Mark my words. But that can wait for the time being. If Lance and the others are successful, he won't matter nearly as much...at least in the short term. Keep me posted with any further developments."

"All right. What about Stevenson and Diehl?"

Brenner's voice dropped an octave. "Have them collect the girl from the warehouse and bring her to the island. I'll send a helicopter." He recited a set of grid coordinates for the rendezvous point. "And Nina... No more mistakes. It would be a shame for Green Castle to lose you."

Marlowe knew what that meant. Brenner did not suffer failure lightly. Any further missteps and she would be marked for death.

"Okay. I—"

But Brenner had already terminated the call.

52

East Providence, Rhode Island

Press had managed to talk the East Prov. PD scene supervisor into grabbing him shoes and a change of clothes from the house. He quickly dressed in the garage, collected some gear bags from his truck then slid into the front passenger seat of JK's Chevy Malibu. It would double as both his office and bed for the next few hours.

The two of them stopped off for some coffees for everyone while Gabby and Tank each made a quick pit stop at their own homes. The four of them had agreed to link back up at an exit on the other side of the Massachusetts border just off I-95 due north of Pawtucket.

Killian now eased onto the shoulder and engaged his flashers as Press was finishing up with the last of a series of phone calls to authorities in Wolfeboro. He had been right. Police there were short-staffed and working with minimum manpower. It seemed the same problem plagued every police department these days: No one wanted to be a cop. Even in a place like Wolfeboro. Only one officer was currently on duty. Two others would be coming on to relieve him at shift change which wasn't until 6:00 a.m. The chief and captain were expected in at 8:00 a.m., but according to the seasoned officer with whom Press had spoken, no one ever knew what their schedules were—they seemed to come and go as they pleased and did not keep the rank and file apprised of their daily movements.

When Gabby and Tank pulled in behind them, Press exited the car with their coffees. After handing them over, he called for JK to come join them. The four detectives stood along the passenger side of Gabby's Fusion.

"Before we head out, I need to tell you all something," Press said, a tinge of melancholy in his voice. "I *know* why I was targeted, why those men came to my house."

No one said a thing.

"Before this all started, even before Riley Talbert was found dead..." Press averted his gaze to a string of passing vehicles then settled his eyes on those looking back at him. "He'd written me a letter. I found it in my mailbox on Friday, the fourteenth—in the evening, mixed in with a stack of mail."

"The fourteenth," Gabby said. "Talbert was abducted on the fourteenth...and killed later that night."

Press nodded.

"What did it say?" said Tank.

"Talbert wanted to meet with me, to give me something the next day. He offered no other information but for the fact that he cautioned me not to tell anyone and that I shouldn't try to contact him. He also said that if something were to happen to him that I would know where to find whatever it was he wanted to give me."

"Weird," Tank said, one hand in his pants pocket, the other cradling his coffee.

"You're telling me."

Gabby sipped her coffee, staring at him intently. "You never got the chance to meet...obviously. And you never made any attempt to contact him?"

"No." Press worked his sore jaw. "I went to the location at the specified time, but Talbert never showed. At the time, I figured something must have spooked him. Maybe he was being followed or at least thought he was and decided meeting with me wasn't safe. Now I know it was because he was already dead."

No one spoke for several seconds.

When the mournful silence had passed, Gabby said, "Any idea what he wanted to give you or what it was regarding?"

"None."

She folded her arms beneath her breasts, one hand still on her coffee cup. "But it would stand to reason it had something to do with Seth Barnett."

"No doubt."

Killian shook his head, not revealing the fact that Press had already told him about the letter. "Freakin' mystery, bro."

"I just wanted y'all to know everything. The people who killed Talbert and Barb Stanley, the ones who were in my house *are* professionals. When we get to Wolfeboro, I want your heads on a swivel. These people are extremely dangerous. If they find Seth Barnett, it's not hard to imagine what they'll do to him. Assuming Barnett *is* up there, and we locate him, I want him stuffed in a car and back on the road immediately. If we should get separated for any reason, we will link back up at the Dunkin' Donuts just south of Pittsfield. I'm texting y'all the address right now.

"And by the way, if anything happens to me, the Talbert letter is locked in my desk back at the office, envelope and all."

"What's the plan when we get Barnett back here?" Tank said.

"We'll have to put him in protective custody. But we'll cross that bridge when we come to it. Any other questions, concerns?" When no one offered any, he said, "Now, let's find that kid."

53

Wolfeboro, New Hampshire

With a plan in place to meet up with officers when they arrived in Wolfeboro, Press reclined his seat, and made an honest attempt at sleeping. But whether it was his pounding headache, sore body, or the energetic thoughts filling his mind, he could do nothing more than doze for a few minutes at a time.

The sun had already slipped over the horizon by the time they were rolling past Morrisseys' Front Porch Family Restaurant. The Wolfeboro Police Department was just a little further up, sleeping peacefully beside the town's public library. Once JK and Gabby had backed into parking spaces, everyone climbed out, stretched their legs, and got the inevitable yawns out of their systems.

Press immediately detected the fragrant smell of pine trees and lake air as he took stock of his surroundings.

Corporal Tony Fitzpatrick and Officer Greg Bowersox greeted them in the parking lot. When the introductions were over, they all made their way inside to a small conference room.

Press kept the briefing short, describing Seth Barnett as a material witness in a homicide investigation. He further described how and why they believed Barnett's life to be in danger and thus the reason they needed to move swiftly but cautiously to get him into their custody and back to Providence. Press's own battered face was illustration enough to drive home his point.

"You can't force him to go with you. What if he refuses? Do you have a material witness warrant?" asked Bowersox.

Press smiled. "No, but he won't."

Bowersox shrugged his shoulders. He looked like he lived in the gym. "What if he's not there?"

"Then we drove a long way for breakfast," Tank said.

"He's here. I can feel it," said Press before further addressing the Wolfeboro officers. "As you know, our target location is at the end of Many Pines Road."

"Yeah, that's right on the lake," said Fitzpatrick. "Just a heads up... The roads back there are narrow and can get confusing. It's easy to get turned around and lose your sense of direction."

"Good to know."

"What about comms?" Gabby said. "Is there a way for us to stay in touch with you guys?"

"Yes," said Fitzpatrick, adjusting his vest at the neckline. "You guys plan to stay buddied up? I only ask because radios are in short supply around here."

Based on the man's bearing, salt-and-pepper brush cut, and assertive voice, Press figured him to be former military. "We do," Press said.

Fitzpatrick asked Bowersox to grab the spare portable radios from the charging station in the patrol room—there were only two. When the younger officer returned, Fitzpatrick had him dial both radios to the "TAC 1" channel and hand them to Press, who promptly passed one to Gabby.

Press glanced down at the radio to be sure which knob controlled the volume, before clipping it onto his belt. "All goes well, we'll be out of your guys' hair quickly and y'all can go grab a nice breakfast before the chief comes in."

Bowersox smiled. "Spoken like a true veteran."

"How do you want to do this?" said Fitzpatrick.

Press moved to a large, laminated map of the greater Wolfeboro area that was affixed to the wall on one side of the room. "I was thinking that one of you guys could go to the front door with JK and me. Seeing a local uniform should put him at ease." He turned toward the table. "Gabby and Tank, I want you to keep eyes on the back of the house. You know the drill. Give a shout if he would try to bolt."

"What about me?" said Bowersox.

Press pointed to a spot on the map approximately a quarter of the way down Many Pines Road from the intersecting Keewaydin Road. "Hang out here and watch our backs. Alert us to any traffic that tries to come in or out. The marked car should serve to calm the nerves of any curious neighbors and also keep anyone from surprising us from behind like a FedEx truck, et cetera."

Fitzpatrick alerted his county dispatcher by phone about what was going on and where and asked her to pend all non-emergency calls. Soon afterward, everyone mounted up and headed out.

54

Lance Cheney stood in the living room, hands on his hips. He drew in a long breath and let it out in one quick burst. Meanwhile, Marcus Zug gazed through the wall of windows at the back of the house, which yielded a glorious view of the lake. A breeze caused the trees in their springtime bloom to swish and sway and the surface of the water beyond to dance in the morning sunlight.

Brenner had dispatched additional men to assist them—shooters, with whom he and Zug had worked on previous assignments. They had kept their vehicles out of sight and patrolled to the house through the woods, keeping twenty yards off Many Pines Road the entire way in order to avoid spoiling their element of surprise. The outdoor clothing they each wore would allow them to blend in with area residents if need be, though their plan was to remain unseen to the extent possible.

"Now what?" said Zug.

Cheney adjusted his ball cap and met Marcus's eyes. "He's been here." Though Barnett's car was not parked outside, the signs were everywhere: dishes in the sink, the bed that had been slept in and remained unmade, the fresh water on the shower walls and damp wash cloth hanging on a railing in the master bath, the accumulated trash in the waste bins. But nothing screamed computer geek more than what was right there in the living room.

"You think he's coming back? What if he heard us and bolted?"

Cheney evaluated the bounty before him. A 17-inch laptop rested on the coffee table. Next to it were a wireless mouse and a spiral notebook with pages of handwritten notes scribbled inside. A blue, rugged backpack outfitted with a pocket to carry a computer lay on the sofa. He stepped over to it and explored the various pouches, finding numerous flash drives, a Kindle, an iPad, a mini laptop, charging cables, and an assortment of other peripherals. "No, he'll be back. He wouldn't have left all this behind."

"What do you want to do?"

Cheney considered their options. It seemed the kid had just stepped out. Maybe he had gone into town for groceries or down to the lake to do some early morning fishing. "Now, we wait. He's going to come back. And when he does, he's going to have the biggest surprise of his life."

The corners of Marcus Zug's mouth crept upward, forming a wicked smile.

"Grab all this stuff and take it outside. I'll meet you out back in a few minutes. I want to take one last look around."

Zug scooped up the laptop and other materials as Cheney made his way slowly through the house once more. He wasn't sure what he was looking for this time but felt compelled to take one last pass through every room, every hiding place.

Cheney heard the back door close and Marcus's heavy footfalls on the wooden decking that ran the length of the house at the end of which were several flights of stairs that doubled back on themselves down to ground level.

He was alone now. The only sound was the distant buzz of an outboard motor from somewhere out on the lake. He was close. He could feel it in his bones. Seth Barnett was a smart, elusive prey. But they had found him and soon the thrill of the hunt would be gone. For Cheney that was everything. He wanted to soak it all in. Oftentimes the actual kill or capture was anticlimactic. Though he wanted nothing to thwart the success of their mission, a part of him was secretly hoping that would not be the case with the apprehension of Seth Barnett.

It was during this private reverie that radio traffic suddenly came alive in the earpiece nestled in his left ear. "Look alive, all. Cops are heading your way." It was Eddie Olsen, one of the men posted out along the road. Each of them had callsigns to be used over the radio. Olsen was called Joker. Cheney, Lucky.

Cheney keyed his radio. "Cops? Are you sure?"

"Roger that. Two marked units and two plain wrappers just turned down Many Pines. I count six tangos in total."

"Okay. Copy." Cheney was about to run downstairs and exit the house, but a thought occurred to him. If the cops did not get an answer at the door, they would probably sit on the house, maybe even enter and check for the kid—they had an articulable reason to fear for his safety. But if they could be diverted, they might clear out in time for Barnett to fall right into their trap.

"Everyone, hold your position," he said. "And keep your eyes out for our little friend."

After hearing affirmative responses from his team, Cheney used his finger to slightly nudge the blinds aside in a window in the upstairs master bedroom. A Ford Explorer with a lightbar on the roof and black-and-yellow striping on its sides was just now pulling to a stop in front of the house. Two unmarked sedans—a black Ford Fusion and a white Chevy Malibu, both with Rhode Island tags—parked in the driveway behind it. He watched the officers dismount. He only counted five cops. The other marked car must have stopped further up the road, probably to guard against a rear attack or perhaps just be a visible presence.

Cheney focused on two of the plainclothes cops. He instantly recognized them—the pretty, dark-haired woman and the short, powerful-looking guy. He'd seen them at Barnett's apartment building as he had been getting off the elevator. A flood of anxiety washed over him. If they recognized him, it would all be over. But in the next instant, his fear subsided; the pair was headed around the corner, to the back of the house. He turned his attention to the others. A single uniformed officer—a corporal, based on the two stripes on his sleeves—led two men toward the front door. The tallest of the trio was the detective, Nathan Press. He looked like he'd been thrown off a cliff and survived. Damian and his team had obviously failed to do their job.

Cheney quickly walked to the bathroom and checked himself in the mirror. He removed his ball cap and tried on a friendly, good-natured smile.

Good to go.

55

Press surveyed the area for blind spots. The woodpile down a slight grade off to the right. The outbuilding that was set back in the woods on the left flank of the house. He figured it probably contained landscaping equipment, jet skis, ATVs, or other expensive toys. The house was bigger than the "cottage" he had expected to see. It was three stories high and constructed of stone and clapboard siding, the type commonly seen on homes along the New England coast. The spouting was aged copper. The front door, a mammoth slab of wood.

"His car's not here," said Killian.

"Maybe it's in there." Press motioned to the giant, detached garage off to the right. The three overhead doors were tall enough to accommodate a lifted 4x4 with a camper rig.

Killian was already moving toward it. He kicked over a fat log, stepped up on it, and peered through a small window on the side of the building. When he had rejoined them, Press quietly said, "Anything?"

"No. Just a couple of dirt bikes, some kayaks, and a bunch of tools."

"He might have stashed the car elsewhere...or maybe he ran into town."

"Or maybe he's not here," Fitzpatrick said.

Press hated to consider that possibility. Barnett *had* to be here. It just made sense.

They climbed a path of wide flagstone steps to the front door as JK remained by a tree near the corner of house, looking for movement in the windows. Colorful beds of hydrangea, coneflowers, peonies, and marigolds covered the sloped ground on either side of the entryway, portraying an artful welcome worthy of a postcard.

"Ever been here before?" Press said, as he and Fitzpatrick ascended to the front door.

"Nope. First time." Fitzpatrick pushed a fancy button on the wall. A rich, multi-tone chime came alive on the other side of the door.

Press stood a few paces away from the door, peering through a void in the shades of one of the first-floor windows. Through the foyer, he could see just a sliver of a stair railing that curled downward from the ceiling to the floor. Save for that, his view deeper into the house was obstructed by a thick pillar that rose to the second level.

"See anything?" the corporal asked, after ringing the bell again.

Press maneuvered his head this way and that. "Nah. There doesn't appear to be anyone home. *Wait.* I just saw movement." He tilted his head to the right. "Someone's inside. They're coming to the door."

Press and Fitzpatrick instinctively stepped to either side of the door and placed their right hands on their pistols but in such a way that would appear non-threatening to the homeowner. A casual lean rather than what it really was: tactical preparedness.

The deadbolt snapped free of the frame and the door swung inward. A man of medium build with early gray hair and a vanilla face appeared. He was clad in a black-and-barley-colored flannel shirt, tan Ariat work pants, and hiking boots that were new and unsoiled. A flash of surprise gave way to an engaging smile. "The police," he said, as if the sight of an officer all the way out here was beyond the realm of his comprehension. He stood straighter, his eyes moving from Fitzpatrick to Press before refocusing on the man in uniform. "Yes, Officer. What can I do for you?"

"We're looking for this man." Fitzpatrick held out a photo that Press had supplied him. "His name is Seth Barnett. We have information that leads us to believe he may be staying here."

"Bar*nett*?" The man shook his head. "I'm sorry, but there is no one here by that name. What's this all about? Is he some type of criminal? Should I be worried?"

"The man in the photo is missing and we're trying to locate him. He may be in danger," Press said, assuming command of the conversation.

"And you think he might be *here*? Good gracious. *Why*?"

Press was congenial but all business. "Do you have some ID, sir?"

"*ID*? What do you mean? This is *my* house."

"Yessir, but if you could just humor me. It's just procedure that we document the identities of folks we speak with. The bosses back at the office will be all over us if we don't verify ID." Press's Spidey-sense was firing on multiple levels. If this were Ocean Enberg's grandparents' house, who the heck was this guy? He was clearly not old enough to be her grandfather. And there was something about the way he smiled. It didn't seem genuine, like he was hiding something.

Cheney perceived that Press wasn't buying his acting performance. Or maybe he was just the type of detective who dotted every "I" and crossed every "T." This was the first time he had seen him up close. The man's demeanor at first had been friendly yet professional. But now his gaze was steely.

He knew.

"Sure, Officer. My wallet is on the kitchen table. Just let me go grab it." He closed the door partway and retreated into the foyer, whistling a tune as he went.

Then suddenly Olsen was in his ear. "All, from Joker. I see the kid. He's in his car and coming down Keeywadin. Passing my pos right now."

At that moment, everything changed. They had the kid in their sights. And no one was going to stop them from taking him. No local cops. No detectives from Providence. No one.

Cheney quietly keyed his radio. "Grab him. But do it quickly."

56

Seth Barnett drummed the steering wheel as he hummed along to an old '80s song spilling from the car radio. He had gone into town for breakfast and to pick up some groceries. Despite the Enbergs' gorgeous lakeside retreat and all the toys at his disposal, the cupboards had been bare when he'd arrived a week ago. He had been to Wolfeboro only once before. The previous autumn, he and Ocean had come up for a week with her mom and stepdad. He loved everything about it. The house on the lake. The quaint little town. The mountain trails and streams. The soul-taming scent of pine. The radiant colors of the trees performing their annual ritual. It truly was heaven on earth.

One morning, he and Ocean had risen early from their beds and biked into town for breakfast at the Downtown Grille Café. They'd sat outside on the deck, just like he did today, enjoying their omelets and watching boats come and go from the docks. It was a day he'd never forgotten. Not because of the breakfast or the bucolic lakeside scenery but because later that afternoon, on a hike up near Mount Washington, his life changed forever. Standing on a wooden bridge overlooking a glorious waterfall known as Crystal Cascade, he'd decided that he wanted to spend the rest of his life with her.

Thoughts of Ocean now percolated in his mind as he turned out of the Hunter's Shop 'n Save parking lot and headed back to the house. He remembered her smiling at him over her glasses. It was a look that blended mischief and intelligence and beauty into one. She was the total package. He'd imagined sharing a lifetime with her. Having children someday and living in a place like Wolfeboro, or perhaps in a simple ranch-style house on a remote mountain somewhere out west. Far away from the world and all its ugliness. But now that was impossible. That dream had been ripped from him. When he had first set out, he'd told himself his efforts would all be worth it. He was doing the right thing after all, the difficult thing. Now he wasn't so sure. He'd already lost his true love—the woman he so desperately wanted to marry, and his career, which had been a large part of his identity. Now, with people after him—people willing to kill, he faced the very real prospect of losing his life altogether. What options did he have left? Where could he go? Whom could he trust?

He was calculating ideas and their probabilities for success and failure as he made the left onto Keewaydin from North Main Street. His deep thoughts kept him from noticing the dark gray GMC Yukon parked on the shoulder as he neared his destination. It wasn't until he'd turned onto Many Pines Road and saw the marked police cruiser blocking his path that a bolt of fear shot through him.

Then came sharp cracks of gunfire, and in that same instant, the idyllic lakeside paradise devolved into absolute mayhem.

Gabby and Tank had taken up positions at the back of the house, doing the usual: watching the doors and windows for movement, preparing for the kid to come running outside at any moment like a spooked deer. Gabby had already climbed up on the decking that ran the length of the house and was doing well to stay out of view from the large bank of windows that surely offered a sublime view of the lake behind her. She crouched behind a handcrafted wooden bench set amidst five Adirondack chairs that all faced one another. She imagined a large family gathering here with steaks and burgers sizzling on the grill, several generations of men talking sports and smoking cigars, women gabbing about their children's latest accomplishments and school activities, maybe planning an upcoming holiday party over glasses of wine. And, finally, kids somewhere out there, endlessly exploring and getting into mischief like all good boys and girls should in the great outdoors.

She was entertaining all these thoughts while focusing her eyes on the interior of the house. The doorbell chimed from somewhere deep inside. She ducked down further out of view and stole a quick glance back to Tank who was posted up behind a large oak tree in the woods that skirted the house. He offered no signal, whispered no words, just peered toward the house occasionally scanning the perimeter, ready for anything.

The sound of the doorbell came again and suddenly she felt movement. It was in the form of vibrations beneath her feet. She prepared herself to spring into action, expecting at any moment Seth Barnett to throw open the back door and come bursting toward her. Instead, she saw a man through the windows, crossing the foyer. Though his back was toward her, she could plainly tell he was not Seth Barnett. The man walked to the front door, pulled it open, and began talking with Nate and the corporal. After a brief conversation, the man turned around, and despite the sun reflecting in the glass, Gabby caught a good glimpse of his face. Something registered. He looked familiar, but she couldn't immediately place the face. Then, just as the memory surfaced in her mind, she caught a glimpse of the object in the man's right hand, held flat against his thigh.

She instantly keyed her radio and yelled, "GUN! GUN! GUN!"

Hearing Gabby's shouted alert, Press instantly dodged to his right. Had he not done so, he would have been shot dead. Fitzpatrick on the other hand had no chance whatsoever of avoiding the hot lead. But by the grace of God, Gabby's rabid alert had caused him to drop his center of gravity. As such, the round that would have hit him right between the eyes, cut a path along the top of his head. Nevertheless, the Wolfeboro corporal dropped on the front landing unconscious without ever knowing what had hit him.

Press leaned left and fired three rounds in quick succession just as the heavy door slammed shut. Bullets suddenly tore through the adjacent wall from the inside out, forcing Press to dive to his right. He landed in the flowerbed with a thud and quickly scrambled on his belly toward the walled edge of the stone and concrete porch. Press kept his head down for several beats then stole a quick peek toward the house while preparing to move to a different position of cover.

"See anything?!" he yelled to Killian.

"No!"

Press quickly scanned his surroundings. His head snapped back around as several gun blasts thundered from somewhere behind the house. They were sporadic and clearly fired from different caliber weapons. One gun was much louder than the others. A long gun.

Not good.

Press heard Bowersox yelling on the radio for backup from neighboring jurisdictions. In the next breath, Bowersox was back on the radio. "Press! Your witness is here!"

"Barnett?!"

"10-4! He's—" The radio transmission abruptly ceased as gunfire cracked and boomed from seemingly every direction.

Staying low, Press made several attempts to raise Bowersox on the radio, but the officer did not respond.

Something flashed in the woods off to the right. At the same time, wood splintered on the deck and chair beside her. Gabby dropped to the wood planks, flattening herself like a pancake. Shots she knew had to be from Tank's gun answered back.

"Gabby! I'll cover you. Move!" he yelled. He fired two, three, four more times.

Gabby glanced up, gun in hand. "Moving!" She bolted to her feet and, while hinging over at the waist, sprinted down the deck stairs. When she was safely behind a tree and had her gun pointed toward where the shots had originated, she yelled, "I'm set!"

There were two threats, two gunmen, to deal with. The man still in the house and whoever was shooting at them out here. But the man outside had a long gun and that was a real problem. Projectiles fired from a rifle had much more energy than those fired from a pistol. Though she preferred not to get hit by either if she could help it.

"Any movement on the deck?" called Tank.

"Don't see any." The sound of glass breaking echoed through the woods. "I think the guy inside is coming out a side window!"

The computer bag slung over his left shoulder, pistol in his right hand, Marcus Zug was about to make a run for it. A few seconds ago, with the stock of a rifle pressed to his cheek, Vinnie Trich—callsign Vandal—had yelled for him to go, that he would cover him. Zug nodded and sprinted for the next grouping of thick trees. After only a few strides though, he heard Trich issue a pained grunt and his gun fell silent. As soon as Zug hit the trees, he spun. Trich was writhing on the ground with several wet flowers of crimson blossoming on the front of his jacket. Zug could have easily made it to safety, but for a soldier like him there was no hesitation, no debating what to do. He had been trained to never leave a man behind.

Zug fired three shots toward the enemy then sprinted back to Trich, snatched him up and threw him onto his shoulder. He sprayed more rounds before taking off again through the woods, this time with reckless abandon, Trich hissing curse words with every bump along way. This time he wouldn't stop until he reached the car or was arrested by a bullet.

Zug almost ran into Cheney as he bolted past the east side of the house. Cheney had apparently kicked out a side window and shimmied down the exterior wall somehow, probably by way of the water spouting. He'd seen Cheney do that type of thing before. An exchange of words was not necessary. Both men knew what to do: get the kid and get the hell out of here.

"Bird, Pepper, this is Lucky. Tiny and I are coming out hot with Vandal. He's been hit. Cover us. Joker, gimme a sitrep on the kid." When no response came, Cheney barked again. "Joker! Sitrep!"

Gunfire crackled ahead. Both men simultaneously ducked their heads and veered right, plowing a path through the brush as they ran.

"Stand by! Working here!" screamed Eddie Olsen.

Press noticed two men running through the woods on the far side of the driveway. One of them looked to be the man with whom only moments ago they had spoken at the front door. The other was the size of a refrigerator, and yet somehow, he was moving with impossible speed and agility.

Press was about to stand and give chase when automatic gunfire lit up the Wolfeboro cruiser behind which he was currently crouched. The shooter then turned his attention to Killian just as he popped out to return fire. Both unmarked vehicles as well as Fitzpatrick's patrol car were shredded with hot lead. Somehow, the shooting had caused the trunk of JK's car to unlatch. It now hung partway open.

"JK! Cover me!"

"Okay!" Killian fired toward the gunman in the woods.

"Moving!" Press sprinted to the back of the car, grabbed his and JK's plate carriers—tactical vests that held thick armor plates, extra ammunition, and other items. He threw them on the ground beside him and next reached for their patrol rifles, thankful he'd thought to bring his along. Press's was a suppressed BCM MCMR with an 11.5" barrel. It was the same gun he'd used throughout his time on SRU; he still trained with it often. The gun was outfitted with an Eotech EXPS3 holographic site and a G33 magnifier optic. Killian's, meanwhile, was the standard department-issue Colt AR-15 A3 Tactical, chambered in 5.56, and carried an Aimpoint PRO red dot. Press shrimped back down behind the car's rear wheel as a barrage of gunfire found the spot he had just vacated.

Staying low, he dragged the items forward and joined Killian. They took turns covering each other as they donned their vests and charged the rifles.

Press took a few quick peeks in several directions. At the far end of Many Pines Road, roughly 800 feet away, Seth Barnett's silver Nissan Rogue was smashed into a tree. Flames were crawling out of the engine compartment and sending thick, acrid smoke into the trees above. More bullets pinged against and through the vehicles behind which they were huddled.

"Whadda we do, Nate? They're going to kill the kid!"

Press glanced toward the garage. "Wait here and cover me." In the next instant, he gave an emphatic nod. JK leaned from behind the front end of his car and fired several times in quick succession as Press burst from his position and ran for the corner of the large garage.

The pedestrian door along this side of the garage was locked though that didn't much matter. Press launched his shoulder into it without slowing. The wood of the door frame splintered, and he immediately fell inside. He kept his head low as several times gunfire from outside found its way through the overhead garage doors and walls.

Press adjusted the rubber pull tab on his sling, drawing the rifle close to his torso before letting it hang. He examined the first dirt bike, a Honda CRF450. The front tire was flat. A definite no go. Parked next to it was a KTM 250 XC. The tires looked good. Press unscrewed the cap on the fuel tank and peeked inside. It was half full. Now, would she start? A stray round tore into the garage and clanged off a metal hanger. He swung his rifle around to his back, climbed astride the dirt bike, and thumbed the ignition start button. The motor came to life, sputtered a few times. He wound the throttle, delivering a bit of gas, and the idle evened out, filling the garage with exhaust fumes.

Keeping his head down, Press walked the bike toward the man door, eased the front tire over the threshold and twisted the handlebars, so he could get her outside. Once there, he circled the bike around in a quick walk while keeping his torso flat against the fuel tank.

Killian was still engaged in sporadic return fire, but when he saw Press on the bike, he did a double take. "What the—?!"

"You ready?!"

"For what?!" yelled Killian.

"To go on offense."

57

Press used the trees along the corner of the garage as cover, while revving the dirt bike's motor and mentally preparing to speed right into the belly of the beast. He peered through the gaps in the tree trunks, at the woods on the opposite side of the drive.

Killian fired a burst of rounds, ducked back down to perform a mag change, and crawled to the other end of his mortally wounded car—the end closest to Press. "You sure about this?!"

"No! But it's the only way!" Press nosed the bike forward.

Keeping his rifle turned toward the threat, Killian jumped up and sprinted over to the bike. He hopped on, threw an arm around Press, and yelled in his ear, "Go!!!"

Press released the clutch and twisted the throttle. They instantly shot forward and curled around the knot of trees at the corner of the garage, emerging onto the wooded drive, which was now saturated with the haze of gunfire and a growing fog of heavy, black smoke.

Gus Evans, known to his teammates as Pepper, stood within a thick stand of pine trees. He had heard the radio broadcast about Seth Barnett. He had also seen with his own eyes, Keith Wrigley—callsign Bird—engage the patrol officer parked just off Keewaydin in a fierce gun battle that lasted close to half a minute. Somehow during this sudden chaos and confusion, Barnett had crashed his vehicle into a large tree along the wooded lane. Flames now licked from beneath the mangled hood and smoke poured forth.

Evans turned back toward the two plainclothes cops holed up behind the unmarked police cars in front of the house to his left. He let loose with another burst of automatic gunfire then paused, hoping one of them would stick his head out, so he could shoot it off.

Sirens wailed in the distance seemingly from every direction. They were drawing dangerously close and doing so quicker than he believed was possible for this tiny little hick town. Wrigley was suddenly in his earpiece. "I'll get the kid. Joker, bring your car up next to the cruiser out by the road!"

"Roger," came the response.

"Pepper, hold your pos."

"Roger that," said Gus Evans.

Next, it was Lance Cheney on the radio net. "All, Tiny, Vandal, and I are exfilling back to our vehicle. Advise as soon as you have the target in custody. We'll link back up at the rally point."

"Joker copies."

"Bird copies."

Evans keyed his radio, relating the same message.

Then something unexpected happened. The big detective, Nathan Press, and one of his plain-clothed colleagues came screaming around the far side of the garage on a dirt bike of all things.

What in the world?

Evans shouldered his rifle, centering the optic's reticle on Press's torso. He tracked him from left to right, pulled the trigger. But the detective tandem was moving too fast. With all the trees between the muzzle and the dirt bike rocketing down the lane, hitting either man proved to be incredibly difficult.

Determined, Evans took aim again.

Seeing Press and Killian race down the lane on the dirt bike, Gabby motioned to Tank and together they sprinted after them. A gun burped loudly from a tight grouping of trees somewhere ahead and to the right of their position. They ducked but immediately realized the shots were not directed at them.

Gabby detected movement. *There.* A figure was secreted within a natural hide of leaves and pine needles—a man clad in a black windbreaker and faded blue jeans. He shifted his firing stance and let loose again toward Nate and JK, all of this happening in a mere few seconds.

Gabby pushed against Tank's left shoulder and they both immediately cut to the right, took up firing positions. She steadied herself with her forearm against a beech tree and took aim with her duty pistol. The gunman was thirty yards away and still focused on the dirt bike and her squad mates astride it. She fought to slow her rapid breathing that was right now causing her chest to heave up and down. She exhaled again and held her breath for a quick beat. Then squeezed the trigger, sending four steady rounds toward the gunman. A red mist burst from within the pine branches. The man tumbled forward and, as if in slow motion, rolled down the slight grade, eventually coming to a halt in a bloody, lifeless heap.

She whipped her eyes back to the speeding dirt bike. At that very moment, it disappeared into the large cloud of black smoke billowing from Seth Barnett's car.

Gabby scanned the woods for more threats. Seeing none, she yelled to Tank, "Come on!"

Press wound the bike's engine as bullets whirred and whizzed past them, some scorching the worn pavement, others snapping branches and boring holes into tree trunks. For a moment, he rode blindly through the black cloud of smoke that was rapidly filling the forest. As he emerged on the other side, he observed a dark green sedan pulled in next to Bowersox's patrol car. The driver was alert and amped up but far from panicked. A man armed with a carbine sprinted to the passenger side and hopped in.

Press eased off the throttle and at the same time noticed a frantic runner, plowing through the thick tangle of pine trees and undergrowth to his left.

Barnett.

The kid stumbled and fell, picked himself up, and continued bounding through the woods away from the dark sedan whose occupants were entirely focused on him now, too. The driver threw the car into REVERSE, its tires chirping loudly against the mottled pavement.

Press skidded to a stop next to the police cruiser. Its windshield was pocked with bullet holes, the open driver's door, too. The Wolfeboro officer lay on the ground not far away, the sun reflecting off pools of bright crimson all around him.

"Check on Bowersox! I'm going after the kid," yelled Press, steadying the dirt bike with both feet on the ground.

Killian leapt off, rifle at a high-ready, and ran toward the downed officer.

Press squeezed the bike with his thighs, leaned forward, and ripped down on the throttle. The front wheel rose a few inches off the ground before it found purchase as he screamed away. Press reached the end of Many Pines Road just as the green sedan was screeching to a stop and the driver was dropping the car back into DRIVE. Press zipped past him and wound the throttle. He went about fifty yards then slowed before swerving into the woods. He rose into a slight standing position and allowed the bike's fork and rear suspension to absorb the rocks and uneven ground. The bike caught air for an instant as he raged through the forest on a direct line for Seth Barnett.

Press quickly overcame him, slid to a stop in the pine needles and dead leaves, and planted one foot on the ground. "You want to stay alive?! Get on!"

Wide-eyed, Barnett seemed to be caught in a moment of sensory overload, unsure of what he was seeing or if he should trust the man on the motor bike.

"Hey! Seth! Let's go! Get on! Do it now!"

Gunfire thundered from the road. Chunks of tree bark exploded all around them. Rounds caroming off nearby rocks sang a song of high-pitched squeals, pings, and zings.

Barnett hustled to the bike, threw a leg over the seat.

"Hold on! Tight!"

Press felt Barnett grip him in a desperate bear hug. He leaned forward and twisted the throttle toward the ground. The bike responded instantly. He wove through the trees, over several earthen obstacles, and back to the pavement just as the green sedan came whipping around the bend. The car yawed sideways, throwing up stones and a cloud of dust. One of its wheels dropped into the rutted shoulder causing the men inside the cabin to rock violently.

Press veered to the left, leaned forward on the gas tank, and redlined the throttle. After a hundred yards, he took a quick peek over his shoulder to see how close the men in pursuit were. They had fallen behind but were still giving chase.

Wind ripping through his hair, Press recalled the map on the wall of the Wolfeboro police station. He remembered that this road eventually terminated somewhere not far from here and that another road—Mandalay Road—ran parallel. If he could just make it through the woods over to Mandalay, he could double back and shoot out to 109, then really put some distance between himself and these gun-toting mutts. Right now, that was his best hope for keeping Barnett—and himself—alive.

"Hang on! This could get bumpy!"

Barnett closed his eyes and clung to him even tighter.

58

By the time they had reached the spot where Keewaydin bent north and intersected with Mandalay, there was no sign of the green sedan or anything else that posed a threat—man or machine. Press brought the bike to a stop. Red and blue lights now flared through the trees in nearly every direction. The siren of a fire truck howled as it swept past. He could hear more sirens in the distance.

Press turned back toward the Enberg house and the center of the storm of activity. He maneuvered the bike around vehicles alive and flickering with bright LEDs. There were two that belonged to the state police as well as a collection from several other departments. A policeman in a florescent yellow vest armed with a carbine and a red-coned flashlight eyed him carefully. At first, the officer gave the signal to stop, but then, seeing the POLICE patches on Press's plate carrier, waved him past while immediately mouthing something into his radio: an update to others on scene.

Press entered the woods in order to avoid the firemen and the burning vehicle with which they were engaged. He bumped back out onto Many Pines Road a safe distance away and coasted back toward the shredded police vehicles and the house beyond. Aside from the clamor of a fire truck's diesel engine, cartridge cases littering the pavement, bullet holes seemingly everywhere, and the scent of fresh gunfire in the air, the setting had returned to its previous serene state.

JK and Tank were tending to Fitzpatrick on the porch while Gabby was pacing the driveway, a cell phone to her ear. She glanced over at him, nodded with relieved recognition, then said something into the phone before holding it to her shoulder and walking toward him.

Press killed the engine and steadied the bike for Barnett to climb off. The young man appeared sheepish and dejected. Press flicked the kickstand down and quickly dismounted. He wordlessly gazed at the carnage before him then cast his attention back toward the end of the lane. Firefighters had pried open the car's hood and were poking and prodding various spots inside and out. The front half of the vehicle was now heavily charred and soaked to the bone. Sunshine glistened from its wet veneer as an impotent tendril of smoke slithered upward from the engine compartment.

"EMS is en route for Fitzpatrick—he's still unconscious, but he's breathing and appears stable." She took a few steps closer. "Major's on the phone, Sarge. He wants to talk to you."

Major Harold Booth was the commander of Detective Division, the chief of D's, as it were. Press didn't care for the man. He was pompous and foul-mouthed and smoked as many cigarettes as a four-dollar hooker. At one time he may have been a decent investigator, but office life had turned him lazy and soft and pious for policy adherence above all else. Press had seen this happen to more than a few good street cops in his time.

"Yessir?"

"Press! What in the name of all that's holy did you manage to get yourself into this time?! And by the way, who gave you the approval to go up there and start a war with God's knows who?!" The cursing commenced from that point forward and did not end for close to thirty seconds.

"What do you need, Major? I'm kind of busy."

Booth exploded. "You're *busy*? You're *busy*?!"

"That's what I said." Press nodded and offered a string of mm-hmms and uh-huhs into the handset then said, "Okay, Major. I gotta go." There was a burst of profanity as he disconnected the call. When he looked up, Gabby was just shaking her head. "He'll get over it," Press said.

Barnett quietly stood off to the side, shuffling his feet and fidgeting with his hands.

"You okay?" Press asked him. "You're not injured, are you?"

"No, sir. I'm okay."

A horn honked twice and caused everyone to look back up the lane. A shiny black Chevy Tahoe with red and blue visor lights flashing, slipped past the firemen, and continued toward the house. It was followed by an ambulance that no longer had its lights or siren activated. Both vehicles lurched to a stop. EMTs hopped out of the ambulance, grabbed their bags, and fast-walked to the porch to begin their assessment of Fitzpatrick.

Meanwhile, a burly man in a shirt and tie, dark slacks, and dress shoes, stepped from the Tahoe, followed the EMTs up the stairs. Press noticed the gold badge on the man's belt next to his sidearm. He carried no handcuffs.

The police chief.

The man bent over his wounded officer, said a few words near his ear and patted him on the shoulder. He then descended to the grouping that consisted of Press, Gabby, and Barnett. "Which one of you is Press?"

"I am," said Press without hesitation.

The man held out his hand and Press shook it. He had an iron grip to go with his iron-colored hair.

"Bill Walton, Chief of Police." He scanned the house, the bullet-riddled cars. "What a mess. What an *absolute mess*."

"Yes, sir. It is."

"Did you get your witness? Was he here?"

"You're looking at him, Chief." Press nodded toward Barnett.

Walton shifted his gaze to the slight, young man, who immediately averted his eyes. Walton then turned back toward the burned-up car in the distance, the body of his dead officer beyond. Someone had dutifully draped a yellow, disposable blanket over him. A state trooper moved about at the terminus of the lane, stringing up crime-scene tape.

"I thought I'd left all this crap behind when I got out of the Big Apple."

"I'm very sorry about all of this, Chief," Press said. He would later learn that Bill Walton was a retired and highly decorated NYPD inspector with his last post having been commander of the 19th Precinct.

"Me, too, Detective. Me, too."

Walton again fixed his gaze on Barnett. "A good man lost his life here today. His family lost a husband and father." He looked toward Fitzpatrick then back to Barnett, gritting his teeth as a swell of emotion rippled across his face. After a few seconds, he took an unsteady breath. "I just hope you're worth it."

59

Press had a brief conversation with Chief Walton in private then strode over to Killian's car from which he reclaimed his briefcase and large duffel from the back seat and empty rifle case from the trunk. He shook off the glass fragments and dust then examined each of them for bullet holes. Seeing none, he walked to the back of Walton's Tahoe and stowed his gear then slipped out of his slung rifle. He shoved a fresh magazine into the lower receiver and clicked shut the dust cover on the ejection port before placing the gun in front of the driver's seat inside the cabin of the vehicle, the muzzle angled toward the floor alongside the center console.

Killian saw all of this and approached him. "What are you doing?"

Press ducked out of his plate carrier, propped it on the back seat. "Chief Walton has kindly granted me the use of his vehicle."

"For what? Where are you going?"

"Our mission hasn't changed. In fact, it's now more important than ever to get Barnett out of here, get him somewhere safe. I want you, Gabby, and Tank to remain here. This thing is going to generate one heck of an after-action investigation. Here and back home. You know the drill. We're all going to be put on admin. leave. Booth and some people are already en route." By now Gabby and Tank had joined them. "Hang around, answer their questions. It was a good shoot. We all know that. Booth or anyone else gives you crap, you tell them exactly what I just told you. As far as you guys are concerned, you're just following orders."

"Where are you taking him?" Gabby said.

"I'm not sure yet. But he can't stay here." Press looked over at the ambulance. Chief Walton was talking to one of the EMTs as they loaded Fitzpatrick inside and closed the back doors. Turning back, Press looked each of them in the eyes. "I'm proud of the way you guys handled yourselves out here. We didn't choose for things to turn out this way, they did." He pointed toward the trees. "We did what we had to do. No one did anything wrong here except for those hired guns. Don't forget that." Press paused to let them digest his words. "I know we're all tough, but I need to ask. Are we good? Anyone need anything right now? Don't be shy about it if you do."

No one said a word.

"Okay. I'll touch base with y'all after I get this kid someplace safe. In the meantime, if anyone needs anything hit me up. Understood?"

They all nodded.

Press waved Barnett over and directed him to get in the front seat of the Tahoe. He was about to join him when JK grabbed his arm.

"Yeah, bud. What is it?"

"You be safe. You hear?"

Press patted him on the arm. "You know me."

"Yeah, brother. I do."

Press donned a Wolfeboro PD ball cap he'd found inside the vehicle, pulled it low, and ordered Barnett to stay down in his seat until they were well clear of the scene. They were on the road for only two minutes when Barnett said he needed to pull over.

Press massaged the steering wheel, scanning the terrain for suspicious vehicles and characters, as he listened to the kid puke his guts out for close to five minutes. He handed him some napkins from the glove box then hurried him to get back in the car.

A mile further down the road, they passed several news vehicles heading in the opposite direction. This kind of thing just didn't happen in a place like Wolfeboro. It would probably be the lead broadcast for days, maybe even weeks to come.

For the next five miles, Press rigorously checked his mirrors and the road ahead as well as those jutting out at all angles along the way. Anywhere a vehicle could be hidden or gunmen might think to stage another ambush. But he saw nothing that registered as a threat.

Finally, he turned to Barnett. The kid was staring straight ahead, a vacant look on his face. Trauma had that effect on some people.

"You okay?" Press said.

Barnett shifted his gaze from the roadway ahead to the trees zipping past his window.

"I know something like what happened back there can be hard to deal with. Don't try to think about it right now. Just let your mind and body rest. It sometimes helps to think about something else."

Barnett said nothing in response.

"Name's Press. Nate Press. I'm a detective from Providence."

"I know." His voice was flat and weak.

"My team and I came up here because of what happened to Riley Talbert."

Barnett met his gaze for a second then turned back to the windshield.

"I'd like to understand what happened to him and why. I think you can help in that regard. At some point, I'd like to talk to you about it. Once we get to where we're going."

The young man offered a slight nod. A good sign.

Press was pleased that Barnett didn't ask about where that might be, because he, himself, currently had no clue. Before they'd arrived in Wolfeboro, he had made a few calls to several of his trusted contacts within the Rhode Island Attorney General's Office regarding their witness protection program, but they had yet to get back to him. It was trial term, so most of the prosecutors were busy preparing to argue their cases at trial or were already doing so. Thus, he wasn't surprised that no one had called him back yet.

He pulled into a Cumberland Farms store in Hillsboro on account of Barnett needing to use the restroom. While he waited with a watchful eye, he phoned Gentry.

"Man, Nate, you sure know how to piss off the wrong people."

"Why? What's up?"

"Booth is *all* wound up. Shot outta here spewing fire and brimstone. Fantroy, too. Except he's waiting here...for when you show your face. I think he wants to chew it off. That and your backside."

"Yeah, well... I got the kid. He's safe. For now, that is." Though Press knew Gentry would always be in his corner, he didn't want the man's career to suffer harm on his account. He figured Gentry had a good shot at becoming chief someday. "AG's Office hasn't called me back. We need to squirrel this kid away someplace safe."

"He tell you anything yet?"

"No. I'm still trying to earn his confidence. I figure once we get tucked in somewhere, I can go at him then. He's still in shock over what went down by the lake."

"I got you."

An idea came to him as he was eyeing the kid through the convenience store's large front windows. Barnett was standing in line at the register. He looked dejected, his shoulders sloped, eyes straight ahead and seemingly unfocused.

Press voiced his idea to Gentry.

"Well, there's no guarantee they'll help. But I guess it's worth a try. Let me know if you need anything else."

"Will do. Thanks."

"And Nate."

"Yeah?"

"As your supervisor, I need to tell you—"

"I know, I know. Administrative leave garbage."

"I don't have a choice, Nate. It's policy, you know that. And it's just until this stuff from New Hampshire is sorted out."

"Yeah, yeah. Well, let me at least get this kid somewhere safe and take a crack at him. I'll give you a buzz later. You good with that?"

"All right. Call me as soon as you're tucked in and can talk."

"Thanks, Lieu."

Grumpily, Press scrolled through his phone and landed on a stored contact. He tapped on the screen then held the phone to his ear while the call connected, his eyes still on Barnett inside the store.

"Nate. What's up?"

"Hey, Clint, buddy. I need a big favor. And I mean *big*. This is kind of sudden and out of left field, but would the Bureau have someplace out of the way where I can hide a witness?"

"Why? What's going on?" said FBI Assistant Special Agent in Charge Clint Hickman.

"You know the Riley Talbert murder case?"

"Yeah?"

"I've got someone in my custody that is going to blow this thing wide open." Press explained what had happened by the lake in Wolfeboro.

"Holy freakin' cow, dude!"

"So, can you help? This needs to be kept quiet. Some dangerous people are trying to kill this kid. And just about did this morning."

"Okay. I need to do some checking, but yeah, I think we can assist."

"Great. And Clint, utmost discretion. The fewer people that know about this the better. I know you'll do your best."

"Understood. Where are you right now?"

"I'd rather not say over the phone."

"Okay. Give me fifteen minutes and I'll call you back with an address."

"Awesome. Thanks, brother."

"Happy to help. Stay safe."

60

Scituate, Rhode Island

True to his word, Hickman called back in fifteen minutes on the button. He provided an address for a small, ranch-style house on Dorr Road just off Route 14 due west of Providence. It was only about fifteen minutes more to the Gwynn home from here. Press turned onto the narrow, unlined pavement, briefly reflecting on the afternoon he'd spent with Avery and her family. Why hadn't he joined Sunny for a Sunday service sooner?

The tires of the Tahoe kicked up dust as he maneuvered into the dirt-coated driveway. The FBI safe house was nothing fancy and that was probably the point. Just another boring house in an unglamorous quadrant of Rhode Island.

Press threw the vehicle in PARK and stepped out, scanning the wooded surroundings before sizing up the house, which sat in a ring of sunbaked earth and bore the essence of a lonely and forgotten old man. The front door was faded and dull. It may have been burgundy once, but now looked brown with a pinkish hue. The lawn was brown, too, marred by a riot of clover and the occasional dandelion. Small shrubs that were wasting away to nothing dotted the earth along the front of the house.

"Stay here," Press said as he slung his rifle. He walked the home's circumference, checking for any signs of danger. Seeing none, he returned to the back door. Hickman had said there was a key hidden inside a dusty rock near the southeast corner of the house. It didn't take long to find it. Press popped open the fake rock and used the key to enter the back door. A red light flashed from an alarm panel on the wall just inside.

He entered the code Hickman had shared with him and waited till the blinking red light turned solid green.

The house smelled of dust, stale cigarettes, and a trace of cleaning product—the domain of federal agents on babysitting duty. Press imagined them playing cards under a cone of light, veiled in second-hand smoke, their reluctant charge in the middle distance, watching cartoons, a baseball game, or endless re-runs of Law & Order.

The furniture in the living room was purely functional, so too were the appliances in the kitchen. But they were clean and orderly at that's all that mattered in such a setting. The rest of the house was no different. Someone likely tidied up once a month or so. Enough to wipe away the cobwebs and the dust from the surfaces, keep the plumbing in shape, and the house ready to receive the next government witness, intelligence officer preparing for a term abroad, or even a fateful foreign spy waiting to be debriefed.

He wondered if there were cameras secreted in the house. Out of curiosity, Press examined several nearby light fixtures and wall outlets as well as the hallway smoke detector. But the tiny devices could be anywhere, even buried inside walls and ceilings. He would just have to take his chances.

Barnett was still obediently seated in the Tahoe when he returned out front. Press stepped close to his car door, waved him out. "C'mon. Back door's open. I already checked out the house. It's safe."

Press removed his briefcase and other gear as Barnett looked on in silence. He led him around back and through the unlocked door, dropped his stuff on the floor next to the sofa. Barnett stood stock still halfway between the living room and kitchen, seemingly unsure what to do next.

"Make yourself comfortable, Seth. There's no telling how long we're going to be here."

"Do my parents know that I'm okay? I'd like to let them know if I may."

"I understand. We'll contact them when it's safe to do so. But first, I'd like to sit down and hear your side of what it is that has everybody so hellbent on finding you. Are you up to talking for a bit?"

Barnett had the tired eyes of a man who'd been running on fumes. Press had seen the same exhausted features in fugitives who had been hiding from the long arm of the law for weeks and months on end. The difference between Barnett and those fugitives was the absence of a defiant fire in his belly to mask the fatigue. The only thing Press could see in Barnett was a mix of relief and anxiety. Not uncommon for someone in his position. Now to go about the careful extraction of information that would solve his case or at least unearth some fruitful leads.

Press walked into the kitchen. The cabinets were mostly bare, save for a bounty of K-cups and a slim variety of canned soups, baked beans, and other foodstuffs that could be stored for long stretches of time without spoiling.

"Care for some coffee or tea?"

"Coffee, please."

Press fired up the machine on the counter and examined one of the pods. It indicated a medium roast blend from Ethiopia. "This looks promising." He grabbed another one and popped them one at a time into the coffeemaker. "How do you like yours?"

"Black with two scoops of sugar."

"Perfect. Because the only cream in this joint," Press held up a canister with a faded red label, "is this *powdered* crap."

A few minutes onward, he and Barnett were seated at the modest dining-room table beneath a hanging, faux-brass light fixture with bulbs that resembled candles, each of them cradling a chipped enamel mug. Press took a sip from his and let the liquid register to his palate. "Mmm. You know, that's not bad."

"Thank you...for saving my life, I mean."

"Part of my job, Seth. Happy to do it." Press lowered his mug halfway to the table.

"The officer that died..." He trailed off, but his eyes said it all.

"Bowersox."

"That other officer said he had a family."

Press patiently waited.

"I'd like to tell them that I'm sorry...and thank you."

"I'm sure that would mean a lot to them. We'll see that you get the chance at some point down the road. As police officers we know that there may come a time in our careers in which we might have to sacrifice our lives so that others might live. Bowersox knew it. We all do."

Barnett was staring into his steaming mug.

"So, let's not let his sacrifice be in vain." Press gently continued. "How about we start at the beginning?"

Barnett nodded solemnly.

Press held up a small, digital voice recorder he had withdrawn from his briefcase. "You mind if I record our conversation?"

"No."

The narrative that followed was nothing short of earth-shattering. Press could scarcely believe the significance of Barnett's account. And yet despite the magnitude of the moment, he willed himself to remain steadfast and clinical throughout his examination. The kid obviously knew this was explosive stuff, he didn't need further drama injected into the situation.

"Why'd you pick Riley Talbert?"

"Based on my research, I knew he had the legal chops to handle this and the honor and integrity to be unaffected by the media and the political firestorm that was sure to follow. The moment and the subject matter wouldn't be too big for him. Add to that the fact that he was one of the best criminal defense attorneys in the country *and* was right in my own backyard."

Barnett's voice grew softer. "This may sound strange of me to ask, but... How did he die? I saw on the news that he was murdered, but no details were given."

"Technically, he died from a heart attack, but for all intents and purposes, he was beaten to death."

Barnett sighed heavily. "All because of me."

"You didn't kill him, Seth. Those men did. Don't blame yourself for the actions—the *evil deeds*—of others." Press felt sorry him. Carrying the burden of another man's death, whatever the cause and whatever the justification, was no easy thing. "Who chose the zoo for the meeting spot?"

"I did. I've always liked it there. And I wanted a place that was public yet discreet...in case I was being followed. Talbert was one of the zoo's biggest donors, so it wouldn't have seemed out of character for him to visit as well."

"How did you initially communicate with him?"

"In person. I watched him for a few weeks, so I knew he frequented the GPub on Friday evenings after work. I waited until he went to the restroom then made my move. He was incredibly gracious and agreed right away to meet with me the following Sunday afternoon at the zoo."

Press considered mentioning the letter Talbert had written him but then decided against it. "You gave him a flash drive?"

"For him to review and vet my findings. And for the sake of redundancy, I suppose."

"How many total digital copies are there?"

"Three. The original, of course... I'd decided to keep it with me at all times. One copy I kept in my gear—I was planning to hide it somewhere up at the lake house. I can only assume you guys or those other men have it now."

"And the other copy you gave to Talbert?"

Barnett nodded. "I gave it to him during our meeting at the zoo. I suppose it's a dumb question, but you didn't happen to find it, did you?"

"No. And to my knowledge, we don't have the one you left in your stuff back at the lake house either." Press sensed he already knew the answer to his next question. "What about the original? Where is it now?"

Barnett sunk in his chair. "I must have lost it somehow when I was running from those men. I wore it around my neck on a leather shoestring."

"What exactly is on those drives?"

"*Everything*. Those data files are going to put a lot of people behind bars. Every state in the Union will be forced to open investigations. Probably a few foreign countries, too. The public is going to be livid. Of course, that's assuming the files ever see the light of day."

When Press could think of no more specific questions, he asked his old standby, "Is there anything you've left out, anything else you think is important that I should know?"

Barnett shook his head. "I knew there would be repercussions, but I never meant for any of this to happen."

"No, I'm sure you didn't." Press twisted the ends of his pen with the index finger and thumb of each hand as he thought.

"I debated early on between keeping quiet and doing something. I kept coming back to Ocean's father and my neighbor. You know about Ocean, right?"

"Yes."

Barnett now teetered with emotion. "I broke up with her because of this, you know. For her safety. I never told her why I..." A tear slid down his face.

"Tell me about your neighbor."

Barnett composed himself. "Growing up I had this neighbor: Miss Irene—that's what everyone called her. She was elderly and lived alone, kept her house immaculate...like a museum. Anyway, she had this room. It was full of all kinds of interesting things: medals, patches, pins, framed citations, challenge coins, some foreign flags, and other items that documented her son's incredible military service. Above the fireplace, there was a folded flag—an *American* flag—and next to that was a small, framed banner. The banner was plain white with a band of red that ran around its edges. In the center of the banner was a gold star.

"When I was about twelve years old, I asked her what the gold star on the banner meant. Do you know what she said?"

"Her son was killed in combat."

Barnett seemed to have renewed energy. It was obvious that this was the thing motivating him, the source of his drive. "She said it symbolized the sacrifice her family had made for our country. For America. For *my* family. For *me*."

The weight of the story as told by a computer nerd from Wisconsin materialized in Press's throat.

"I have never forgotten those words. And I hope I never do."

Press swallowed. "Powerful stuff."

"Do you know about Ocean's dad?"

"Yeah, I do."

"That's why I did what I did. And while it pales in comparison to my neighbor's sacrifice, the lives her son and Ocean's father gave for this country, *this* is my sacrifice. I felt it was my duty to do something. What they were doing wasn't right. It was criminal. It was *wrong*."

Press clicked off the recorder, pushed aside his notepad and pen, and for a moment the two of them sat in silence.

Barnett's shoulders finally sagged, his eyelids hung halfway closed. "I'm tired."

"There's a bedroom back the hall. Why don't you go lie down. My FBI friend will be here soon. We'll get all of this sorted out. I promise you."

61

Press watched him push back from the table and shuffle from the room. Before this morning, Seth Barnett had been just another slippery witness in another difficult murder case, albeit one that involved a dangerous cast of professional killers. But now, knowing everything Barnett had done, the steps he'd taken to investigate and document the massive criminal conspiracy he had stumbled upon despite the obvious personal risks, Press had a whole new respect for the man.

And yet now there was a huge problem. All that documentation might never see the light of day. Barnett had lost the flash drive he wore around his neck. The backup copy he had secreted in his computer bag and left in the house back in Wolfeboro might still be there but more likely had been snatched up by the shooters. Press was pretty sure it was a lost cause, but he needed to check regardless.

He phoned JK.

"Yes?"

"It's me. Can you talk?" Press didn't want any of the brass from his department or Wolfeboro's, and especially not the people from the Office of

Professional Responsibility, colloquially known as internal affairs, listening in on their conversation. Neither he nor any of his squad mates had anything to hide, but a direct order from a superior to come in and relinquish his firearms and sit for a battery of lengthy interviews would hamper his plans, at least in the short term. He was already in violation of a handful of departmental policies, but so far, with the unusual circumstances and Barnett's safety and security being paramount, he could likely talk his way out of trouble. But any leeway he had would not last forever.

"Nate, it's an absolute circus. OPR has already placed all of us on admin leave. The FIT team is up here tearing things apart. They've taken our weapons, ordered us to stay put, and submit to interviews. Have they gotten to you yet?"

"Not yet."

"The whole thing is one giant cluster."

"Then I'll be quick. I don't want them to catch wind of my talking to you. Mantoy's had it out for me for as long as I've been with the department. So, listen. Did the locals search the house yet?"

"Yeah. Well, the state police did a couple of hours ago."

"They find anything? Laptop, computer bag, flash drives, that type of thing?"

"I don't think so. From what I've been able to gather, it was pretty cleaned out. Why? What's up?"

"I was afraid of that. Okay. I interviewed the kid."

"Yeah? What'd he have to say?"

Press frowned into the phone. "It's bad, JK. *Really* bad." He quickly explained the nuts and bolts of their conversation. After he'd finished, Killian emitted a low whistle. "I need you to check the area up there for that flash drive."

"I don't know, Nate. They've got that scene locked down tight. I don't think any of us is getting anywhere near that place any time soon especially with the FIT team guys breathing down our necks."

Press sighed. "You're right. Well, any chance you can get word to one of the troopers? It's a long shot, but unless I find the flash drive Barnett gave Talbert, it might be our only chance of getting our hands on any hard proof of the conspiracy and thus Talbert's and Barb Stanley's killers."

"Understood. I'll do my best."

"Good deal. How are Gabby and Tank doing?"

"They're fine. Bummed like me about being put in timeout."

Press grinned. "I hear ya. Well, keep your spirits up. Y'all did a phenomenal job. When I get the chance, I'm going to write letters to the Commendation Board for each of you." He didn't give JK time to be humble. "All right, brother. I'll holler at you when I can."

He switched his phone to airplane mode, so the brass couldn't reach him even if they tried—and when he was interviewed down the road, he could honestly say he had never received any messages—then pushed his phone inside his pants pocket and stared at the ceiling.

The Force Investigation Team (FIT) was a panel of three PPD officers, whose job it was to investigate any incident involving the use of force that was likely to cause serious bodily injury or death even if no injury actually occurred. The panel consisted of a Weapons Bureau training instructor, a representative from OPR, and an officer who was specifically designated by the chief of police. As acting chief, Denny Fantroy would surely designate one of his "special people," to the team. Someone he was sure would eagerly do his bidding, to wit, bring the wild and reckless Detective Sergeant Nathan Press to heel.

Press spent the next thirty minutes feverishly scribbling notes in his legal pad while the information from his interview with Barnett was still fresh in his mind. Notes were crucial. He had no idea when he would be able to sit down and type out his many reports. Such was the life of a busy police detective.

The soft thud of a car door drew his attention. Pistol in hand, Press stepped quickly to the darkened window at the front of the house and peered through a crack in the shades. A figure swept through the shadows en route to the front door.

For another couple of beats, Press scanned the man's vehicle and then the road beyond in either direction.

Holding his gun by his thigh as he opened the door, Press allowed Clint Hickman into the house. Once the door was closed and locked, he holstered the pistol and returned to the dining-room table.

Hickman's eyes greedily searched every nook and cranny available to him but in a casual way before landing on the coffee machine on the counter. "Where is he?"

"In the bedroom."

"How's he holding up?"

"He's exhausted."

"I bet," said Hickman, walking to the machine. He studied it for a second then began pressing buttons. He stood with his hands on the counter as the contraption began hissing and spitting hot, dark liquid.

Press finished putting a few more thoughts to paper. "He's got an incredible story to tell."

"Yeah?" Hickman carried his steaming coffee to the table, blew into the mug, and motioned toward Press's battered face, the bandage on the back of his head. "What the heck happened to you?"

"Blanket party and I was the guest of honor."

"Ouch." Hickman eased into the chair across from him, pointed at the notepad. "May I?"

Press nodded. "If you can read my chicken scratch."

The FBI man pulled the pad toward him, rotated it on the table.

"The Bureau is going to want to be in on this. DHS, too," Press said.

Hickman's eyes narrowed. "Why?"

"Just listen." Press set the digital recorder on the table and pressed PLAY.

62

The sounds of rustling papers and a creaking chair burst forth. Press held up his hand, signaling to wait a moment, and quickly adjusted the volume on the digital recorder just as his own voice declared the date, time, and setting of the interview followed by the names of the principals involved. Next, he announced that the interview was being conducted pursuant to the murder investigation of Riley Talbert and recited the relevant case number.

Press and Hickman relaxed back in their chairs, each of them staring at the recorder on the table as the interview played out.

Press had set the stage by first asking Barnett about his education and employment background. Once all that was established, the real questions began.

"Tell me about Riley Talbert."

"He was a lawyer that I hired."

"For what purpose?"

"I wanted legal protection and also someone I could trust to look out for my interests." A brief pause. "Through my employment with Donstar, I learned that various actors were conspiring to deceive the public."

"How so?"

"They were going to rig elections by manipulating the voting machines Donstar was contracted to certify."

"Please explain."

"How much do you know about how elections work in this country?"

"Assume very little," said Press.

Barnett sighed. "So, theoretically, you show up on Election Day, fill out your paper ballot, feed it into the electronic voting machine where it's recorded and logged, and you go home and await the results on the nightly news. Right?

"In practice, there is a lot more going on with a lot of room to cheat. Without getting too deep in the technological weeds—there are a lot of moving pieces to this criminal conspiracy...things like qualified voter files, electronic poll books, mail-in ballots, and signature verification...all of that stuff requires co-conspirators or at a minimum pliable people put in key positions of trust in various states and counties around the country—but where I come in is with the voting machines.

"Donstar was tapped to perform the certification testing on the latest and greatest batch of AccuTab vote tabulators, which were designed and built by a company called Ascendant Election Systems, or AES. Donstar was also to certify AES's election management systems and network devices. Everything runs on SecurMark 5.0, a software suite that was allegedly designed by AES systems engineers."

"What do you mean allegedly?"

"I'll get to that in a minute," Barnett said.

"Now, just so you have all the background...Janelle Holt, Donstar's president and CEO, used to work for AES. In fact, she was one of the very engineers who designed the AccuTab machines and their management systems."

"Isn't that a conflict of interest?"

"To any honest, reasonably intelligent person it is. However, sadly, as I've come to find out, it's business as usual for the election-industrial complex.

"Fast forward to the certification process. Whether Holt was too busy running the company, or she wanted to avoid the appearance of impropriety, or maybe it was to have some measure of deniability in the event some curious citizen journalist did some digging, she tasked Albert...uh, Albert Roten, that is...to do all the hands-on testing. It would be his name that would appear on all the certification documentation.

"Albert had worked at Donstar for years. He was smart and loyal...a true professional. Unlike a lot of people in the tech industry, he wasn't political, just went about his work with quiet modesty and class. Perhaps that's one of the reasons we became fast friends.

"At some point during the initial testing, Albert came across something that he just could not make sense of. It was a series of complex algorithms in the source code that seemed to have no legitimate purpose. At least none that he could discern."

"What happened?" said Press.

"Though against protocol, Albert quietly came to me since I have a strong background in both coding and deconstructing network systems...what some people might call troubleshooting. I'm also an expert in white-hat hacking. At first, I, too, didn't understand why the code was there in such a software. But as I played around with it, I realized something: the code's object...it's intended purpose. It was specifically designed to alter votes and in a number of different ways.

"First, I found when the overall vote tally in the machine reached a certain value, the votes for candidate X would suddenly be worth half the value of votes for candidate Y. Next, I discovered a feature that would allow for the fractionalizing of votes based on a set of variables prescribed by an authorized user. Really anyone with an administrative password could log in to the management system and activate this specific algorithm at any point in the process. So, for example, a person could set vote ratios to say 0.67 to one, or 0.25 to one."

"Why on earth would a system be designed to fractionalize votes? One vote should equal one vote, period."

"Exactly right. Why? The only answer is to make it possible to cheat. But that's not the end of it. I also found source code that would cause votes to completely flip if a certain threshold ratio were to be reached in the tabulation. To keep it simple, if the ballot threshold was set for 400 and at that time candidate X had 100 votes and candidate Y had 300 votes, the algorithm would flip the totals. Candidate X would suddenly have 300 and Y would have 100."

Press interjected, "But there are paper ballots. How would they explain the discrepancies between the computer tallies and the paper ballots if there were ever a recount?"

"Enter the recent push for mail-in ballots and ballot drop boxes on street corners. And the abandonment of signature verification. And the need to extend vote-counting days or even weeks. If, based on the voting machine computers and my remote access, I know what the vote numbers are in real-time in any given election, I can backfill paper ballots into the system even after voting has ended. In fact, I might conjure up a reason to halt all counting for a spell in order to give my accomplices time to dump more paper ballots into the system, say a power outage or some kind of emergency. See how that works? Realistically though, you only need a few key people in a handful of counties and states to make an election go your way. Easier still if you own or control the company producing the mail-in ballots.

"Finally, I discovered a line of code that would do two things if the system was accessed remotely in a particular fashion. In effect, it was a kill code. One, it would delete all the vote-altering algorithms. And two, it would wipe the entire audit trail, so there would be no trace of the cheat."

"Let me get this straight. The tabulators and management systems are all connected to the internet?"

"A hundred percent. All the AES products allow for remote network access. Each can also be accessed locally via a USB drive. Bottom line: Anyone with an administrative password can access the system and trigger these algorithms at any point in the process. And I haven't even touched on the capabilities of nefarious foreign actors. Anyone in the cyber community with half a brain could design something far more secure. You don't create a vote tabulation system with this many glaring vulnerabilities and bizarre algorithms—what AES calls features—unless you want to cheat at elections. It's without a doubt intentional."

There was a pause and a perceptible scratching noise on the recording that was the result of Press scribbling notes into his pad. "So, what happened? How did Albert end up dead?"

Barnett's voice hardened. "He trusted Dr. Holt, that's how. See, he didn't know about her background and neither did I until my subsequent digging. Before AES, she worked for the CIA. She was one of their tech wizards. In fact—and I can prove it with the information I uncovered—while at CIA she was the one who designed the first version of the SecurMark software though it had a different name then. See, the CIA has been using it to manipulate elections overseas for years."

Press's headshaking could not be heard on the recording, nevertheless he found himself doing the same thing yet again as he stared across the table at Hickman, who bore the appearance of someone studying a hand of cards without revealing a trace of his internal monologue.

"Albert went to Dr. Holt with all of this—not the CIA stuff mind you, just the things about the cheat code I had found. He told her that he could not certify the machines and that he was considering going to the authorities. They argued quite vehemently. She directed him to certify them anyway, that she would give him a big, fat bonus, and that his future would be set for life. But he had to keep what he knew quiet.

"*Afterward, he came to me, shared everything. In a weird kind of way, he may have been trying to protect himself in the event something happened to him, I don't know. Whatever the reason, I can tell you that he didn't want to fabricate a report for certification, but he also didn't want to ruin his career either. For a brief time, he waivered. He considered taking the money and going along with her orders. But in the end, I convinced him to do the right thing. He went back to Dr. Holt and said he would not certify the machines. She told him to take a week off and think about it some more.*"

"That's when he went out west?"

"*Yeah. To Colorado. He loved to climb.*" Barnett's voice grew louder. "*They killed him. I know it in my soul. I can't prove it, but I know they killed him somehow. He was an expert climber. Grew up in Switzerland.*"

"So, what happened next?"

"*Dr. Holt gave me the AES assignment. But I already knew what I was going to do. I began digging and digging. And logging everything I found. I even placed a keylogger program on Dr. Holt's machine, accessed her cell phones and personal computers.*"

"That's why you needed an attorney."

"*Right. I was going to blow the whistle on their whole stinkin' operation. I had accessed Dr. Holt's emails, phone calls, text and voice-mail messages, her bank accounts. Everything. I knew for instance that she received nearly twenty million dollars from a shell corporation based in the British Virgin Islands. Money which she promptly deposited in an offshore account she has in the Seychelles.*"

"What's so special about Donstar? Is it because Holt is in their pocket?"

"*Yes, but also because Donstar is a federally accredited laboratory per the EAC—the Election Assistance Commission.*"

"Who verifies the accreditation?" asked Press.

"*It doesn't matter. It's all a meaningless pile of horse crap. What I mean is that the accreditation process is comprised of an incestuous web of politicians, federal employees, and corporations to whom they are beholden, including voting machine vendor companies like AES. Dr. Holt was paid to make sure the AES machines were certified, period. Albert's refusing to carry out her wishes threatened to undermine everything. It was going to bring down their entire house of cards."*

"But why try to rig elections? Why take that kind of risk?"

"One word. Power. *Marty Kendall wasn't supposed to win the presidential election last year. But he did. This was going to be their way of assuring that no election here in America would ever again be outside their control."*

Press said, *"Now for the big question... Who's* they? *Kendall is a Republican, so does that mean the Democrats are behind this?"*

Though there was no evidence of this on the recording, Barnett adamantly shook his head. Only his voice could be heard. *"You have to understand something. The* they *is a tight little cabal of elites from* both *political parties and their shadowy puppet masters. They're globalists. They want a* New World Order, *one without national borders or a pesky Constitution or duly elected government officials legitimately voted into office by the people to represent them in free and fair elections. They're all in on it together. And they will do* anything *to cover this up. Count on it. Just look at what they've tried to do to me already. That's why I contacted Riley Talbert and why I ran. Talbert was an honest man, a feisty litigator, and someone who could not be bought at any price. I did my homework on him."*

63

It was here during the interview playback that Hickman's phone vibrated inside his jacket pocket. Press paused the recording and noted the word "Restricted" on the phone's screen as Hickman quickly accepted the call and brought it to his ear.

"Yes? Yeah, it's all good. I'm here with him now. Of course, no worries. We're still a go." He switched the phone to his right ear, glanced down at his watch. "Understood. Okay. I got it. Bye." Hickman returned the phone to his jacket. "Sorry about that. My boss, the consummate worrier." He adjusted himself in the chair. "The Marshals will be here soon to take custody of the kid."

"Marshals?"

"Yeah. I pulled some strings. They've agreed to accept the kid into their WITSEC program for the time being. The Marshals Service is the best organization in the world at protecting witnesses, bar none. They'll keep him safe somewhere for as long as we need them to."

Press nodded and resumed the playback.

His was the first voice to be heard as the recording recommenced. "*There has got to be someone pulling all the strings. Someone coordinating everything. Do you have any idea who that is?*"

Barnett spoke in a self-confident tone. "*That's the trillion-dollar question. And the answer is yes, I do. Throughout all my digging,*" Press interpreted this to mean *hacking*, "*one name kept coming up over and over.*"

"*And that is?*"

"*Henrik Vandenberg.*"

"*Vandenberg. Who's he?*" said Press.

"*The short version is, he's money. Lots of it. In the late eighties, Henrik Vandenberg co-founded the Brayden Group, a multinational private equity, alternative asset management, and financial services corporation in DC. Right after 9/11, his company moved heavily into the arena of the military-industrial complex. Made tons—I'm talking* tons—*of money on the Global War on Terror. By 2010, Brayden had become the world's third largest private equity firm. Last year, it moved into the number one spot.*

"*The Brayden Group uses all kinds of political relationships for financial gain. And they are not bound by party affiliation either. Brayden, along with its host of subsidiaries, employs loads of former government types from secretaries of state and treasury to foreign ministers. Brayden even hires former intelligence service directors and officers, and not just from the United States. It's how Brayden weasels into governments and industries alike worldwide. They own large banks on six continents. They've got assets everywhere.*

"*You ever hear of Green Castle, Inc.?*"

"*No,*" said Press.

"*Green Castle is Robert Brenner's private intelligence firm. Brayden financed it, in fact.*"

"*Robert Brenner...the former CIA deputy director?*"

"*That's the one. Remember what I said about Janelle Holt and the Secur-Mark software? The early version of that software—before it was rebranded*

SecurMark by AES—was developed by Janelle Holt when she worked at the CIA. It was called Evergreen and guess who the project lead was at the time."

"Robert Brenner."

"The one and only. He's bad news. Helped rig elections overseas for years. In South America, Europe, Southeast Asia. SecurMark 5.0 is just a brand-new version of Evergreen, and it's designed to fix elections here in America."

"How do you know all this?"

"I like to dig. And I know how to do it without leaving a trail." Barnett could be heard sipping his coffee. "The Brayden Group is linked to all kinds of powerful corporations, banks, hospitals, pharmaceutical- and medical-supply companies, NGOs and think tanks, past and present office holders—at every level of government, too—and even, you guessed it...voting machine companies like AES."

"But why the need to rig elections now if they already have their hands in everything?"

"Because President Kendall has vowed to expose all of the filthy corruption in our government, the Deep State...the Swamp. He's popular with a large majority of Americans and has been building a strong platform of other like-minded candidates to run at every level of government with the objective of returning the power back to the people and away from the insidious gang of globalist elites. That's why those who gather in Davos and Brussels—wine-party snobs from both parties here in the States as well as the open-borders crowd in Europe and abroad—hate him so much. Kendall is a threat to their power structure and global influence. And he's not one to back down or apologize for American greatness."

"So, you control elections, you control the country."

"And states, and counties, and courts, heck, even school boards, district attorneys, and sheriffs. If you can control the vote counting in elections, you control elections. And thus, you control people."

"And you were going to expose all that."

"*I was. I am.*"

Press said, "*So, that's why they abducted Riley Talbert, beat him to death. They were after information on how to get to you.*"

"*No doubt about it. Somehow, they must have found out, or maybe just assumed, that Albert had confided in me. They were probably following me and that's how they learned of my contacting Mr. Talbert. Then, when I disappeared, they figured he knew where to find me.*"

Press clicked off the recording, the word "professionals" flashing in his mind. It all made sense now.

He ran through the entire case for Hickman's benefit: the letter, the Riley Talbert scene, the autopsy, his torched SUV, what the homeless man had said of the men who dumped Talbert's body, the assassination of Barb Stanley, the deadly scrape in his own home, the raging gun battle along the shore of Lake Winnipesaukee. It was all so unreal. And yet it *was* real.

Very real.

A silence descended upon them for several minutes as Press committed some more thoughts to paper. It was a lot to digest all at one time.

Finally, Hickman said, "So you really don't know where Talbert kept that drive—the one he wanted to give you?"

"No." A pause prompted him to look up from his notepad. When he did, Press found himself staring into the business end of Hickman's Glock. "What are you doing?"

"You had to keep digging, didn't you, Nate. Had to keep pushing and pushing. You've been a thorn in our side from the beginning."

"*You're* mixed up in this?" said Press with genuine surprise.

"The funny part is that all this time we've been waiting for the kid to pop up on the grid with that burner phone he'd bought at Walmart. But either he's smart—figured out a way to use it without being tracked—or just never got around to powering it on." He grunted. "And then you and that girlfriend of his lead us right to him. Precious." His smile grew into something sinister. "All because that dumb attorney went and died on us. If I had been the one to dispose of his body, it never would have been found. But thankfully this can still be cleaned up. And that's exactly what I intend to do."

Press vividly recalled Riley Talbert's ominous warning. *Trust no one.* Anger and adrenaline coursed through him. He'd led them right to Seth Barnett.

Hickman's phone buzzed again. "Yeah," he said in answer. "We're good here. Come on in."

A few beats later, the front door swung open and in walked two men who formed the most unusual pair. The shorter one was thin and rangy with a pate of premature gray hair—the same guy who had greeted him at the door of the lake house. His partner was big and muscled and mean-looking—a monster of a man. Trotting in behind them was a third individual, who Press immediately registered as being one of the two gunmen in the green sedan that chased after him and Barnett while they were astride the dirt bike.

Professionals.

All three men bore murderous faces. But it was the look on the big guy's face that caused him to offer a quick and earnest prayer to his Maker. These men weren't just going to kill him, they were going to make sure he died a painful, gruesome death.

Clint Hickman saw it, too—the determined look of a man intent on killing even with his bare hands. Especially with his bare hands. Marcus Zug plowed forward, swept him out of the way and grabbed Press by the shirt, lifted him out of the chair and held him in the air. A massive fist the size of a car battery was already heading for his face.

Press jerked his head to the side at the last minute, and in so doing, managed to avoid a direct hit. Nevertheless, the blow was severe. Another found his stomach and instantly caused him to want to wretch.

"No, Marcus!" yelled Hickman. "You and Lance get the kid. He's back in the bedroom. Brenner wants him on the island ASAP. I'll take care of things here."

Press lay on the floor, coughing and spitting blood onto the worn, patterned linoleum.

"I know you want vengeance for your teammates, but you have a job to do."

There was no way Press could have known that Gus Evans had been shot dead in the New Hampshire woods by Gabby Ibarra or that Vinnie Trich had succumbed to his wounds on the furious drive away from the lakeside gun battle. Reports would later reveal this information along with the names of the two men Morty Sherman had killed inside his home, to wit, Damian Rogowicz and Hector Maldonado. Nevertheless, the desire for revenge poured from the eyes of the big man called Marcus.

"Eddie, you stay here. I'm going to need you to help dispose of the body and get rid of the vehicle out front."

Eddie Olsen nodded, his eyes also morbidly fixated on Press.

Press wheezed and coughed, trying to draw enough oxygen into his lungs to not pass out, thus there was nothing he could do as the odd couple hustled back the hall and exploded into the room in which Seth Barnett was currently asleep.

There were a few seconds filled with primal screams, the sound of furniture scraping violently against the floor. Grunts and growls, too. Those, Press naturally assumed came from Marcus the Beast. Finally, a sickening thud put a morbid end to it all.

With blood now streaking his cheek, Press managed to raise his head in time to see the big guy marching from the bedroom and out the front door, an unconscious Seth Barnett flung over his shoulder.

A dark, sinking feeling of dread set in. Press felt as if he were being pulled toward a bottomless chasm of fatalistic despair. He had to resist. He could not give in.

He would never give in.

64

Hickman and Olsen stood in tandem, looking down at him. Press had finally caught his breath but now had a pounding headache caused by the vicious blow Marcus had dealt him. He had to fight through it and keep his wits about him.

Hickman tossed a pair of handcuffs on the floor in front of him. "Put them on. Slowly. You make a move for your pistol, and I'll shoot you dead right now."

Still on his knees, Press reluctantly reached for them, conscious that any sudden movement could result in a bullet being fired into his forehead. That would be worse than the headache but perhaps only marginally so. He slipped his left wrist inside the cold steel of the Peerless handcuff and ratcheted it closed. His eyes locked on Hickman's, he repeated the action, clicking the second cuff onto his right wrist.

"So, when did they buy *you*?" Press said.

Hickman wrinkled his nose, still pointing his Glock at Press's face though he had now lowered his arm to waist level. "It's not entirely what you think, Nate."

"'Not entirely.' Rationalize it any way you like, Clint. You're a dirty, rotten Fed. That's what I think. Talbert was a good man. You killed him. And Barb Stanley. And this kid? You're going to murder him, too."

"And his girlfriend, yes. But this is about more than just money, old friend."

"I know. It's about power."

Hickman offered a knowing grin. "They're going to make me director someday."

"Riiiight."

"No, seriously. In another couple years, I'm going to be the director of the FBI."

"It's only cost you your soul. I don't get it, Clint. You were a good guy. A dogged investigator. The epitome of a hard-nosed, intelligent FBI special agent. What happened? Where did it all go wrong?"

"'All go wrong'... Listen to you."

"More than that, we were friends. I know your wife and kids for crying out loud."

"Well...things happen in life. You have to take your opportunities when they present themselves. Brenner made me an offer I just couldn't refuse."

"Brenner. What a sack of—"

"Enough talking!" Hickman inclined his head to Olsen, who up until now had been standing a few paces off to the side, watching for Press to make the slightest wrong move. "Get his gun."

Olsen glanced back to Hickman then shuffled around the table toward Press.

Clint Hickman was right in a way. You had to take your opportunities when they presented themselves. And in that very moment, as Olsen crossed between him and Hickman, momentarily stepping into the path of the gun, Press took his.

He launched himself upward, lowering his head and driving his shoulder into Olsen's abdomen. The angle and violence of action created enough leverage to thrust Olsen off his feet and straight back into Hickman. A shot rang out just before the three men tumbled as one pile of humanity onto the floor and slid harshly into the wall. A framed print above them fell and disappeared into the scrum.

Press found himself in the mount position over the man Hickman called Eddie. With his hands cuffed, Press made an awkward and desperate fighter. Yet fight he did. He swung his fists in unison over and over, Olsen's head suffering the brunt of the blows. Blood poured from the man's shattered nose and a wide gash that one of the steel handcuffs had carved on his forehead. The man gasped and heaved, spewing blood that had run into his eyes, across his mouth, and down his chin and neck. Press didn't know for sure if Eddie was armed or not, but assumed he was, and therefore he did not relent in his onslaught of hammer fists and all-out fury. In fact, he only became more frenzied with each blow.

Olsen was caught on his back as Press pounded away, swinging his arms in unison because of the cuffs. Nevertheless, Olsen connected a number of good punches to Press's face and an elbow to the side of his head. Press momentarily saw stars and collapsed to the floor, but just that quickly consciousness returned and so did his will to win.

Eager to press his advantage, Olsen rolled to his knee and put a hand to the floor, preparing to stand. Press saw an opening and flung his locked wrists over the man's exposed head, sinking them deep around his neck. Olsen immediately tried to squirm out of the hold. To counter this, Press swung his body around to gain better leverage and squeezed with everything he had in him. Olsen flipped and twisted like a fish trying to throw a hook. He rocked his body this way and that. But Press only cinched his arms tighter, adjusting his hips to apply even more torque. Olsen soon became docile, yet Press did not release his grip, thinking the man might be faking. And he was glad he didn't, because suddenly, Olsen's body came alive like it had been electrocuted.

Press's arm muscles burned. He couldn't go on like this forever. And what of Hickman? Where was he? Press shot his eyes around the room but Olsen's biting, kicking, and violent flailing forced him back to his current predicament.

He had to end this. Now.

Press felt a sudden renewed strength as a surge of adrenaline coursed through him. In one quick motion, he shifted his hips and swung his leg to the side. This caused both men to rotate in tandem. Press rolled on top of the man, who was still locked within his iron grip. He squeezed with his whole body, planted his shoulder into the top of the man's spine and torqued his arms and hips with lightning quickness. There was a grotesque crack and instantly Press felt his opponent's neck go slack on the body. All life seemed to have left him.

Press waited a beat till he was sure the man was out of the fight for good then released his grasp and pushed him away with disgust. He did not examine his kill. He had to find Hickman who was probably standing spectator to the fierce brawl just waiting to shoot him when he got the chance.

Press rolled to his feet expecting to engage the FBI man in similar close-quarters battle. Instead, he found Hickman with his head propped up against the wall right where he had fallen when the fight began. His shirt was soaked through with blood. His face was ashen and clammy. Eyes unfocused and blinking lazily.

When Press had smashed into Olsen and Hickman, the gun must have been forced backward into Hickman's chest. The wound track appeared to be longitudinal. The bullet had apparently entered the area of his right lung and dove downward across his entire abdominal cavity. Press didn't see an exit wound but the expanding pool of blood on the floor beneath him indicated it was somewhere on the man's lower back. Hickman's internal organs were obviously in bad shape. Death was not far off. And it would come with considerable pain.

Press's breathing soon calmed. A keyring with a handcuff key was hooked to his gear bag. He retrieved it and freed himself from the cuffs.

Press glanced at Olsen, who was sprawled on the floor, his head twisted at an unnatural angle, eyes half-shut and glazed over, staring emotionlessly into eternity.

He turned his attention back to Hickman. Blood continued to spread across the floor beneath him. He would be dead soon. There was nothing anyone could do to help him.

Press walked over to him. With each fading breath Hickman drew in came a phlegmy arrhythmic sound as blood continued to flood into his lungs.

"I'm...dying, Nate."

"Yeah, Clint. You are."

"For what...it's worth...I'm sorry." His face was relaxed and resolved to death. "I love...my...family... I did it...for them."

That was all BS. He did it for one man: Clint Hickman.

Press knelt. "Tell me where they're taking the kid. He has a family, too. Help me end this."

Hickman coughed blood. He grimaced as pain wracked his body.

"Clint. You can help make this right. Do it for Yvonne and Jenna and James."

Tears gathered in the corners of his eyes at the mention of his wife and kids. He swallowed and coughed some more.

"*Clint!*"

A blood-streaked hand inched off the floor, beckoning. Press took hold of it.

"Where, Clint?"

"Okay."

Press leaned closer, clicked on the digital recorder in his left hand, and listened. When he had captured it all, he said, "The kid. Is any of what he said true?"

"Every...word."

"And Albert Roten?"

"Janelle...told Brenner. He had him...killed. Tampered...with his gear...so it...would look like...an accident. Lance and Marcus...did the deed."

"They work for Brenner?"

"Yeah." Hickman's face scrunched up as a wave of pain tormented him. When it had passed, he squeaked, "Lance Cheney. Marcus...Zug. I... I...was there, too. Stayed at...Chipeta Lodge. Under alias...Tim Nelson. Should be records."

"Talbert. Who killed him?"

"Lance...and Marcus... Died...right when...they started...working...on him. His heart...just like you said. He just...keeled over on them."

"And they dumped his body where?"

Hickman swallowed, his eyes slamming shut as more pain came with a vengeance. "Behind the...math place."

Right where Bermuda Bob had seen two men toss Talbert into the water.

For another half a minute, there was silence save for Hickman's raspy, exaggerated gasps for air.

"I'm sorry, Nate."

Press nodded, stared at the floor. He continued holding Clint's hand. The dying man's grip was losing starch.

"Yvonne...and the kids... Tell them..." But before he could utter another word, his eyes drooped shut, head lulled to the side, and he was gone.

Press set the man's hand free and stood, slowly shaking his head.

What a waste. On so many levels.

65

Press dropped the digital recorder on the dining room table and walked to the kitchen sink. He let the water run till it turned hot then, using a bar of soap, scrubbed Hickman's blood from his hands. When they were clean, he leaned over and washed Olsen's and his own blood from his face. He still had the pounding headache and now a severe decision to make: Should he alert his superiors and the local police and further jeopardize the lives of Seth Barnett and Ocean Enberg or maintain the element of surprise and go get them himself? He didn't have to think long.

He fished his personal cell phone out of his briefcase, switched it off airplane mode. There were several notifications for new voice-mail and text messages. Without listening to or reading them, he swiped them all clear of the screen and opened the app for his contacts. It was a long shot this, but he had to try.

He downed some ibuprofen from his bag as he waited for the call to connect.

Come on. Come on.

Finally, the person on the other end answered with a chipper hello.

"Avery. It's Nate. Nate Press."

"Hi there. I figured you forgot about me."

"Impossible," he said.

He could hear the smile in her voice. "What's up?"

"This is a little out of left field, but... You're a pilot, right? You have access to a plane?"

"Wow. That's more than a little out of left field. But yes. Why?"

"I don't have time to explain over the phone. Can you fly me to Nantucket?"

"Right now?" She didn't do well to hide her incredulity.

"I'll pay you, of course." He quickly added, "It's important. Life and death important."

The pause conveyed to him that she was thinking.

"And I need a bike, too."

"What happened to yours?"

"It's a long story. Oh, and there are two more things I need if you can manage it." He told her what they were.

"I don't understand."

"I'll explain later."

"Okay, I guess. Anything else? You sure you don't need me to rip out our kitchen sink and bring that along, too?"

"No, that should be everything."

Her tone softened. She almost sounded disappointed. "I thought at first you were going to ask me to go riding or something."

"I wouldn't ask this of you if it weren't extremely important."

"Our plane is in Idaho right now, but I can use one of the trainers, I suppose. How soon will you be ready to fly?"

"I'm ready now."

Press had loaded his gear into the SUV he'd borrowed from the Wolfeboro police chief and was now throttling down Jenckes Hill Road. He slowed as he entered onto the property of the North Central State Airport. The road drew a straight line behind a series of plain-looking pole buildings that he knew were aircraft hangars.

Avery's Chevy pickup was backed into a space near a hangar displaying a sign that read NORTHPOINT AIR. LEARN TO FLY. He pulled in next to her truck, grabbed his gear, and went in search of her. As he neared a pedestrian door on the side of the building, he heard a sharp whistle.

"Over here."

She wore gray leggings, a navy-blue hoodie with the Gordon College logo on the front, and running shoes that prominently featured a fluorescent-green letter N.

Avery Gwynn moved about in the darkness next to a small—very small—single prop plane parked along the flight line, loosing the tiedowns that kept the plane from being blown about by high winds and prop wash during storage. The dim light did not diminish her features. In fact, she was even more beautiful in the glow of the hangar lights.

Press wound his way through a gate of high chain-link fencing and hustled over to her.

"Oh my gosh! What happened to your *face*? You're bleeding... You look like you got hit by a bus."

"I kind of did." Press chuckled. "You should see the other guys."

"What other guys?"

"I'm fine," he said, hoping to avoid any further comment on his physical appearance. "I really appreciate your help. Is there anything I can do?"

"You can pop the front wheel off that bike; it's not going to fit inside the plane otherwise."

Press opened the cabin door, dropped his gear on the small back seat then walked to the bike lying in the grass. He recognized it as a Specialized Rockhopper, size XL.

"This can't be *your* bike."

Avery laughed. "It's my brother's. He never rides anyway."

"Well, tell him I said thanks. I'll try not to hurt it."

"Why did you need the guitar case?" She looked on as Press transferred his tricked-out SBR from its tactical soft-shell Savior carrier into the guitar case then wedged some other gear inside so the rifle wouldn't bounce around and possibly lose its zero. Press clicked the case shut and smiled.

"I see," she said. "What you're going to be doing is pretty dangerous, huh?"

"I won't lie. It could be. It's best to be prepared for every contingency."

"My father says the same thing."

She tossed him a flannel shirt. "Also my brother's."

"Thanks." He changed out of his blood-stained shirt and pulled it on. If she noticed the puckered scar from the healed gunshot wound on his left shoulder, she refrained from commenting about it.

The two of them worked quickly. Press followed Avery's lead and instructions to the letter. Soon they were seated in the close confines of the cockpit with headsets on and their shoulders touching.

"Small plane."

"It's a Cessna 172 Skyhawk. I learned how to fly on this baby, remember? It's among the most popular single-engine aircraft running in the world today and makes for a great trainer. She might be small, but she gets the job done."

Press considered that Avery might very well be talking about herself. The thought caused him to grin. He spied her out of the corner of his eye. What a beauty. And the fragrance she wore—it was exotic and familiar at the same time, attracted him to her all the more. He had to stay on task, stay focused.

Stunning as she was, he wasn't here for Avery Gwynn. He had a job to do. Lives to save. Just so long as he wasn't too late already.

He maintained a knowing silence as they taxied to the runway. Avery radioed the tower over the ground frequency and navigated into position for takeoff.

She met his gaze and said, "Ready?"

"Ready."

Having been given the green light by the air traffic controller, they began to roll forward, steadily gaining speed. They reached a rate that didn't feel much faster than what a decent lawn tractor could do and in the next instant they were airborne.

Avery worked the pedals and the yoke, banking them to the left before leveling the plane and adding altitude. He could see lights gleaming on the horizon, the City of Providence radiating with life and vitality against a backdrop of utter darkness.

"So, what's this all about?" she said, breaking him from his quiet reverie. Her voice even filtered through the headset was alluring and pitch perfect. "You said it's dangerous. Or, well, it *could* be."

He was reluctant to tell her but did so anyway. From start to finish, he recounted everything that the Riley Talbert murder investigation had revealed. Barnett, Donstar, Brenner, Henrik Vandenberg, what had happened in New Hampshire and the FBI safe house. Every last detail. Truth be told, he didn't know if he would be coming back from this trip. He had to tell someone, so the information would get to the proper authorities in due time. But regardless of the outcome, whether he was successful or not, he was sure that Deputy Chief Denny Fantroy would attribute such intrepid gallivanting to his wild and reckless nature. At least that would be the official department stance.

But what other option did he have at this point? During Hickman's dying declaration, he had said that Brenner owned the entire police force on Nantucket. Surely the man had early warning systems in place. He was a veteran intelligence officer, a former deputy director of the CIA for crying out loud. If word got out that the police or feds were on their way to his oceanside property, Brenner would surely know. He'd probably kill Barnett and Ocean, drive them out to sea and dump their bodies, or bury them in a hole in the sand, and that would be that. Press was hoping and praying that he hadn't done so already.

To say Avery Gwynn was shocked at such weighty revelations was the understatement of the year.

By the time he had finished chronicling the events of the past couple weeks, Nantucket was well within view through the cockpit windshield. It appeared an arrow-shaped mass, pointing toward the black void of the North Atlantic. Small pockets of light dotted the island hither and yon, but due to Nantucket's pious stance against light pollution, the bulk of it lay eerily dark.

He asked her to first loop around the north end of the island. As she did so, Press peered down on Brenner's property through a set of binoculars. A fancy helicopter was parked not far from the outsize beach house, which held a commanding view of the ocean from a tree-studded dune. He spied two vehicles in the forecourt and possibly a third shrouded beneath a carport, the darkness making it impossible to be certain.

"What are you going to do if you find them?" Avery said.

"I don't know yet. I just hope I'm not too late." He gently massaged his sore face. The headache was back with a vengeance, so he popped some more ibuprofen as they made their approach. "I appreciate you flying me out here."

"Happy to help. Just promise me you'll stay safe."

"As safe as humanly possible."

They chirped down and as Avery taxied to a corner of the airport, Press was already scanning the area for a quick and low-vis exit.

Avery seemed to know what he was thinking. "Your best bet is to go right through the terminal. It's quiet this time of night and all the airline desks are closed."

"You're a lifesaver, Avery."

A bright smile formed on her face. Her eyes spoke volumes. "I certainly hope so."

He knew exactly what she meant: Seth Barnett and Ocean Enberg.

The plane lurched to a halt, and she powered off the engine. Avery made to pop open the cabin door, but Press caught her by the arm before she could. She turned toward him with mild alarm.

"There's just one more thing." He motioned to his briefcase on the floor behind them. "Once you're back on the ground in Rhode Island, I need you to contact Lt. Gentry with the Providence Police." He provided her with Gentry's personal cell phone number. "Make sure he gets my briefcase. But only him. No one else. Understand?"

She nodded stiffly.

"Also…" He looked toward a spot in the western sky. "If things, you know, go bad and you don't hear from me in the next twenty-four hours, find my dad. His name is Nicholas. Nicholas Press. He lives in Gauley Bridge. Tell him that I'm sorry and that I love him. And that…I forgive him. Can you do that?"

Avery reached out, touched his hand. If she had questions, and no doubt she did, she refrained from asking them. She started to say something but stopped. Then uttered, "I understand. I'll do as you wish."

He leaned toward the door on his side of the cabin but stopped when Avery hooked him by the swell of his bicep. Her hand slid to his forearm, where it remained. "I'll be praying for you. Remember, Nate. The Lord says, 'Call upon Me in the day of trouble; I will deliver you, and you shall glorify Me.' Whatever you are planning to do, no matter what happens… Call on Him, trust Him. With God nothing is impossible."

The sincerity in her face nearly caused him to become emotional. Her quoting from Scripture, the demonstration of her strongly held faith reminded him so much of his late grandmother.

He hesitated before exiting the aircraft, not fully wanting to depart her company. At last, he twisted back toward her, feeling a gravitational pull like no other. Before he knew what was happening, she lifted her hand and softly placed it on his battered face. She gazed into his eyes with sincerity, with genuine concern. The weight of the investigation and all that had transpired became lost in that moment. Inexplicable as it was—they had only just met, after all, he knew right then and there that he loved her.

She leaned close, tears in her eyes, and kissed him gently on the lips. "Godspeed, Nathan Press."

66

Nantucket, Massachusetts

The house was on the northern tip of the island and perched on a narrow bar of land between the ocean to the east and Wauwinet Road to the west. Based on a search of the area Press had done via the mapping application on his phone, he knew it was an exclusive area with homes that went for seven figures easy and residents who valued their privacy as much as their ocean views. It was the perfect place for hosting quiet parties with wealthy guests, peaceful walks on the beach, or mercilessly interrogating prisoners and disappearing them from the face of the earth altogether.

Avery was right, the terminal was empty save for a few sleepy-eyed, modern-hippie types pushing brooms and emptying trash bins. They never even glanced up as he pushed the bike through, backpack riding on his chest and the guitar case strapped to his back. His lumped-up face and alert detective eyes hidden behind wraparound sunglasses, Press might have been easily confused for an alcoholic rockstar trying to avoid paparazzi, or a dashing, local troubadour back from the holiday from hell.

Once outside, he doffed the sunglasses and pushed them into his pack, then mounted the bike and set off at a casual pace through the parking lot and onto Airport Road. For a normal person, the ride out to Brenner's beachside property would take about 45 minutes, but for a man in his physical condition it would be considerably less even with the added weight and bulk of his gear.

Press worked his way to a bike path that shot in a northeasterly direction. There were no streetlamps here, so to illuminate his way forward, he clicked on a small Petzl headlamp, careful not to agitate the wound on the back of his head. The trick was to blend in. The bike and guitar case helped in that regard. Apart from the fact that he wasn't wearing sandals or flip-flops or boat shoes, he looked like a regular fixture of the island.

In short order, the bike path crossed over Milestone Road and connected with another trail called Polpis Bike Path, which he followed all the way to Wauwinet Road, a desolate two-lane that would carry him north to his destination.

The road was peaceful and traffic nearly non-existent. The late-April night air was cool yet fragrant with the scent of newly budding vegetation, a hint of woodsmoke, and of course, the ever-present sea. Overhead, the stars put on quite a show, sparkling like glitter, the moon nothing more than a single waxing parenthesis in a sky as dark as motor oil.

Press pedaled onward, his headlamp cutting a wedge of light into the black. After another mile, the two-lane macadam of Wauwinet Road terminated at a small, clapboard gatehouse with brown-burgundy trim. A square of sand and gravel that constituted a parking lot lay to the right. From the sweeping tire marks, it appeared to double as a turnaround for the expeditious riffraff. A small yellow sign jutting from the ground in front of the gatehouse proclaimed that this was the end of the road. Thru traffic was *verboten*. The single track of weather-worn blacktop that continued up the beach was for residents and guests only. Vehicles were required to have a permit.

The only weakness to this otherwise impenetrable system was an unmanned gatehouse that bore not a single security camera.

Before he proceeded, Press noticed another placard affixed to the gray clapboard. It instructed that there was to be no biking beyond this point.

Tsk. Press assumed a privileged, self-righteous air—he guessed most of the residents around here would do the same in these circumstances—and ignored the sign completely.

Further on, numerous homes were parked right along the road, others were well out of sight, only accessible by means of quaint, sand-swept lanes that disappeared through the wild thicket and gnarled branches of high bush blueberry, black huckleberry, scrub oak, and sumac.

A man unpacking suitcases from a large SUV outside a single-story house near the road eyed him curiously as he passed by. Press gave a polite wave—one rich man to another. The man, his hands weighed down with luggage, nodded in lieu of waving back.

The posh Wauwinet Hotel came next. The historic beach resort, its windows afire with light, gazed upon him with neither suspicion nor artifice. He rode by without a single employee or guest seeing him, even that handsome couple ambling arm in arm on the well-manicured lawn along the north side of the property. It was nice to see that romance wasn't dead.

Now, the weathered blacktop gave way to hard-packed sand. Puddles had collected in the ruts along its fringes. Large homes, some alive with modest light, others dark and dormant, greeted him as he rolled forward. The lane here narrowed as it curled between them, transitioning to crushed gravel and sun-scarred pavement then back to sand. The bike tires against the hard-packed earth sent up a melody of soft, continuous static—a needle playing against a vinyl record on an old phonograph.

As he rounded a bend and the knotted shrubs and trees gave way to sandplain grassland and coastal heathland, he cut off his headlamp and slowed, allowing his eyes to adjust to the darkness.

To his left, the gray-blue water of Nantucket Harbor jostled with a slight chop. Opposite that was a column of lavish oceanfront homes that stood well off the sandy lane. Each of them looked out toward the Atlantic, broad-shouldered sentries guarding against some invisible enemy flotilla.

Press sneaked past their rear guard without fanfare. Truth be told, most of them appeared empty, patiently waiting for their owners to come calling. One, in fact, was being renovated from head to toe. Various construction trailers and gang boxes were parked at odd angles in the sandy drive with piles of lumber and tarpaulined pallets of building materials stacked about.

He was considering what it must be like to live out here when the sand on the narrow track suddenly became deeper, forcing him to stop. After a quick check of the mapping application on his phone, he climbed off the bike and walked it up to the home that was under construction. He stashed it next to a pallet of hewn stone, likely predestined for the unfinished chimney on the home's northern flank. Press gazed around the job site, noting how the workers had assembled in one area a makeshift campsite, where, he imagined, they shared their meals and coffee breaks. Not exactly the worst working conditions one could endure.

Press decided here was as good a place as any to prepare himself for battle though he hoped it wouldn't come to that. He checked the construction site for cameras and, finding none, slipped off the headlamp, guitar case, and his front-mounted backpack. He removed his rifle and other needed gear from the guitar case and propped it next to the bike. For a few seconds, he wished he'd brought his tactical vest, but there was only so much he could carry with him out here.

From the backpack, Press pulled a battle belt. Like his tac vest, it was something he had used often during his time in the Special Response Unit and still did when executing arrest warrants with the Violent Fugitive Task Force. He removed his pistol from the plainclothes holster beneath his untucked flannel shirt then stripped the belt and holster from his pants. After tucking in his shirt, he strapped on the belt system; it was manufactured by a company called Haley Strategic. Once it was secured on his waist, he shoved his pistol into the belt's Safariland tactical holster and clicked the hood shut, all while keeping his eyes up and scanning for trouble.

Press made several minor adjustments to the ammo pouches and other gear on the battle belt until everything was seated to his liking. He did the same for the backpack after he'd strapped into it. Now that he had offloaded some items, it was considerably lighter. Finally, he performed a series of checks on his rifle, slung it over his frame, and set off.

If anyone saw him now, he would have a lot of explaining to do.

The time for blending in was over.

67

Avery Gwynn sat in the small cockpit with her feet pressed firmly against the tops of the rudder pedals, the plane's engine humming loudly on the apron. She could not yet bring herself to taxi over to the runway. A large part of her wanted to stay here and help Nate. She cast her eyes downward onto the tactical-looking briefcase that she'd since moved to the seat where Press had been sitting only moments ago. He'd said it contained everything his police lieutenant would need to understand what was going on. Most important was the audio recorder tucked into one of the small, outer pockets.

Avery considered what had just happened between the two of them. Never had she experienced such strong feelings for a man, let alone a man she'd just met. She'd told no one that ever since the fateful Sunday afternoon they'd shared together, she could think of little else aside from the big, striking detective. His athletic physique, his charming smile, and my gosh those piercing, gray-blue eyes. They were the color of a New England sky in winter, yet somehow exuded warmth, sincerity, and verve. Doubtless, he could wield them like a weapon but also use them to disarm, to capture hearts. Melt them, too. He surely had hers. But was that it? Just the physical? Could it also be their shared interest in biking? No. There was something more about Nathan Press. But what?

It occurred to her how similar he was to her father. Is that why she had formed such a strong attraction to him so quickly? They were clearly cut from the same cloth. But it was also something else. His disposition, his manner. Nathan Press was a stallion who would not be easily tamed. If ever he could be. She knew in her heart she was not the type of person to shy away from such a challenge, the promise of brazen adventure and derring-do. It was in her DNA after all. Was that what made Press so alluring? The excitement, the mystery? The danger?

Regardless of her complex feelings, she may have just lost him for good. The man was clearly committed to his job of putting bad people where they belonged: behind bars. And what's more, he was willing to risk his life to save innocents. Another trait he shared with her father.

Avery considered Press's instructions. *Contact Lt. Gentry once on the ground back home. Make sure he gets the briefcase.* She looked at the scrap of paper on which Press had written Gentry's personal cell phone number. She *would* call him. She *would* deliver Nate's bag. But first, she had another phone call to make. She only hoped there was cell reception right now in Idaho.

The call finally connected but the line was clouded with static.

"Dad?"

"Yeah, sweetie. What is it?" Lester Gwynn's voice cut in and out. Mountains had that effect on cellular communications.

When Avery had finished what she had to say, she waited. Her father had only a few questions, which she did her best to answer. All the while, static crackled in her ear and the connection faded in and out.

"I care about him, Dad. He needs help. I just know he does."

Now, rolling down the runway, she smeared tears from her cheeks.

Once aloft and heading for home, she beseeched Almighty God with heartfelt supplication. It was a simple prayer that she would repeat countless times throughout the flight. "Keep him safe, Lord. Keep him safe."

68

Press jogged silently along the sandy track. He considered the consequences of his actions both personally and professionally, even if all went well out here. Not only was he in violation of numerous departmental policies already, he was in another state with plans of exerting police authority—authority that by law did not extend across state lines here in Massachusetts, but he would worry about all of that later. Two innocent people were in imminent danger. Surely, *they* didn't care about any precious policies, stuffy laws, or bureaucratic red tape right now. They only needed help. He would do his best to see that they suffered no further harm. He owed them that much.

The narrow strip of land was dark and quiet. The only sounds were those of a beach breeze that whipped up every now and again and the distant whoosh of waves washing ashore and receding back into the sea.

His steady pace carried him past the last house before Robert Brenner's. The former CIA man's dwelling sat off by itself on the northern tip of the island. The road from this point forward was nothing more than loose sand

and accessible only by four-wheel-drive vehicle, thus signifying that the man took his privacy very seriously.

The silhouette of a helicopter soon came into view. It was parked just off the sandy track in a clearing of patchy grass. The primitive landing zone lay far enough away so that such an aircraft would not sandblast Brenner's monster beach house and likewise any guests who might be sunbathing or sipping cocktails on its decks during takeoffs and landings. Several thick groves of trees contributed to this and simultaneously helped shield the aircraft from the view of anyone gazing outward from the house—at least from the lower levels. A thin pedestrian path cut through these trees and presumably emptied out somewhere near the back of the home.

Press slowed to a walk. He moved closer to the helicopter, using the landscape to mask his ingress. He would check the bird first, make sure no one was hanging around nearby who could later sneak up on him from behind. When he was within fifty yards of it, he crouched down behind some thorny bushes, fished out a night-vision monocular. It wasn't one of the more expensive models out there, but it worked reasonably well and had a feature that allowed for digital recording to a microSD card, which had come in handy on more than one occasion.

He saw no movement anywhere inside or outside the helicopter or along the trees that skirted the clearing. He turned to his right and scoped the rest of the grounds, then the house, what he could see of it anyway. From here, all that he could make out was the northwest corner of the home's second floor. Even when he switched to his Steiner binoculars and zoomed in much closer, he could see nothing more than that one exposed corner. The good news so far was that there were no outward signs of a security element patrolling the property.

He crept forward, using the IR scope to navigate the natural obstacles. Now would not be a good time to get poked in the eye by an errant tree branch. The house was just over a slight rise, on the oceanside of a sand dune that doubtless offered exquisite views of the beach and the sea beyond. Press settled into a dark void within the trees at the top of the dune and scanned the area. He swept his field glasses back and forth, the wind causing the trees, grass, and scrub brush to swish and sway.

Alternating between the night-vision device and the binoculars, he focused on the house. He next considered optimal stand-off positions of overwatch but saw no one posted anywhere.

He shifted his attention back to the house and scanned it again more closely. Not surprisingly, he spotted numerous cameras at the usual locations. He doubted, however, that anyone was actively monitoring the feeds from inside. Large as it was, this was a beach house on the edge of sleepy Nantucket, not some fortified military installation where soldiers were garrisoned and kept on alert for enemy combatants. Press calculated that, minus the local cops, probably only a handful of people even knew Robert Brenner had any affiliation with this place. After all, ownership was couched in trust behind a high rock wall of shell companies. At least that's what Hickman had told him before he gave up the ghost.

A stiff gust forged up from the beach, throttling the trees and bushes in which he was nested. Press shaded his eyes from the whipped-up sand. The wind could be a valuable partner, he thought. It camouflaged sound and caused movement in the trees and other vegetation, which likely meant the cameras would not be linked to motion-detection sensors set to trigger an alarm. The same would be true of the floodlights he saw mounted high on the home's exterior. On the other hand, if the cameras and lights were equipped with IR or thermal sensors, he would be royally screwed. A former CIA deputy director almost assuredly had such systems in place.

This was not going to be easy.

Nevertheless, he first needed to verify that Seth Barnett and Ocean Enberg were here.

He had to move closer.

Robert Brenner paced the room, which had been transformed into a kind of interrogation chamber not unlike those he had grown accustomed to using in foreign lands during his time at the Agency. Though it was something he excelled at, rendition was an ugly business. He did not wish to unnecessarily sully his home with blood and flesh and bits of brain matter even if that meant getting the answers he needed. For that reason, most of the furniture had been moved to other rooms. Some of the weightier pieces—a gigantic grandfather clock with gold inlay, for instance, had been carefully shielded in plastic sheeting. Likewise, heavy-gauge plastic sheeting had been spread out and duct-taped across the tiled floor. Every precaution had been made. Every contingency thoughtfully considered. When it was all over, the clean-up would be easy and there would be no physical evidence of any kind left behind. Even the bodies would be disposed of in such a fashion that they would never be found. To that end, a rigid inflatable boat was already beached on the sand a hundred yards away.

Brenner approached the first chair in the center of the room. It had a high back and was made of hewn wood, same as its nearby twin. The chairs were twelve feet apart and had been positioned so that the two people who occupied them were facing each other. The chairs would be broken down later and burned on the beach. Both captives were strapped in, their arms and feet secured by strong cable ties. Their necks, too.

"Tell me what I want to know. What else is there?" Brenner was clinical as if he could do this all night long. He had begun by asking Barnett about the data he'd taken from Donstar and the other information he had since unearthed through his vaunted cyber-related facilities. He and his masters had to be sure there was no one else who knew what they were up to. Additionally, they needed to know what servers to target and destroy. The location of any external data storage devices that he had squirreled away. The names of any remaining witnesses to eliminate. As a result of his questioning, Brenner had already learned that the mysterious item Barnett had given the attorney was a flash drive. They had initially assumed Talbert had already passed it to the detective, Nathan Press, but Brenner was now confident the policeman did not have it or even comprehend its significance. The flash drive was still in play. That fact alone was enough to damn the whole lot of them, bring their plans crashing down. Send people to jail. Almost assuredly result in him being marked for death. It must be located and destroyed. Though he wouldn't like it, he would be satisfied to know that it would never be found. But why take any chances?

A beaten and bloodied Seth Barnett hung awkwardly in his bindings. A string of drool stretched from his chin to his red-stained shirtsleeve. Several teeth now dotted the plastic-coated floor. In their midst was a car battery and jumper cables. The interrogation would not go on much longer.

"I...already...told you...everything," Barnett gasped for air, his chest heaving, eyes—both were now slits and grotesquely swelled—canted to the floor.

Across from him, Ocean Enberg sobbed uncontrollably. Her face was red and wet from having cried too many tears already. "Please stop," she whimpered with a voice that had become hoarse from screaming.

Brenner regarded her with no emotion before turning back to his primary detainee. He had done this countless times. Long ago, he had become immune to emotional outbursts, the desperate pleas for mercy, violent thrashing, and futile attempts at escape. This far along in the process, short as it was, he knew he was close. Close to putting an end to all this madness. Seth Barnett was not a hardened jihadi. Or an operative trained to endure the cruel machinations of enhanced interrogation. If this kid knew anything beyond what he had already confessed, he was not human.

Still, he had to be sure.

69

The house was surrounded by a high stone wall. An iron gate with an ornamental design stood at the southwest corner. Through the iron bars, Press could see two vehicles: a dark green, mid-90s model Land Rover Defender sporting an overland-style roof rack and a black Mercedes G-Class SUV. Beside them, parked beneath a carport, wasn't another SUV, but an ATV, the kind lifeguards used to navigate the beach. Just outside the gate, on what would be the driver's side of an approaching vehicle, was a weatherized, electronic box set atop a four-foot-high steel post. Using the binos, Press could see a numeric keypad and a plate that registered RFID chips from key fobs or proximity keycards. He assumed a microphone and speaker were built into the box as well. A surveillance camera, too.

Press followed the stone wall along the south side of the property. Trees and thick flora pressed up against it. He picked his way through the vegetation, using it to camouflage his movements, stopping every few paces to scan his surroundings with the IR scope. The bottom of the wall followed the contours of the dune to a point a hundred yards from the tideline while the top remained level. Here, the wall was much higher—eighteen or twenty feet, no less—and turned abruptly to the left, cutting parallel to the beach.

Hunkered down at the southeast corner, Press followed the wall with his eyes to the place where it turned away from the beach and shot back toward the western side of the property. An archway and another metal gate stood at the midpoint between this corner and the far one. This gate though was built for pedestrians only and stood above a private boardwalk that extended about fifty feet toward the water.

Before moving, Press scanned the beach. Because of the severe darkness, he hadn't noticed it at first, but there it was. A black, fast-looking, rigid inflatable boat, or RIB, was lurking at the water's edge. It had been pulled up on the sand but appeared ready to put to sea at a moment's notice. He put the IR scope on the boat and confirmed no one was out there safeguarding it.

Press secured the scope, rotated his rifle to his back, and put his foot onto the branch of a gnarled tree that rose from the sand like a mythological snake-like creature. Gripping an adjoining tree for balance, he climbed slowly and silently until his eyes broke the plane of the top of the wall. He now noticed the razor-sharp shards of metal and glass embedded in the wall's crown of concrete. Brenner was indeed serious about his security.

Careful to avoid any sudden movements for fear of setting off alarms or cameras or floodlights, Press wedged himself into the trees with only his feet and thighs. From his battle belt, he unclipped a pair of tactical gloves with hard-plastic knuckles. After yanking them on, he reached out, grabbed the edge of the wall, and slowly pulled himself closer. He brought the IR scope to his eye once more and scanned the back of the property for armed men tasked with keeping watch for interlopers like him. The only things he saw moving were the numerous potted fronds swaying in rhythm with the fibrillating breeze.

Next, he traded the IR scope for the binoculars and studied the back of the house. A wall of windows fronted the beach. There were no shades or curtains drawn. Lights burned freely inside.

A flash of movement on the first floor commanded his attention. He adjusted the knob on the binos. A tall man of medium build with thin, receding gray hair that had probably once been coal black stepped into view. His back was to Press, but his body language indicated that he was speaking to someone out of sight. As the man shifted to the left, Press glimpsed another man, younger and thinner, who was bound to a chair. Press's stomach tightened. The seated man's face was raw hamburger, an absolute wreck. Press didn't recognize him but from the clothing concluded he was Seth Barnett.

Dear God.

He hurried to document the scene with his IR scope by way of a brief video recording then snapped several photos.

The man standing turned in the opposite direction. Zooming in with the digital monocular, Press now saw the face full on and recognized it immediately. Robert Brenner was plain-looking, almost forgettable, in fact, but for his eyes; they were piercing and flagrantly intelligent. Dressed in a white, button-down shirt and pleated, tan slacks, the former CIA man cut a trim, athletic figure. Though Press could not hear what he was saying, Brenner was quite obviously speaking to someone seated directly across from Barnett, however, from Press's current position it was impossible to make out who that was.

Press snapped more photos.

Still suspended in the trees, it took Press another painstaking two minutes to stealthily traverse sideways along the wall to a spot from which he could plainly see the person seated opposite Seth Barnett. This time, there was no doubt about the individual's identity.

Like Barnett, Ocean Enberg was also bound to a chair by her neck, arms, and legs. She bore little resemblance to the beautiful, well-put-together college girl he'd spoken to in the River House apartment. Her disposition revealed horror and abject despair. He made a record of this, too, as more adrenaline dumped into his bloodstream.

He'd found them.

They were alive.

But for how long?

70

Press quickly surveyed the landscape for anything he could use to facilitate a silent descent to the ground from the top of the wall, assuming he didn't get sliced and diced while trying to get there. But without a tree to shimmy down or the lid of a hot tub to leap upon, he was looking at a dead drop of at least 20 feet on either tiered slate rock or a poured concrete walkway. Those were his only options. A broken ankle or torn-up knee now would doom Barnett and Enberg to certain death. Jumping was a no-go.

He ignored the covered, Olympic-size swimming pool and deck chairs glaring back at him mockingly and looked again at the torture scene playing out in the window. He had no time to formulate the perfect plan. He would have to move quickly and rely on his instincts. Seth and Ocean didn't have much time. Likely mere minutes.

Avery's words came rushing back. *"With God nothing is impossible."*

Though he hadn't prayed in a very long time, he mentally offered a quiet, albeit short prayer to the Almighty.

Help me, God. Provide a way.

Press climbed back down to the ground. He considered the pedestrian gate and, with his rifle at a low ready, moved to it with great urgency. Using the edge of the wall as cover, he examined the gate more closely. The lock was sturdy, a strong electro-magnetic type. There was no getting through it, at least with the tools he had at his disposal.

There would be no silent entry. He would just have to go in hard. But maybe there was a way to... He suddenly had an idea.

Press jogged back to the corner of the wall, stopped, peeked around it with the IR scope.

Nothing.

He scrambled his way back up the tree-studded dune and was just about to break cover, when suddenly he heard the whine of an engine. Instantly, he dropped to his stomach and froze. A pearly blue Jeep Wrangler Rubicon 392 wearing no top, or doors for that matter, emerged from around the bend, its knobby tires churning the sand with ease. Press was well within the V of the Jeep's headlights but somehow the prickly scrub brush managed to camouflage him enough so that the driver and sole occupant failed to notice him. Music from the Jeep's open interior leaked into the night. Some dreadful hair band from the '80s.

Press watched the vehicle approach the iron gate. The driver leaned toward the electronic access-control panel then inched forward as the gate yawned open. Once inside, the Jeep bumped onto an elegant drive of stone pavers and parked in front of the Defender. The gate closed without delay.

He crawled to a place where he could see through the gate. When the driver emerged from the Jeep, he was holding two boxes of pizza and singing the song's chorus to himself. If only he had been closer to the gate, thought Press, he might have been able to sneak inside, overwhelm the guy, and gain entry into the house.

But there was no time to lament over could've, would've, should've.

The two boxes of pizza did in a strange way provide him with a bit of intelligence. If each pizza had a total of eight pieces and one man ate two or three of them, he could extrapolate that out to mean there was somewhere between five and eight men inside the house. Not exactly ideal odds considering he was alone. Even assuming he could get inside, he didn't know if Barnett in his condition was ambulatory. Would he need to be carried? And what exactly was the plan from there?

He had no clue. He would just have to improvise. And trust God.

Press moved stealthily back to the trees, hurried through them past the helicopter to the sandy track that Google Maps called Great Point Road. Confident he had not been spotted, he gripped his rifle, and broke into a furious sprint.

The home under construction was just how he had left it. He found a dirty rag in a trash barrel, weaved it through the padlock on the tool trailer hoping to muffle the sound from what he was about to do next. He picked up a cinder block that had likely served someone as an improvised chair and thrust it downward against the lock. It fell away after only one blow.

The inside of the trailer was pitch black. From his pack he dug out a penlight that emitted a blue LED light, clicked it on. He performed a quick inventory. The first thing he saw was a portable generator. Next to it was a red, plastic five-gallon container of gasoline. He rocked it back and forth, determining it to be nearly full. He set it aside and continued searching.

Under some wooden shelving, he found an acetylene torch—the type plumbers use to solder copper pipes. The gauge indicated the tank was full. *Beautiful.* He flicked out his folding knife and cut the hose from the cylinder close to the valve assembly.

Next, he scooped up a pry bar, which he stuffed into his backpack, followed by a three-pound sledge with a 16-inch rubberized handle. He slid this into the ten o'clock position of his battle belt next to his double-mag pouch.

Hanging on a nail was an electric grill starter, doubtless used by workers on the charcoal grill just outside. He snatched it off the wall and pushed it, too, into his backpack.

He walked deeper into the trailer in search of one more thing that would add to his plan in a big way. And there, propped in the back with some shovels and a bundle of ¾-inch threaded rods, he found it. Apparently, some of the construction workers liked to fish along the shore while on their lunch breaks, or who knows, maybe even while they were on the clock. In any case, Press was grateful they did.

He snapped off the reel from one of the rods and again flipped open his folder, put the blade to the braided, fluorocarbon fishing line and cut the bait rig free. Press shoved the reel into his pack, picked up the acetylene cylinder and container of gasoline and hurried back to the clearing where the helicopter slumbered.

A quick check with the IR scope revealed no movement. He sprinted in a crouch to the helicopter. It was a sleek, modern aircraft with a shrouded tail rotor. An Airbus H145 from the small script imprinted into the landing skid.

Press set the cylinder and the gas can down in the sand and gently clicked open the cockpit door. He cupped his left hand over the end of his penlight and shined the blue beam around in search of a button or switch that indicated POWER or something of the sort. On the left side of a cluster of knobs and switches positioned above the two pilot seats, he noted a toggle switch labeled ENGAGE BAT MSTR. Bingo. Master battery. Press clicked it on, and the instrument panel came alive, various lights winking and blinking at him. A number of dings and beeps followed as the helicopter woke from its nap. He prayed Brenner and his men would not see the glow within the cockpit. Soon he found another switch, this one designated for an auxiliary power unit. He flicked it on and, through the glass partition behind him, noted the tiny red LED bulbs now illuminating the power ports in the passenger cabin.

Press toggled both switches back to the off position and climbed into the back of the bird via a rear passenger door. The interior was elegant, sophisticated. The scent of expensive leather was pervasive. The cabin was obviously designed for a busy—and wealthy—executive. It consisted of six tan, Cordovan-leather passenger seats with mahogany-colored stitching. Four of them faced each other. One of these was soiled with small dark stains each in the shape of an amoeba. So, too, was the floor in front of it. In addition, Press could see circular blood droplets on the arm of the chair and a crooked trail leading into and out of the helicopter.

Barnett's blood.

Between two of the seats, in front of some cup holders, was a panel of brushed nickel with woodgrain trim. He slid it backward and nearly smiled.

Pay dirt.

Leaving the gas can and acetylene cylinder next to the helicopter, he hurried to the tree line at the entrance to the pedestrian path. He went twenty yards down the path and knelt, dug into his pack. Using the fishing line, he rigged up a series of tripwires to the pull-rings of the three CTS flashbangs he had with him. He'd kept three in his kit ever since his time in SRU and was glad he had. They were handy little suckers. You never knew when one might be needed, whether during an active shooter situation at a school or a hasty rescue operation on an island within the confines of another state. One was the standard-type bang. The others were a little different. One of these produced a double bang, the other nine separate bangs separated by small intervals of time. With these, he was hoping to create the illusion of a small army. That is if everything went off without a hitch.

When the bangs were set, he ran back to the helicopter, pulled out his phone and fired off a quick text to Avery Gwynn: *Tell Gentry I found them. Both still alive. But don't look good. No time. Going in. Pray.*

He powered off his phone, stuffed it in his pack then picked up the container of gasoline. He dumped its contents evenly throughout the cabin, tossed the empty canister to the back. Next, he engaged the bird's master battery again followed by the auxiliary power unit. The latter supplied power to the passenger cabin and the 12-volt outlets Press figured were normally meant for laptop computers or phone chargers.

Press next hefted the acetylene tank into the cabin and spun open the value. Gas hissed venomously from the nub of cut rubber hose. Finally, after a quick prayer that his improvised explosive contraption wouldn't blow up in his face, he plugged the electric grill starter into the outlet. He figured he had about four to five minutes until the element would be glowing red hot and would hopefully ignite the acetylene and, if not, at least the gasoline. He sliced open one of the leather seats with his blade and pushed the grill starter inside. He wasn't sure if this was going to work, but it was the best he could come up with in the moment. He needed a diversion—one with a time delay that would allow him to get into position before it activated.

Ducking out of the helicopter, he worked his way back down along the wall, posted up at the southeast corner along the beach. The boat was still unmanned. Good.

He crept into position next to the pedestrian gate, removed the pry bar from his pack, and leaned it quietly against the wall. Here, he waited.

And prayed some more.

71

Lance Cheney, Gary Diehl, and the helicopter pilot, a man they all called Mick, though that wasn't his actual name, had already downed some pizza and were now outside loitering on the long, second-floor deck that wrapped around the north and west sides of the house. Each man had a cigarette in his hand. They would all be glad when this operation was over.

They were discussing recreational plans and rumors of upcoming ops when Cheney, facing westward, noticed a strange glow between the trees. "What *is* that?"

"What's what?" Mick said.

"Some kind of light. It seems to be coming from the area of the helicopter."

Diehl blew out a cloud of smoke from the corner of his mouth, squinted toward the helicopter. "Yeah. I see it, too."

Mick soon spotted the same thing. "What on earth?" He walked to the railing, stood next to Cheney. "Call me crazy but it... It looks like the cockpit lights are on."

Cheney dropped his cigarette to the decking, ducked inside the house, and returned with a set of binoculars. He used them to study the distant helicopter. "He's right. The cockpit lights *are* on."

Normally, Cheney might have relied on the floodlights, but he didn't want to blind himself, so he reached back inside and turned a switch that disabled them. He would much rather the element of surprise if someone really was out there tampering with the helicopter.

Cheney drew a pistol from the holster in his waistband, motioned to Diehl, who already had a SIG MCX Rattler SBR chambered in .300 Blackout slung around his frame. The pair descended a set of steps and forged up the sandy path toward the anomalous lights while Mick the pilot lumbered a safe distance behind with a nickel-plated revolver that he'd pulled from a shoulder holster.

Nearing the end of the path, they all crouched and slowed their pace. Diehl was now in the lead and therefore was the unfortunate soul who triggered the first flashbang. The sharp, unexpected blast sent each man diving to the ground. Before they could gather their senses, another one went off. Then another. Cheney remained pressed to the sand as Diehl rose to a knee. Mick, meanwhile, stood up to run when suddenly there came a bright flash and near-simultaneous, chest-thumping boom. A jagged piece of metal whipsawed across Diehl's neck. He fell over into the nearby foliage, dark fluid spurting from his mortal wound.

Wide-eyed, Cheney assessed himself for injuries. Miraculously, he had suffered only knicks and scrapes on his face and forehead. However, but for a loud, high-pitched tone he couldn't shake, his hearing was gone. Blood leaked from his ears. He looked back for Mick and saw him lying lifeless in the center of the path. Something had taken his head clean off. For it was right now rolling the rest of the way back down the hill, grotesquely keeping to the hard-packed sandy track.

They were under attack.

72

A horrific scream pierced the night air. Press knew he couldn't wait any longer. He couldn't stand by out here while these monsters killed Seth and Ocean. His plan had failed. He picked up the pry bar and focused on a specific spot in the gate's locking mechanism. He reared the tool back and was about to thrust it forward when he heard what sounded like a shotgun blast on the opposite side of the property.

He flinched, at first thinking someone had fired a shot at him, then it registered. And suddenly Nantucket came alive like the fourth of July. But the next sound trumped them all. There was an enormous flash of light followed by a thunderous explosion from the vicinity of the helicopter—the mother of all diversions. Debris and shrapnel clattered against the house, vehicles, and landings, some of it filtering through the trees and falling mute into the sandy earth.

His helicopter IED had worked.

Press jammed the pry bar between the frame and the door lock. It took several swings to get a good bite. He drew the hammer from his belt, gave the heel of the pry bar a good whack then torqued it with all his strength. At first the lock didn't budge, but slowly it began to slide. Then all at once it gave way and the gate flung open.

Press dropped the pry bar in the sand and bent down, picked up the hammer, slid it back into his belt. Rifle poised, he moved across the threshold of the gate, stepped quickly to the right to avoid potential straight-on fire. He was now in the danger zone. He expected to be immediately blinded by floodlights but oddly they remained dark.

He mounted a set of stone steps, swept past a small clapboard shed with a tiled outdoor shower, then the dormant swimming pool. He ascended another more elaborate system of tiered landings that funneled onto a long flagstone patio. Wood decking ran the length of the house overhead. There was a door at the center of the patio dead ahead and another off to the far left. He went directly to the center door. The room in which Seth and Ocean were being held was immediately beyond it.

Through the glass, he saw a giant man—the one Hickman had called Marcus at the safe house—run from the room and head deeper into the house. Press was about to move when another guy armed with a carbine stepped into view. The man had not yet seen him. Press put two rounds of 5.56 through a window and into his back, dropping him instantly.

Keeping his rifle shouldered and pointed forward, Press kicked the door just below the brass knob. But it didn't want to give. He kicked it again with the same result, a sturdy sucker. Press drew the three-pound sledge from his belt and, with a two-hand grip, blasted the door just above the knob where the deadbolt was located. It did the trick.

He was in.

73

First, there were a few cracks of gunfire. Then an enormous blast shook the entire house, blew out windows, and lodged bits of sharp metal into the exterior walls. War had come to Nantucket. The sound suggested an offensive maneuver had been initiated on the side of the property opposite the beach. Marcus Zug hadn't even had a chance to get started on the girl. Both he and Brenner sprinted from the room to see what had caused such a clatter, leaving Stevenson alone to guard the prisoners.

Zug ran through the kitchen, but stopped when Brenner, a shock of worry on his face, grabbed him by the shirt.

Keith Wrigley swept past, darted down a hallway. He returned a few seconds later holding a suppressed Colt M4 and bolted outside.

"What on earth was that?! Sounded like half the island blew up!" Zug said.

"I believe we're under attack," Brenner clapped back, a pistol now in his hand.

"What do you want me to do?"

"Get back in there. You and Dale watch Barnett and the girl. In fact, no. Kill them. Do it now. And hurry."

Zug nodded and spun on his heel. He veered through the kitchen and plucked a long carving knife from a wood block on the counter and jogged back to the interrogation chamber, what would normally be a large sitting room from which to watch the ocean or untold beautiful women sprawled out by the pool.

When he flung open the French doors, what he saw caused his eyes to jolt wide open. Dale lay in a heap on the floor. And an athletically built, serious-looking man clad in a flannel shirt and cargo pants, with a rucksack strapped on his back and a rifle slung across his chest, was cutting the girl free. And it was not just any man. It was the detective, Nathan Press, no less.

Zug immediately charged for him, murderous intent in his eyes. He would finish him this time for good.

Press looked up to the sound of the doors being thrown open. Suddenly, a freight train of a man was bearing down on him, a blade in an outstretched hand. The name Hickman had mentioned back at the FBI safe house shot through his mind.

Marcus Zug.

Instinctively, Press dropped his knife and drew his pistol. With the man's speed and closing time, going for the rifle was a no go. But in the split-second it took him to angle the muzzle of the pistol forward just clear of his holster, Zug was already on him.

Press got off one round, which went low, caromed off the plastic-covered floor, and lodged into the far wall. Zug clamped onto Press's right wrist—his gun hand—and shoved it downward while at the same time he slashed wildly at his neck with the knife. In a desperate reactionary maneuver, Press grabbed at his slung rifle with his left hand and ripped it upward. The blade struck the upper receiver and threw a spark. Zug's forward momentum and shoulder, which was now buried into Press's sternum, sent both men crashing against the wall, where they remained locked together. Each man's face was a mask of strenuous physical exertion as they struggled for position. Press had no leverage. His feet barely touched the floor. Zug's power was extreme.

Along with the rifle, Press's left arm was now pinned against his body. He released his grip on the pistol, rotated his right palm clockwise, and snapped his hand down on the back of the big man's wrist. This action freed his right hand. Without hesitation, he shot his hand upward and jammed his gloved index finger directly into Zug's left eye socket. It went in deep. Far deeper than he imagined it could go. He hooked something stringy and squishy and violently raked it outward.

Zug bellowed in agony, moved back a step, and swung the blade blindly back and forth across his body. Press ducked once, twice. The second time, the man's forearm slammed against his temple and teetered him off balance. He tried to shove the large man backward to create space, but the mass of humanity didn't budge. Rather, Zug plowed forward again and bear-hugged him, driving him back into the wall once more. Where was that blade?

Press quickly leapt upward, drew his heels up to his butt, and using the wall as a springboard, planted his feet against it and lunged, essentially leg-pressing the giant in a horizontal direction. This forced Zug backward several steps. Press fell on his stomach as the two men separated. He scanned the floor for his pistol, saw it down along the wall well out of reach. It must have gotten kicked in the melee. Press focused again on his adversary's hands. *Crap!* The knife was still there.

Zug advanced toward him yet again, his one good eye wide with alarm and lusting for vengeance, the ruined one grotesquely hanging on his cheekbone by a thick cord of flesh.

Press scrambled to the right, dropped onto his rear end, and leaned backward, again trying to create enough space that would allow him to get the muzzle of his rifle up and on target. But his sling caught on something, which prevented him from rotating the weapon. As Zug lunged forward, the knife already on its way, Press's hand landed on something familiar. He immediately claimed it from the floor and torqued his whole body like he was throwing the mother of all haymakers. The three-pound sledge connected with Zug's ear and caved in the entire left side of his head. Zug's knife, too, connected but not nearly with the intended velocity and force. Regardless, it managed to carve a line across the outside of Press's upper left arm.

Zug crashed on Press's legs with Press swinging the hammer again and again just to make sure the massive guy was out of the fight permanently. It took several seconds for Press to catch his breath. By then he noticed Ocean Enberg along the wall, his pistol in her shaking hands.

"Easy, Ocean. It's Detective Press. Remember me? I'm one of the good guys. I've come to take you and Seth out of here."

Her eyes were red and wet. Her hair knotted and twisted across her face.

"Please. There isn't much time. We have to move." He cautiously stepped closer, keeping his frame angled and out of the line of fire. When he was within reach of the gun, he gently plucked it from her grasp. She immediately fell into his chest, sobbing. He hugged her as a father would, wanting to console her and wipe away every tear. "I know. Believe me, I know," he said. "But we need to move."

"Okay. Okay," she gasped, her voice quivering.

Press found his knife on the floor and quickly freed Barnett from his bindings. The kid just about slid to the floor. He was barely conscious. Press tried not to focus on his face, which was a pulpy, red mess. His own parents wouldn't recognize him.

They exited via the patio door, Press with Barnett over his shoulder and Ocean close by his side. Once through the iron pedestrian gate, he said, "This way. And stay quiet."

74

Brenner stood just outside the wall several paces away from another arched and gated pedestrian entryway, this one issuing onto the grounds of the west side of the property. He studied Wrigley, who was halfway up the foot path at the crest of the dune, lying prone at the base of a tree. From his position, Brenner could not actually see the burning helicopter, only the flickering light cast against the bosky terrain and dark firmament above.

"Well? Anything?" he impatiently called.

Wrigley turned his head toward Brenner, shook it slowly and deliberately so as not to give away his position by making a sudden movement or an undisciplined sound.

Lowering his pistol, Brenner sighed and let his mind work. He suddenly knew what was happening.

"The beach! Get to the beach!" He raced back into the house, found the ghastly scene in the interrogation room. Dale's and Marcus's lifeless bodies were the only human forms inside. The side of Marcus's head had been bashed in. Who could have done such a thing? To Marcus of all people?

Brenner proceeded cautiously through the doorway and out onto the patio that presided over the rolling ocean. With that infernal wall in the way, he could not see the entire width of beach, only a slim strip of sand. Beyond that, gray-and-black-tinted seawater, white splotches of foam and froth as the tide churned about.

He hesitated briefly at the gate then thrust himself through it, immediately ducking down. Kneeling with his pistol up and pointed toward the unknown, he scanned left, right, then left again but saw nothing save for the unoccupied RIB, the rising tide now licking at its stern. Then something—a sound—drew his attention back to the right. He stared into the blackened void above the sand, which converged into a solitary point within the darkness due south.

There it was again. A muffled gasp.

He quickly pulled his phone from his pocket and dialed Cheney.

"Yeah?!"

"Where are you?" he said, keeping his voice low.

"WHAT?!"

"Where are you?!"

"I'm up by the helo!" Cheney shouted. "Looks like it was hit by a Hellfire missile! It's gone! So are Gary and Mick! I can barely hear!"

"Never mind that."

"What?!"

"Never. Mind. It was a diversion. Someone came and took Barnett and the girl. They're on the beach headed south. Don't let them get away." Brenner ran back into the house, grabbed his keys. Though it had been sitting for a month, the Defender started right up. Before dropping it into gear, he pulled out his phone again and dialed another number. He hated to do it, but he was left with no choice. It must be done. He tapped the green circle on the screen.

The call did not connect immediately. In the few seconds he waited, he contemplated how Hickman must have sold them out. But why wasn't there a huge police or federal law-enforcement presence here? The locals would have warned him. That's why. So... Press was smart and resourceful. He'd managed to somehow get to the island and launch an assault likely by himself. All that intelligence and resourcefulness notwithstanding, Press was going to die tonight. Brenner would see to that.

Still, he had to consider all the angles. Were more people coming? How would Press get Barnett and the girl off the island? Perhaps he hadn't thought that far ahead.

The call connected.

A man's voice. "Yes, sir. What is it?"

Brenner explained what he wanted with great urgency then before ending the call, he hissed an ominous warning. "Do not fail me. Or I will have you and your family chopped up and fed to the sharks."

The helicopter—what was left of it—was a charred, black husk. Its peeled-open carcass was still hot and smoking. Flames from the ruptured fuel tanks feverishly wiggled and wagged on the ground in a haphazard pattern that extended in all directions. Some nearby trees had been turned into titanic tiki torches.

Firelight flickered and danced in Cheney's pupils as he hunched over Mick's decapitated body. He still had the phone pressed to his ear. "Where are Marcus and Dale?!"

"Dead," Brenner said.

Hearing nothing further, Cheney looked at the phone. Brenner had apparently terminated the call. A wave of grief washed over him followed by white-hot rage as he pocketed the device. He shoved his pistol into his waistband, grabbed Diehl's short-barreled rifle, and ran.

Once back inside the walled compound, Cheney snapped his head to the driveway. Wrigley was already firing up the Jeep. "Wait for me!"

Wrigley feathered the clutch long enough for him to hop into the front seat. As soon as he was inside, the Jeep lurched forward against the slowly opening gate, forcing a metallic screech. Once clear, Wrigley gunned the engine. The Jeep's knobby wheels chirped free of the stone pavers and threw sand.

Cheney pulled the charging handle part way back on the rifle, making sure a round was chambered.

"What happened to the others?" Wrigley said, spinning the wheel and throwing the gear shift forward.

"What?!"

"The others! Where are they?!"

"Brenner said they're dead!"

Wrigley jerked his head, swore through clenched teeth. "Do we know who or how many we're even up against?"

"No. But the helo and flashbangs were clearly a diversion."

Wrigley shifted again, wind buffeting his hair and pullover jacket. "If there was an assault team, then why the diversion? Why blow the chopper?"

"My thoughts exactly. We're probably talking one or two men. No more." Cheney clung to the grab bar in front of him as the Jeep bobbed over the sand and nosed down the dune. "They couldn't have gotten far."

Press kept a swift pace, doing his best not to lose his footing with Seth Barnett looped over his shoulder. His breathing consisted of heavy gasps and grunts as he negotiated the soft, uneven ground. Ocean Enberg was closely in tow, her former demeanor of morbid hopelessness now transformed to alert obedience.

"I don't see them."

"They'll be along soon enough. Keep running!" Press whispered. "A little further... I know a place where you and Seth can hide."

"Shouldn't we stay together?"

Press grimaced as the toe of his shoe caught in the sand. He nearly toppled over but managed to kick his foot out and catch his balance in the nick of time. His forehead was already slick with sweat and blood. His shirt clung to his back. He was a fit guy, but he had never sprinted in sand while lugging someone in a fireman's carry. Every muscle fiber in his thighs and calves was on fire. But he could rest later. After he'd gotten them all to safety. He pushed the pain from his mind and ran harder.

"We can talk about it later. Just do as I say."

Ocean acquiesced with her actions, but anxiety and confusion were all over her face.

The first house they came to was situated further back from the beach than Brenner's place. Just beyond the property's wooden dune fence, sat a small clapboard shed with porthole windows and a decorative antique lifesaver ring on the wall.

"Here!" Barely slowing down, Press stomped over the three-foot fencing, lumbered up the rising dune, and swung Barnett from his shoulder to the ground alongside the structure as delicately as he could. The heavy shadows made the poor kid's brutalized features all the more grotesque. Press knelt beside Ocean. "Stay here with him and be very quiet."

"You're leaving us? But—"

"Look at me." When she did, Press whispered in a slow, stern tone, "I need you to trust me. Can you do that?"

Ocean nodded courageously. "Okay."

"Good. Now give me one of your shoes."

She pulled off her canvas slip-on, handed it to him, then, with the back of her hands, smudged a fresh set of tears from her face.

Press leaned to his right, scanning around the edge of the shed. In the very next instant, he heard it: the growl of an engine. It was the Jeep. He was sure of it. But no sign of headlights.

He looked at the fence they had forged through, paced to it, and tramped it down some more. He threw the shoe twenty yards back in the direction from which they had come. Then he ran back up the rise to Barnett and Ocean, held his finger to his lips. Ocean nodded while Barnett, though conscious and breathing, appeared out of it.

Wrigley turned parallel to the water, downshifted, and the Jeep's engine dutifully responded.

"We don't want to over-pursue them. Slow down. And turn off the headlights," Cheney said, peering into the darkness. Studying the contours of the sand took him back to a nighttime operation on the outskirts of Riyadh. He'd been posted to the US embassy's regional security office there when he was a younger man. It seemed like a lifetime ago now. "Hit the spotlight when I give the signal."

The vehicle slowed to a predatory crawl. Creeping forward, Cheney wordlessly pointed. There in the sand was the outline of a solitary woman's shoe. He suspected its matching partner wasn't far away. "Easy now." They glided forward, the Jeep bucking slightly in the low gear.

Cheney next noticed the broken fence. He squinted, thinking. *Where would I go?* Just up a small rise, in the sand beyond the fence, was a shed. Something about this felt too easy and yet the evidence spoke for itself. With his eyes still scanning, he leaned toward Wrigley, quietly explained what he wanted him to do.

Wrigley gave him a thumbs up.

Via the IR scope, Press watched the Jeep creeping along the beach. The gray-haired man in the front passenger seat he recognized from the FBI safe house and the shootout in Wolfeboro before that. Armed with a short-barreled rifle, the man pointed then said something to his fellow confederate. They had seen the shoe.

The vehicle rolled closer. Press could hear the Jeep's transmission holding the engine back. He adjusted his position in the sand, cinched the rifle's buttstock to his cheek and waited.

A grouping of bushes blocked his view for a moment, but the sound of the Jeep indicated it was still on the move. Could they be ignoring his enticement, figuring it for a false trail? When the Jeep appeared on the other side of the shrubs, its occupants were minus one. Press quickly shifted his focus, glancing back to the shed. Suddenly a bright, vehicle-mounted spotlight lit up the side of the building where Barnett and Ocean were currently huddled. The former passenger—the man with the short-barreled rifle—suddenly emerged around the corner. He had obviously reasoned that he would find his prey right where they were. Ocean shrieked and, with her arms already flung around Barnett, pulled him closer to her body, whipping her head away from the gunman as he drew down on them.

And yet there was a moment of hesitation. In those few seconds of extreme calculation, the man surely must have considered he was the victim of an ambush. For where was the man or men who'd dared to penetrate Brenner's compound and stolen away Seth Barnett and Ocean Enberg?

Lance Cheney instantly lunged for cover.

Press saw all of this through his rifle's optic. He gave the trigger three quick pulls. At this range, Press's rounds found Cheney easily, evidenced by the fast, black blooms on his shirt and thigh as he thudded into the sand, grunting like an injured bear. Press immediately snapped his muzzle toward the Jeep's driver. The bright spotlight made him easy to find. The driver must have realized this, too, and urgently clicked it off. But Press's trigger finger was already moving. Keith Wrigley caught four of the five rounds in his head and torso. But not before he somehow managed to stomp the accelerator. Lifeless, his body shifted and then tumbled from the driver's seat. In doing so, it caused the steering wheel to jerk to the right. The Jeep responded. Its front right wheel struck a log half-buried in the sand and the entire vehicle rolled onto its back.

Press ran to the first man—the passenger. Cheney was squirming violently in the sand next to a cement walkway. The arterial spurt flooding from the area of his shattered femur was his sole focus. Press approached in a tactical crouch with his muzzle trained on Cheney's sternum. He considered leaving him to bleed out, but the police officer in him quickly decided it would be wrong to do so. Press scooped up Cheney's rifle, heaved it into the dark shadows. Then yanked one of the CAT tourniquets from his battle belt, tossed it to him.

Cheney offered a brief look of professional respect after staunching the flow of blood from his femoral artery. He was probably still going to die, thought Press. That chest wound was no joke.

Press stripped the pistol and knife from Cheney's waistband, flung them far away, then cuffed him to a nearby cast-iron fire pit. He shot Seth and Ocean a quick appraising glance then in a tactical crouch, moved toward the overturned Jeep. Using the corner of the shed as cover, he assessed the driver and quickly concluded that he was beyond any kind of help. The man was quite obviously dead. Not only had a portion of his face been ripped away by gunfire, but the Jeep had rolled on top of him.

A familiar sound.

The throaty growl of a 5.0-liter V8 engine.

Press turned toward it with a budding sense of relief. Hurtling up the beach from the south was a Ford F-150 pickup. The feeble moonlight had transformed its otherwise white and blue markings to an almost shark-like gray. The truck wore a push-bar, giving it the countenance of an angry NFL linebacker with a menacing faceguard. Press could just make out the lightbar on its roof. It was dormant. So, too, was the police siren.

Press eased upward as he cautiously prepared to welcome his fellow lawmen to a scene that was going to be supremely difficult to explain. Then all thoughts of fraternity were gone.

The truck's nose dove into the sand and the back end whipped around, throwing a healthy amount of powder in his direction. Two men alighted with long guns and immediately began firing.

Gunfire raked the overturned Jeep and the sand nearby. A sharp pain erupted across his shoulder and upper back. Press scurried around to the far side of the vehicle. He yelled more than once, "Police officer! Don't shoot!" And yet the gunfire continued to rage.

"Yeah! We know!" one of the men finally shouted back, adding a string of coarse words for good measure.

He heard Hickman's fading voice. *Brenner owns the cops on the island. Don't bank on them helping you. They'll tip him off for sure.*

Press hated the idea of engaging fellow law enforcement officers in a gun battle, but they left him no choice. He popped out behind the Jeep's inverted engine block. He quickly centered his optic's reticle on the first man's neck just above the sternum, accounting for a possible armored plate in the center of the guy's body armor, pulled the trigger. The man fell backward into the sand, dead.

The second officer soon noticed his partner was no longer shooting and turned to see why without ducking his head behind cover. As he did so, Press put a round through his temple.

Silence descended like New England snowfall. Press could hear himself breathing. He waited, expecting more threats to come. But none did.

Then he noticed it.

Up the coast about two hundred yards. The Land Rover Defender with the roof rack sat idling, exhaust from its tailpipe rising into the night air—the moonlight caused it to shimmer and glow.

Brenner.

75

**Providence PD
Central Station**

Lt. Tevaughn Gentry stood in the Major Crimes Unit office, one hand on his hip, the other gripping a phone that was firmly pressed to his ear. He had just taken a call from a woman named Avery Gwynn. She'd told him the most alarming story. And apparently had the goods to back it up. Right this very minute, on Press's strict instructions, she was on her way into the office to turn over material evidence in the Riley Talbert murder case. Evidence that was utterly explosive. The kind of stuff about which books are written and movies are made.

Apparently, Press had taken it upon himself to wrangle her into a hastily conceived rescue operation. Gentry loved the guy. He was the smartest, most tenacious, valorous—and stubborn—investigator he'd ever known. And when Nathan Press had his mind made up about something, he was an unstoppable force. But sooner or later his luck was going to run out.

Gentry considered what Deputy Chief Fantroy had said. The man had given specific orders that he was to be notified if anyone were to hear from Press or had the slightest inclination of where he might be.

Screw Mantoy, thought Gentry. There was no time for his BS right now.

"Marjorie. Get me the Coast Guard. Whichever station covers Nantucket. And hurry. It's an emergency."

A few detectives burning the midnight oil looked up at him as he related the urgent message to the Providence PD dispatcher.

"Patching you through to their dispatch center now," she said.

When the Coast Guard operations duty officer came on the line, Gentry rattled off what he knew of the quickly developing situation. Before he could be asked, he supplied the exact coordinates of Robert Brenner's beach house, however, did not dare mention the former CIA man by name for fear that a thick door of bureaucracy and bumbledom would be slammed in his face.

"We know," the duty officer said. "We've already got personnel headed that way. Mass. State Police and others are also en route."

"You *know*? How is that possible?"

"We received a tip through one of our partner agencies."

Gentry shook his head in confusion. "Okay. Just hurry."

76

NANTUCKET, MASSACHUSETTS

Robert Brenner watched it all unfold via a pair of night-vision binoculars. Fifteen minutes ago, he had called his contact within the Nantucket Police. The chief, in turn, had dispatched two of his officers to respond, guns blazing, while he and another officer would lock down the airport.

Since then, whatever hope Brenner had of extinguishing this little flash fire had gone out the window. Press had gotten lucky in killing Dale and Marcus. And yes, the helicopter exploding...that was bad. But he could still spin the situation. A catastrophic mechanical problem he would say. Information warfare after all was one of his specialties.

The running gunfight on the beach, however, put him in a grave position. There was no way to spin that. Even if the two local cops had managed to end it quickly. But Press had dropped them rather easily. The idiots.

Brenner eyed him now through the binoculars with pure hatred, calculating what options he had left. He couldn't figure a way out of this without bringing in heavy reinforcements. And that would take time, time he didn't have. He had to disappear.

But first he had to run.

Press glanced back at the police pickup truck. A small engine fire had flared beneath the hood. Flames were getting more intense with each passing second.

He called to Ocean.

"We're here. We're okay," she replied.

"Good. The next house over is under construction. There's a tool trailer in the drive. It's black. The door is unlocked. Do you think you and Seth can make it there by yourselves."

Ocean looked to Barnett. The computer whiz acknowledged Press's question with a slack thumbs up. "We'll manage," Ocean said with conviction.

"Okay. Go there, wait there. Don't open the door for anyone but me. I'll come back and meet you there."

"What are you going to do?"

Press sized up the overturned Jeep. He took another glance back at the Defender, watched as it turned in the sand and began fleeing northbound. "My job."

He peeled off the backpack, pulled the nearly empty mag from his rifle, and slipped it into his back pocket before slamming a fresh one into the gun and swinging it to his back. Then, he squatted next to the Jeep. With his aching shoulder pressed into its side, he gripped the rollbar, and exploded upward at an angle. He did this three times, finally rocking the Jeep back and forth with enough force that it rolled over and landed right-side up.

Press found the Jeep's key fob in the pocket of the man who lay lifeless in the sand. He fired her up without a hiccup—it was a Jeep after all—and he tore off in pursuit of the Defender. If Brenner made it to that rigid inflatable, he would be gone.

As Press cut the wheel toward the hard-packed sand along the tideline and clicked on the headlights, he detected the thumping sound of a rotary-wing aircraft. Nay, there were two helicopters. They swooped in from the north low over the water and shot past him. The pickup truck, now fully engulfed with fire, was what probably had the bulk of their attention.

Slamming home his seatbelt, Press shifted again, stomped the gas. He was beginning to close the distance between himself and the slower Defender. In the sheen of the Jeep's headlights, he saw the former CIA man twist in his seat and look back, which inadvertently caused the Defender to veer dangerously close to the water. Too close, in fact. Suddenly, the wheels on its right side caught the incoming tide. An enormous splash sprang forth and arced over the frothy water. Brenner somehow saved the vehicle from crashing, but his error had allowed Press to gain even more ground.

Press shifted again. Before long he was right behind the Defender.

The two vehicles raced along the beach at a frenetic speed. Brenner tried to shake him several times, even firing a pistol from the open driver's window. But Press would not be deterred. They rocketed past the beached inflatable.

It's now or never.

He gripped the steering wheel tightly with both hands and nosed the Jeep into the back left fender of the other vehicle while at the same time giving the Jeep's engine more gas—a maneuver known as a precision immobilization technique, or PIT. The Defender began to yaw and Press, attempting to give her a final nudge, steered through her. Something went wrong though. This was sand not asphalt. The Defender teetered on its right wheels and for a moment both vehicles locked together like two stags fighting over a doe. Press downshifted, ripped the steering wheel to the left. Miraculously, the Jeep whipped free. However, both vehicles dug into the sand and rolled several times.

Press must have blacked out for a few seconds. When he awoke, he was hovering over the beach, the Jeep on its side. Recognition soon came thundering back. He clicked out of his seatbelt and fell into the sand, forced himself to his feet. His whole body ached and now he tasted fresh blood. Something, probably his rifle, had smacked him in the mouth during the violent crash. He grasped for it now, pointed the muzzle at the Defender. Only then did he realize the vehicle was upside down and half in the surf. He limped toward the big SUV at an angle, prepared to send rounds into the driver. A target glance revealed a man hanging upside down, dazed and wounded as ocean water poured into the cabin. Brenner's arms dangled uselessly, the fast flow of water pushing and pulling them about. He had a nasty compound fracture to his left wrist. The other arm looked to be broken, too.

Press stared at him. Then flicked out his folding knife.

After cutting him loose, he dragged Brenner by the collar up onto the beach, dumped him in the dry sand. Having checked the former CIA man for weapons and found none, Press plopped down next to him. Both men were huffing and puffing, shivering, too, as their clothing, sodden with cold, Atlantic seawater, clung to their bodies. It was impossible to tell which man was the victor. Blood continued to leak from the knife wound in Press's arm and the long bullet track on his upper back, the reopened gash in the back of his head, and now his mouth. Press desperately wanted to collapse back and rest but knew he couldn't. Not yet anyway. Instead, he leaned forward with his elbows on his knees and looked up at the two helos now circling in a low hover. Sea spray and sand whipped and whirled, forcing him to avert his eyes. One of the helicopters, a shiny black Blackhawk with gold striping, landed a hundred yards away, its rotors still humming, while the other moved into a cover position. A sniper was poised on her starboard side ready to destroy anything that posed a threat.

Four kitted-up men in olive-drab, battle-dress utilities, armed with tricked-out M4s, sprinted toward him. Three of them pulled security, forming a tight circle around him and Brenner, as the fourth man took a knee beside him. The man's shoulder patches indicated he was a member of HSI's Special Response Team out of Boston.

"You Press?" the medic said.

Exhausted, Press nodded. "Yeah." In a kind of information triage, he quickly related the critical facts, including what Brenner had done and why he needed to be taken into custody. "There's also a man down the beach who may still be alive. He took some serious rounds and is not ambulatory. He's secured to a firepit but consider him dangerous."

The medic keyed his radio and relayed this to fellow operators aboard the second helicopter. It immediately banked to the left and nosed southward. "Looks like we missed all the fun," the man said, as he worked on Press's arm.

"Who called?"

The medic smiled. "Let's just say you've got some good friends."

Next on scene was a Massachusetts State Police STOP team in a bird of their own. The Coast Guard, too, had deployed two Sikorsky MH-60T Jayhawks out of Air Station Cape Cod to assist with CASEVAC.

A short time later, bandaged and his left arm in a sling, Press led a small contingent of HSI SRT operators and MSP STOP team members to the tool trailer. He called out to Ocean Enberg and Seth Barnett to alert them to his presence before opening the door.

"It's over. It's all over," he said.

They shared tears of joy and a sense of elation he had never before experienced. The three of them were immediately airlifted off the island by the Coast Guard.

After that, Nantucket became infested with officials from every level of law enforcement in existence including multiple federal agencies. Nantucket Police though were denied access on information provided by Press and Lt. Tevaughn Gentry of the Providence Police Department. Command posts were established. Evidence tents erected. Men and women in uniform, tactical gear, raid jackets, evidence collection attire, and coats and ties were everywhere. Emergency lights flashed nonstop up and down the island as onlookers congregated in hopes of snapping photos and video clips that would quickly make their way to various social media platforms. The small Nantucket airport was overrun with constant government activity.

As morning broke, news crews had already descended upon the island to cover the sudden, shocking events. Helicopters and drones dotted the skies. All of New England was abuzz.

77

Rhode Island Hospital
Providence, Rhode Island

The sunlight cutting through the blinds and streaking across the room seemed impossibly bright. Nathan Press lay in a hospital bed. His battle wounds had been stitched up and bandaged. Gentry sat in a chair by his side. The lieutenant detective had taken on the role of an angry pit bull, defending its injured owner with extreme vigilance. No one came near Press without Gentry's explicit approval. The man was a born leader and knew how to take care of his people.

"The good news is that all the doctors and nurses here know you," Gentry said. "The bad news... All the doctors and nurses here know you. This is kind of getting old wouldn't you say?"

Press grinned then immediately grimaced away a sharp pinch of pain. The bruises on his face were beginning to darken though the swelling had begun to subside. "How are Seth and Ocean?"

"Physically they're going to be fine. Seth is likely going to need reconstructive surgery for his face, but considering what he endured, he's doing well. Ocean will not leave his side. She's been adamant about that. The psychological trauma is another thing. Probably going to take a good amount of time for them to deal with everything."

"Robert Brenner and Lance Cheney are alive. They're at Mass. General in Boston in a secure, isolated wing under armed guard per the State Police. The feds are making a stink, but for now they're not going anywhere."

Gentry related that a long list of detectives, special agents, and lawyers were chomping at the bit to interview him, Barnett, and Enberg. They would all have their chance, but Gentry was doing his best to keep them at bay while the security arrangements could be ironed out.

Thankfully, the Rhode Island AG's Office had stepped up and agreed to place Barnett and Enberg in protective custody upon their release from the hospital. Until then their adjoining rooms would be under heavy guard.

Press's squad mates were allowed in to see him briefly. Of course, they teased him mercilessly the way cops do, even christening him with a new nickname: Dodger...for dodging death yet again. Gabby joked that he must be Batman. After the good-natured ribbing, JK broke the bad news that the flash drive Seth Barnett had worn around his neck had not been recovered in New Hampshire. Though police there would continue to search for it, the prospects of finding it before it was damaged by weather were not good.

Sunny, too, stopped in to see how he was doing. Her church would be praying for him. Again.

Avery Gwynn had called him on his personal cell and said that she and her mother wanted to visit, but the police would not allow them on the floor. Security was tight for good reason. They did not have police credentials and were not family. Press thanked her for everything and assured her that he would see her soon enough. They still had a bike ride to share.

"Nate, some people from OPR and the FIT team are out in the hall," Gentry said. "I've run interference for as long as I could. They want to get some of the preliminary stuff out of the way. They'll take your full statement after you're discharged."

"Mantoy probably wants my head on a platter."

Gentry stuck out his bottom lip, nodded.

"I appreciate everything you've done for me, Lieu. You can let them in. I'm a big boy."

"There's one more thing."

"What do you mean?"

In answer, Gentry walked to the door, opened it. Immediately, two men and a woman in starched uniforms and wearing stern faces stood from a line of chairs that had been placed outside the room. "For crying out loud, it's about time," one of them said. However, before they could enter, a man in an expensive suit with a military bearing squeezed in front of them. He held up his photo ID for them all to see. Gentry blocked the man's path, turned back to Press, who nodded curiously.

"Give me a few minutes to meet with my client," said Roland Finley to the PPD brass.

Gentry permitted him entry and closed the door.

Finley switched his briefcase to his left hand and extended the other to Press. "I'll get right to it, Detective. It would be my honor to represent you in any and all matters stemming from the Riley Talbert investigation. No charge."

Press looked at Gentry.

"I owe it to Riley and his family. And you, of course, for solving his murder and bringing those responsible to justice."

"It was a team effort," Press replied.

"I expected you to say as much."

Press shook his hand. "I accept. Thank you."

78

**BROWN UNIVERSITY
PROVIDENCE, RHODE ISLAND**

Even prior to his hospital discharge, Press had been placed on suspension since technically he was under investigation for a variety of felony criminal offenses. In the week that followed, he was forced to endure several marathon days of interviews with people from the Office of Professional Responsibility and the Field Investigative Team. It was abundantly clear that despite all he had done, the lives he'd saved, Deputy Chief Denny Fantroy wanted his hide nailed to a wall. If not for the considerable amount of public praise the story had generated for both him and the department, Press would have likely been terminated already, according to Roland Finley, though he should not consider the matter closed. Everything was still on the table, the attorney warned. The criminal and internal investigations would take weeks, if not months to complete. Meanwhile, Finley would do his best to keep any of about ten law enforcement agencies from filing criminal charges.

Press worried about none of this. He knew he'd done the right thing. He spent his ensuing convalescence checking on Seth Barnett and Ocean Enberg and pouring over reports—Killian had smuggled them out of the office for him—that in any way involved Riley Talbert. After years of criminal cases, there were many.

With his personal 9mm pistol, a Smith & Wesson M&P 2.0 Compact with an Apex Flat-Faced Trigger—Thin Blue Line Freedom Edition—and Trijicon RMR red dot along with two extra magazines with +6 extensions from Taran Tactical, concealed beneath his untucked flannel shirt for protection, Press had reclaimed a familiar post in the back corner of the Willis Reading Room within Brown University's John Hay Library. Some of the people working here knew him by name and not just from his college days. During some of his more difficult cases, he'd often come here to prepare for trial or to sift through investigative reports, witness statements, and case law. He did some of his best thinking in libraries for two reasons. One, it was deathly quiet here; and two, he enjoyed being surrounded by books, a trait he shared with his late grandmother. She would have particularly enjoyed the Henry David Thoreau and George Orwell Collections here, if she were still living.

With several neat stacks of police reports on the table before him, Press focused again on the letter Talbert had written him. This one was a copy; the original had been removed from his desk and secured as evidence in the property room at Central Station. He picked it up and read it one more time.

Nate,

I have something important that I need to give you and only you. Meet me tomorrow in the mezzanine at the Robert at 10 AM. Come alone. Tell no one! Trust no one! Don't try to contact me. It isn't safe. If something should happen to me in the meantime, I've put the item someplace safe. I trust that you'll be able to find it. Again, trust no one! I'll explain when I see you.

Riley

He set the letter down and smoothed it against the table. His eyes shifted back to the reports. Bits and pieces of passages from officers' narratives flashed in his mind. *You'll be able to find it.* You *will be able to...*

Something clicked. He read the letter once more, now seeing the answer in sharp relief. The logic of it made perfect sense. Nevertheless, he was a veteran detective. He knew to temper his expectations. Investigative leads, even the really good ones, could vanish like a desert mirage. And yet the more he reasoned through Talbert's own thought process, the more he knew he was on to something.

79

**TALBERT RESIDENCE
PROVIDENCE, RHODE ISLAND**

Press switched off the engine of his Toyota 4Runner—on top of his badge and department-issued firearms, his pickup truck had been seized from him pending the outcome of the OPR investigation. Even though he was technically restricted from police duties, he had been wanting to update Mrs. Talbert and the family on the status of the case. And he wanted to do it face to face. He owed them that much.

After being shown inside, Press explained to the widow Talbert and her son, Riley Jr., everything that had transpired since they had last spoken minus a few details that needed to remain confidential for the follow-on investigations. He promised to come back and relate the same information to Christine and her husband if they wished.

"It's all over the news," said RJ. "Is it true what they're saying? About New Hampshire and Nantucket, I mean. You're a freakin' hero!"

"I appreciate the kind words, but, honestly, it was teamwork. I work with a lot of great people. There are a few things I'm not supposed to discuss, for legal reasons. You understand."

"Of course, but—"

Gwen Talbert held up her hand. "He can't discuss it, RJ. Just leave him be."

Press offered a gracious smile. After a moment had passed, he said, "Now, I must ask one last thing."

"Ask me anything, young man. You and the other detectives are doing God's work. I'm so thankful for everything you've done for our family." Her son nodded at the sentiment.

Press produced the copy of the letter Riley Talbert had written him. He read it aloud.

"That's why you wanted to search the house the last time you were here."

"The letter was certainly part of it. I apologize for withholding that information back then, but sometimes in an investigation such as this one, we must tread carefully with disseminating such things."

"You needn't be sorry, Detective. I was married to an attorney. I understand completely. Now, ask your question."

"I appreciate that." Press inched forward in his chair. "Would you mind if I had another look inside one of the safes in your husband's closet?"

She provided him with the new combination and sat on the bed just outside the walk-in closet as he approached the safe in the number two position as Riley Talbert had cleverly indicated in his letter. Christine and her family had since arrived home, the kids were playing with some newly bought Matchbox cars in a playroom in the basement. She and her husband along with RJ stood at the closet's threshold looking on in suspense.

Press entered the combination and pulled the heavy door open. He knew the pistol was there from having performed the inventory previously. It was sheathed in an upholstered pocket built into the interior side of the vault door. It was the same pistol that had once been stolen from Mrs. Talbert's car—a SCCY Industries CPX-1 Gen 3 9mm with stainless-steel slide and white frame. Press had recovered it from the thieves who'd taken it and, after the actors pleaded guilty to the crime, saw to its return. Press recalled the look on Riley Talbert's face when he had first broken the news about the firearm's recovery, the many conversations they'd shared in halls outside courtrooms and over the phone throughout the time they'd known each other. A moment of remembrance settled in. Riley Talbert had been a good man.

Press held the pistol in his hand, looked up at his audience. No one said a word.

The SCCY was immaculately clean like all of Talbert's firearms. He dropped the magazine and pulled back the slide, verifying the gun was empty. Then set the pistol on a shelf and turned his attention to the magazine in his hand. There were no rounds inside. Visually, it was no different than any of the other pistol magazines in the safe. Using his thumb, he pressed down on the follower. It didn't spring back up like it should have. Adrenaline and curiosity caused his heart rate to tick up.

From an outer pocket on his briefcase, he extracted a Gerber Diesel Multi-Plier, flicked open the can opener tool and inserted its pointy tip into the dimple in the magazine's base plate. He worked the plate free, careful not to let the magazine's spring fire into his face or across the room. Instead of a spring, though, he found a bundle of tissues. Slowly, he peeled back each layer until all that was left was a titanium-colored 1TB flash drive.

Christine, her husband, and RJ exchanged glances then in unison turned back toward Gwen Talbert who was seated on the bed with her hands folded neatly in her lap. She regarded them all, leaned forward with a tear streaking her face, and focused on Press, who was now standing.

"You found it?" she said.

Press nodded. "Yes, ma'am. I found it."

80

East Providence, Rhode Island

Three days later, the news media were finally catching up. There were bombshell revelations all over social media. Federal indictments had been handed down for Robert Brenner, Lance Cheney, Janelle Holt, and others. "And this is just the beginning," a fierce Justice Department spokeswoman was quoted as saying. Press noted how Henrik Vandenberg's name was conspicuously absent from the list. He could only speculate as to why.

Some of the more scrupulous outlets were drilling down on an exposed plot to steal elections. Federal, state, and local authorities were promising to open investigations all over the country. A congressional inquiry was even underway.

The warm spring air carried the scent of flowers and cut grass. His neighbor, Evangeline Sherman, was outside toiling away with some potted tulips beneath a wide-brimmed straw hat. Dark, rich soil from the bag propped beside her caked her gloved hands. For a moment, she reminded him of his mother, how she'd gone about tending to her flower beds when he was just a child. She always did love her flowers.

As he walked to the garage, he ruminated on the highlights of the Talbert investigation. In a blink, memories of other difficult cases he'd worked throughout his career came calling, some good, some he tried hard to forget.

But the hugs, like the ones Gwen Talbert and her daughter had given him, always seemed to bring him back to why he did what he did. Why he took such risks. Why he fostered an ember of rage deep within for all those times he was called upon to go to war with the worst of humanity.

He was still engaged with these thoughts as a little girl on a bike with a colorful basket strapped to the handlebars pedaled by on the cracked and faded asphalt. The sunlight gleamed against her golden pigtails jutting from beneath her pink helmet. Her father, slightly out of breath, trotted behind with one hand gripping the back of the seat, the other swinging vigorously as he endeavored to keep pace with his free-spirited, little girl. From the looks of it, she'd be riding on her own in no time.

Press waved as they drifted past and turned the corner onto Waterview Avenue.

As a warmup, he performed a series of stretches, squats, and slow jumping jacks. He adjusted the bellyband holster in which he had secreted a Springfield Armory Hellcat OSP—his bike gun—then smoothed his jersey. His wounds were healing nicely though he still had some tightness in his left shoulder. The doctors had told him that riding his bike would cause his trapezius muscle no harm. In fact, the intense rehab would only help generate blood flow, break up the scar tissue, and even restore some range of motion.

Finally, he flicked off the lights, walked his brand-new Orbea Orca M20iLTD out of the garage, and closed the overhead door via the keypad mounted on the door's frame. He eased down the steep dirt track that zig-zagged through the brush not far from his house to the East Bay Bike Path, clicked into his pedals.

Avery Gwynn was already waiting for him. In her bike attire, she was the picture of athletic beauty. No wonder all those cycling magazines and sponsors were after her. On top of being one of the top pros in the country, she was drop-dead gorgeous. A publicist's dream. Maybe a certain police detective's, too.

"Finally," she said as he coasted up to her. "I was starting to think you weren't going to show."

Press grinned, making a minor adjustment to his helmet's chin strap. "And miss my chance to ride with a pro."

"I just hope you can keep up."

"Is that a challenge?"

They stared each other down in mock seriousness before sharing a smile.

"I'll do my best," he said. "Don't go easy on me."

"Oh, don't worry. Ready?"

"Ready."

ACKNOWLEDGMENTS

First and foremost, I'd like to offer heartfelt thanksgiving to my **Lord and Savior, Jesus Christ**. I've been through many ups and downs not only during the writing of this book but also in searching out a proper home for its publication. As always, God knows best. His ways are indeed not our ways. And they are never wrong. Where this book and the intended series go from here is firmly in His hands. All glory to God.

To my lovely and intelligent wife **Jill**, words alone cannot describe just how thankful I am for you. May we share many more years together, years filled with love and laughter. And books. Lot of them.

Claire and **Jackson**, I love you both more than you will ever know. Thank you for seeing your old dad through the writing process once more. And for abiding my studious bouts of researching, editing, proofreading, formatting and all the countless other tasks that go into producing a book worth readers' time and money. You are forever my pride and joy.

My **mom** was such a great influence on my life. And by her legacy, she still is. She was an ardent Christ-follower and a voracious reader. I can only hope that my writing makes her proud.

To the rest of **my family**, your love and support have been invaluable throughout my life. I cherish you all.

Dr. James Gill, former president of the National Association of Medical Examiners (NAME), graciously offered his keen medical expertise in the realm of forensic pathology for which I am immensely grateful.

To **Karen Comery, Esquire**, it was great working with you over the years when you were at the DA's Office. I've always appreciated your feisty spirit in prosecuting violent offenders. It's what hard-working cops expect and deserve of their prosecutors. Thank you for the legal insights you provided during the researching phase of this book.

Det. Susan Cormier (Pawtucket Police Dept.) and **Det. Robert Santagata** (Cranston Police Dept.) were super gracious in aiding a fellow LEO with on-the-ground information about the Providence area and local police procedure. Thank you both!

For bike intel, I turned to my good friend, **Jason Dickensheets**. I look forward to tapping your cycling expertise for many books to come. Thank you for the information and for your family's ironclad friendship. We love you guys.

Army veteran and fellow police officer **Richard Geiger** assisted me with parts of the book that touched on military matters. Many thanks, brother.

My Swiss friend, **Alex Konig**, brought me much laughter over the course of writing this book. Her posts on Twitter (now X) were often spicy and full of biting sarcasm, and therefore, struck a familiar chord with this veteran police detective. Laughter is survival in police work. Her contribution to the book related to her expertise as a helicopter pilot. Thanks, Alex.

To the men and women of the **US Coast Guard**, particularly **USCG Air Station Cape Cod**, I appreciate your kindness and quick response to my inquiries. May God be with you as you carry out your important function in a dangerous world.

Beth Murray, **Joshua Hood**, and **Chris Miller** each provided valuable feedback on early manuscripts. I appreciate you guys. You are super kind.

Ryan Steck, aka the Real Book Spy, was extremely gracious and longsuffering as he offered his time and considerable expertise as both an author and a thriller aficionado. I could go on for pages, but I know you're a busy man. So, I'll just sum it by saying thank you for everything!

To agent extraordinaire **Gina Panettieri**, I am so appreciative of your kind assistance with early queries and industry insights. While I'm not represented by you or your agency, I can attest from having studied countless book agents over the years, you and your staff are the gold standard.

Speaking of the gold standard, the super-talented writing duo of **Andrews & Wilson**, has been particularly kind to me. For that, I am immensely humbled and grateful. **Brian Andrews** and **Jeffrey Wilson** are two men at the top of their game. And yet they reached out to offer their support, knowledge, and friendship to a nobody still clawing around at the bottom of the mountain. Thanks to you guys, I've got my eyes on the summit and am ready to climb, ready to blaze my own path forward.

The following folks deserve special thanks for having me on their respective podcasts prior to the publication of this book. I'd love to be invited back sometime to talk about *Murder by Half*. You know where to find me. Each of them is an author, too. I encourage readers to go check out their books.

J. Ryan Fenzel and **Keira F. Jacobs** — The Write Note
Travis Davis — Author Ecke
John Stamp — Writer Stuff

To the immensely gifted **Tosca Lee** and **Ronie Kendig**, thank you for your kindness and gracious support. You ladies are not only great authors and wonderful ambassadors of the industry, you're also pure class. Thank you as well for the killer blurbs.

I would not be where I am today as an author and student of the business without the friendship and support of fellow authors **Eric Bishop** and **Luana Erhlich**. You've both given me words of encouragement when I desperately needed to hear them. Thank you.

To **Jan Thompson**, a dynamo of industry knowledge and verve. Jan, I hold you in high regard. Your joyful Christian spirit is constant. You're always quick to offer a helping hand or a crucial bit of advice and you do it all with a smile. Thank you for your encouragement, guidance, and friendship over the years. May God bless you in ways you cannot fathom.

Thank you as well to **Steve Wilson** and **John Robinson**. Both are super authors. If you love action-adventure fiction, you need to check out their books. More importantly, Steve and John are strong men of God. Iron sharpens iron. I appreciate you guys!

And to the countless others who wish to remain nameless, thank you for your technical knowledge and friendly conversations. This book could not have been written without you.

I especially want to express my love for and solidarity with all **the men and women behind the badge** to include your supportive families. Whether on the local, state, or federal level, law enforcement has never been an easy gig, but today's culture presents unique and difficult challenges to not just those of us in the trenches but to our families as well. Regardless, the profession is still a noble one and requires smart, courageous, honorable, and resolute individuals who are willing to sacrifice everything to protect and serve our communities. My family and I stand with you. May God bless and protect.

Finally, to my **readers**. This book was a long time coming. I hope it fulfilled your expectations. I will always consider myself a reader first, so I understand that waiting for books from your favorite authors can be insufferable. I promise to always do my best to deliver books worth reading, books worthy of your time and money. Reading is definitely an investment. When you finish each book I write, I hope you can say it was time and money well spent.

Our journey together has only just begun!

If you enjoyed this book, I strongly and humbly urge you to tell a friend or family member. Share the love on social media, too. Word of mouth is perhaps the best way for authors to reach new readers. What's more, if you could please submit a review on Amazon, Goodreads, and any other platforms that accept reviews, I'd be forever in your debt. Like it or not, reviews are critical for authors to succeed these days. More reviews equal more of the books you love.

Whether you're a reader, the host of a podcast, a book-club member, or someone who just wants to talk books, please don't hesitate to reach out. You can always find me through my website at **DonyJayBooks.com**. And don't forget to sign up for my email newsletter, what I call my **Reader Intel Bulletin**. Subscribers are the first to learn about news, contests, deals, and more.

God bless!
DJ

ABOUT THE AUTHOR

DONY JAY attended Penn State University and York College of Pennsylvania. He holds a BS degree in criminal justice. Dony is a police detective with over 21 years of law-enforcement experience. He has served on a US Marshals Fugitive Task Force and is currently a member of a county-wide Child Abduction Response Team (CART) and his department's forensic unit. When he's not reading or writing, Dony loves spending time with his family, staying fit, and cheering on the Philadelphia Eagles. Above all, he's a follower of Jesus Christ. He resides in south-central Pennsylvania.

To learn more about the author, go to **DonyJayBooks.com**. He invites you to sign up for his email newsletter—Dony Jay's Reader Intel Bulletin—to stay up to date with the latest news. And don't forget to follow Dony on social media.